Motherless Soul

Steve Lindahl

Motherless Soul

ISBN 13: 978-0-9840984-9-1
ISBN 10: 0-9840984-9-6
Library of Congress Control Number: 2009909444

Cover design by All Things That Matter Press

Published in 2009 by All Things That Matter Press

To Toni

ACKNOWLEDGEMENTS

I would like to express my gratitude to my wife, Toni, and my daughter and son, Nicole and Erik for their help and constant encouragement. I would also like to acknowledge the following sources I used for research: *Discover Your Past Lives* by J.H. Brennan, *Everyday Life in the 1800s* by Marc McCutcheon, *The Civil War Paintings of Mort Künstler* by Mort Künstler, *Eyewitness to the Civil War* by Neil Kagan and Stephen G. Hyslop, *Civil War, a Complete Photographic History* by William C. Davis and Bell L. Wiley, and the National Park Service websites for Gettysburg and The Battle of the Wilderness.

One

On the eightieth anniversary of her mother's death Emily wrote a letter to a hypnotist. Her mother had died when she was two, so Emily's only memories of the woman were imagined events inspired by old photographs. She'd polished those conjured recollections to the point where she could feel the thick fabric of a cotton skirt against her mother's strong thigh and smell the Ivory soap on her mother's bare arms. But as Emily's body grew slow and soft and the reality of her own mortality became clear, she found that her lifelong desire to know the person from whose body she'd come was overwhelming. She thought that a hypnotist might help her reach into the back corners of her mind to make her dream a reality.

"The death of your mother was probably more important than you realize," Glen Wiley wrote back. The rest of his letter followed the theme of his first sentence. He wrote of the particular importance of a mother's role in the life of a woman, stating that it went beyond the need for a loving, nurturing environment that all children share. He said that daughters often grow up to be images of their mothers. "Without that clear role model," he continued, "a woman runs the risk of feeling worthless."

Mr. Wiley's response felt exploitive to Emily, as if he were attempting to raise the importance of her situation so she'd be certain to pay for his services. She wrote him back, this time by email. Although his words had been phrased in a generic manner, she took them personally and felt the need to defend herself.

Emily Vinson told Glen Wiley that her life had not been worthless. She had been a teacher before she retired and she continued to serve others through her church work, which recently included teaching Sunday school classes and volunteering as a cook in a mission program that helped feed and shelter homeless families. She was proud of how she had lived.

"Those are good things," Glen wrote, "but you should know why you do them. Are you expressing gratitude for the life you've led? Or are you looking for something that you've never known? There's a world of difference. The relationship between a teacher and a student can be intimate and powerful, but it isn't family. The student will eventually be in someone else's class and the teacher's role will shift from molding a supple young mind to nodding hello in the hall. I'm not saying a permanent relationship and children are for everyone, but maybe you've always been too scared to know for sure. Without a mother to show you how to love, you may never have learned how."

Emily had read an article in TIME about successful hypnotists, notably in the people section, not the science section. The article had said that Mr. Wiley had succeeded in pulling memories from the early years of his patients' lives and that those patients sometimes included celebrities. Emily wrote him in the hope that she could reawaken experiences she'd had during the first two years of her life, when her mother was still alive. That was the only reason she had contacted him. She didn't need or want any help regarding the quality of the life she had led. But Glen Wiley's words infuriated her because there was some truth to what he said.

Her mother was twenty-four when she died. Emily often found herself looking in her bedroom mirror and trying to imagine what her mother would have been like if she'd had the same opportunity for a long life that Emily had.

Emily had very pale skin with numerous age spots all over her body, especially on her chest, neck and the back of her hands. But she had inherited her light skin from her father, so her mother would probably not have had the same issues. Emily used special toothpaste to keep her teeth from becoming too yellow. Her mother wouldn't have had that choice, so she probably would not have shown her teeth when she smiled. Emily's hair had been similar to her mother's, judging by the old photographs. It was currently solid gray, thin and just barely long enough to pin up when she wanted to get it out of her way. She thought her mother's would have been the same. Emily's eyes were dark brown and hadn't appeared to grow lighter as she aged. That was unusual, so she imagined her mother's would have been a lighter color. Their statures were similar, so since Emily had not gained weight as she had aged she didn't believe her mother would have either. One disparity she was certain of was their height. She was five foot seven. Her mother had been two inches shorter. Emily thought about that difference every time she pictured her mother giving her a hug. And Emily couldn't remember a day in her life when that image hadn't been there.

Emily's father had reacted to the loss of his wife by throwing himself into his work and ignoring her. The sense of abandonment from the death of her mother and her father's reaction to it had affected every relationship Emily had throughout her life. Glen Wiley was right. She liked the bonds she had with her students because there were predefined ends to them. She made sure her relationships had the same limitations. She had been in love a few times when she was much younger, but she had always pushed the men away rather than risk being hurt by them.

"I'm a different person than I would have been if my mother had not died when I was so young," Emily wrote. "I realize that, so it's not a point you need to make. It also seems clear that having an idea of what my mother was like would be pleasant, even now. So I'm asking, can hypnotism bring out the early memories? And, if so, would you be willing to try?"

In Glen Wiley's next email he told her he would love to hypnotize her. He said that everything we've ever experienced is buried in our brains. That includes our earliest memories and more. He switched the topic from the subject of Emily's personal life and began discussing a broad philosophy.

"Everything we know is part of something bigger than itself," he wrote, "while at the same time consisting of elements that are smaller. This is true of our world and our solar system and of our own bodies and the bones, blood and flesh that make us the people we are. It is also true of our souls."

Emily liked the turn in the tone of Glen Wiley's emails. She wrote back with numerous questions and a few guarded opinions. During that process she stopped addressing her notes to Mr. Wiley and switched instead to calling her new friend Glen. She was careful with how many of her own beliefs she revealed in her writing because her thoughts on some topics, especially life after death, were very different from traditional Christian teaching. Her church had always been the place where she had discussed the broad questions of life and death, so Emily had become accustomed to holding back. But Glen's ideas touched on concepts that she liked to consider.

"We all lead multiple lives through reincarnation," Glen told her. "My work has given me the opportunity to experience many cases that can't be explained in any other way. I've also observed that there's a tendency for specific events to occur in multiple past lives, especially when those events create major disturbances and emotional trauma. There could be a possibility that your mother's death might have occurred previously and not just once. It probably happened over and over and, I believe, will keep on happening until someone stops it."

Emily had thought about multiple lives and even repeating events, but she hadn't considered the hell of a never ending repetition of her mother's death. Her stomach twisted. She took a deep breath and managed to control her emotions.

Glen Wiley also told Emily that he had found some success recovering experiences from the past lives of a few of his patients. His theory, if true, would mean that there were memories hidden in the recesses of Emily's mind that might have affected every moment she'd been alive. Glen was offering to help her identify those past wounds so she might deal with them. The concept was frightening, but enticing.

Emily found herself scratching and picking at it as if it were a physical wound.

"I would like to come up there," was the next thing Emily wrote to Glen.

She lived in Greensboro, North Carolina. He was in Charlottesville, Virginia. According to Yahoo Maps, the trip would take her a little over three hours. The length of that drive had made her hesitate. She was a careful driver, but her responses weren't as quick as they had once been. Still, the idea of learning why she had lived the life she'd lived proved to be tantalizing enough for Emily to overcome any fears she had.

"Everything spins," Glen said in his next email. "The planets spin around the sun. The moon spins around the earth. The electrons in a molecule spin around their nucleus. So doesn't it make sense that our souls have a similar pattern? Imagine the model of a solar system with the events of a lifetime spinning around a cluster of individuals. The events would keep passing by us again and again. Incidents that happen at one time will occur again at another time. At the center of the system is a group of individuals or what I call the soul of a family. The family is, of course, a spiritual family, not a physical family. It's made up of friends and enemies, of relatives and non relatives. What makes them a group is the fact that they are always a part of each others' lives, time and time again."

As she read his note, Emily felt disappointed that Glen didn't appear to be responding to her suggestion that she make the trip to his home. But after the first paragraph he switched the subject back to her.

"A few hours won't be enough time with you," he wrote. Emily was pleased with that comment and thrilled with what he said next. "I've researched hundreds of people throughout the course of my career. I know potential and you've got it. I promise you that. I'll pay your mileage and cover your meals."

He wanted to talk to her in person enough to pay her expenses.

"There's an Econo Lodge a little over a mile from my place," he added. "I'll pay for that, too. You can get to my apartment from there with very little trouble. And one more thing. Bring loose clothing with you."

"I call the concept Circularity," Glen wrote at the end of his email. "When you come here I'll tell you more about it. I think I can help you understand."

Two

Emily turned her beige Buick up route 29. She took a spot in the right lane and started to cruise north at about sixty mph. That was much slower than the cars around her, but she was fine with that. There was no need to hurry. It was noon on Saturday. She'd eaten lunch before leaving and Glen wasn't expecting her until sometime between four and five. She always tried to give herself extra time when planning a trip. If more people would drive the way she did there wouldn't be nearly as many accidents.

Emily started to think about circularity. Somehow having a single word to identify with the concepts made them easier to accept.

As the years had passed there had been a gradual shift in Emily's thoughts from a focus on the future to a focus on the past. That change in her thinking was as much a part of aging as the physical changes her body had experienced. But since she had no family or close friends, her memories were mostly of dead end events that had no relevance to anyone other than her. And for that reason each year seemed to be a little sadder than the one before.

Circularity changed that.

Emily felt a purpose and a hope that had been lost from her life. If Glen could prove the ideas he spoke of, then Emily would have a reason to look forward again. He had told her that it was possible that the tragic events she'd experienced would repeat themselves, but they were not preordained. Maybe the next time she could get it right.

The radio was turned off and her window was half open, so she could hear the repetitious sound of her car's tires against the concrete pavement.

When she was a young girl there were no highways, only the narrow, often unpaved roads that wove through small towns and countless tobacco fields. Her father's car had bounced a great deal as he had driven it over the rough surfaces. The wide open windows invited in the smell of the forests and ponds they drove by. Though today's highway smells were more exhaust fumes than fields of crops and the ride was more akin to sitting in a living room than riding in an open wagon, Emily was still carried back by the feel of travel.

Her father was a successful real estate broker. His business dealings kept him away more often than he was home. But it wasn't her life as a latch key child that she was thinking about, it was the summers when she was not yet a teenager. Her father used to bring her to her uncle and aunt's country home during the polio season, to get her out of

Greensboro and into a rural area that was less likely to suffer an outbreak.

The summer of her twelfth year was the summer of Bobby Champ.

Her friendship with Bobby was her first close relationship with a boy and also the first in a long pattern of abrupt endings that followed her throughout her life.

Bobby's mom felt sorry for Emily because her mom was dead. That was why Bobby had to play with her even though she was a year younger than he was and just a girl. He told her so much on the first day they met, but Emily could tell that his attitude changed after he got to know her. She wasn't afraid of snakes or toads or even the family of raccoons they discovered under the footbridge by the pond in the backwoods. She could climb trees faster and higher than he could and when they skipped stones hers would always bounce more and carry further.

Bobby talked Emily into a series of adventures which were all fun since they never got caught. They climbed through a window of the Wilson house when the family wasn't there and stole two mason jars of home canned pears. They each ate a couple of slices and then threw the jars away. They spied on the Fisher girl who was sixteen. She had her boyfriend over when her parents were out of the house, but all they ever did was read books and drink iced tea. Bobby also convinced Emily that they should jump in the pond on his property with all their clothes on, and then he lay beside her while the sun dried them. He told her how he intended to be an athlete someday, but couldn't choose between baseball and football. Emily replied that she had no idea what she wanted to be.

When the summer was over Emily returned to Greensboro and to a life that was very different. She didn't play much. She never asked to have her school friends over and her father never brought the subject up. Emily became accustomed to being alone. There was always a great deal to do around the home because she had no mother to take care of day to day tasks. Her aunt had taught her how to cook and clean, so that's what she did. Her father never thanked her for taking over chores he had once been forced to do himself. Instead, he spent more time away from their home.

The next summer Bobby came over to see Emily as soon as she arrived in the country. Emily was polite but after a few days she made it clear that she no longer wanted to hang around with him. The previous summer has been fun, but that was the problem. The sense of duty that had grown out of Emily's solitary life ran counter to a child's natural desire to play.

* * *

Before Bobby Champ, Emily had no close friends but she did have her dolls. She called the first one Virginia. Virginia was a cloth doll with painted brown eyes, real blonde hair and a glazed, molded head. The second one was all cloth with yarn hair, a red beret and a small doll of her own, sewn to her right hand. Her name was Alma. Her baby doll was Millie. Those toys were all gifts from her father and in many ways they were more important to Emily's life than he was.

The first time she tried to talk to her dolls, she made sounds that were little more than baby coos. Emily was six. She might have been imitating the wind whistling against her window or a nest of sparrows up under the eaves. But by the time Emily was eight she was speaking to both the dolls in a clear voice and she was often talking about her mother.

Her mother had died from a fall into a deep ravine behind their home. All Emily could remember of the woman came from images in old yellowed photos. She seemed to Emily to be the most beautiful woman she had ever seen, but that was through the perspective of a lonely child. Apparently, Emily's mother had been walking in the woods in one of her finest dresses when she had slipped and fallen. She'd hit her head on a large rock near the bottom. The blow had killed her. No one was able to explain why she was walking in the woods, but there was a fresh campfire near the ravine. Emily's father always said there had to be someone out there, someone who had attacked her. He couldn't get the police to agree.

"I thought of another reason my mother might have had for walking in the woods," Emily told her dolls. "A stray cat could have been stuck up a tree, calling for help. The poor thing might have been thirsty and scared. Her cry could have been what drew my mother to the woods. When she saw that the animal was stuck she might have gone over to see if she could help and passed too close to the edge of the ravine. She died because she cared. It was that simple and that sad. My mother wasn't foolish at all. She was wonderful."

There was a sense of optimism that Emily maintained before the summer of Bobby. It came out in the stories she told her dolls. The short friendship Emily and Bobby shared broke the hold the dolls had over her, but it didn't break her focus on her mother. And after her twelfth summer was over, Emily returned to the life she was used to.

Emily put her dolls away and didn't bring them out again until, at age forty-eight, she rediscovered them while cleaning her attic. By that time they smelled of mildew and she'd grown too old to talk to them.

* * *

Glen had told Emily that it was the big events, the huge tragedies that were destined to repeat themselves. Those were the important occurrences, the ones that had to be changed. But perhaps it was the smaller things, the attitudes, the perceptions and mind-sets that mattered most. Life would have been very different if Emily hadn't spent so much time thinking about her mother and reaching for a father who wasn't willing to reach back.

"Maybe I'll get it right the next time," Emily said to herself, feeling her old optimism in a way she hadn't felt for years. She smiled as she thought of how much Glen had done for her already just by changing her attitude. Who knows what would happen when he hypnotized her?

Three

Emily had packed for a week and booked the motel near Glen's apartment for the same length of time. She wanted to be prepared in case the conversations went on longer than she expected. She could cancel the last days if they didn't.

The drive to Charlottesville turned out to be fairly easy. What was hard was getting from the parking lot up to Glen's apartment. His home was on the third floor and Emily couldn't climb stairs as well as she used to. She used the railing and took her time. When she felt a little dizzy she stood in place and let the flow of her blood get back to normal. Eventually she made it. Emily knocked on Glen's door and he invited her in.

Glen Wiley's smooth voice reminded Emily of a man she'd known in the sixties. The man's name was Charlie. He was a house painter who was ten years younger than she was. Charlie was tall and had a thin moustache. He loved to talk, write poetry and take drugs at parties. One evening they sat by a lake in the back seat of his Rambler Classic. She pretended to be asleep while Charlie took more than an hour and a half to slowly slip his right hand up her blouse and under her bra. That's all he did that night, but it was enough to make her shiver. Three days later she invited him to her house and gave him her virginity. She was thirty-four. Charlie enjoyed himself enough to call more than a dozen times, but Emily kept putting him off. He finally gave up and she never saw him again.

Unlike Charlie, Glen was not attractive. He had thick glasses that exaggerated his eyes, puffy cheeks, short, curly hair with too much gel in it and a very wide mouth. He looked like a poodle that had just been swimming. That thought made Emily smile, but she caught herself quickly. She didn't want him to think she was laughing at him, even if she was.

"I believe in patterns and repetition," Emily told Glen after they had begun to discuss his ideas, "but also second chances. I'm an optimist. Every time the earth goes around the sun, there's a new year." She liked to call herself an optimist, because it surprised anyone who knew her well. But she was just getting to know Glen, so he seemed to take her comment seriously.

"Every new year brings us closer to our deaths," he said. "True optimism has to come hand in hand with a belief in something after that." There was a funny little upturn in his voice at the end of that sentence. Emily thought he might have been questioning her, testing her beliefs. She wanted to believe in reincarnation even more than she wanted to believe in the Christian version of the afterlife.

"Death is part of the cycle," Glen said, "but only a single part. It's something that can't be eliminated, of course, but death's method and timing can be changed. Cycles without change are prisons. You don't think we're in prison, do you?"

Emily shook her head.

"I've always thought of fate as a creek," he told her. "The flow of water that's already gone by has carved a path over time. It's hard to change that path, but not impossible. The other part of my theory, and what I think you will find most intriguing, is the idea of a community path. People are like drops of water in that creek, clinging to each other as they flow by. There is one soul, just as there's one creek, but individuals each have their own souls that are all parts of the whole. Our souls are like the air in our lungs. What we breathe is us, but we also exhale and that sustains life around us. Again, everything is a cycle. Everything spins."

"Being part of something bigger than my simple life sounds nice, but complicated," Emily told him. "And it isn't why I'm here."

"I suppose not," Glen said. "You want me to hypnotize you, to help you look back at your earliest memories. I can do that. Everything you've ever experienced is recorded in your mind. I can help you pull out what you've forgotten. Your mother is in there even though you were so young when she died. I can help you retrieve your memories. I can give you the woman you don't remember knowing."

"That's what I want."

"But Emily, I can do more. If you let me I'll not only introduce you to your mother from this lifetime, I'll help you find others."

"I'll try the first step," she told him. "If you can bring back memories of my mother, the one from this lifetime, then we'll see where we go from there. All right?"

Glen nodded and smiled so wide he looked like a Disney cartoon, happy like Tigger, not sly like the Cheshire Cat.

* * *

Emily drove back to Glen's place the next morning. It was a wet day with a constant light rain interspersed with short downpours. Fortunately, Emily missed the heavy showers, but the humidity caused her legs to ache which made the climb to the apartment even harder than the day before.

She was wearing the loose clothing she'd brought per his instructions, a long skirt and a large, long sleeve sweatshirt. She had a pair of flats on, but Glen had her remove them before the process began.

He took Emily to a guest room and had her lie on the bed with no pillow. He explained that to pull memories of her mother, he would make her recall a specific event in her life that had occurred before her mother had died. Then he told her to stare at the ceiling. Over the years a nail had worked its way through the spackle that had originally covered it and now its head lay exposed on the white sheetrock. It made a perfect point of focus.

"Your eyes are growing tired," Glen told her. "Your lids are heavy."

She was nervous at first, but Emily let that feeling flow out of her. She tried to put herself somewhere else, in a gentle memory from her past. She knew that was the wrong thing to do. She should have been focused on what Glen was saying, but Emily needed to relax and using her imagination was the way she did that best.

Emily's eyes were closed so she could put a different face to Glen's soothing voice. She chose Clark Gable, her favorite actor when she was a young woman. She imagined the scene in *Gone with the Wind* when he was dancing with Scarlett after paying a hundred and fifty dollars in gold for the chance. There were other actors Emily liked, but Clark Gable was the man who came to her imagination on the days when her solitary life made her feel more lonely than independent. And now that she was too old for the silliness of sexuality she found she was still not too old to think and feel.

"Look back in time," Glen said. "You're a child. Your mother is near you. You're learning to walk, to take your first steps."

Emily let Rhett Butler drift away. She tried to imagine clouds or cotton—enormous spans of white, soft nothingness.

"Your mother's helping you," Glen told her. "She's coaching you through the process. You want to cross to her, to be near her where you feel warm and secure. She's calling you."

Emily was starting to see her there. The dress she was wearing was white muslin, almost the color of the clouds she was wrapped in, but her brown hair was clear. It was like an island on a sea of snow.

The memory didn't jump into her head as she had expected it would. Instead it gradually seeped its way in, becoming clearer and more defined as each instant passed.

"Her will is overwhelming. All you want is to please her."

Then suddenly the memories poured into Emily's head as if a dam had burst. Her mother was there, the woman Emily had spent most of her life imagining. She wasn't calling her as Glen had suggested. She was

11

standing across the room, looking at Emily and smiling. Emily was looking back at her from the odd perspective of a child sitting on a floor. Yet she could tell how beautiful her mother was and she could see the warmth in her eyes.

The experience was very much like normal memories only more intense. Emily was looking through the eyes of the child she had been and feeling what she had felt back then. But at the same time she had the perspective of the woman she had grown into. She could see her mother. She could think about how she looked and sounded, but she also thought about herself and what an amazing experience she was having.

Her mother walked across the room and lifted Emily to her feet. Then she stepped back and left her daughter there. Emily's legs were wobbly and weak, but she was able to stand. Her mother held her arms out to her daughter and called her name. Emily wanted to be upright and tall. She wanted to be big like her mother. But more than that she wanted to hold her mother, to smell her skin, to wrap her arms around her mother's leg and rest her head against her soft thigh.

Emily had to reach her mother to feel secure and protected. She took a step in her direction. She wobbled a little more, but she wasn't going to stop there. She took another step, then her legs gave out and she sat down abruptly. Her mother came to Emily and bent down.

"Good, Emily. Very good," she said as she lifted her daughter once more. Her arms were powerful but soft, like a gentle river that's always there, always flowing. Yet in the back of her mind, Emily knew that always was the wrong word. "Try it again," her mother added.

Emily stepped back and tried once more. This time she took three, four and finally five steps. She fell into her mother and was home in the arms of the woman she'd loved and longed for her entire life.

"When I count to three you will wake up," Glen's voice called out from a lifetime away. "You will remember what you experienced. One. Two. Three."

Emily woke up in a stunned state. The experience had been so emotional that it had left her groggy, almost as if she were drunk. She worked her way to a sitting position on the side of the bed and stayed there for a moment, breathing heavily as she tried to comprehend what she'd just been through.

"Are you all right?" Glen asked.

She looked down at her hands in her lap. The wrinkled skin on her wrists and her palms and across the backs of her hands and her fingers was pale pink with blue veins peeking through and a couple of dark blemishes. They were the hands of an old woman and they were empty hands. The memory of her mother reminded her how empty they'd been throughout her life.

She tried not to cry, but the tears started rolling down her cheeks. She brushed her hands across her face and then looked down at the floor as she rubbed the back of her neck and sucked in a deep breath. She'd lived a life without her mother. She had gone on from that tragedy to lead a life with few friends and, after her father had died, without any family at all. No one cared who she was or what she had done throughout the years she had spent in the world. And now she had a picture of what she'd missed. She felt what it was like to watch someone take pride in the smallest of her accomplishments, even the simple ability to walk.

Emily forced back her sobs. "I'd always known my mother was beautiful, but she was much more. The experience was like finding the comfort of a warm bed after a hard day, but it was a hundred times more than that could ever be. This was about being part of a person in a way I can't remember ever experiencing. I know those feelings were in me. That child was me, of course, but it wasn't a me I remembered. There were so many strange new, wonderful experiences in just the short burst of time you gave me. All I can say is thank you. Thank you so much."

Glen leaned over and hugged her. He didn't hold back and hurt Emily a little. But she was so excited she didn't care.

"Can we go again? Now?" she asked.

"Not now," he told her. "There's a great deal of emotional strain in an experience such as this. You need to work up to longer sessions, just like an athlete needs to get in shape before a game. But you are clearly an excellent subject, so it won't end here."

"You'll send me back?" she asked.

"I was serious about going back further, back into the memories of your soul. You have my word on that."

"And you have my word that I'll be back on your bed tomorrow."

Glen laughed at how Emily had phrased herself, but she could tell he was looking forward to what they were about to go through.

Four

The next day Emily stopped for scrambled eggs and coffee on her way to Glen's apartment. But even after she ate, her stomach was tense as if she were still hungry. Her hands were also shaky and she was short of breath.

She was much more anxious than she had been the day before. She'd been through her first successful trip into her memories, so she understood the process. She also knew how much further Glen wanted her to go and believed that his powerful hypnotism could take her there.

"You seem edgy," Glen told her as she walked into his guest room. "Remember, the first step in a successful regression is always the same. You need to relax. Would you like a cup of tea before we start?"

"No, thank you," Emily said.

He told her he had Chamomile tea and insisted that it was very soothing.

"I'll be fine," she told him.

"I'm sure you will."

Although Glen's personality was very clinical, it seemed to Emily that he had a new age side to his character that was epitomized by the fact that he had herbal tea in his kitchen cabinets. He seemed similar to Carl Sagan in the way he mixed science with marvel, but without Sagan's looks and charm. That was all right with Emily. It was Carl Sagan's mind that most people had admired and, after the experience of the previous day, Emily felt the same about Glen Wiley.

She continued to think about Glen as she sat on the edge of the bed and watched him pull a pine desk chair toward her. The day before he had stood, which had made taking notes a little awkward. Apparently, this day he planned to sit. Maybe he was tired. Perhaps he had tossed and turned all night thinking about the success they had experienced. He seemed like someone who could be consumed with the results of his work.

"Were you always interested in hypnotism?" Emily asked. "Even as a child?" Glen had quickly become an important person in her life. She was trying to get a feel for his background.

"I use it because it works," Glen told her, "but my interest is more accurately with people's minds and memories. At least that's where it began. Now I'm a step further. I'm also interested in their souls. People are supposed to be a combination of their experiences and their genetic makeup, in other words, nature and nurture. I suppose that's true, but incomplete. Souls are part of the equation. They are the components that hold everything together. The individual souls keep each person basically the same from one lifetime to the next and the group souls are the glue that keeps us together on our journeys through eternity."

Glen was proving that first impressions are often wrong, even about appearances. He had looked odd to Emily when she first arrived at his apartment, as if he had never grown out of a shy, bookish stage he'd been through as a teenager. But now his thick glasses made him appear intelligent, and even his gelled hair seemed to be a quirky choice rather than bad taste.

"I'm going to send you back much further than I did yesterday," Glen told her. "Are you ready?"

"I am," Emily said.

Emily lay on the bed and straightened her skirt. She was wearing the same skirt she had on the day before, but this time with a heavy blue T-shirt.

Glen asked her to count backwards from one hundred. When she passed fifty-nine he started to guide her saying, "Go back, back further to a time before you were Emily Vinson. Keep going back." His words seemed to run right through her body, like a shot of whiskey. Glen seemed to be growing distant, although she knew he was right next to her. She kept counting toward zero, even as he spoke.

Emily lost track of the counting. She was certain she'd repeated some numbers, but she tried to keep them coming. She knew she had to do what Glen told her to do. She closed her eyes. Shortly after that the dim light she could make out through her lids faded into absolute darkness.

"You're slipping through time and space into a place that's been buried in your heart for ages upon ages. Something important happened to you in this place. You're starting to remember what it was like: the smells, the sounds, the texture of the world around you."

Her eyes started to burn. Memories were flowing into her head after a period of nothingness and those sensations were different from what she'd experienced the day before. This time it was as if she were two people. The person she had been before the session began, the old woman nearing the end of her life, was now watching someone else from inside that other person's body. The other person was very young, but in trouble.

"Talk to me, Emily. Let me know what you're feeling."

Emily started to cry. She wasn't able to hold back. Her cry was the loud wail of a hungry baby. But Emily knew what she felt wasn't only hunger. Something was very wrong.

"I can smell smoke and feel heat," she told Glen. She was in a trance, but able to speak. "Images are coming into my head. I see my mother sitting beside me. She's reaching over to pick me up. I'm an infant, too young to say words or understand what's happening around me. There is so much noise, groans from men lying on the ground near us and shouts from other men behind the bushes and trees. There are blasts of gunfire and the sounds of branches breaking and feet pounding as men run in every direction imaginable. My mother's lifting me to her face and kissing me. Her face is wet with sweat, so are her hair and her arms. She's rocking me, comforting me. This isn't the mother I saw yesterday, when I was still Emily. This is a different woman with light brown hair, blue eyes and two small moles under the left side of her mouth. She is covered in soot and dressed in a torn, filthy cotton dress that hangs loosely on her thin body.

"And then there is the voice of my mother. *Everything will be all right, my darling. We'll be home again soon. We'll be with Charles and with Grandma. This will all be over. I promise. Remember what God tells us, Charlotte.*

"Charlotte is my name. I'm so very young, but I recognized my name. I also know this isn't the first time my mother has prayed with me. We have been walking for what seems like forever and during that long walk my mother often held me to her chest and talked with a soft, rhythmic voice that comforted me. *Yea, though I walk through the valley of the shadow of death, I will fear no evil; for thou art with me; thy rod and thy staff, they comfort me.*

"The words aren't enough this time. The noise around us is too loud and the sting from the smoke hurts too much. A burning tree is crashing down behind us. I'm crying. I'm crying so hard.

"*Remember that I love you,* my mother tells me.

"My mother kisses both of my eyes, then my cheek, three long, deliberate kisses. She holds me on her shoulder and turns my face against her neck, as if her body can be a filter from the smoke.

"My mother starts singing and I listen. Her voice is so beautiful and no matter what else is happening, I can't help but listen.

"*In Scarlett town where I was born…* I know the song. My mother sings it often. It's one of her favorites."

Emily was Charlotte, so she could feel what the baby felt, but she could also understand it with the background her age offered. Charlotte's mother was protecting her the only way she could. She couldn't stop what was happening, but she could ease the fear for both of them. "*…there was a fair maid dwellin'.*" It was a folk song. The tone was gentle and soft. If Charlotte concentrated on it she wouldn't hear the gunshots or feel the heat of the fires. She would be at peace.

"*…her name was Barb'ra Allen.*"

Then a nearby gun exploded loudly. Her mother stopped singing and fell to her right side, still holding Charlotte in her arms.

Charlotte lay still. She was too young to move, too young to do anything other than cry.

Emily was there, too, lying on the body of Charlotte's dead mother. She could see the same blood the baby saw and feel the same warm but lifeless flesh. Charlotte didn't understand death, but that didn't lessen the sense of loss. Grief for the baby was instinctual and hurt in ways that were more akin to physical pain than the sorrow of an anguished adult. For Emily it was different. She understood death all too well.

"I won't let you burn," the man's voice said clearly. He was the one who had walked with them. Now he was standing above her, where Charlotte could see only his legs. "Even Charles' bastard deserves that much." He leaned close to her. His breath smelled bad, worse than the smoke. He had a knife and he used that knife to cut her. He sliced her throat with one quick slash and, at that instant, Emily spun back to Glen.

She was lying on the bed, shaking as if she had Parkinson's, but all her tremors were from fear. Her thoughts swirled around what she had just been through. The baby she had been in that past life was murdered and she had experienced the death. That horrible, violent act is what had woken her from her trance and brought her back to her present life. She struggled to take a deep breath and to sit up. She couldn't lift herself; her body was trembling too much. She tried to speak, but her words wouldn't come out.

"Are you all right?" Glen asked her.

He took Emily's hand. She let him hold it for a moment, but he let go when she was able to swing her legs around and pull herself into a sitting position. She was still breathing hard. Glen grabbed her upper arm and stabilized her.

"I don't want to talk about it."

"You don't have to," he said.

But despite her reluctance to speak the words started to flow out of her mouth.

"It was hot, smoky and horrible," she said. "I was a baby and with my mother, but she was different from the woman I saw yesterday."

"It was a different lifetime."

"Of course, but it was so much worse than you can imagine. That baby was me! She died! I felt myself die! It was the most horrible, the most frightening thing I've ever experienced."

"It's all right. You'll be all right. You need to put it out of your head. Let me help you into the kitchen."

Glen told Emily to sit at the kitchen table and watch him while he cooked. He said only heaven could balance the hell she'd been through, so he would make her a meal fit for paradise. He poured her a glass of sangria then started preparing baked squash. While that was in the oven he thawed a couple of tilapia fillets in his microwave then seasoned and fried them.

They drank coffee after they ate and finally talked about what Emily had witnessed.

"Were the people around you speaking English?" he asked.

"Of course they were," Emily told him. "I understood them and it's all I know."

"In another life you might have known another language and if it were your native language you would have felt the same comfort level you currently feel with English. That's not uncommon with past life experiences. I don't think that was the case with you, because you were speaking English while you were in the hypnotic state. But I want to be sure. Some subjects can speak to their hypnotist in one language even though the memories they're experiencing are in another language."

"I'm sure it was English."

"Good. That limits the location and time period to some degree. From what you were saying I'm certain you were in a war zone, a mother and a baby caught up in a battle. That must have been overwhelmingly frightening."

"The fear was a different kind. I was too young to understand what was happening, so it was something I can best describe as immediate fear. I wasn't wondering how I got there or how I could escape, I was just consumed with pure terror."

"I'm so sorry," Glen said.

"Don't be," she told him. "What comes next?"

"Your mother died in two lifetimes. That tells me I was right about the circle you are stuck in. Now you take what you learned back to Greensboro and you use it to start the search for the woman who currently shares your mother's soul. It's been years since she died. It's possible, even probable, that this woman is someone you know and someone of child bearing age. You think back on what you've just been through and you analyze it. You write down everything you remember and you compare it with what you see in the people around you. It will be tedious and difficult, but it's the only way."

The second hypnotic trip had been to a past life. The woman she saw was Charlotte's mother, not her own. But aspects of that woman *were* her mother because according to Glen those two people shared a single soul. Seeing Charlotte's mother in the midst of a crisis had given Emily a chance to see how her own mother would have reacted and also taught her things she needed to know to help her identify the current person who possessed her mother's soul.

Yet Emily realized the importance of the problem they were facing with the lack of information brought back from her soul's memory. Charlotte was a baby. Her senses were still developing. She had no concept about what she was seeing and feeling. That fact was offset somewhat by Emily looking through Charlotte's eyes and hearing through her ears with the experience and knowledge of an adult, but she worried that it might not be enough.

"Suppose we find this woman," Emily said, carefully choosing her words. Her brow was furrowed and she stared at Glen as she spoke slowly. "And suppose she gives birth to this hypothetical child you're talking about. Then where will I be?"

"That's the point," he told her. "The child will be you."

"Then you're saying I'll be dead? And what's worse you're telling me it doesn't matter because I'm old. Isn't that what you're saying?"

"Of course it matters. But the idea is to move on to a better life. You can't do that while your spiritual family is stuck on the same tragic path."

"And what about Charlotte? She died along with her mother. I didn't die when I lost my mother. If everything is the same, then why isn't that the same?"

"That was your life," Glen said, "just as where you are living now has been your life."

"*Is* my life," Emily told him. "I'm still alive."

"I'm sorry. I chose my words poorly."

"I'd say you did."

"Each life is different which means there's always potential. But when a powerful event takes the same path enough times to get stuck in a circle, then everything around it is influenced by that event. Perhaps the outcome for you is a lonely life or maybe it's a short one, but either result is tragic and that's why something has to be done. To do that we need to identify the woman."

"Then I have to find as many things that have passed down from my mother's other lives as I possibly can. And the only way I can do that is by letting you regress me again and again."

"Exactly, but we have to be careful. The last session put a great deal of strain on you."

"Isn't this important enough to take that risk?"

"Of course, but that doesn't mean we shouldn't be careful."

"Yesterday went extremely well," she told him.

"That's right, but yesterday I didn't try to delve into your memories from a past life. All I did yesterday was help you to know your mother."

"But that's the point, isn't it?"

Emily was starting to grow fond of this young man and part of the reason was that she identified with his capacity for conflicting feelings. He felt she was a good subject and he wanted to use her. But he couldn't rationalize putting her at risk.

The fear Emily had experienced during the last moments of the regression had started to fade like a child's nightmare. She was left with the amazing concept that she had experienced her mother once again, just as she had the day before. This woman had existed in a different time and lived in a different body, but she was the same in everything that matters.

Knowledge does not come in a gradual even flow. It comes in waves and Emily had just experienced a tsunami. There was nothing equivalent to it in her eighty-two years. What would the religious leaders of today think if they'd been through what she had? The Pope? The Dalai Lama? The TV evangelists? Where would Christianity be? Or Islam? Reincarnation is a fundamental tenet of Hinduism, but it didn't seem to Emily that it conflicted with other religions. She didn't think it disproved the afterlife. Although Glen talked of life after life extending on into eternity, Emily believed that concept represented an assumption on his part. Perhaps there was an end somewhere in time. If there was, it would be in the future and Glen's ability to delve into Emily's memory could never show that.

"Hypnotize me again," Emily said, "but don't put me at risk. Repeat what we did yesterday. Don't send me back to some unknown past life, just bring out another set of memories from the first two years of this life. We know that was a safe time."

"We do know that," Glen agreed. "It might not give us everything we need, but it would be a start."

"Us?" Emily asked.

"Yes. I'll have to wrap up some loose ends here, but I'd like to follow you back to Greensboro. If you don't mind."

"Mind? I'd love it."

"Good. I intend to stay with you for a while. I can give up this apartment. I sublet it and it came furnished, so it will be easy for me to move. There are a few other people I've been working with here in Charlottesville, but they aren't nearly as promising as you. They'll have to understand."

Emily understood what she would get out of this arrangement, but the benefit to Glen was less clear. She wondered if this might be research for one of his books. He must have read her question in her expression because he added, "I've traveled all over the world looking for people with your potential. You're very rare."

Glen agreed to hypnotize Emily later that afternoon, as she had asked him to. But he insisted that they first identify an innocent moment they were both certain existed in her first two years. He didn't want to accidentally pull out memories like the ones from the battle. "If the moment isn't there to latch onto," he explained to Emily. "I could touch a memory from almost anywhere."

They chose waving bye-bye, something everybody teaches their babies to do. It was not a milestone on the level of the first step, but it was important, yet sweet and Glen explained that it had to be somewhere in Emily's head. He was right.

* * *

"Say bye-bye, my bunny," Emily's mother said as she held Emily against her body with her right arm and used her left to wave the baby's little hand. "Wave to Papa. He won't be gone long."

"That's right, Emily. I'll be back in a few minutes." He turned to her mother and asked, "Do you want anything other than bread and coffee?" When she shook her head, he turned back to Emily, walked toward her then leaned over and kissed her forehead.

Emily's father was tall and thin with a full head of surprisingly bushy dark hair, but his smile was his most startling characteristic. Emily remembered him as always being grim. She knew that the death of her mother had caused him to become that way, but the difference was more than she'd expected.

She was suddenly struck by the fact that she couldn't remember this happy father anymore than she could remember her mother. He had changed so completely after the accident.

Emily's father had been like an indifferent foster parent. It was hard to know why. Perhaps the hurt of losing his wife had been so great he'd avoided attachments to anyone, even to his own daughter. Or perhaps he felt his loss was symbolic of a failure so he had to strive harder to succeed in the area still open to success— his career. Whatever the case, he stayed away most of the time and when he was home he was too stern to allow Emily to love him.

Holidays had been difficult times during Emily's childhood, especially Christmas. There hadn't been a lack of gifts. In fact her father had always spent too much. But the presents disappointed her because they were always a little different from what she wanted. He didn't know her wishes as well as he should have. He gave her a ruffled skirt when she wanted pants and gave her Indian drums and cowboy cap guns when she wanted a rocking horse. Even the dolls disappointed her at first. But she grew to love them, perhaps a little more than she should have.

Her gifts to him were more of a problem. She made her presents: cards, pictures and paper ornaments among other things. He looked them over, said his thanks then tucked them to the side. His reaction was always the same, but she kept on trying year after year.

When Emily was fifteen she wrote a note to Bobby Champ. She hadn't spoken to him in years, but she couldn't think of anyone else to address the letter to. Bobby was a ploy. The note was actually to her father. She explained in her writing how much she wished her father would take her places and talk to her more. She left the note upside down on her bed then she took a hair from her brush and placed it on the back of the letter, with its furthest curl positioned exactly one thumb width from the right edge of the paper. She left it there for two weeks, moving it to her dresser at night and carefully setting it back out during the day.

The letter was a test of her father's concern and he failed. The man she was watching from her mother's arms would have cared enough about her to read the note.

Emily's father stepped into his blue Chevrolet and drove down the dirt driveway. She watched him. He stopped the car and waved just before he turned onto the road.

Emily waved back.

"That's right Emily," her mother said with the sound of joy in her voice. "Wave bye-bye. You're an amazing little one, you are. I love you so much. So does Papa."

Emily lay on the bed for a while after Glen brought her out of the hypnotic state. She thought of her father and how she had lost two parents when her mother died. That realization made it twice as important to change the course of the future.

Five

Julie had dinner on the table when Michael returned from the library. It was only a couple of turkey subs from Jersey Mike's, but it meant he didn't have to think about cooking. Michael was the one who prepared most of the meals for the couple, although Julie was the one whose appearance indicated that she loved food.

She was five foot eight with light toned skin and red hair. She looked Irish or German, which made sense since she was a mixture of the two, with a little Dutch thrown in. She had straight hips and a broad waist which gave her a look that was closer to a column than an hourglass. Some of that look was due to the fact that Julie was large boned and slightly overweight.

Michael was just shy of six feet tall and a little on the thin side. His dominate feature was his thick, almost pure black hair and dark eyes. His background was French and English, but he thought he might have a little Native American buried somewhere in his genes.

Michael thanked Julie for the night's meal, perhaps a little too profusely.

"You normally don't like fast food," Julie responded, after looking at him for a moment and tilting her head slightly. "What's different this time?"

There was a small white lie within his gratitude and Julie recognized it immediately. When he had something he needed to confess, something he knew she wouldn't like, she could read his thoughts as if there were subtitles on his forehead.

"The last test is taking longer to grade than I thought it would," Michael told her. "I'm not complaining. In fact, I'm proud of the kids. In the test on the War of 1812, I asked for essays and all I got was a series of disjointed paragraphs. I was expecting the same thing this time, but they wrote a lot of material and a great deal of it is good. It happened last year, too. That's why I'm certain it's me. When I move a class into the Civil War era something changes with my teaching and the kids start to pay attention. It's always been my favorite period, but I'm surprised by how much influence my interest has on them."

Michael could also read Julie's expressions fairly well, so it was easy for him to tell that she had stopped listening about halfway through what he had said.

"You plan to grade them tonight, don't you?" Julie's question was clearly rhetorical.

"It can't be helped."

"If just once you surprised me with a plan that didn't exclude me, I would find your excuses a little easier to take."

Michael had promised Julie he'd go shopping with her. She'd been harping about his beat up kitchen furniture for at least half of the two years they'd been living together. He knew she was right. He'd had that table close to ten years, since he was in college. And it looked as if it had been through a few too many parties.

"We can go tomorrow or on the weekend," Michael said. "It's not as if the stores are going to close or there's some sale we're going to miss. Things come up. Be a little flexible."

"Flexible?"

Julie's eyes puffed up as if they were suddenly inflated with helium. Michael knew he'd said the wrong thing, but it was too late to take it back.

"I'm always the one who needs to adapt," Julie told him, "the one who's consistently being put off to tomorrow or the weekend. But not this time. I'm going shopping. You can come if you want or you can just live with whatever I pick out. I couldn't care less."

The "couldn't care less" part was a lie. If she went alone, Michael knew Julie would never let it go. Every meal served at the table she chose would be a reminder of what a disappointment her boyfriend was. She would mention it over and over and over again.

"All right," Michael said. "I'll finish grading the papers when we get home even if I have to stay up all night."

* * *

Michael and Julie went to three furniture stores which were all similar to each other. They were one story buildings with large open areas containing clusters of furniture set up to have the look and feel of comfortable rooms. There were bedroom and living room sets as well as a variety of tables comparable to what they were looking for.

The sales floors were designed to give the impression of comfort and warmth, but that was just a marketing tool. Michael considered his relationship with Julie to be similar to those stores. Although they tried their best to create the impression of a caring couple, that act was more of a show for others than an honest display of their relationship.

Michael was going to be up most of the night and he was feeling angry about that. Still, he knew the problem wasn't solely with Julie. He needed to care from his heart, instead of from the momentum he'd built up over the years they'd been together. The trouble was he didn't know how to do that. It was as if there was nothing to build on.

"This would fit," he said as he ran his hand over a small table with a light birch top and thick white legs. The chairs were similar with white legs, white backs and light birch seats. He liked the set and didn't think he was overly influenced by his intense desire to make a decision, purchase it and head home.

"It's nice," Julie agreed, "but it looks too much like Cecelia's."

"Who's Cecelia?"

"She works with me in the school office. She's only been there about three months, but you must have seen her— wavy brown hair and a wide butt. She looks young. You might have thought she was a student. Anyway, she has pictures on her desk and her kitchen table is just like this one."

"So?"

"So if we have the staff over someday she'll see it and our house will look like a copy."

"That's simple enough. We never have her over. Problem solved."

"Or we find a different table, if spending some more time with me isn't too much effort."

It wasn't always this way, Michael thought as he watched Julie move on to the next kitchen set. *There was once a time when we enjoyed being together.*

* * *

Michael liked to say he met Julie at the chess club because it sounded nerdy enough to be funny. But that wasn't the complete truth. They met at work, like so many other couples. Michael was a teacher and Julie worked in the school office keeping track of grades and SAT scores and attendance records among other things. He didn't pay much attention to her until she approached him and offered to help start the club. He took her up on her offer. He suggested they play a game. It turned out that Julie was fairly good at chess. Michael lost that game and most of the ones they played after that. On the rare occasions that he did win, she always told him she had intentionally lost. He didn't believe her, though. She was too competitive to take a fall.

"He brings his queen out too early," Julie once told Michael as she described one of the students who showed potential. "Early in the game players often trade pieces because the board is crowded. If a player loses his queen too soon it will generally destroy his game."

"Where did you learn to play so well?" Michael asked. He could tell she wasn't just a player, she'd studied.

"My father taught me the basics and then left me alone. He piqued my interest then wouldn't let me play against him until I was ready. So I learned by watching and practicing. His method of teaching was a strategy worthy of his chess game."

"Sounds devious."

"It worked."

Chess wasn't the only way they competed. When they watched game shows they would try to beat each other to the answer. Julie kept track of who got the most right and celebrated when it was her. So did Michael, but not as much. They also joined a club where they played duplicate bridge, but that didn't last long. They fought too much afterwards because they both consistently felt the other one hadn't played as well as possible.

They even competed with the interests they had in common. The Civil War was an example of that. Michael had written his Master's thesis on the Battle of Vicksburg and considered himself to be fairly well versed in all the campaigns. So it was quite a surprise when he discovered that Julie, who had no formal education beyond high school, was as knowledgeable as he was in that area. And she loved to debate.

"Sherman's march through Georgia is always thought of as cruel," Julie said. She knew Michael's thoughts on that subject, so she was apparently trying for shock value. "But it served a good purpose."

"He murdered thousands of innocent people," Michael replied. "His troops stole crops and livestock from the farms they passed then destroyed what they couldn't eat or carry. The men were off fighting the war. The people he shot or left to starve were women, children and the elderly. If ever the devil was on earth he was William Sherman."

"It was politics. Sherman knew the Southerners would hate him for what he did, but he didn't care. He also knew they'd blame Jefferson Davis for leading them into the bloody war and that was what was important. His goal was the death of the Confederacy. Those people were just a means to an end."

Michael's face went pale. "Just a means to an end?" he spurted out, his shock clear in his trembling words. "How could you say that?"

Michael's relationship with Julie was complicated from the beginning. He enjoyed living with a competitor because the competition kept him sharp and because when he did win it felt good to beat someone who was trying as hard as she could to beat him.

Yet it was also missing some of what he'd always expected from a relationship. Their common goals felt good, but there was no pride in playing a support role for each other's individual accomplishments. And there were never any moments when Michael felt the struggle was done and the prize had been won.

* * *

The next table that caught Julie's attention was a light wood, stained with a red hue. The chairs were pine and the table appeared to be as well, although the knots that were present on the chairs were missing from the table. The table had, in the style of nineteenth century furniture, two drop leaves that could fold down to allow it to fit in a narrow spot. With the leaves extended the table was about four by six feet and had thin, square legs.

Julie ran her hand over the top and then pulled up a chair and sat down. Michael stood near her looking down. They were almost alone in the store, probably because it was a weekday night. Michael had noticed two women and a Latino couple along with the sales people, but all of them were looking at living room furniture.

"It's too big," he said. "It'll block the door to the living room."

"Not if we keep the leaves folded down," Julie told him. "When we need more table space we can pull it away from the wall temporarily. That way we have a decent size table when we need it and plenty of room when we don't. That seems like an efficient use of space. I think I'd like that."

"Space can be good, in the right circumstance," Michael said.

"Perhaps," Julie agreed. She moved her chair back from the table and turned to face Michael. "But sometimes space isn't a place for opportunity," she added. "Sometimes it's just emptiness."

Michael pulled up the chair next to Julie's and sat facing her. He leaned toward her, resting his forearms on his legs and clutching his hands.

"If what's in the space now isn't good," he said, "then emptiness is a step in the right direction."

"We're not talking about the table, are we?"

"We've got problems," Michael said.

"I know we do, but we had some good times, too. Think of the movies we went to and the dinners we shared. Remember the football games on Friday nights and the ballroom dancing class we took. We went out every weekend when we first got together. And don't forget the time you brought me home and couldn't stop kissing me. Remember that? You pulled me to the floor of the foyer and barely closed the front door. That had to mean something, didn't it? We've had time together, memories that are good, very good. We should at least try to change."

"I don't think that's possible."

"We're not the first couple to have problems. That's why there are counselors. I could set up a session for us, with Stephie."

Her suggestion was a surprise. He'd expected arguments and excuses, but not an offer to work things out. It seemed to be an indirect admission that she'd been a part of what went wrong between them. That was a rare thing to hear from Julie.

"Stephie can help us," she said.

It also surprised Michael that Julie suggested Stephie. Most of Julie's friends were a little awkward or insecure, just enough to give her an advantage. Stephie was the one exception. She was self-confident and strikingly beautiful with thick black hair, high cheek bones and attentive green eyes. She even looked good in a choir robe.

Stephie was the youth minister at their church. She also worked with couples who needed guidance through troubled times. Apparently, she was fairly good at it. Their situation might be a little awkward because Julie and Michael weren't married, but Stephie would probably agree to help them. Besides, if she couldn't help they'd just be back where they were now. What did he have to lose?

"All right," he said. "I'll give us another try. But it's not going to be easy. You have to promise me you're going to listen to what she tells us and try to do what it takes to make us better."

"I promise," Julie said. For the first time since they'd walked into the furniture store, she was smiling. "We can go home now, if you'd like. I'm sorry I kept you from your work."

At first Julie's reaction left Michael with a sense of contentment. It seemed that he and Julie were finally a couple with some hope for the future. But as they walked out of the store, hand in hand for the first time in more than a week, he noticed that Julie's grip was a little tense. He knew Julie well enough to know that when she was trying to win at something, a game, a debate or something more important, she always revealed her competitive spirit by becoming tense. He wondered about that.

Julie had been very quick to suggest counseling and Stephie's name had been at the tip of her tongue. It seemed as if she had been prepared for the conversation. Perhaps, Michael thought, he'd been manipulated toward an idea Julie already had in mind. And perhaps she was taking pleasure in the joy of another victory, right then and there as they walked together. He wondered if the day might come when he would regret what he'd just agreed to do.

Michael dropped Julie's hand as they left the building and walked toward the parking lot.

Six

Three days after Emily returned to Greensboro, she took Glen to Northside Presbyterian. He had told her to keep following her regular routine, and spending Sunday mornings in the sanctuary was part of that. But there was a greater reason she felt the need to attend the weekly service. She was caught in a never ending cycle of personal tragedy that could last for eternity. Emily needed God's comfort.

"This is my nephew, Glen," she told a heavyset woman who happened to be entering the church at the same time as they were. The woman had only been visiting a short while. It was highly unlikely that she was the person they were searching for. That was good, because Emily knew very little about her personality. Of course, she knew even less about her mother's.

Emily decided to introduce Glen Wiley to the people at her church as a relative because she didn't want anyone to think he was her caregiver. That would have made her seem feeble and would evoke too much concern. This was not a pride issue. Emily couldn't afford to be the focus of the congregation's concern. It would be a distraction.

They took a seat in a pew in the center section three rows from the back. It was Emily's regular place and had been since the new sanctuary had been built twenty-five years earlier. Church was important to Emily. She enjoyed having the constant reinforcement that came from spending time among people who shared her belief in Jesus' divinity and studied his teaching. But most of the people in her congregation were not as open to nontraditional beliefs as she was. She warned Glen to be careful of what he said.

Since she'd met Glen, Emily had been exposed to a multitude of ideas that were strange and difficult, but the concept of the souls of her parents being among the people she already knew was still hard to accept. This was especially true of her mother's soul. Emily thought of her mother as perfect, while the people around her were nice, but flawed.

She looked around, hoping she would see something that would at least make someone worth a second look.

There was Teresa Bazer, a forty-two year old single woman with blonde hair she wore in a short, blunt cut. She generally dressed for church in light colored suits with knee length skirts that gave her a conservative, neat appearance. She was sweet and intelligent and would have been a good candidate for the current presence of Emily's mother if it weren't for her age and the occasional slurred speech and uneasiness in her walk that indicated an alcohol problem. And there was Sherry Coats, a thin, dark haired woman who had joined the church about ten years earlier. Emily had served on a committee with Sherry. They had been charged with developing plans for a remembrance garden, a carefully landscaped area in back of the church that would be serene and secluded. It was to be surrounded by a large brick wall. Church members who wished to have their cremated remains preserved in containers within the wall could have their resting place on the property of the church they loved. But Sherry saw the wall as a money-making project and insisted that the spaces be sold for substantial amounts. It turned out that when Sherry had an idea she became pushy and uncompromising. The project stalled, the committee disbanded and Emily was convinced that Sherry's soul was imperfect.

On most Sundays, Emily's mind would roam as she sat in the peaceful church listening to the organist play a prelude to another Sunday service. It was one of her favorite times of the week. Generally, her thoughts went to recalling events in her life, but sometimes her mental wanderings would take her into fantasy worlds from a life that was much closer to the way she would have liked hers to be.

This Sunday her mind drifted again, but this time it was very different. Emily envisioned a series of terrifying incidents in which she continued to watch her mother die. No matter how hard she tried she couldn't pull her focus from all the horrible possibilities she could imagine.

She pictured her mother falling from a galloping horse, drowning in the surf at a beach and being shot by a mob gunman. None of these scenes were real. None of them had been pulled from her mind during a regression. They were just pure manifestations of her fear. She tried to push the thoughts out of her head, but they kept relentlessly marching through her mind like an army of soldier ants.

Emily started to shake. Glen reached over and touched her arm. His hand felt comforting and brought her thoughts back to reality.

"Are you all right?" he whispered.

She nodded.

"This congregation is a perfect place to start looking," Glen told her. "But remember that there's no guarantee they're here. Your father could be your plumber and your mother the cashier at your grocery store for all we know. But still, we are lucky to have your closest acquaintances together in a single place."

Emily nodded again, to acknowledge Glen's comment. She turned her focus to Stephie Howell as she watched the young minister step up to the pulpit.

Emily enjoyed the Sundays when Stephie delivered the sermon. She was young, animated and fun to watch. Could Stephie be the one? Emily wondered. She didn't think so. Stephie was single and, according to church rumors, did not have a significant other hiding in the wings. It seemed to Emily that when they found her mother's soul, her father's soul had to be nearby. Of course a person's single status can change in an instant. There were just too many variables, too many. Emily shook her head and stared at the patterns in the large stained glass window in back of the altar. She felt Glen's hand on her arm again and the realization that she was not alone in her struggle helped ease her fear.

Stephie's sermon was on persistence and was exactly what Emily needed to hear. The scripture reading included the ninth verse of Luke 11. "So I say to you: Ask and it will be given to you; seek and you will find; knock and the door will be opened to you."

The conclusion of the sermon was that hard work in the pursuit of a worthwhile goal was the best way to ask God for help. Emily liked that interpretation.

It had been a week and a half since Glen had last regressed Emily. Moving his things to Greensboro took up some of that time, although Emily was surprised by how few possessions Glen owned. Most of the items he brought with him were books. There were some concerning parapsychology including three about Edgar Cayce and four written by Edgar Cayce. Emily had heard that name and knew the man had been a psychic, but she didn't know any specifics. She was pleased to see that one of the books was entitled, <u>Edgar Cayce's Story of Jesus</u>. It gave her hope that Glen wouldn't be adverse to her odd mixture of spiritual beliefs.

There were also a dozen books about reincarnation including three that were each called, <u>Discover Your Past Lives</u>. Those had different authors and didn't appear to be related other than the coincidence of sharing a title. The rest of the reincarnation books included a mixture of past life stories, philosophical discussions on the subject and how-to books of which the three singularly titled books were included.

His fiction collection was more eclectic and included authors ranging from Herman Melville and F. Scott Fitzgerald to Richard Preston, Nora Roberts and Toni Morrison. Emily had read about half of those books, which indicated to her that she had a great deal in common with Glen beyond their shared desire to explore her past lives.

Glen had told Emily that there were two tasks he wanted to complete before he would regress her again. The first was to move into her apartment. It took Glen a few days to clear the accumulated junk out of her spare bedroom, unpack his stuff, buy a few groceries and settle in.

The second was to begin the process of meeting and studying the people she knew with the hope of associating people from her memories with people in her present life. That was why she had brought him to her church and why she had plans to include him in as many parts of her daily routine as she could. He would go with her to buy groceries and clothes. He would join her on her daily walks through her apartment complex and the adjacent park.

Stephie was winding up her sermon, talking about a connection between the grace of God and the goals we set in the rest of our lives. It was a clever and interesting way to draw together all her comments about that day's scripture reading.

A few days earlier, Emily had snuck away from Glen long enough to stop by Stephie's office to ask the young minister what she thought of reincarnation and how it could co-exist with Christian beliefs.

"The traditional answer is it can't," Stephie had told her.

But Stephie's pretty face had lit up when Emily asked her that question. Apparently, it was the type of issue she enjoyed discussing. Maybe it was a refreshing break from the problems that generally draw people to a minister's office. Her eyes seemed to take on a little extra intensity as she explained.

"Reincarnation is generally considered to be a part of a process which has what amounts to a long series of judgment days. When a soul is successful at one level they move to a higher plane. If they fail, they drop down a notch or two. The goal is to keep moving up until your soul eventually reaches Karma. But Christian philosophy is the other way around. We teach that God's grace is a gift. What we do with our lives is a result of accepting that gift, not a standard by which we earn it.

"However," Stephie said, smiling a little. "There have been many scholars throughout the ages who have believed that Jesus was the return of Elijah. So there's at least one case where some mainstream Christians accept reincarnation." She shrugged when she added that last part, as if she enjoyed letting Emily know how complex and interesting religious studies could be.

After Stephie finished her sermon the service moved on to the collection of the offering, the third hymn and the benediction. There was a slight pause between the spoken and sung parts of the benediction as the choir stood and opened their music.

On the Sundays when Stephie wasn't preaching, the young minister stood in the choir next to Julie Bullard. There was something interesting about the way the two women looked when they were side by side, dressed in identical white robes. Stephie's solid black hair contrasted with Julie's strawberry blonde, like the offsetting colors of a morning glory. And they both had colorful eyes, Julie's were blue and Stephie's were green. They were the only two choir members with that striking trait.

Emily also enjoyed the quality of their voices. Generally, they blended with the rest of the choir, but sometimes she could hear them individually. She enjoyed it when that happened.

Emily introduced Glen to Stephie as they left the church, again with the harmless deceit of identifying him as her nephew. He shook her hand and complimented her sermon.

"Sometimes I think Christians are too much like sheep," Glen said. Emily was taken aback by that comment and hoped he wasn't about to embarrass her. But he redeemed himself as he continued to speak. "We hear that metaphor all the time," he told Stephie, "and we like to think that we'll follow Christ anywhere he leads us. But still, it's nice to hear an emphasis placed on people's own responsibility for their choice of goals instead of simply asking them to support objectives the church has already chosen. Your attitude showed respect for your congregation. I like that."

Stephie thanked him as Emily hurried him out of the church.

Glen and Emily walked across the church parking lot toward his silver Camry. When they reached the car, Glen held the front passenger door open for Emily.

"That's a nice group of people," he said. He shut the door and walked around to the driver's side. After he took his position in the driver's seat, he added, "It's convenient having so many possibilities in one location. But we can't forget the other places that are part of your daily routine."

"It's going to be so hard to find the right people," Emily said. "And I'm scared of what happens if I don't. I can't stand the idea of losing my mother over and over. I don't know what I did to deserve this, but it has to be Hell."

"We can solve this," Glen said. "We just need more clues, more personal traits that can help us narrow our choices."

But they couldn't make progress unless they could find connections between the people from her past lives and the people she knew now. They both understood that.

"I'm ready for the next regression whenever you are," Emily told him, as he pulled out of the church parking lot and headed toward her apartment.

Through Glen's regressions Emily had met two people with whom she had experienced an intense intimacy. The first was her mother, the woman she had dreamed about most of her life, but could not remember until Glen sent her back. The other woman was also her mother. Although her physical bond was different, her spiritual bond was the same. Emily needed to reach back into both of those experiences to find similarities.

Patience was a term Emily could use to describe her mother, and so was persistence. But those terms were common for mothers and even more common for mothers at the time when they were teaching their children to walk or wave bye-bye. Emily needed something specific to latch onto, some trait of her mother's that would transcend countless lifetimes.

Nothing jumped out, so she turned her thoughts to the other woman, the mother whose life ended on the smoky battlefield. There were moments during that horrific experience when the woman demonstrated an extraordinary strength of character powerful enough to endure through time.

"I believe we need to focus on my mother's faith," Emily told Glen.

Glen's head perked up and Emily could see interest in his eyes. Like many advocates of self-spirituality, Glen acted somewhat condescending toward traditional religion. His reaction to Emily's invitation to attend her church services had revealed a little of his preconceived notions, but he went with her and he observed the people he met there with respect. Most likely it was prejudice that had kept him from looking for the clues he was after in demonstrations of faith, but this time a light seemed to go on as he considered her suggestion.

"The usual process is to lock onto an important occurrence from the previous life," Glen said. "But theoretically a spiritual event could be better than a physical one, since for many people God is the sole reason for life."

Emily continued to think about the woman in the battlefield. She had demonstrated a faith that was not a death's door conversion and in the process she had quoted scripture, which meant she must have studied the Bible. She also used her faith to ease the fear her daughter was experiencing. That meant God was a source of strength for her and a gift she wanted her child to have. Her faith was important enough to be a quality that could pass from one lifetime to another.

Glen pulled his car into a parking spot in front of Emily's apartment and opened his door.

"I'd like to get started as soon as we can," Emily told him.

"Then let's do it," Glen said, as they reached the front door and Emily started searching through her purse for her key.

Seven

Glen had already sent Emily back to a time when she was about a year old and after that to a time when she was about ten months. With this session, his plan was to send her back to a point in her current life that was earlier still. Emily listened to his explanation and accepted it as the best she could get. There wasn't going to be another trip to one of her past lives as long as Glen suspected it would be too great a strain for her.

"I'm going to steer you toward a feeding," he told her. "Of all the events in an infant's life, eating is the most important. Your most basic need is being satisfied while at the same time your mother is touching you and holding you. I'm certain those memories are strong for you, as they would be for any of us."

"I hope so," she said.

Emily wasn't sure she would be comfortable remembering every detail of such an intimate act, but she knew how important each regression was. She was ready to travel into whatever section of her mind Glen sent her.

Emily's apartment had two bedrooms, hers and the one Glen had moved into. Neither seemed right for a regression. Glen told Emily that hypnotizing her in the room where she was accustomed to sleeping might cause her to nod off and she didn't feel she could relax in his room because his possessions were scattered all over. Glen suggested the living room and she agreed.

Emily changed her clothes first. She put on the same dark blue skirt she'd worn for the previous sessions. It was the most comfortable skirt she owned and wearing it was becoming a bit of a tradition. This time she wore a long sleeved floral blouse with it. She skipped the flats and opted to do this hypnotism barefoot.

Glen suggested that she lay on the floor instead of the couch, so Emily spread an afghan on the carpet. Glen must have noticed her hesitating over the intimidating prospect of maneuvering her old body down to floor level so he offered a hand. With his help, she got down on her back.

"I'm going to try a different method this time," he told her. "I start by rubbing your ankles until you're thoroughly relaxed. Then you imagine that you're stretching. Begin by thinking of your legs extending a couple of inches and follow that by picturing the top of your body lengthening by the same amount. After you can picture the change from both your perspective and the viewpoint of a soul floating above your body, then you increase the length of the stretch to about twelve inches. Once you've mastered the second step, you picture your body inflating, like a balloon.

When that is complete your soul will be free and ready to drift back in time."

When Emily first accepted the idea of Glen moving to her apartment she thought of him as a mentor and a spiritual guide. After a while his effect on her seemed to also take on the power of a potent drug. He replaced her pain and loneliness with a sense of purpose. His presence made her feel younger than she had in years, but not so young that she forgot the difference in their ages. She was old enough to be his grandmother.

The concept of lying on a blanket with Glen hovering over her seemed more like a young girl's fantasy than a plan for an old woman's regression. Emily wasn't sure what Glen was thinking, but there was no question that this would be an intimate act. For her, it was also tantalizing. She had lived a solitary life. No man had ever rubbed her ankles. The fantasies she had in her youth had rarely been realized and she thought that any chance of them becoming real was gone. Apparently she was wrong.

"You're not sending me back to a different life, right?" Emily asked, looking up at her reflection in his glasses. It seemed to her that Glen had chosen an elaborate method and that confused her.

"If you get this process to work," he told her. "I'll be able to send you anywhere."

Glen's answer was vague, but it sounded like the response Emily wanted to hear. At this point there was little association between the people in her current life and the people from the past. She would do anything in her power to change that. Yet the stress of the regression to the battlefield seemed to have intimidated Glen.

He knelt at her feet and started to rub her ankles. At first his touch tickled, but when she grew used to it she liked the feeling. The soft motion of his hands relaxed her mind and body, like soothing music. A picture of Jesus washing the disciples' feet came into her head and that idea comforted her even more than the physical sensation.

Glen started to step her through the process, asking her to imagine that her body was stretching as if it were taffy. He told her to picture herself drifting up to the ceiling and looking down on her own body. She did that and soon after found herself following Glen's direction back in time to when she was an infant.

Emily was hungry and her mother was there to feed her. This was a year or so earlier than the time when Emily was being taught to walk. Her mother's hair was out of the bun she had worn in that other regression and flowed down her bare shoulders like a dark stole. She was wearing a black dress that buttoned up the back, but it was unbuttoned now and pushed down to her waist. She'd pulled her arms out of the white chemise she wore underneath and had also slipped that down to her waist.

Her skin was white, with hints of pink and light blue. Her breasts seemed larger than Emily had thought they would be. Perhaps they were full with milk or perhaps they had just seemed smaller underneath her clothing. Her nipples were dark pink and more distinct from the rest of her flesh than Emily's own lighter nipples had always been. They were a little swollen and damp. They had started to lactate slightly.

Emily's mother was beside the bassinet where Emily was lying. She leaned in to pick up her child and held Emily to her shoulder as she walked back to a pine rocker. Then she sat down, brushed her long hair back and offered her breast to her daughter.

Emily could feel her mother's breast in her tiny mouth as she started to suckle. The flesh was soft and the smell of skin was fresh and clean. The milk was the most satisfying food she'd ever had. It wasn't the taste as much as the warmth and the way it seemed to fill her entire body. She was an infant living entirely in the moment and at that instant every need she had was satisfied. She couldn't remember any time in her life that came close to offering her the pure pleasure she was feeling. When baby Emily opened her eyes and looked up, adult Emily found herself just inches from her mother's face, staring at the gentle brown color of her irises and seeing a love in them that was more than she had ever thought possible.

Emily had no children, so she'd never experienced breast feeding as a grown woman. That made her experience as an infant even more important to her. She wondered if it was important to everyone in ways they didn't realize. Perhaps the reason people like to socialize over meals is because the act of sharing food is reminiscent of the intimate joy each of us experienced as we fed from the bodies of our mothers.

When Emily's mother finished feeding her, she placed Emily on her lap then bent forward and kissed her. She kissed both of her eyes, then her cheek, three long, deliberate kisses.

There was something familiar about the way her mother kissed her. It left her with a sense of déjà vu, but she couldn't quite remember from where or when. Perhaps the kiss was something her mother had done each time she'd fed her. Emily decided she would ask Glen to send her back to a different feeding, so she would know if the kiss was a regular ritual. She wouldn't mind if he did that. Of all her memories, hidden or clear, present life or past, this had been the most pleasant she could remember.

"You're smiling," Glen said as Emily slipped back into the present and took a moment to continue lying on the afghan thinking of what she'd been through.

"I suppose I am," she said without any further explanation.

Emily's relationship with her mother had always been the biggest void in her life. Now, in the final years of her life, she was filling that empty space and filling it in a way that most people would never experience. How many others could remember, with absolute clarity, feeding from their mothers' bodies? How many knew of a time when they'd lain stretched out on their mothers' laps with their toes touching a stomach and their heads not quite reaching knees?

Thank you, God, Emily thought. *Thank you for Glen.*

* * *

Emily made tuna salad for lunch and served it with crackers. They sat at her kitchen table after the meal, sipping coffee and talking about the regression. Glen thought he remembered Emily describing a similar kiss from her mother during the session that had taken her to the battlefield. Emily remembered something about that, too, after Glen brought it up. But the fear she'd experienced during that regression had left her foggy on the specifics.

"I'm ready for a real regression, again," Emily told Glen. She spoke with certainty, but she was actually testing the waters. When it came to regression, Emily treated Glen's opinion with the same deference she might treat a doctor's diagnosis. "When you are," she added to show him the respect she felt he deserved.

"I think we've done enough for today."

"I didn't mean right now," she said, backing off a bit. "But I'd like to do it soon. I want to know if my mother kissed me like that all the time. And even more than that, I'd like to confirm that she kissed me that way in our past lives. It seems to me this could be important. It could be the first thing we've seen that's significant enough to show up in multiple lives."

"That's one idea," Glen said. "But I'd like us to take a different approach. I keep thinking about how unusual your situation is. I've always worked with younger people whose parents hadn't been gone long enough for their souls to be back, at least not in adults. With you the timing is different. Now that you've been back to see your mother a few times and learned some important things about her, I think it's time to focus on the other side of the equation. You've gotten to know her in the most intimate of ways. What you don't have is any sense of someone alive today who is enough like her to be her."

Glen reached over and laid his hand on Emily's shoulder, gripping it softly. She moved back a bit, surprised by his touch.

"So you're saying no more regressions for a while?" That idea felt bad. She suspected it came from his fear for her safety.

"Sending you back repeatedly will take too long."

Too long meant that Emily was so old she didn't have time to waste. But his logic was twisted. Avoiding regressions would take more time, not less.

This was the first time Emily remembered caring enough about life to fear its end. It was ironic. Why did she have to wait until she was in her eighties to have that feeling? And worse yet, why did she have to wait until after she knew what eternity had in store?

"Who do I look for?" she asked, once again deferring to Glen's suggestion. "How can I expect to recognize her in the women around me today? Tell me that and I'll do whatever you say."

Eight

Michael and Julie's first counseling session with Stephie Howell was on a Thursday evening, just one week after their conversation in the furniture store. He was annoyed that Julie had scheduled their meeting for a school night, but he didn't tell her so. Instead he cleared his schedule for that evening. He could do that with a little creative effort. He hoped Julie wouldn't ask why he hadn't done it before.

Stephie's office appeared to be decorated in leftover furniture from church yard sales. Her desk had scratches across the top and severely chipped veneer on both pedestals. Her computer was on one of the tattered folding tables that had been purchased for the monthly lunches in the fellowship room and her tarnished brass floor lamp had a yellowed shade with a prominent tear. Despite the worn furniture the room was very neat, with the few papers that weren't filed gathered into orderly piles.

The room was paneled, like a den or a rec room, but the paneling was painted a soothing pale pink that made the space feel warm. The view out of the large window was of the church's backyard where there were swings and monkey bars for the young children and a volleyball court for the older ones. And for her guests, there were two mismatched couches: one off-white with patterns of lilies and the other with light and dark beige stripes. Julie and Michael sat on the striped couch while Stephie sat across from them on the lilies.

"I don't like to start with specifics about your problems or why you're here," Stephie told them after she'd offered them each coffee or water, which they both declined. "I'd rather start with a broad question. It's a little childish, but it should be fun. When I was a young girl I used to imagine that I would somehow come across a magic genie who would offer to grant me a single wish. I wanted to be prepared when that happened, so I planned carefully. At first I was going to wish for something like a toy or pretty clothes, but as I grew the wish became more about school work or relationships with friends. I think the process kept things in perspective and sometimes that's all we need in life. So that's the first question I'm going to throw out to both of you. If you could have a magic genie grant you one wish, what would it be?"

"Can it be anything?" Michael asked. He'd imagined something similar when he was a child and he'd come up with a loophole.

"The only rule is that you can't wish for all your wishes to come true," Stephie said, smiling broadly. Apparently, she knew what Michael was thinking. "That's cheating. We could flip a coin to see who goes first, unless one of you would like to volunteer."

Michael looked at Julie, who shook her head. He turned back to Stephie and said, "I'll give it a try. My wish would be to resolve this problem Julie and I are having. Is that what you're looking for?"

"No," Stephie told him, "because trying to give me what I'm looking for isn't honest. I want you to forget that Julie and I are sitting here. Make the wish purely selfish."

"So selfishness is a rule? I thought there was only one rule."

"Let's just call it guidance," Stephie told him. She was shaking her head but still smiling.

Michael smiled back and then turned his head to see Julie's emotionless expression. It was her suggestion to arrange this counseling session yet she was sitting beside him in silence. Michael imagined that Julie was planning her arguments and wondered if the warrior inside of her was hoping for peace or for victory.

He wondered how much chance there was that something better might eventually grow out of his relationship with Julie, especially now that they were seeking help. He wanted compassion in his home, compassion and consideration. It was what he imagined most people wanted, but not Julie. Something else drove her, something he never could comprehend. The understanding he hoped he'd get from this session was about the strange force inside Julie, but he couldn't put that into words without sounding critical.

"I had a dog when I was eight," Stephie told them. "She was a boxer mix, at least that's what the vet called her. She crawled under the fence where we kept her and got hit by a car when she was less than a year old. She died."

"That's so sad," Julie said. Michael thought she sounded sincere, but she had never been an animal lover.

"A dog is something I wish for every day," Stephie continued, "but also something I'm afraid of getting because I remember how much it hurt to lose the one I had. That's what I'm looking for, something you've always wanted. See what I mean?"

"I've always wanted a rifle," Julie told her.

"A rifle?" Stephie asked, clearly startled.

Julie had never mentioned guns before. It seemed to Michael that she was trying to shock Stephie, that her words were a distraction, as if she was agreeing to have their relationship examined under a magnifying glass but then cracking the glass so severely no one could see through it.

"You had a dog when you were eight," Julie continued. "We had a neighbor, a boy who used to shoot. He was a teenager, sixteen or seventeen and he owned a .22 he used to play with in his backyard. His yard was backed by a wooded area, so it was safe. He let me target shoot sometimes and I was fairly good at it. I'd like to do that again, sometime."

Maybe, Michael thought, *this isn't a ploy*. With Julie it was always so hard to tell. Everyone has something that draws them back to the tranquility of their childhood, but hers wasn't a sled named Rosebud. It was hard to put tranquility, children and rifles together in one clear, nostalgic thought.

"How about you, Michael?" Stephie asked, turning away from Julie. "For the purpose of this one exercise forget about complicated concepts like understanding or respect. We'll work toward those, of course, but for now isn't there some single material object you want, something like my dog or Julie's rifle?"

"That's a good question," Julie said. "What do you want? It can't be more simple or straightforward than that."

It didn't seem that it could be simpler, yet nothing came to Michael's mind. He never had a desire for expensive items like sports cars or lavish vacations. And when he wanted something less expensive he just bought it. At least he did before Julie moved in. Now he had to explain anything that was even a little extravagant.

The thing about Julie and Stephie's wishes, Michael told himself, are the negatives that come with them. A rifle comes with a stigma, of course, and a dog, when treated right, comes with dedication and hard work. What would he want that would change his life? What would be something he wouldn't just put on a shelf and forget about?

"I'm thinking of a clarinet," Michael said finally.

"Why?" Julie asked. "You already have a guitar and a piano."

"You don't have to explain," Stephie told him.

"That's all right. It's a piece of my childhood, just like a dog and a rifle are for you two. I played in junior high and high school."

"You never told me that," Julie said.

"And you never told me you used to shoot."

"That's part of the reason for this exercise," Stephie said. "You live with somebody, so you think you know him or her. But there's much about us that's hidden, that's buried inside our heads. A lot of those facts we can't even remember, yet they're important to the people we are today."

As Michael listened to Stephie he wondered how well he actually knew Julie and how many of their problems would fade away if their understanding of each other could increase. People change every day. The cells in our bodies renew themselves entirely every seven years. So what keeps us connected with the people we were eight or nine years ago? That was the part of Julie he needed to know better. In fact, that was the part of himself he needed to know better.

"I didn't realize music was important to you," Stephie told him. "That's good. It's something you share with Julie."

"No," Michael said, glancing at Julie then turning back to Stephie. "We go our separate ways. She sings and I play. We're in different worlds."

"They don't sound so different to me," Stephie argued. "Music is something you share. I could arrange for you to do the anthem in church one Sunday. Julie, you could sing. And Michael, you could accompany her. It would give you something to work on together and I think that would do you both a world of good. There's no better exercise in trust than sharing music."

"I haven't played in public since I was in high school," Michael said, looking at Julie then turning toward Stephie.

Julie was never one to accept his excuses, so Michael wasn't surprised when her comment was that she liked Stephie's suggestion and wished he would agree.

"I'll do it if you both think it will help," Michael told them as he shrugged his shoulders and smiled weakly. "But give me some time to practice, a few months perhaps?" It wasn't performing in church that worried him. It was making another commitment with Julie, one that she would fret over and use as an excuse to complain about his effort or lack thereof. That was the core of their problem. Whenever they tried to do things together, they just didn't seem to fit.

Michael knew that many of the problems were his, but not all of them. A gun seemed angry and anger described Julie too perfectly. Life could be much more pleasant. And it *would* be, if the woman Michael was with wanted something from her magic genie other than a rifle, something positive, something more like Stephie's dog.

Nine

Julie selected the song she wanted to perform in church then ordered the sheet music on line. She picked *How to Say Goodbye* by Michael W. Smith. It was a song about the grief of letting go of a loved one. The theme of people choosing paths that pull them away from their loved ones was recurrent throughout the Bible from the tale of the prodigal son to the story of James and John dropping their nets and leaving their father to follow Jesus. But the real reason Julie had picked the song was because singing it to Michael would be an effective way to mask her most common complaint in a veil of tenderness. It would be interesting to see how well he understood her message.

Julie convinced Michael to accompany her on a piano rather than his guitar. The sheet music was written for both so there was a choice to be made. Michael preferred the guitar and had even worked out a short rift, but Julie wanted him anchored behind a keyboard where it was less likely he'd be the center of attention. When she suggested he switch, he shrugged his shoulders and agreed. That was exactly how she had expected he would react.

They worked on the song in the evenings after dinner. Michael suggested they run through it a couple of times each night. Julie insisted they work on it much more. They ended up practicing at least an hour a night, even when Michael claimed he had school work to complete. Julie liked those times best, but not for the music. Pushing Michael to do something he didn't want to do left her with a sense of victory. It felt better than taking his queen in the first few moves of one of their chess matches. Yet the music was every bit as intoxicating for Julie as the power. Whenever Julie sang, the notes gave her an endorphin like sensation that was one of the few ways she could still feel happy.

Julie's relationship with Michael had the same problem her relationships always had. Once she was recognized as part of a couple by their friends and family there was nowhere left to go. She was like a gymnast in her post teen years relegated to delivering motivational speeches and weight loss commercials. But the music wasn't boring, at least not for her.

"There's no emotion in what you're playing," Julie told Michael. "It's all comfort, like a bride wearing tennis shoes to her wedding. Put some feeling to it. Get up on those toes, so to speak. Make the music attractive." The imagery was feminine, but she was certain he got the message.

Michael ran through the song again, yet he was still dragging. It was clear that he was tired or bored, which made Julie wonder why he had told Stephie he wanted a clarinet. A wish such as that implies a love for music that should rise above his weariness. Perhaps the clarinet just brought back memories of his childhood. Her own wish wasn't like that. The very thought of a rifle gave her a feeling of power that clearly existed in the present. She wished she had bought herself one years ago. She shouldn't have given up on her desire just because she believed other people wouldn't understand it.

Neil was the neighbor boy who used to shoot his .22 when Julie was young. She could remember him more clearly than she had implied at Stephie's session. He was thin with wavy brown hair that covered his ears and a large nose that gave his profile the appearance of a hawk's. He was also hawk-like in another respect. When he was target shooting, small mammals were among his choice of targets.

Julie was twelve when she knew Neil, but her age didn't cause him to hesitate when it came to sharing his rifle and she quickly found that she could pick off a squirrel or a rabbit better than he could. Neil was impressed by her marksmanship and used to tell her it was as if she was born with a gun.

"That's it for me," Michael said, sounding defensive as he stood up and stepped away from the piano. "I've got a busy day tomorrow and I need to get some sleep."

"OK," Julie said quickly. She was happy Michael suggested quitting for the evening. Her mind was no longer on the music.

He left the living room where they kept the piano and headed to the kitchen. Michael didn't have an office, so he marked papers on the kitchen table, the old one they still hadn't replaced.

Julie grabbed her copy of last month's *Elle* and settled in the chair with the ottoman, the best seat in their house for reading. She started to skim an article on Reese Witherspoon, but the magazine slipped to her lap and her thoughts drifted to the topic that had been tucked in the back of her mind since Stephie's session.

Despite the fact that Neil had been sixteen and Julie just a prepubescent little girl, she never had a crush on him. In fact, Neil's rifle had stuck in her head more than Neil himself. She could still feel it in her arms more than fifteen years after she'd last picked it up.

It had a barrel that was just shy of two feet long and a smooth wood stock that was most likely walnut with a flat finish. Of course, Julie didn't know terms such as barrel and stock when Neil was showing her how to shoot. She just knew that the rifle felt as if it were part of her body, a part that could reach out and snatch the life from the grey squirrels that lived in the woods near the family garage.

The gun took one bullet at a time, unlike many modern rifles. But Julie liked that. She felt part of every shot as she went through the ritual of pulling back the bolt, slipping in a bullet, lifting the gun to her shoulder, sighting her prey and softly squeezing the trigger. And each time she took down a squirrel she would pause to think of how the small animal would no longer jump from tree to tree because she, Julie Bullard, had decided its life should be over.

Julie reached through the neck of her T-shirt to scratch her shoulder then leaned back in the chair and closed her eyes. The magazine fell from her lap as she drifted off to sleep.

Ten

Glen was pushing Emily to start her search for the right woman, the one with significant traits in common with her mother. But she wasn't sure she knew her mother well enough to recognize the traits that mattered. *If only Glen had allowed one more regression,* she told herself, yet she understood his reasons. She would always feel a need for another regression and eventually they had to move forward.

"Use your intuition," Glen said. "Pick someone and get started. You'll need personal details to make a determination, so you'll need to be a detective. If you discover aspects to this woman's personality that seem to conflict with your mother's soul then you move on to the next woman. If you can't find any conflicts then I take over. I'll need to regress her, so we can be certain we have the right person. I'm not sure how we convince her to let us do that, but we'll cross that bridge when we get to it."

Emily felt pulled to a gardener she had seen tending a furrowed patch of vegetables beside a brick house about two miles from her home. She thought the woman was in her late twenties, but she wasn't sure. She was horrible at estimating ages.

Emily saw her almost every day, as she drove toward the side of town where both her church and her grocery store were located. The woman was always out there: weeding, digging or picking, depending on the time of year. Emily didn't know her name, but she was determined to find out. She hoped she could accomplish that without making a fool of herself.

"If you don't mind me saying so, this gal doesn't seem to fit with how you described your mother," Glen told her, his tone expressing surprise. "You do have something in mind, right?"

"You said to *pick someone and get started*. That's what I'm doing."

Emily couldn't think of a connection between the women, but that didn't surprise her. She didn't know the gardener and she barely knew her mother. Yet there had always been something comforting about seeing the woman working in the same place each time she passed, consistently dressed in jeans, a straw hat and whatever shirt suited the temperature. Now that Emily was looking for a connection to someone around her she thought this could be a real possibility, even if the maternal feeling the woman invoked was something she had longed for from her mother rather than something she had experienced.

"Think of getting to know her as a game you have to win," Glen told Emily after she expressed concern that she had never been good at making friends. "Imitate your father. He sold real estate, right? And he was successful. He must have had a technique for chatting up clients."

"I didn't see him at work that often."

"That often?"

"Well— there were a few times."

"Think of him, Emily. You'll do fine."

A couple of days after she had discussed her choice with Glen, Emily stopped her car at the woman's home and got out to talk to her. She was bent over with her back toward Emily as Emily crossed the lawn. Apparently she was tying tomatoes to wooden stakes. Emily had to use tiny steps to make her way down a slight incline, like a Chinese woman with bound feet. But she needed to be careful. She certainly didn't want to meet the gardener by falling in her yard.

"Hello," Emily said when she was about ten feet away. She was trying to avoid surprising her by speaking unexpectedly from too close a distance. The woman still reacted with a start.

"I've been admiring your garden for years," Emily said. "I thought I'd finally tell you that."

"You're not Jehovah's Witness, are you?" the gardener asked, her brow in a little scowl as she stared at Emily's eyes.

Emily had been expecting a thank you for going out of her way to complement her, not the abrupt response she received. "I'm just someone who saw you working and stepped out of her car to talk," she told the woman.

The gardener's light brown hair was pulled back in a ponytail that stuck out from her straw hat like the train of a dress. When Emily stood close enough to speak with her she could see bags under her eyes that gave her a sad appearance. Her skin was tan and her neck had begun to wrinkle, probably from spending too much time in unprotected sunlight.

Why do you spend so much of your life out here, alone? is what Emily felt like asking. Instead she said, "Your garden is huge. Do you sell the produce? Seems like a big job for one person to tend it."

"I do sometimes grow more than I can use," the gardener said from a kneeling position. She was still facing away, her hands working the twine as if she were weaving. "If you'd like some snap beans I have extra."

The conversation lightened up from that point and they finally introduced themselves. Her name was Jeri. They started to chat about what Jeri had chosen to plant and why. She showed Emily the beans, tomatoes, spinach, and eggplant. In the far end of the garden she had a couple of rows of sunflowers, but she said she didn't dry and eat the seeds. They were there because she liked the way they looked. She also had zinnias to help attract bees and marigolds to repel moles. The conversation moved to the possibility of rain before Jeri invited Emily in for coffee.

At Jeri's kitchen table the conversation became a little more personal. It was Jeri's boyfriend's decision to make her garden so large. "He's gone now," she told Emily. It was a bad sign that she was single since Emily was searching for someone who would be a mother. But perhaps the boyfriend would return or another man would show up to father a child with this woman.

"I'm sorry to hear that," Emily told her. She wondered how the man had left her. Had he walked away or had he died? There were similarities with her own family, although her father had left emotionally rather than physically. And that hadn't occurred until after her mother was gone. After they each had a cup of coffee Emily told Jeri she had to leave, but she said she would stop by again soon. Jeri led Emily out of her house and went back to her garden while Emily went back to her car. It was easier to walk up the incline than it had been to walk down.

"You're studying her overall attitude," Glen said when Emily got back to the apartment, "and trying to evaluate your own instinct. Those are the right things to do, but the fact that you didn't know this woman still gives me pause. Before you stopped your car she was more of a landmark than an actual personality in your life."

"If you think I'm on the wrong track, I don't have to go back," Emily told Glen.

"I didn't say that. We won't know anything for sure unless I can regress her. So try to become her friend. Let's see where it takes us."

Emily worked Jeri as Glen had suggested she should and was successful much quicker than she had imagined she would be. She played the caring mother role, which turned out to be a powerful path into Jeri's good graces. She felt uncomfortable with the calculated nature of her actions, but she understood what was required of her. If Jeri turned out to be the woman she was seeking and if she and Glen managed to change fate, Jeri would gain as much as anyone.

Emily learned that Jeri had lost her dog a couple of years earlier, about a month after her boyfriend walked out on her. In Jeri's case the loss of her man was not nearly as devastating as the loss of her pet. Whenever Jeri mentioned the beagle to Emily, tears welled in her eyes. For twelve years Jeri had fed the dog, cared for her and watched her grow old. It was clear Jeri was still mourning Chelsea even after two years had passed.

Emily never had an animal in her life. Loving a dog was something she'd always equated more to the love of a possession, something such as a car or jewelry rather than another soul. But she could see the emotion in

Jeri's eyes and hear the sorrow in her voice as the gardener put the pain of her loss into words. Emily felt her face grow flush and her throat tighten as she empathized with the story of Jeri's loss. That compassion helped the two women connect quickly.

Because Jeri had an emotional void to fill, Emily rushed in like air into a vacuum. She was soon listening to whatever Emily said and willing to do whatever she asked her to do. If Emily had been conning her for her life savings, it would have been gone within a few days of their meeting. But what Emily was after was more complicated than that and it took a little longer.

"His name is Glen," she told Jeri a week later. "He'll help you discover your past lives. He's good at it. I know because he did it for me. It's an amazing feeling. What he can give you provides proof that there's something more than this life and at the same time it can reconnect you with the most important people in your life. I don't know if the same is true with animals, but they do have souls. And if Chelsea's soul is traveling through time with yours then Glen can help you reconnect. You don't have to believe in reincarnation, but you do need an open mind. He'll tell you it's important to relax and go wherever the process takes you. If you can do that, you'll be amazed where you can go."

"If you say so," Jeri told her.

"I do say so."

Emily learned quickly that Jeri was not the woman she was looking for. Glen sent Jeri back successfully, but the life she had led before had not included Emily. Still, the time had not been wasted. The search was beginning and Emily had proven herself to be capable of getting people to do what she wanted them to do by reaching into their hearts. That was a talent she had not known she possessed.

Emily also learned that gender is not always consistent in reincarnation and that the circumstances of one life can intensify the relationship between souls in another, often in unexpected ways.

When Jeri lay on the couch in Emily's apartment, with Glen hovering over her and Emily standing off to the side, her first words were the pronouncement that she was a man. She seemed surprised by that fact, but not at all upset. She then described the life she was revisiting in these words.

"I've stopped. I'm in a forest, by a stream. I'm alone and I'm certain that no one is anywhere within miles of where I'm working. It's autumn. I can tell by the leaves. The colors on the trees are powerful, bright reds and yellows. There are also fresh leaves covering the ground and falling around me. They have the crisp smell I love so much. The temperature is comfortable, even warm. I've taken off my clothes, so I can wade out into the water and work there. I'm using a knife to shape the dirt under a shallow part of the stream, to make it flat for the trap I'm about to place. My legs and arms are in the water, but my body and my head are still dry. The trap is a steel jaw with a stake attached to it by a chain. When I have the ground prepared properly I'll place the trap and drive the stake into the earth a yard or so away. If I catch a beaver he'll be waiting for me when I return, or at least his coat will."

"A trapper?" Emily asked. She hadn't expected Jeri's other life to be based on the killing of prey. "It's solitary, much like gardening. I can see the consistency, but it doesn't work. My mother was a very social person. I can't see her as someone who lives her life alone. Jeri's the wrong person."

"You're right about her being the wrong person," Glen told Emily, "but there's a clearer reason. The woman we're searching for is stuck in a repeating pattern that includes, among other things, being your mother. She can't be the right woman if she was a man in any other lifetime. Switching genders happens sometimes, but not in the case we're looking for."

"I'm dressed again," Jeri continued. "I've collected my things and I'm on my way upstream. There are too many thick shrubs along the water line, so I work my way into the woods. I keep my eyes on the stream. I can't wander too far away. My traps need to be set in the water."

"We've put her through enough," Emily says. "We need to find someone else."

Glen brought Jeri back and helped her sit up on the couch. He offered her cheese and crackers along with coffee to wash the snack down. Jeri asked for water instead. When she said she felt rested, Glen drove her back to her home.

Jeri was left still mourning her dog, but the session had helped her a little. The concept of reincarnation comes bundled with the emotion of hope. Proof that she had been on the planet at a different time and in another form helped Jeri look forward to a vague, but now clearly possible, future when she would reunite with her Chelsea.

Emily wanted to spend more time with this new, young friend, but she knew she couldn't. She was a soldier on a mission to save her own family. Along the way there would be many people she would get to know and they would all have their own problems. Emily couldn't allow herself the luxury of further involvement with any of them, no matter how inhuman that detachment made her feel.

"People sometimes change genders from one life to the next," Glen told Emily when he returned. "We put a great deal of emphasis on it when we discover a case such as Jeri's because gender is emphasized in our current lives. But it isn't any different than changing any other major trait and we shouldn't think of it that way."

"What surprises me most about Jeri's past life," Emily said, "is what she did for a living. Trappers are like ranchers, they have to think of animals as product rather than living beings. Yet Jeri was devastated when her dog died. It has affected her for years. How could someone like her have led a life as a trapper? It just doesn't add up."

"Her dog didn't just die," Glen said. "It grew old and she had to have it put down. What if her dog's soul was in one of the animals she trapped? She would have killed the same soul in two lifetimes. If her subconscious mind realized what she'd done it could be reason enough for her emotional reaction, even if she could rationalize one of those deaths as a mercy killing."

"That's circularity," Emily said. "Isn't it?"

"Yes. A much less significant case than the one your family is caught in, but still powerful."

"I see. Interesting, but useless. For all the effort we put forth, we haven't made any progress."

"What you tried made sense," Glen told her. "You need to keep it up, even if we didn't succeed this time. Look for somebody who feels right and use the same charm you used with Jeri. Keep trusting your gut. It's the best weapon we have."

Jeri went back to her garden and Emily went back to driving past. Every once in a while Jeri would stand up from her work and stare at Emily's car as she slowly rode by, but Emily never stopped. There was no time for friendships. That is to say she didn't have time for friendships with anyone other than Glen. When he suggested they attend a concert to help them both get over the failure, Emily quickly agreed. She had a season ticket to the Greensboro Symphony Orchestra and had already suggested that they might pick up an extra ticket for him to one of the performances. Fortunately, one was scheduled for the coming weekend.

There was an attractive young flutist who drew Emily's attention from the orchestra's first note until the final bow. This wasn't the first concert where this musician had pulled Emily's attention away from the others in the orchestra, but this time she was looking for a woman who could affect her that way. She remembered that the mother on the battlefield had sung to her daughter. Perhaps music was a connection. That wasn't much to go on, but it was something. Before they rose from their seats to leave the hall Emily leaned over to Glen and whispered, "I think we have another candidate."

Emily used the internet to discover what she needed to know about the musician. Her name was Tina Eversole and she was thirty-two. She lived with her boyfriend, Hal Wilkowe, a furniture designer who appeared to be a few years younger. Emily watched their house from her car for a week and often followed them when they went out. She learned enough about their habits to form a plan to meet Tina. The couple ate out every evening, generally at the K&W cafeteria, a choice which seemed a little removed from the artistic set Emily had expected them to run with. But that restaurant was a place where Emily felt comfortable approaching them. She brought a concert program with her and asked Tina for an autograph.

"I had the program in my car," Emily lied. She was doing too much of that recently. "I recognized you, so I went out to get it. The Brahms Overture you performed last month was so powerful I shook in my seat." The last part was true.

"That's sweet of you to say," Tina told her as she signed the program.

Emily's technique had been polished somewhat by her work with Jeri, but Tina was trickier. She had a boyfriend and a successful career. While Jeri was escaping as often as she could to the solitude of her garden, Tina's choice of a life spent with music meant her time included socializing and working with the other members of the orchestra.

Tina was, however, tickled to have a fan approach her. Although she was a performer, she was not, by any reasonable definition, a celebrity. She said that it was unusual for any of the concert attendees to seek her out. "I like the fact that you did that," Tina told Emily. "My friends all love my music, but I've often wondered what it would take to make a fan out of a stranger. Could you give me a hint?"

Emily used that question, to get Tina to meet her for lunch a few days later. During their second meeting, Emily discovered that Tina was neither depressed nor mourning a lost friend, family member or pet. If she was going to convince Tina to allow Glen to regress her, she needed to come up with a fresh method.

Glen, as always, had an idea that they both thought would work. All artists— poets, painters, but especially performers, have moments in their lives that they could live in for eternity. If Tina knew she could revisit whatever her moment was and hear a special musical phrase that had sent shivers through her audience, she would jump at the chance. Perhaps it was when she was a student and performed better than anyone else in her class. Perhaps it was her finest professional solo, in front of over a thousand people. It didn't matter when it was, artists have large egos and her vanity was surely the key they needed. Emily had already touched on that by posing as a fan. The next step was clear.

It turned out that Tina did have a special moment she considered the most important performance of her musical career. The music was an arrangement of Chopin's *Nocturne in E flat* adapted for flute, not by any means one of her more technically challenging pieces. She played it at the funeral of Brianna Stahl, her favorite student, ever. But that wasn't the performance Tina wanted to relive. A month earlier Brianna had requested that Tina come to the hospice where she'd been since it was determined that her cancer treatments were no longer helping. Tina had agreed to perform a selection of pieces for Brianna, so the young woman could choose the music she felt best summed up her short, but precious life.

"That's it," Brianna had said when Tina completed the Chopin. "That's the sound I want my family and friends to remember whenever they think of me."

"Shouldn't it be your own music?" Tina asked, trying not to cry.

"You're the one playing it," Brianna told her, "but that *is* my own music."

Glen sent Tina back to that special moment three times before he brought up the possibility of sending her back further. He told her that there might be another, similar moment in a past life and he could help her find it. As with Jeri, that line was true, but not the complete truth.

Tina had not been a part of Emily's life and, oddly, the past life of hers they discovered had very little music in it. Tina had spent a lifetime in a Native American tribe that was probably located in New England. She was a maker of pottery. Some of her work was beautiful, but most was simply practical.

"Where did the music come from?" Emily asked Glen when Tina wasn't with them.

"It would be hard to tell without spending more time with her and we can't afford to do that. It does, however, explain her attraction to a furniture designer. As I've said before, everything has a reason."

After Tina, Emily approached Michelle, her dental hygienist and after Michelle, she had Glen regress Anna, who worked the counter at the Market Street Post Office. Others followed those two. Every woman except one had a past life that came out under Glen's guidance, but none were connected in any way to Emily.

Three months passed, yet Glen still refused to regress Emily. He continued to make the argument that they had enough information from her past lives and they would find the woman with her mother's soul if they just looked around. But as time went by, it became clear that he believed sending her back to a past life would be dangerous. The battlefield session had scared him more than Emily had realized. She liked the idea that Glen cared whether she lived or died, but she was frustrated with their lack of progress. She'd had a birthday during this period and was now eighty-three. She knew she was running out of time.

Emily decided to reassert an argument she had made once before. She pointed out that the battlefield woman had demonstrated a great faith and that it would help if she knew if that faith existed in the woman's life prior to that day. Glen didn't buy into that argument the way Emily had hoped he would. Instead he suggested that they should take a closer look at the women in her church.

Emily had been avoiding her congregation because the church members would most likely find her new belief in reincarnation to be in conflict with their own beliefs. Getting their cooperation without appearing to be a heathen would be quite a trick. But Glen was right. This was something that had to be done.

Eleven

Emily sat beside Glen in what was now their regular place in the sanctuary— center aisle, three pews from the back. He had been attending church with her since he moved down from Charlottesville. Everyone knew him and he knew them. It seemed that he had more friends than she had, because he didn't put them off the way she did. Glen seemed to fit into a church family while Emily always backed away from getting too close to the other members.

She glanced through the bulletin to see what to expect. The sermon was entitled *Who do you say I am?* Emily looked forward to hearing that one. She imagined it would be about Christ's divinity, but she wasn't sure because the title was vague, probably on purpose. It could be about each person's search for his or her identity. If it was, she could tell the minister a thing or two about that, but, of course, she wouldn't.

Emily looked over at the choir and noticed that Stephie Howell was next to Julie Bullard. As always, there was something about seeing them together that evoked a sense of déjà vu. This time Emily dwelled on that feeling more than she had before. Her intuition was telling her something about those two. Why would she think they were connected any more than the other people she knew at the church? She never had that feeling about the married couples she knew. Could it be that there was something about one of them, or even both of them, that she recognized from another life? She looked back at her bulletin to see what they were singing that day and discovered that there was going to be special music during the offertory. Julie and her boyfriend, Michael were credited. Apparently, she was going to sing and he was to accompany her. This felt better than the gardener, the flutist, the dental hygienist and the postal worker put together.

Emily tugged on Glen's sleeve and whispered in his ear, "Something's going on in the choir."

"What?" he asked, also in a whisper.

"I think I have our next candidate."

"One of the choir members? Which one?"

"I'm not certain yet."

"How can you have a legitimate instinct about someone when you don't know who that someone is?"

"That's what I'm trying to figure out."

"Just be careful. You've got two, maybe three chances to approach someone before you get a reputation as a kook."

The service moved through one of the scripture readings and on to the anthem. The music was *Be Still My Soul,* a title that was strangely appropriate for what Emily had been going through. She thought how her mother's soul could use a little stillness. It was like a moving target. The piece was sung by the entire choir, but Emily could hear a woman's voice through the others and that voice gave her chills. She couldn't tell if the sound was Julie, Stephie or some other woman since they were all singing the same words. This was so confusing.

The second scripture reading came next, then two sermons, one for the children and one for the rest of the congregation. Emily didn't hear the message from either. Her mind was still focused on the two women. She was trying to determine where the feelings were coming from and beyond that, just what the feelings were.

Emily caught Julie's eye as she stared at the women a little too intensely. She turned her gaze quickly, like a young girl caught gaping at a boy who was the object of her crush.

As she contemplated the woman a burning smell came upon her, or more specifically she seemed to feel a smell. This sense of smoke brought her back to the regression that had sent her to a battle in a forest that was ablaze. The smell might have been from the candles on the communion table, but it appeared to be a connection if ever there could be one. She was growing excited.

"I'm sure this is right," Emily whispered.

"I hope so," Glen replied.

The service reached the offertory. Julie stood up while her boyfriend, Michael, stepped out of the congregation to take a seat at the grand piano. Emily wasn't sure why she felt strange about both of them, but she did. As they started their music Emily's intuition told her they belonged together, but not like the carefully crafted harmonies they were creating, more like the brash rhythms of a marching band's cymbals and snare drums. Yet that was enough for her. Something seemed right and Julie was the thread that connected it all.

"She's the one we need to regress," Emily whispered to Glen. "I'm sure of that."

Emily sat up straight and listened while Julie's clear alto continued to fill the room with the words of the Michael W. Smith song.

Here I stand arms open wide
I've held you close, kept you safe
Till you could fly

It was a beautiful performance of a lovely song. The balance between Julie's voice and Michael's piano music was perfect. They had obviously put in many hours rehearsing, but there was also a clear connection between them that went beyond preparation. Emily couldn't help but wonder if their music had carried through time and if they'd ever played something similar in another life.

* * *

"Have you heard anything about Julie Bullard from the B-L express?" Glen joked as he and Emily drove back toward the apartment after the Sunday service was over. B-L stood for Bessie and Lynn, a couple of talkative women in their seventies who sat one pew up from Emily and Glen almost every Sunday and had been attending long before Glen arrived. They didn't talk during the service, but they got their gossip in by arriving a few minutes early each week and Emily made it a point to eavesdrop as inconspicuously as possible.

"She and Michael work at the high school," Emily told him. "He's a teacher. She works in the office. They've been living together for a while now. I'm not sure exactly how long, but the relationship isn't fresh. I heard they're in counseling."

"Interesting," was all that Glen said to that.

Since Julie worked at the school, Emily decided to offer her services as a volunteer. The plan was a first step, a means of starting a conversation. Schools were always looking for tutors and people to help with extra curricular groups such as the band or the cheerleaders. She would never follow through, but the act of volunteering would give her an excuse to talk to Julie away from the church.

Julie's desk was in a crowded room outside the private offices of the principal, the assistant principal and the two guidance counselors. Two other women sat near her, their three desks arranged in a horseshoe shape, allowing them no privacy at all. They all had computers on their desks and shared a printer that was on a credenza behind Julie. On her left side there was a wall of cubbies where the teachers received their mail and on her right side was a row of chairs where students or parents sat while awaiting meetings with the staff.

"What group do you want to work with?" Julie asked after Emily approached her. "Or do you have a specific skill? We can always use math tutors."

"Math is not my strong suit by any means. I like history. Maybe it's my age. So much has happened over my lifetime. It's interesting to see how it all fits together. Don't you get that feeling sometimes?"

"Me? I'm no tutor. I spend too much of my day here already."

"I suppose you do. You are a busy one, between this place and church. I enjoyed your music on Sunday. You have an excellent voice and your boyfriend is quite the musician."

"Thank you. We worked hard on that piece."

"It showed."

Once the conversation turned to Julie's life, the topic of volunteer work disappeared in a flash of flattery. Emily successfully used the technique she had honed on the flutist to convince the young woman to talk to her away from the distractions of her office. After school they met at a small Chinese restaurant. It had a modest but sufficient buffet and booths that offered the privacy Emily wanted. The subject of volunteering never came up again.

"It felt good to see a nice young couple such as you and Michael performing your music in church," Emily said after they had been chatting, eating and sipping tea for more than half an hour. She was continuing the conversation that had begun at the school. "You should consider doing it more often."

"Thanks, but things aren't always what they seem."

"What does that mean?"

"Nothing, I'm just rambling."

"I don't mind rambling. I'm a good listener." A year ago that would have been a lie, but Emily's listening skills had developed as her search had progressed.

"I'm just saying we have our problems," Julie told her. "We aren't always the nice young couple you say we are."

"He mistreats you?"

"Sometimes it's his fault," Julie told her, "but other times I act in ways I don't understand. I say things to Michael that I know are going to make him mad, but I can't help saying them. It's as if his anger is the only way I can be confident he cares about me. I seem to want the anger and I make it happen. The entire time I'm doing that, I know my actions are pushing him away. Yet I can't stop."

Emily had her opening. She said, "We're all influenced by events that occurred many years ago. It's complicated, but there are always reasons. The trick to controlling them comes through learning what they are." Emily knew she shouldn't move too quickly, so she did her best to charm Julie. She must have succeeded. After the meal Julie admitted she had enjoyed the conversation and they agreed to meet again a week later.

That night in bed, before she drifted to sleep, Emily lay on her back and thought about Julie. Michael was the one who had switched churches when he and Julie became a couple, so Emily had known Julie for a longer time, more than three years. But she didn't know either one of them well. In fact, she had learned more about Julie during their conversation at the restaurant than she had over all the previous years put together. Emily was trying to picture Julie with the same loving nature she'd seen in her mother during the regressions. That was hard to do. Although Julie was a living person and not simply a memory in the recesses of her mind, she still knew less about her than even the battlefield incarnation of her mother. All Emily had to go on were Julie's comments about herself (mostly about her relationship with Michael) and the few impressions she'd drawn while watching Julie sing.

Oddly Julie's smile was the most negative image that remained with Emily from the day she'd watched her and Michael make their music. After the music was over, as Michael walked back to his seat in the pews, Julie had paused and looked out over the sanctuary. She stretched her lips as wide as her eyes and seemed to say, "It's all right to applaud." But the congregation remained quiet.

Julie had some issues, as everyone does, but Emily was glad she had picked her. Someone who was murdered in countless previous lives certainly has as much right to issues as anyone else.

Twelve

While Michael and Julie had been preparing their music the process had helped their relationship. Although there had been small squabbles over how much to rehearse, making music had brought them together. But when their performance was done, the intimacy they had tried to nurture soured quickly.

"You were too loud on the refrain," Julie had told Michael as they drove home together after that service.

"Thanks for letting me know that," he'd replied, trying to sound sarcastic. Her constant criticism irritated him.

"I'm just saying that I doubt the congregation could hear what I was singing. Words are important."

"The refrain should swell a bit. It has more emotion that way."

"There's a difference between emotion and noise. You do realize that?"

"I doubt what I realize makes much difference."

* * *

The counseling sessions with Stephie continued. Michael was impressed with Stephie's creative suggestions. They'd worked on developing new thinking patterns that were gracious and supportive, rather than competitive and aggressive. Stephie told them that the past was to learn from not to dwell on. She also said that problems in a relationship need to be dealt with by both people. Even the victim needs to make concessions sometimes.

Despite the well intentioned efforts of Stephie, Julie's attitude grew worse. It was becoming more apparent to Michael that both their lives would be better if they were to go their separate ways. He was becoming bitter and almost as sullen as she was. They were competing in a new game, one Stephie called *who is the biggest victim?*

"Money is an issue," Julie said, talking mostly to Stephie at one of the sessions.

Michael thought that was a sucker punch. She had never mentioned a concern over money in the past. It was true that they couldn't afford to splurge very often. Neither of them made a fortune, but their combined income seemed adequate.

"In what way?" Michael asked.

"You spend on yourself," she said, "There's never anything left for me."

"Sure there is. We go out. We do things together."

"And that isn't for you?"

"I have no idea what you're talking about. Give me one example."

"Your gym membership costs us over three hundred a year, right?"

"It's for my health. Think of what it would cost us in doctor bills if I didn't take care of myself."

"That's a rationalization."

"It's not as if I don't use it. I go at least three times a week."

"Don't you think I know that? I eat alone every evening you're there."

"That's your choice. You could join. We could exercise together."

"Right— as if my life isn't enough of a treadmill."

"Hold it there," Stephie said. Michael could tell she was growing frustrated. He and Julie were a difficult case. "This isn't helping. I can understand why you want to get this stuff out, but throwing it at each other isn't a good way to do that. We need to move back a step or two. I'd like to start meeting with both of you individually. It would help if we could talk things over without hurting each other."

The idea sounded all right to Michael, but the look on Julie's face told him she wasn't pleased with the new plan. Perhaps she didn't want to spend more time away from him, but it was more likely that she saw Stephie's suggestion as a retreat. Julie hated retreating.

* * *

The counseling sessions Michael had gone to with Julie had been salt on his wounds, but the new sessions, the ones when he was alone with Stephie, were a balm.

"My expectations are probably naïve," Michael told Stephie at the first solo session. "What Julie and I have isn't close to what I thought love would be. There have been good times. She loves to play games and follow sports and that can be fun, but things aren't consistently good."

"They never are," Stephie said. "Even the strongest relationships go through rough periods."

"I know that. Still, I wish I could tell the difference between weathering a storm and not having enough sense to come in out of the rain."

"There are times when relationships become so destructive that ending them seems the best solution. That's something only you and Julie can determine, but it isn't an easy thing to do and it shouldn't be. Tell me what it is you expect from a relationship."

"Love," Michael answered, smiling a little because he knew it was the specifics she was after, not the quick and easy response he had offered.

"And what is that?" she asked.

Michael told her how lately he'd been spending most of his waking time thinking about that question. How he would drive past exits on highways because his mind was on a vision of a pretty smile, one that was more pensive than filled with laughter and that always turned down a little at the corners. How he would lie awake at night thinking of legs that were thinner and longer than Julie's with skin as smooth as jazz. How he told himself this was love, although he imagined that Stephie would be more likely to label his thoughts as fantasies.

"What is odd," he said, "isn't the visions themselves as much as the feeling that I knew someone from a time long passed, a time that's so far back all that remains are those few vague images."

"Oh," Stephie said. She stopped taking notes and stared at him with her eyebrows raised slightly. She was so still that Michael could see her chest rise with each breath she took. Her reaction worried him a bit.

"That's all you can say?" Michael asked her. "I pour my heart out and that's all I get?"

"I'm sorry. It's just that— maybe your words are not as odd as you think, not nearly so odd at all."

Stephie ended Michael's fifth session by trying to cancel the sixth. Kathy McDowell, one of her suite mates from her college years, was in Greensboro. Kathy had become a fairly well known artist specializing in paintings of the Civil War. She lived and worked out of Pennsylvania, but traveled a great deal. She had come to North Carolina to work on a commission. Her project was to paint a series of murals on the walls of a theme restaurant that was scheduled to open in downtown Greensboro. Stephie was canceling Michael's counseling session so she could meet her old friend at the restaurant to see how her work was progressing.

"I've got an idea," Michael said. "Why don't I go with you?"

"I'm not sure that's a good idea," Stephie responded. But Michael didn't hear conviction behind her words. That made him think she might be open to his idea. He felt a connection to her that caused him to always look forward to their counseling sessions and he wanted her to feel that same connection. Sometimes they would get so involved with their conversations that they'd lose track of time, which would, of course, irritate Julie.

"I teach history," he said. "I know something about the 1800s, so I might be the perfect one to look over your friend's work."

"Perhaps." Stephie spoke hesitantly. She brought the fingers of her right hand to her lips and frowned a little.

"I could pick you up. We could talk on the way over," he told her. "I'd rather do that than skip the session all together."

Stephie had not taken sides in Michael's disputes with Julie, but he could tell she agreed with what he was saying. She had often told them in their sessions that they spent too much time questioning each other's choices. It seemed to Michael that was Stephie's way of acknowledging the issue of Julie's controlling nature.

"It might be fun to meet your friend and see her work," he said. "Do you think there's something wrong with that?"

"I guess not," she said shrugging her shoulders.

"Then I'll pick you up at seven on Thursday?" he asked.

"Make it seven fifteen," She said.

Stephie had agreed to Michael's suggestion quicker than he had thought she would, which made him wonder why. She had to have the same mental picture he had of what was going to happen in three days. He would knock on Stephie's apartment door. Then she would answer and they would walk to his car together. It wouldn't be a date, but it would feel like one.

* * *

Thursday evening did not turn out as Michael had pictured it.

"I'm running a little late," Stephie told him when she answered the door. "Come in and wait in the living room. I'll only be a few minutes."

She was wearing a floral print dress with black flowers on a white background. It had a v-neck, short sleeves, and a skirt that stopped right below her knees. It was a casual dress, but more formal than anything Michael had expected her to wear. They weren't a good match. He had on a green polo shirt and khakis, as if he were on his way to play golf.

"The restaurant is closed, right?" Michael asked, fearing there could be a dress code he wouldn't meet. He spoke to Stephie's back as she left him standing in her living room.

"Yes," she shouted. "It should be just us and Kathy. She said she likes to work in the evening after the construction guys have gone home."

"You look very good in that dress," Michael said, raising his voice so Stephie could hear him from the living room.

"Thank you," she said. "I want to impress Kathy. I haven't seen her in years."

The living room had light green walls and an off white carpet. The furniture included a white couch, two green arm chairs and a white, upright piano set in a corner. There was also a coffee table and a wall unit that had a mixture of books and porcelain figurines on it. There were photos on the piano, pictures of an older couple who were probably her parents and also pictures of young people he recognized from the church.

There were no photos on the walls. Instead she had two framed prints of old farms. One was a summer scene while the other was set in winter. They made the room very peaceful.

Michael stepped into the hall, so he could talk to Stephie without shouting. She was in her bedroom, leaning into the mirror behind her bureau as she fixed her eyeliner. She had her hair pulled back. She moved her hand across her face with a relaxed manner that was very different from the on edge gestures he was used to seeing when Julie put on her makeup. For a brief moment, he was surprised by how enticing it felt to be watching Stephie, as if he had stolen his way into a private moment. But the moment also felt a little voyeuristic. He was uncomfortable with that sensation.

"For some reason I thought your friend had been in Greensboro for a while," he said, revealing his presence.

Stephie looked at him standing in the hall. She stepped over to her door and closed it most of the way. But she left it open a little so they could continue to talk. "Kathy's been here for almost four months," she told Michael.

"And you couldn't get together before tonight? I suppose that's a sign of the times. Everyone is too busy for their friends." That sounded as if he was being critical so he added, "I'm glad you're doing this. It shows you've got your priorities right."

"I didn't know she was in town."

"Oh? She didn't call?"

"No. Kathy and I were once best friends, but we had a falling out. That's why it's so important to me that this reunion go well."

"I hope I won't be in the way."

"You won't. Kathy will love talking to you about day to day life during the civil war."

Michael felt compelled to be near Stephie and had hoped that she felt the same way. She appeared to be more concerned with Kathy than with him, which disappointed him, but he forgot all that as soon as Stephie stepped out of her room. She looked even prettier than she had when he had arrived at her front door. Her makeup was nice, not overdone. Her lipstick was on the pink side of red and matched her subtle rouge perfectly. She had liner on both her upper and lower lids and her lashes seemed exceptionally long. She rarely wore makeup at church and, except on Sundays, she was usually dressed in jeans. He said, "If you're out to impress this friend of yours, you're definitely on the right track."

Stephie smiled then gestured toward the front door. It was time to meet Kathy.

They walked to the parking lot together, as he had imagined they would. When they reached his Grand Prix, Michael held the door for Stephie and she slid into the passenger seat as he tried not to look at her legs. His car was over five years old, but he kept up with the maintenance and it ran well. It was rare that anyone other than Julie rode with him, so the night before he had cleaned and vacuumed it specifically for Stephie. He hoped she was impressed, but she gave no indication.

"Have you and Julie thought of something else to work on now that you're not practicing your music together?" Stephie asked.

Stephie jumped right into the planned counseling session as soon as they were driving. Michael was pleased. He didn't have much hope left for his relationship with Julie, but he enjoyed talking about it with Stephie.

"No. We haven't," he said. "We've gone back to our old habits and separate ways."

"There are plenty of things you can do together," she told him. "Be creative. Go for walks or schedule regular movie marathons. I worked with one couple who picked a local high school and started going to the football games there. They enjoyed the experience so much they were soon going to basketball games, plays and concerts, all at the same school. The idea is to spend time together and have fun. You can do that, can't you?"

"Did you suggest this to Julie?"

"I did."

"I couldn't picture Julie enjoying a high school play even if her own child was in it."

There's something to that, Michael thought as soon as he had said those words. *Truth is I could picture a rock as a mother easier than I could picture Julie. There's nothing maternal in her at all.*

He'd just had a breakthrough in his understanding of his feelings toward Julie and it was momentous enough to cause a chill to run down his back. Julie's self centered attitude was something he could live with if it was just the two of them, but there would come a day when he would need more than that. And Julie could never be anything beyond half a couple. He was certain of that. He knew there was no future in their relationship and that meant there was no reason to work at salvaging it. That realization left him feeling empty, but free, like a hitchhiker with nothing to his name but the clothes he was wearing.

Stephie let the conversation stop. She seemed to sense that Michael needed a moment to be lost in his thoughts. She stared out the side window as they drove passed the stores on Battleground Avenue while making their way toward downtown Greensboro.

It took them about fifteen minutes to get to the restaurant and another two to park the car and walk. When they arrived Stephie tried the door. Kathy had left it open for them, so they stepped inside.

One of Kathy's murals was almost complete on a wall in the foyer. It was an evening scene, a party on a garden patio outside a large two story home that might have been on a plantation. Confederate flags hung from the railing around the upstairs balcony. Azaleas and Magnolias framed the picture.

The women were in vast, colorful, bell shaped dresses stuffed with crinoline that made them look more like decorative topiaries than people. That night must have been warm since most of their dresses had short sleeves and low necklines. A few were even worn off the shoulder. Every woman over ten years old had a man in her gaze.

The men were all dressed in the uniforms of southern officers, formal and buttoned up with swords at their sides. It was clear by the way they stood tall that their notion of war was still associated with pride and glory rather than blood and death. This party must have been a farewell to the confederate troops as they went off to preserve the traditions they loved.

Michael had wondered how the concept of a civil war restaurant would work in Greensboro. The battle history of the city was tied to the revolutionary war, not the war of the states. But as soon as he saw Kathy's mural he understood. Her painting was about the emotions of people pressed into a conflict they couldn't and most often didn't want to avoid. If she maintained objectivity and continued to demonstrate her understanding of behavior and personality, her work would be amazing.

"Let's go," Stephie said, tugging on Michael's sleeve. "I want you to meet Kathy."

Michael was impressed by how much of Kathy's soul was in her work. He turned from the wall and followed Stephie. He was looking forward to meeting the artist.

Thirteen

The restaurant was deeper than it was wide, with a bar on the left and a fireplace further back on the right. There were no tables or booths, so Michael had to use a little imagination to picture how the room would look when it was finished. The walls were covered with murals. There were five small works, each of them no more than two feet across and three large pieces, four counting the one in the foyer.

Kathy was on a ladder, working on a five foot wide battle scene. Union troops were standing on a hill at the left while confederates rushed down a hill on the right. The fight was occurring in a small valley in the middle of the work. The gray sky was filled with smoke from gun fire and dust from galloping horses. Flags were flying, swords held high, men charging toward the fight. The work was about bravery and, indirectly, death.

Kathy came down from her artist's perch and hugged Stephie with all the energy of one of the soldiers she had just painted, welcoming her friend with enthusiasm.

"Look at you!" Kathy cried out, shouting the words. "You're an absolute joy to see and as pretty as ever! I've missed you so much."

"I've missed you, too," Stephie told her, hugging her friend back. "You haven't changed at all."

Michael wondered how accurate that comment was. It had been, according to Stephie, more than five years since the two women had seen each other.

Kathy had on a gray sweatshirt with baggy khaki pants. The long shirt hung over her hips like a skirt. Her shoes were well-worn, brown loafers with flat heels. She was dressed for work, not for company and Michael wondered if Stephie was disappointed since she had put on such a pretty dress. If she was, she didn't give any indication.

Kathy had a strong body with broad hips, muscular arms and large breasts that dominated her appearance. She would have fit well in one of the colorful dresses the women wore in her paintings, but modern styles are more suited to thinner women. Her hair was long, with thick waves of light brown that made her large, oval head appear even larger. Her hairstyle seemed to point out features most women would try to deemphasize, but it gave her an impression of independence that Michael liked.

Stephie had told him that her relationship with Kathy had been severely strained and that they would probably get along better if they had a third person in the room with them. Yet Michael sensed no tension between the women. They didn't take their eyes off each other as they held hands and circled around in a move that could have passed for a dance. Then they started reminiscing about their college days while Michael hung back and tried to stay out of their way. He had noticed this type of non-sexual intimacy between some of the girls he had as students and had concluded it was a natural part of being young and female, a state he considered extremely complicated.

After Stephie introduced Michael to Kathy the threesome chatted for a few minutes. Then, thinking it would be nice to give the two women some time to get reacquainted, he politely left them alone and busied himself by studying Kathy's work. Her murals appeared to be finished, although she had been on a ladder fixing something when they had arrived. Perhaps she was at the point where she needed to stand back and assess what little changes here or there would make a piece better.

There were scenes of military officers from both the north and the south in realistic settings: Stonewall Jackson parading on horseback in front of cheering troops, George McClellan standing beside his tent with two enlisted men, James Longstreet riding at full gallop through a snow covered field and Ulysses Grant and William Sherman studying battle plans while sitting in their camp.

But the painting that captured Michael's attention had no soldiers or even a hint of the war, just a man and a woman on the porch of a tin-roofed farmhouse beside two empty rocking chairs. They were holding hands. They both had brown hair, but hers was a lighter shade with a red tint. Her sky blue eyes were her most striking feature. The man had on homespun button-fly pants with a long-sleeve white shirt. The woman wore a light blue dress with a diamond pattern in the material.

Michael could not pull away from that painting and found himself staring at the woman in it. She had the gentle expression that had been in his thoughts so often, the one he had told Stephie about, with the pensive smile that always turned down at the corners. Her legs were longer than Julie's, just as they had been in his imagination. He could tell that even through her skirt. He kept wondering how smooth her skin would be if he was looking at it directly instead of at the brush strokes of her image. He imagined touching a lake on a still, spring morning without breaking its surface and thought that's how this woman would be, soft and fragile on the outside, but deep and powerful within.

"Time to go," Stephie said, speaking from behind Michael. Her voice brought him out of his reverie.

"Are you done?" he asked. It was a foolish question.

"Yes," Stephie replied. "Thank you for letting us talk alone. It was wonderful, as if no time had passed."

"Do you like that painting?" Kathy asked Michael. "It's not my most dramatic or even my most detailed work, but I felt as if I had to paint it."

"There's something evocative about the people in it," Michael told her.

"I can see that, too," Stephie said, "especially in the man. He seems strong and at the same time kind."

"He's good looking," Kathy added. "I don't suppose that hurts."

Michael hadn't thought of that. Apparently Stephie had, since she blushed slightly. The man was tall with thick brown hair that swooped across his forehead. He had close-set eyes and very straight eyebrows. He wasn't smiling, yet he seemed happy to be next to the woman.

* * *

"What was it that came between you two?" Michael asked Stephie as he drove her back to her apartment.

"It's a long story."

"I'd like to hear it, if you feel like talking."

"Kathy can be a little overwhelming at times. At least she could back then. And I was in a mixed-up state where I needed both independence and guidance. Kathy couldn't find the right balance. I rebelled against what I saw as an effort to control me, but she clearly thought of as well intentioned advice. There wasn't a single fight, just lots of little ones that put distance between us."

"I can't picture you needing guidance."

"We all do. But I was on my own for the first time in my life and I didn't want a pseudo parent looking over my shoulder. There was one incident that started the problems. It was strange because I needed Kathy that night and she was there for me, like always. But it ended up driving us apart when it should have brought us closer."

"What happened?" Michael asked. He pulled his eyes off the road to glance at Stephie and noticed she was looking out the window as she spoke, apparently absorbed by the lights in the store windows they were passing. He was disappointed that she wasn't looking at him, but when he noticed her hand on the console between the seats he took the wheel with his left and set his right on top of hers. She didn't pull away.

"Friday nights used to be what we called best friend nights," Stephie said. "We would go out together. Sometimes we'd do something on campus, like a play or a concert, but mostly we used it as a time to get away from the school. This one night we were shopping. We went to the Rose Hill Mall and while there we went into a lingerie shop. We looked over the displays, but we didn't buy anything.

"On our way out of the store I glanced up at a hosiery display and noticed a leg form, one used to display socks. I had a bizarre reaction to the image of a detached leg sitting alone on a shelf. It left me unable to catch my breath. I felt as if I couldn't walk.

"Kathy asked me if I was all right. She reached out for my arm. But I couldn't answer her. It was as if something inside of me had kicked my lungs.

"I swayed and slipped. Kathy caught me. She eased me to the floor and offered to call 911.

"I told her I'd be all right. I tried to stand, but I fell back. I remember the dress I was wearing because it was a new outfit and I didn't want to ruin it. Isn't it weird how something like that stuck in my memory? Anyway, I looked up in Kathy's eyes and pleaded for her to get me out of there."

Stephie pulled her hand out from under Michael's. Her action caused him to turn to her again and he saw that she was now staring at his eyes. Her gaze felt almost as nice as her touch.

"Kathy helped me up," Stephie continued, "then half carried me out to a bench in the center of the mall aisle. Once I was away from the store, I could breathe again. We sat there for ten to fifteen minutes as my strength slowly came back. I felt better after that, but the episode had left me shaken."

Michael was transfixed by Stephie's story and a little jealous that Kathy had been there to help her, instead of him. "Any idea what it was that caused you to have such a reaction?" he asked.

"Ever since I was a child I've had a repeating dream that's frightening. There's a huge pile of human limbs and I have to keep going back to it to throw more on top. Sometimes I'm carrying legs and sometimes arms, but there is always blood and the skin is always warm as if the limbs have just been cut off. That dream is the only one I've ever had that has a smell about it and it's an awful odor, rank like raw sewage. When I saw that leg form, images from that dream came back to me like a giant wave. My heart raced, my legs gave out and I couldn't breathe. I can't explain it any better than that."

Michael could hear the emotion in Stephie's voice and he knew how much it bothered her. He started to suggest that she not speak about it, but he decided that getting the words out might help. "It sounds horrible," was all he could say.

"It was. But anyway, Kathy went into this crazy protect mode after that incident. She would insist that I check in with her whenever I did anything out of the ordinary. She always wanted to know where I was going and who I was going to be with. And she constantly complained about how I made her worry. I was eighteen and that was the first time I was on my own. I knew she was acting that way because she cared about me, but she was stifling. Eventually I told her I needed space and I requested a different roommate. She argued, but I was insistent and she finally agreed. We often ran into each other on campus and I always had mixed feelings about trying to resurrect our friendship. I suppose she did, too. But we let it go and when we graduated we went our separate ways. We've been apart ever since, until this week, when she called to let me know she was in Greensboro."

The story made Michael realize that he felt something for Stephie he had never felt for Julie or any other woman. She had shown a fragile side that made him want to wrap his arms around her and keep her safe forever. But it wasn't only a desire to help her overcome her weakness. It was also a need for her strength. They would be better as two, like sticks that can be broken one at a time but not when they lie side by side. Yet Stephie was Julie's friend and she was the counselor who was trying to repair their damaged relationship. The situation couldn't be worse. Michael had noticed that Stephie seemed to like him; and right then he decided to convince her that she needed him as much as he did her. Julie worried him. Oh, Lord, she worried him. But this was something deep in his heart that he knew he had to follow.

Fourteen

"Julie's a competitor," Emily told Glen as she mashed potatoes for their dinner and he cut carrots for their salad. The smell of a cooking meatloaf filled the room. "It shows up in everything she does, from her appearance to how she keeps her house. It seems to be especially strong when it comes to her relationship with her boyfriend. I asked her why she feels the need to compete and that turned out to be a question she didn't know how to answer. But she wants to know. I think I can convince her to look into her past if she believes the reasons might be buried there. That could be our foot in her door."

"Go for it," was Glen's response.

* * *

Julie agreed to talk to Glen, but the first time she came over she started saying things such as, "I feel silly," and "Glen seems like a quack." She ended up leaving before he even tried to hypnotize her. Emily caught up with her the following day and convinced her to come back. On her second visit, Glen talked Julie into lying on the sofa.

Emily was concerned about Glen's plan for Julie. He asked her to name a specific event from her childhood that she thought might help explain some of her relationship problems, but she had been unable or unwilling to name one. So Glen said he intended to focus on buried feelings of distress.

"I'll have to monitor her carefully," he told Emily while Julie was in the bedroom changing. "And if I think I'm putting her through too much, I'll pull her back and instruct her to forget the session."

"Just be careful," Emily said.

Julie was young and healthy, but re-experiencing a disturbing event with absolute clarity could hurt anyone. Yet Glen was insistent. "This is the way it's done," he told Emily. Still, she wasn't sure if it was the way it *should* be done.

When Julie came out of the bedroom Glen started the session, guiding her back to the event she subconsciously thought of as the most upsetting incident of her life. It took only a few minutes for Julie to enter a trance and to start talking. She was back in the memory of an event that had to do with her younger brother Trent.

"It's dark," Julie said. "I'm in my room, in bed. I hear a shot and I know it's Neil. I don't understand what's going on. He always insisted that we shouldn't shoot at night, because he's careful about safety. I'm worried about him. I get up, strip off my nightgown and pull on my underwear, jeans and a T-shirt. I also slip on a pair of sneakers without bothering with socks. It's warm enough to go barefoot, but I might need to run.

"I leave my room and walk down the stairs as quietly as possible. My parents are watching TV. My dad can see the hall from where he's sitting, but he's focused on the show. I manage to get out the front door without drawing their attention. I turn the knob carefully to close it without a click then I take off for where we always go shooting.

"I see Neil. The moon isn't quite full, but it's bright enough to light the clearing where he's standing. Someone is with him. I crouch down and approach carefully. It turns out to be Trent, my brother. He's ten, that's two years younger than me, which makes me closer to Neil's age. Trent shouldn't be out here with Neil. He's my friend, not Trent's.

"As I get closer I have to move off the path and slip carefully from tree to tree. This section of the woods has no undergrowth, but it is still hard to move in it. There are fallen trees and dead branches all over the ground. And there's a thick layer of wet, dead leaves that smell like muck when you dig down a couple of inches. It's hard to walk and even harder to quietly crawl. But I'm good at it. I want to find out what's going on with my brother and Neil.

"They have cans set up on a fallen tree, beer cans, the same type he used to teach me how to shoot. Trent tries two more shots, as I watch. Neil helps him aim, but he still misses. So Neil takes the rifle and shoots twice. On the second shot he hits a can and that causes Trent to whoop.

"Trent is our dad's favorite and mom always goes along with whatever dad says. I have to clean dishes after every supper and fold laundry on the weekends, while Trent does nothing. It's always been like that. He gets everything handed to him. Now this. Shooting was my thing. But if Trent asks for a gun they'll give him one. Not me. They'll say girls shouldn't play with guns. How did Trent get out here anyway? He's supposed to be in bed, which means he must have snuck out here way before I did. I wonder how often that happens.

"Neil sets the rifle down, turns toward Trent and hugs him. He hugs him way too long. Then he pushes his hands up Trent's T-shirt as if he's trying to lift it over his head. Trent squirms back and pushes Neil away. That's when the real weird stuff starts to happen.

"Trent makes eye contact with me. At first he looks confused and uncomfortable. Meanwhile, Neil is backing away from him and saying something that I can't hear. Trent seems startled that I'm watching and appears to be a little frightened as if I've caught him doing something wrong. Neil picks up an open can of something. He drinks from it then tosses the can. He says something else I can't hear while Trent stands still for a second or two, his arms limp, still looking at me. Then Neil moves toward Trent and pulls his shirt off. Trent actually lifts his arms to help him. In a quick motion Neil drops the shirt on the ground.

"Neil hugs Trent again. He has no idea I'm there, but Trent knows. He's doing this to spite me. Neil is my friend. He and Trent barely said two words to each other before this night. Truth is Trent would do anything to get to me. He is like that.

"Neil's putting his hands down my brother's pants now and kissing his chest while he does that. I want to shout at them both, but I know what Trent would do. He would just laugh at me. So I stand up and walk away, not even trying to hide. Trent says something else, but he's talking to Neil not me. I still can't hear what he says.

"Neil was my friend. I was the one he taught to shoot first and I was good at it. It will never be the same now. I hate Trent. I hate him so much. I run back to the house."

* * *

"Trent was ten years old," Emily told Julie, as they sat in the back seat of Glen's car while he drove Julie home. "Neil was sixteen. I don't see how your brother had much control over that situation."

"You didn't know him."

"That's true. I didn't."

"You and Trent had problems before that night, didn't you?" Glen asked from the front seat.

"I suppose."

"Then those problems most likely came from further back than where I sent you, probably a previous life. You've got those memories buried in you, too. And I can bring them out, if you'd like. "

"He can," Emily told Julie. "He did it for me."

"You sound like a quack," Julie said to Glen again, without any hint of humor in her voice.

"That's what you thought when I suggested using hypnotism to bring out your childhood memories. Yet you saw how clear those can be when you tap into them the right way. This is no different. Your past is in your head and I can pull it out. I've done it for many people."

"It's not my past that matters," Julie told him.

"The past controls the future," Emily said.

"You're just as weird as he is," Julie replied.

It took some convincing on both their parts, but before she got out of Glen's car, Julie had agreed to a second hypnotism session. This time the goal would be to go back in time to the source of her problems with Trent.

"I thought you were going to cause her to forget the session," Emily said when she and Glen were driving back alone.

"Julie's coming back to us, isn't she?" was Glen's response.

Those words seemed hard to Emily, but she understood Glen's focus. His approach was the best chance they had.

"Do you really think her brother was raped?" Emily asked, changing the subject back to Julie's story. "Trent was only ten years old and Julie was twelve. They were both too young to understand what was going on. Chances are what she told us was just flat out wrong, probably some crazy mixture of an upset adult mind looking through the eyes of a child. That's possible, isn't it?"

"Julie told us what she saw," Glen said. "I'm sure that part was true, but you're right about her interpretation of what Trent was thinking. That's another story entirely. To us none of it matters. We've got an opportunity. We can find out if Julie's the woman we're after. That's what we need to care about now."

Emily knew Glen was right, but she also had mixed feelings about Julie as her reincarnated mother. She had hoped the woman they would find wouldn't be so troubled.

* * *

"I'm a man," Julie said. "I don't know about birthing babies."

Emily looked at Glen. His startled expression showed he was as surprised as she was. They had latched on to another subject who had switched genders. Julie was like Jeri, the gardener. It meant she couldn't be the one they were looking for, but they kept her regression going. Glen shrugged his shoulders. He continued to ask Julie a series of questions to find out where her memory was located and what was happening around her.

"I'm in a barn constructed with split log walls and a tin roof. There are eight stalls and I'm in one of them. There are no animals, but there is still a smell of hay and manure. I'm with a woman who is about to give birth. We're alone. This is sometime during the Civil War and we are following a union corps. I don't know if we're in Maryland or Virginia, but I know we're headed south. There are camp followers in the farmhouse, two whores and the man who protects them. That's why we are in the barn and not the house.

"The people around us think the woman I'm with is a whore. I know because I was approached twice about using her services. I couldn't call those men out as the pigs they are; instead I told them they would have to wait until after the baby came. She deserves better than that, but I've let the rumors happen to protect us both. Traveling alone would be dangerous, especially since we are heading south. People would think I was a confederate deserter until they heard my accent, then they would think I was a spy. The union army protects us, although there are dangers here as well. I can't let any of the camp followers discover that we stay alive by my stealing, especially since I sometimes take things from them.

"She tells me to close the gate. I ask her if she wants anything else. She tells me she needs something to tie off the cord. Then she wants me to leave her alone. I offer more clean straw, but she says she has enough. I take my laces out of my boots. I toss one to her then close the stall gate and sit on the dirt floor. I listen to her groans as I cut my other lace in half and use the pieces to tie up my shoes.

"She is groaning so loudly it's almost a scream. I ask her if she's hurt. How could I ask such a foolish question? She tells me that if I want to help I should pretend that I'm not here. I can't blame her for wanting to punish me. What I've done is wrong. But I've done it for love. I wish she could understand that. If she would accept me I would even raise her bastard as my own."

Emily jumped back at the mention of the word bastard. That label was one she would never forget. It was what the man at the battle scene had called her before he'd shot her. Glen's eyes were wide with astonishment.

"There are too many similarities for this to be a coincidence," Glen whispered. "There's the battle, the distance these people were walking, the fact that a man was traveling with a woman and her infant child, the fact that another man was the father of that child. Something finally seems to be going our way, but we can't be certain. Not yet."

"Move forward in time," Glen instructed Julie. "Does the baby live? Does the mother live?"

"I can't hear anything from inside the stall. I'm standing up and looking over the gate. There's a great deal of blood around, on the straw and her skirt, but she is alive and smiling. It is the first time in months that I've seen her smile. The baby is also alive, wrapped in her shawl and feeding at her breast and she's singing something softly to the child. It's the old hymn *Leaning on the Everlasting Arms*. She has such a pretty voice. I offer her the water in my canteen to clean herself and her daughter."

"There's another similarity," Glen whispered to Emily. "She's singing to her daughter. Still not much, but little things add up."

They listened for a little more time before Glen brought Julie out of her trance. This time he specified that Julie would remember nothing of the experience and that she would be left with a very pleasant, soothing sensation.

"Why didn't you want her to remember?" Emily asked after they had taken Julie home and were once again riding back in Glen's car.

"Think about how skeptical Julie is. At first you had trouble even getting her to talk to me. And her competitive nature indicates that she's insecure as well. How do you think someone like that would respond to the concept that she was a man in at least one of her past lives? She'd be calling me a quack once again. We can't risk that. If what I suspect is true and Julie is the one destined to cause your next mother's death, then finding her is almost as important as finding the woman with your mother's soul."

Fifteen

Stephie was in a session with Julie when she realized there was a problem. Julie wasn't just Julie anymore. She was Michael's girlfriend. The change in how Stephie perceived Julie happened in spite of the fact that she had known her for some time. Now it was difficult to see her without thinking of Michael.

Ever since the evening when he took her to see Kathy, small qualities of Michael's were consistently in Stephie's thoughts. She liked how he pushed his thick hair away from his eyes and she enjoyed the fact that it was as dark as her own. She liked how he held his lips when he was contemplating a point she had made. She thought of the verse in *Song of Songs*: *His lips are like lilies, wet with liquid myrrh*. She had never understood it as well as she did now— a fact that complicated her life.

Stephie was drawn to Michael and that left her feeling guilty and confused. This wasn't a normal attraction. She'd had her share of those and could recognize the pull. This was different, as if some force inside of her was compelling her toward him.

She wasn't just an acquaintance of Michael and Julie, she was their counselor. She had to control her feelings and deal with the situation in an ethical and professional manner.

"When did you first notice that things weren't going as well as you had hoped?" she asked Julie. It was a safe question, a standard one. She had asked other couples the same question, many times before.

"We have a picture of Vicksburg National Park on the sideboard in our dining room," Julie told her. "One of Michael's students took the shot and had an eight by ten copy printed for us because Michael has such an intense interest in the Civil War. It was a nice gesture, but it was also the first sign that things weren't right. Michael put it in a frame that already had a picture in it, one of me at the beach. He could have chosen another photo to replace. We have four pictures of his mom in the dining room alone. Besides, he picked a cute shot of me. The wind is blowing my hair and I'm wearing a loose, black T-shirt over a white, long sleeve top and a pair of light blue capris. I was upset when I found out my picture was tucked in a drawer. I told Michael so, but he didn't put it back."

Michael was as courteous as any man Stephie had ever met. Julie had to have her facts wrong. If Michael understood that something bothered Julie, or anyone for that matter, he was the type who would find a solution. She did see how he might have been embarrassed by the photo Julie had described. It couldn't have looked good. Julie's thighs were too thick for capris. Stephie realized her thought was catty. She felt some remorse over that and promised herself she wouldn't let Julie see even a hint of attitude in her expression or her body language.

"If the picture was a gift from one of his students," Stephie said, defending her new friend, "I can see why Michael felt an obligation to display it. And if Michael likes pictures that remind him of people he doesn't see regularly then I can understand why he chose to replace yours instead of one of his mother.

"You're taking his side?" Julie asked, with more surprise in her voice than resentment.

"I'm not taking anyone's side. I'm just saying there are ways for him to rationalize his actions. Perhaps what he did is a sign of his taking you for granted rather than a sign of him losing interest in you. If so we have something that's easier to deal with."

"There's also been a disconnect in our conversations recently," Julie told her. "That might be a sign of something. If I make a comment to Michael about chess, he might respond with some statement about art. It's as if he isn't paying attention."

"Art? What did he say about art?"

"I don't remember what he said, but you're missing the point. I talk about chess, he talks about art. I talk about art, he talks about the Civil War. I talk about the Civil War, he talks about chess. We're never on the same page."

"There must have been good times," Stephie said.

"Good times?" Julie said, pondering the suggestion. "There were the early days. Those were good."

"Tell me about them."

"The first few games of chess we played were interesting. I think Michael would agree with that, although I'm not sure because I hustled him. He had this attitude that he would teach me what he knew about the game. That sounds nice enough, but it went hand in hand with an assumption that I knew nothing. I'm not sure where that idea came from. I'm a woman, I'm a secretary and I'm not a college graduate. It could have been any one of those things or all of them put together, but whatever it was he treated me like a child. So I let him win a few times, then I told him money would make the game more fun. He laughed at that and said he'd play for kisses. So I told him I'd give him kisses if he won, but if I won I wanted dollars. He agreed. Then he did this trick he used back then, he brought out both his knights. That's great when you're playing against beginners because knights are different. They don't move straight and they can jump other pieces. New players have a tendency to overlook them. Of course, that didn't work with me. I checkmated him in about twelve moves."

"And you think Michael enjoyed this."

"Yes. I took him for a hundred dollars, but I gave his money back to him when he agreed to use it to buy what he said he wanted. Fact is I sold him more than just kisses, so he ended up winning big. I believe he liked that." Julie smiled at Stephie as she spoke.

If Stephie was counseling a married couple, she would cover sex. She would read from 1 Corinthians and talk about concepts such as satisfying each other's needs and the verse that states that in a marriage the husband has authority over the wife's body and the wife has authority over the husband's body. The subject might be a little uncomfortable for some of the couples she spoke to, but she would help them through that discomfort and make sure they talked about their physical relationship. But Julie and Michael were not married and that meant her approach had to be more careful.

Stephie did not accept a literal interpretation of the Bible. She drew her religious and moral conclusions through contemplation and prayer as well as through a thorough understanding of the cultural differences between twenty-first century Americans and the people who authored the Bible. In modern America, extra marital relations are wide spread and divorce is acceptable. And although she knew that most of her congregation would cringe if they heard her saying so, she thought there were some advantages to the current morality. Many couples would be better off if the relationships they were in would end. In their cases trial marriages made some sense, because they revealed the truth.

Stephie wanted to tell Julie straight-out that when she looked back on the good times, she should have found something other than a successful hustle and sex for money. But those words were harsh, so instead she said. "It sounds as if you did something similar to what Michael did when he brought out his knights. Your moves weren't straight with him and you were jumping over normal steps in a relationship. The results you're seeing are similar to what he ran into. It worked when he was a beginner, but now that the relationship's older he needs to understand where you're coming from and know where you're headed. Life is similar to chess in some ways."

* * *

The following evening it was Michael's turn for a counseling session. After he arrived at Stephie's office and took a seat on her couch, she asked him, "When did you first notice that things weren't going as well as you had hoped?" It was the same question she'd asked Julie. She wanted to see how different his response would be.

"There wasn't a specific problem that told me things were ending," Michael told her. "It was an attitude difference and it was my attitude not hers. It was as if I woke up one day and realized we weren't right for each other, that I had always enjoyed aspects of our friendship and still do, but that there's supposed to be something more in a relationship. Julie is a different person than she used to be. She's always picking fights for one thing and that's tough to live with. But she changed because she needs a commitment I'm not willing to give her. Does that make sense?"

"No," Stephie said, "You sound as if you're taking on too much of the blame. The causes of relationship problems are generally shared. You say you've always enjoyed her friendship. Can you tell me what it is you like?" If Stephie was asked that same question, she could come up with a number of things she liked about Julie. They'd been friends for as long as Julie had been in the choir, which was almost a year now. Julie was friendly and fun in that situation. Stephie often chatted with her after the rehearsals, about things such as music and church activities. They had never quarreled or picked on each other, although there was one time when Stephie was offered a solo and Julie was irritated that she hadn't had the same opportunity. The solo was small, just a single verse, which might be the reason the issue never came to a head. But Julie did make a snide comment about how it pays to work with the choir director.

"She used to push me to be a better person," Michael said. "But when the competitions morphed into fights the pushing turned in the wrong direction."

"And now there's nothing about your relationship that makes you better?"

"I don't see it, but like I said, it's my attitude. Quirky traits of hers that I used to find interesting now irritate me, from the way she hangs onto first impressions like a dog protecting a bone to the way she rolls her eyes and shakes her head when she believes the people around her are all idiots. What was decisive about her hasn't suddenly become opinionated; it's my perspective that's different. I can't run from that."

"When relationships are young they can appear perfect," Stephie told him, "but as they age reality starts to poke through. It's like candy. When we're children we only understand the taste, but when we grow we realize that along with the sweetness we get calories and cavities. Knowledge doesn't mean we stop eating candy. We just strive for a better balance."

But some relationships aren't candy with side effects, they're poison and Stephie was starting to think this could be the case with Michael and Julie. Something about them felt wrong, as if they belonged together about as much as a cat and a bird. Michael had given a great deal of consideration to what was wrong with the relationship, while Julie had spent her time fretting over her picture. That alone spoke volumes about the difference between the two. She was the cat. He was the bird. If the relationship came to an end, she might go hungry but he would live.

Stephie had seen this happen with a few other couples she had been working with. Those times she had always reacted responsibly. She had explained to the people that she couldn't work with them and had tactfully told them why. It was up to them to decide if they wanted to find a different counselor. But Michael made this case a little different. She cared about him in a powerful way that she couldn't quite identify. It would be unbearable to simply leave him in such a toxic situation. She decided instead to think before she did anything and pray for guidance.

Sixteen

When Emily asked Julie if Glen could regress her again she answered, "I enjoyed it the last time." Emily was certain that wasn't true. Julie thought she'd had a good experience, but only because of Glen's hypnotic suggestion that left her with a pleasant sensation. Emily wondered if there was any difference between enjoying something or thinking you enjoyed it, since enjoyment is purely a state of mind. In any case, what he'd done had worked. She was still a willing subject.

This time they decided to send Julie back to the person she had been when Emily was a child, to the time when Emily's mother had died. If Glen's theory of circularity held and if Julie's soul was, as they now suspected, the dark force that had followed her mother through life after life, then Julie's soul would have to have been present on that tragic day. The person she was back then would have affected the events somehow.

Emily had always believed there was something more to her mother's death than the simple explanation of an accident while walking in the woods. Now the combination of Glen's theory, the regression that sent Emily back to the battlefield and Julie's regression to a man witnessing a birth in a Civil War era barn added up to the involvement of Julie's soul. Emily had dealt with the uncertainty and lack of closure for more than eight decades. Suddenly she appeared to be on the verge of knowing and although she wanted the truth, she was also terrified of the emotions that truth would force on her.

"Go back through the years," Glen told Julie in a soft, chanting voice, "to the twenties. It's the middle of prohibition. People are wearing raccoon coats and flapper dresses. The newspapers are filled with stories of Henry Ford, Al Capone and Charles Lindberg. But you have your own life. Tell us about that. Tell us what you're doing."

"I'm waiting for Edwin. That's what I'm always doing lately; at least, that's how it seems."

"What's your name?"

"Anne."

"Tell us about Edwin, Anne."

"I like the way it feels to be with him, as if people can't put us down no matter what we do. And we do a lot. Edwin's strong and he's a looker, too. He's got a full head of curly brown hair and a rock solid chest. He's also got connections. People like him and that's what counts. I'm in his house now, waiting. He was supposed to be back from Canada a couple of days ago, with a full load. He gets the best Canadian hooch anyone can get and he sells it. Like I said, he knows the right people. One run and we're set for a few months, maybe more. But it's risky. If Edwin gets caught I could end up alone. I don't like waiting and I don't like not knowing."

The story was beginning and Emily was braced to hear it. She was in a near hypnotic state herself as she listened to the words Anne was spouting out through Julie's trance. And thanks to her own regressions, Emily now knew her mother well enough to wrap an extra layer of emotions around this experience. She had to clasp her hands in front of her body because they were shaking beyond her control. She also had to concentrate just to keep breathing evenly. She stared at Julie, watching the young woman's lips move as her story unfurled.

* * *

The lock turned softly with a slight scraping sound and immediately after that the door slowly started to slide open. It had to be Edwin. Anne had been waiting for him to return, sometimes pacing the room, but mostly just sitting on the ragged, tweed couch in his small, shabby home and staring at the front door like a cat studying birds at a feeder. Two days and three hours had passed since he was due.

Anne was dressed in a tube style, pink chiffon dress with a wide band around her hips, a loose tie around her neck and a skirt that stopped just below her knees. Wearing the elegant outfit while sitting in such a dump made her feel like a four carat diamond set in stainless steel, but she wore it anyway, every day. Edwin had helped her pick it out and had told her to put it on when she expected him to return, even if he was three months late. He told her that the thought of her dressed so pretty would keep him safe, although she imagined it was *undressing* her he had on his mind. She had added a special touch by taking time with her hairstyle. She finger waved her locks into soft curls that suited her short style perfectly, like Mary Astor only blonde. Edwin would like that, since he had a thing for the young actress. But her name made Anne think of Mary Vinson and she couldn't stand that woman. She called her a bluenose.

* * *

Emily's head shot up at the same time as Glen's. The look on his face made it clear to her that he was as excited by the mention of her mother's name as she was. Then he tilted his head slightly, smiled and winked at her, so it was also clear that he was pleased.

A bluenose is a prude. Emily remembered that term from years ago when it had been common slang. She doubted Glen had any idea what it meant, but the look he'd shot her made it clear that he knew it was negative. Anne had hated Emily's mother and that was one more indication they were looking in the right direction.

Emily wasn't so sure about her own feelings. She wanted to know about her mother's death and needed to understand its connection to the future. But Anne had said she couldn't stand Mary Vinson and that talk brought more clarity to the worst event of Emily's life than she had experienced since she was two. Of course, there was still a chance that Anne wasn't the right person. Everyone who hates doesn't kill. If they did, there wouldn't be much left of humanity. Emily needed to hear more. She sat in her chair and waited for Anne to continue her story.

* * *

After the door opened Edwin stood outside for a moment, staring at Anne. Then he stepped in, looked at her and said, "I don't want to talk about it." He was wearing his navy blue, long sleeve shirt, baggy black pants and a grey flannel cap. These were the dark clothes he had left in and Anne knew that was an awful sign. Clothes were important to Edwin. If he'd made money, his first stop would have been to buy something fancy. If he'd shown up in a new suit with pleated pants, a vest and a bowler hat they would have been hugging and kissing as soon as he had arrived. As it was, his anger was evident in his balled-up hands and in the way he looked at what she was wearing.

Anne backed away from him and as she did she started pulling her dress off. This had happened to her before. She was supposed to be Edwin's celebration. Instead she was a pink reminder of his failure. But undressing was impossible. She had to undo the tie around her neckline then pull everything up over her head. She couldn't do all that and get away from him at the same time, so he caught her. There was whiskey on his breath. He'd gotten at least one bottle, maybe more, and he had drunk some of it himself. He must have lost the hooch somehow after he had it across the border or maybe the buyers cheated him.

"What happened?" she asked. Edwin sometimes told her stories about his work, but they mostly seemed like lies to Anne. There was this long tale about outrunning cops while climbing narrow mountain roads somewhere in southwestern New York. She'd heard the story more than once. She never knew what to believe, but that was what life was like with Edwin. His lying kept her dizzy most of the time, but she was as addicted to him as he was to his whiskey. She had also learned not to question his honesty, because he got mad if she did.

Since she couldn't get her dress off without his help, she held her arms straight up. That was a risky choice. She hoped he would simply pull her clothes off her and that would settle him down, but he was drunk and he was frustrated. There was every bit as good a chance that he'd get violent.

Edwin grabbed her dress on either side of her waist and lifted it up over her head. He threw it at the couch then stood back and stared at her. She was now dressed in black cross-strap shoes, silk stockings with a garter belt, bloomers and a brassiere. She started to fold her arms across her chest, but she knew that would drive him crazy, so she held them down by her side and faced him.

"You dress like a whore," he said to her. "You know that?"

"Sorry." She was in her underwear. What did he expect?

"Sorry? Maybe sorry isn't good enough."

"Please, Edwin."

He grabbed her by her shoulders and started shaking. She pushed on his arms to free herself, but her resistance only made him more aggressive. He slapped her across the face, twice, drawing blood on her lips. After that he hit her in the stomach. She fell forward toward him, but he let her slip to the floor then said, "I'm going for a walk. When I get back you better be out of my place."

Anne stayed on the floor listening to Edwin's hard breathing as he stomped around the room for close to a minute before leaving. After the door closed and she thought it was safe to stand, she struggled to her feet and looked out the window. She could still see him. He was a good distance down the street, walking away from the house at a decent pace. She had time to clean her face up a bit and get dressed before he would turn around. She might even run a comb through her hair before she left.

She stepped into the bathroom to check on her face. The blood would clot if she put some pressure on it. Her lips were swollen and her left cheek was starting to puff up, but he hadn't hurt her eyes. That was good. She took out some lipstick and pancake base that she had left in his bathroom vanity more than a month earlier. She tried to cover the damage but applying the makeup hurt, so instead she grabbed one of Edwin's hand towels to take with her. She would hold it to her face as she walked home.

She went back to the living room and picked up her dress. It was missing a button, but other than that it had not been torn as he had ripped it off her. And her stockings hadn't been ruined as she fell. Anne could get herself back together and, hopefully, be relatively presentable. This wasn't the first time she'd been through this, so she knew what came next. She would hide out in her house for a few days then Edwin would come calling. He'd be all apologies and promises that it would never happen again. The cuts and bruises would heal, so she'd be all right. In fact, she could probably get a few extra favors out of him as part of the process.

She left the house and turned in the direction away from where Edwin was walking. That meant she would have to go home the long way. It also meant she would pass the Vinson's home, which she hated to do. If Mary looked out a window and saw her holding a towel to her face that would be the worst possible ending to a disastrous day. Anne kept walking, the leather soles of her shoes clicking against the stones as she tried to avoid the muddy spots in the dirt road.

Anne knew Harry Vinson when they were teenagers, before Mary came into his life. There was a time when Anne thought they might have a life together. Harry even kissed her once, in the woods behind the house where he now lived with Mary. They had been talking about a spring that flowed into a creek a short distance into the forest. The water poured out from among some rocks that were under a massive Oak tree. Anne told him it was clean enough to drink and when Harry said he didn't believe her, she said she'd show him. She led him into the woods then cupped her hands and took a drink. She filled her hands a second time and offered the water to him, but instead of drinking he pulled her to him and kissed her. She still remembered how that kiss felt all these years later.

Life has a tendency to work out well for some people, but Anne wasn't one of those lucky ones. Here she was sneaking by the Vinson house with a towel to her face to hide her bruises while Mary and Harry were inside, most likely playing with their two year old daughter. They had the perfect life and she had nothing. Anne wondered if Harry ever thought of that kiss and the possibilities that might have existed.

That's when the plan came to her, flowing into her mind like water from that old spring. If she could help Harry's memory a little he might start thinking of what he was missing. He might even try to kiss her again. And after that, who knows?

Edwin would come crawling back in a day or two. When he asked her what he could do to make it up to her, she'd tell him to bring some whiskey and a blanket into the woods behind the Vinson house. She'd say she wanted him to kiss her where Mary and her brat kid could see. He would never suspect the kiss was actually meant for Harry's eyes because Edwin knew how much Anne hated Mary. It was a perfect plan.

Seventeen

Glen ripped a clean sheet of paper from the pad he was using to take notes. He scribbled something on it and handed it to Emily. "Are you all right?" it read. "Should I let her continue?"

Emily nodded for him to go ahead with the regression. It was sweet that Glen was concerned with her emotional state, but there was no way she wanted this to stop. There were, however, things that bothered Emily more than they should. For one, she couldn't get it out of her head that her father had kissed this woman, Anne. She understood the timeframe, how the kiss was years before that. It was before her mother's death, before her father even knew her mother. Still, he had held Anne in his arms. He had touched her lips with his own. Emily couldn't help but feel betrayed.

And what about Julie? Emily had watched her standing in the choir week after week. Julie's face was so expressive that Emily had picked her out as the singer she most enjoyed concentrating on during the music. Now she was looking at her as she lay on the couch in a hypnotic trance, wondering what kind of a monster might be hidden inside. If the story kept unraveling in the manner it appeared to be then it was her soul that had killed Emily's mother and it was her soul that had left Emily with such an empty life.

"Did it work?" Glen asked Julie. "Did Edwin agree to go with you to the woods?"

* * *

Edwin showed up at Anne's door a few days later as she had predicted he would. He told her the fight wasn't her fault. He said he loved her and he'd never hurt her again. She let him in, kissed him and even cooked him a dinner, but she was careful to avoid asking him what had gone wrong with the whiskey run. She knew the subject could set him off once more. He offered to make everything up to her in whatever way she chose, just as she had known he would.

"I can't stand that Mary Vinson," she told him.

"I know that," he said.

"I want to aggravate her by showing her what she's missing. Here's the scoop. We'll have a picnic on her property. She'll see us in back of her house getting tanked. It'll drive her crazy. Mary's jealous of people who know how to have fun, especially me."

"That's it? That's what you want? We can do it tomorrow."

"I think we'd better let my face heal first," Anne said. "Don't you?"

"Oh, yeah. Of course." There wasn't much Edwin could say to that.

* * *

Mary was on a committee that supported classical music. Anne knew that because it was in the paper and because she kept track of Mary's life. It was, after all, the life that should have belonged to Anne; at least, that's what she believed. Anne also knew that Mary's committee had a meeting scheduled in a few weeks, one of those Big Daddy Party's they throw to raise money. Mary would be there and Harry would be home alone with the brat. It was a perfect time for Anne to schedule her own eye popping event, so that's what she did.

Anne and Edwin had to be careful when they sneaked around the Vinson's house. It was a surprisingly cool June evening that felt more like autumn than summer. There would be at least an hour more of enough light for Harry to notice them, but she didn't want him to see anything before they had a chance to set up. About twenty-five yards of a grass covered clearing existed behind the home. The grass was about ankle high except for a worn path that led to a woodpile.

Anne led Edwin into the woods then she spread out the blanket and poured the whiskey while he started a small campfire. Harry would surely remember their kiss when he saw her making love to a man in the forest behind his home. Once the fire was going, Emily tossed some damp leaves into the flames. She wanted to create smoke to draw Harry's attention.

As the smoke swirled up into the evening sky, Anne removed the simple, homespun dress that she had chosen because it was easy to get on and off. They each took a couple of sips of hooch then lay down on the blanket. It was exciting and daring to be lying outside where Harry might see her, especially without her dress on and in the arms of a man like Edwin. The feeling that she had the power to shock Mary's husband was more intoxicating than the whiskey. Edwin put his leg over hers and rubbed her thigh as he started to kiss her on her neck. He tugged at her underwear. He still had all his clothes on and seemed more concerned with hers. She helped him with her brassiere.

It took a little more than fifteen minutes before someone in the house noticed the smoke and reacted. Unfortunately, it was Mary not Harry who came running into the woods.

Anne's brassiere was on the ground and her bloomers were down to her ankles. It would have been such a thrill if Harry had been the one to see her in that position. He would have stood there gaping for Lord knows how long. But Anne hadn't wanted Mary to catch her like this no matter what she had told Edwin. She pulled at the blanket to cover herself and in the process she spilled her whiskey. That was a shame. With the failure of Edwin's last run there wasn't much Canadian bootleg to spare. The angle of the ground allowed a small amount to stay in the glass. Anne took a swig and emptied it.

Mary was yelling while Anne's head spun from the hooch and the smoke that surrounded them. She was having trouble knowing what to say and even more trouble getting her underwear back in place. Luck never came Anne's way. Mary must have been running late. She was probably leaving for the party when she noticed the smoke behind her home. In any case, Anne didn't have the date wrong. She knew that because Mary was dressed in an expensive dress with a rich pattern of beads shaped like rays from the sun. Anne could have lived for a year off what that dress must have cost. It was the perfect dress to make Anne hate Mary more than ever.

"You have whiskey," Mary shouted, "and I have a two year old daughter. She could have been the one to look out and see you drunk and half naked."

Anne thought that *half naked* was an understatement since all she'd had on was a pair of bloomers and they'd been wrapped around her feet, but she was too soused to argue the fact. When Anne didn't say anything, Edwin spoke. His words were slurred. It appeared he had drunk more than Anne had. He laughed and added, "We thought the campfire would be fun. Have you any marshmallows we might roast?"

Mary spun around and started shouting at him. "I'll call the police," she yelled. Rich people had all the laws on their side. When someone like Anne broke one of their precious rules they would whine for help like pampered children. They never had the guts to fight their own battles.

"We didn't do any harm," Anne said. She had her clothing back on by this time. "We just wanted to sit in the woods."

"You have whiskey," Mary repeated. "That's harm enough."

"It was my idea," Edwin said. "Don't blame Anne."

"I assumed you were the one," Mary told him. "You're not getting away with this, not on our property."

"As always you're too smug," Anne said, her voice causing Mary to turn back toward her. Mary was angrier than Anne had ever seen her and every part of her short body was losing control. Her shoulders were tense and her fists clenched. Her eyes were wide open and her face flushed. The reality of Mary's anger had somehow brought the two women to the same level and Anne enjoyed the sight. In fact, the picture of Mary shaking with rage made it almost worth getting caught by the wrong Vinson. "Underneath your fancy dress and impeccable life you're a bore and you know it," Anne told her nemesis. She was egging the haughty woman on, hoping to irritate her even more. "I bet you give your old man about as much thrill as sitting in a church pew," she added.

As Mary started to yell back, Edwin came from behind and grabbed her around the waist. She thrashed about and tried to hit him, while he kept her from screaming by covering her mouth with his free hand. He pulled her down to the ground. Suddenly things were going very wrong. This wasn't what Anne wanted.

Anne looked nervously in the direction of the Vinson house. She didn't want Harry to see this. "What are you doing?" she yelled at Edwin. If he hurt Mary there'd be Hell to pay, serious Hell.

Edwin dragged Mary toward a large stone then began to bang her head against the rock. He kept knocking her head against it until she hung as limp as a pile of wet blankets.

Anne pulled on Edwin's arm with as much force as she had in her, but she was too late. He let Mary's lifeless body drop to the ground in an awkward, uneven heap. Anne' head was swirling. She reached for Mary and pulled her body straight as if making her appear uninjured would help somehow. Mary's eyes were open, but without any focus. She wasn't breathing and there was nothing Anne could do about it. Mary was dead.

It was common knowledge among almost everyone Anne knew that she had hated Mary enough to wish her dead. It wasn't her idea to kill the woman, but Anne could scream those words for the rest of eternity and no one would hear them. They would say she was jealous and call that a motive. They would put the motive and the opportunity together and call that guilt. Edwin, God damn him, would just walk away.

"I couldn't have her calling the cops," Edwin told Anne. "Now give me a hand."

Anne wasn't the one who had died, but it was her life that was passing in front of her eyes.

"I said give me a hand," Edwin told her forcefully. "We need to set something up to make this look like an accident."

"I'm not going to jail for what you did."

"Help me quickly and neither of us will. We'll drag her to the ravine and toss her down. By the time she reaches the bottom she'll be cut and scratched to Hell. They'll say she was walking too close to the edge. They won't even look for us."

"There's blood all over."

"We'll clean it up. We'll toss the bloody leaves and stones in the ravine with her. Come on. We can do this. No one will know."

* * *

"That's enough," Emily told Glen. She now knew what she'd yearned to know for most of her life. Listening to the details of the clean-up of her mother's remains was more than she could stand hearing.

Glen brought Julie out of the regression after he carefully instructed her once again to forget the memories that had been brought out.

"I guess I dozed off," Julie said as she spun her legs around and sat up on the couch. "I must not be a good subject."

"I guess not," Glen said, trying to sound indifferent. "But we can try again."

Emily hoped to God they never would. She hoped she'd never see Julie again, either in a trance or out of one. But she was confused by aspects of what she had learned. If Anne and Edwin hadn't been in the Vinson's woods, her mother might have lived a long life. Everything might have been different. But where did the guilt lie? Edwin was the murderer, but Anne was also to blame. Which soul was coming back time and time again to cause such pain? Or was it both?

Emily's father had spent most of his life believing that her mother had foolishly walked too close to a deep ravine and had fallen. At least that was what he had said he believed. Emily had never accepted the explanation or his belief in it. Now she knew the truth. She also knew that the people responsible for her mother's death had never been punished, while she had paid the price for their actions throughout her life.

Emily needed a place to be alone. She went to the bathroom, locked the door then sat on the commode. The bathroom was narrow, just a vanity with a single sink, a tub-shower combination at the far end, and a toilet between them. The wall across from the vanity had floral wallpaper, with large brown and yellow daffodils outlined in white. Emily had bought that wall covering fifteen years ago and had always regretted her choice. As soon as the paper hangers had it hung, she realized she made a mistake. At this moment she needed something soothing, something blue or dark green. She wanted water images, clear water: a lake or an ocean scene. She needed a cry, an eyes open, head-shaking cry, but the daffodils made her want to scream instead. So she stood up, lifted the toilet seat and stared at the water in the bowl. The tears finally came and as she cried she thought of how this was a metaphor for her life, hiding in the bathroom, seeking peace in the still water of a toilet bowl, while Glen was in the kitchen with Julie making small talk and sipping coffee. The damn world was as unjust as ever and she had to do something about that. She had to break the circle.

Eighteen

Kathy was in Stephie's office talking about an opportunity at the restaurant where she was painting the murals. She had arrived at the church with two lattes which made it apparent that she had a favor to ask. Bringing expensive coffee was the type of friendly gesture with a purpose that Kathy might have done years earlier when they were in college. It made Stephie smile to realize she hadn't lost her ability to read her friend's motives. She was finding it difficult to concentrate on what Kathy was saying because she had her own problems on her mind. She was looking for a graceful exit from her role as Michael and Julie's counselor. It had become clear that she favored Michael and, to make things even more awkward, that she was attracted to him.

"The restaurant is owned by a couple who moved here from New York," Kathy said. "Maddie, that's the woman's name, wants to have a singer for her grand opening. She wants someone dressed in period costume, performing songs that were popular in the mid 1800s. She plans to advertise the performance to help get people out to try the food and see my murals. Maddie decided that since I'm artistic I ought to be able to find a good singer for her. That was a bit of a jump, but I told her I know you and you'd be a good choice."

"Me?"

"You've got a great voice and I'd help you find the songs and a costume. You'd look great in one of those off-the-shoulder party gowns the southern belles used to wear."

Wearing the type of dress Kathy was talking about would be fun, like trying on a prom gown. And she had always enjoyed singing. That's why she joined the choir. A couple of the ladies in her church might object to Stephie participating in something so theatrical, but most of the members wouldn't take the few grumblers seriously. That's when the idea came. Stephie could give the opportunity to Julie at the same time that she told her she was done with the counseling sessions. It would distract her, like tossing a bone to a dog. *A dog?* she thought, cringing a bit. *My thoughts are turning nasty. I've got to get out of this situation.*

"I won't do it," Stephie told her friend, "but I know someone who will."

"You'd be perfect," Kathy argued.

"You're sweet, but believe me this other arrangement will be ideal."

* * *

Julie had expected Stephie's sessions to slant a little in her direction but, if anything, they had gone the other way. She had known Stephie for years and although they weren't the closest of friends, she believed their relationship was cordial. Perhaps Stephie was overcompensating, but whatever the reason Julie was left feeling slighted and was as pleased as she could be when Stephie suggested they end the counseling.

The opportunity to make a little money with her singing sounded interesting to Julie, especially since the gig would have a civil war theme. Michael could assist her by recording tapes she could sing to. He would enjoy that since he was such a fan of the period. And if she handled the opportunity well it might help bring him back into the fold.

"There are dozens of internet sites where we can get suggestions for songs," Stephie told her. "I've looked at some. There are mourning songs such as *Comrades, I am Dying*, proud songs such as *The Bonnie Blue Flag*, and humorous songs such as *Jeff in Petticoats*. Overall, the civil war was a good period for music, as wars often are. People need to put their pain into song."

"Why are you doing all that?" Julie asked. She hadn't realized Stephie was part of the package, not that she objected.

"Kathy told the owner she would help you pick out the songs and a costume and I told Kathy I would help her. I hope that's all right with you."

"I don't have to split the money, do I?" Julie asked. It was the first thing that came to her mind and she regretted saying it. She tried to brush it off with a smile that implied a joke.

"Of course not," Stephie told her, smiling back.

"Michael and I can pick the music," Julie said. "We'll do that while you and Kathy choose the costume." Stephie nodded in agreement.

Stephie ordered a period dress from a costumer in California. It took a couple of weeks to ship, but as soon as it arrived she brought it to Julie. The dress was floor length with a broad train and a cage crinoline to be worn underneath. It had ruffles across the front of the blue skirt and the neck. Black gloves and a black, tie-on bonnet came with it. It seemed like more clothing than an astronaut would wear, but Julie thought she could be attractive in it if she maintained the right attitude. Rather than simply play a civil war era singer, Julie had to step back in time and capture the romance of that woman. If she did all that right, Michael would notice and she would avoid being labeled as a loser who can't hold on to a man.

She put on the wool stockings, chemise and pantaloons by herself, but after those items were in place Julie required help and Stephie was there to give it to her. A short, boned corset had to be laced in front and the cage crinoline had to be held in place while Julie fastened the waist band. Finally, the dress had to be slipped over her head.

The corset slimmed her waist and increased her bust size. The crinoline hid her straight hips. In this dress Julie was more attractive than she had ever been, like a fantasy come to life. She loved her image in the mirror, but it was the slightly envious look on Stephie's face that made her realize what she had. She knew that if she could sing the right music with the right intensity, she could create a weapon rivaling any of her gun fantasies in its power to control. She could knock Michael to the floor and dance on his heart.

* * *

On the night of the grand opening, Michael sat at a table with Stephie and Kathy, while Julie and a young musician from UNCG made their music in the corner of the room. Michael had offered to accompany her on his guitar, but Julie had told him that a fiddler would be more authentic.

"None of the customers will know that," he said.

"But I will," she replied.

Julie sung most of her songs from a small platform in a corner between a confederate painting of Longstreet and a union one of Sherman. But after six or seven songs, her fiddler took a break while she wandered among the tables singing a selection of *a cappella* songs. She did that to allow the diners to experience her up close in her elegant replica of a civil war era dress. When she reached Michael's table she sang Stephen Foster's *Beautiful Dreamer*.

"She sings quite well," Kathy commented as Julie moved on to the next table.

"And she looks good," Stephie added. "That dress is the real deal, exactly what a southern belle might have worn to a coming out party before the war."

"Or a going away party for the men *during* the war," Michael added. Although they were talking about Julie's dress, Michael's mind was focused on the way Stephie looked. She was wearing a floral wrap dress with short sleeves. The dress she had worn on the afternoon when he had taken her to see Kathy was as attractive as this one, but since that time he had only seen her in conservative outfits at church and casual attire at the counseling sessions. This was a light dress, appropriate for the August heat outside but perhaps a little thin for the restaurant's air conditioning. Yet she didn't look uncomfortable, just pretty, very pretty.

Julie was with her fiddler once again, in the corner of the room singing *The Graybacks So Tenderly Clinging*, a union battle song that disparagingly compared the confederates to biting insects. Michael cringed a little on the line "Who went with us marching through Georgia" because it reminded him of the argument he'd had with Julie about General Sherman's place in history. He knew that subject was, like so many others, her way of irritating him for the pure joy of watching him get upset.

"The murals look remarkable," Stephie told Kathy. "That isn't just me talking. I heard a few comments on the way in. You have a right to be proud."

"I thought pride was a flaw," Kathy responded. "Are you granting me an indulgence?" Michael could hear the teasing in her voice and wondered if Kathy had a problem with Stephie's choice to become a minister. He looked at Stephie, hoping she wouldn't take the comment wrong. But Stephie, unlike Julie, had a sense of humor and gave people the benefit of the doubt.

"Some things are worthy of pride," she replied, shaking her head and grinning as she spoke. Then she tried to change the subject. "I'll be surprised if you don't get a few commissions from tonight."

Michael flipped his menu to look at Kathy's name on the back. Her paintings weren't exclusively murals. She worked with oil or acrylic on canvas and had played around a little with watercolors and even some clay sculpture. This event was giving her a lot of good publicity. He wondered if she had lowered her price to get them to print her name or if her status was such that the restaurant gained prestige by listing her on the menu? Either way it was a move that made sense for Kathy, since there had to be a lot more people who wanted paintings than people who wanted murals. Michael had attended a number of civil war reenactments. He knew how fanatic people could be about the subject. And most of those fanatics had dens and rec rooms that needed decorating.

"I'm going to wander around the room a bit," Kathy said as she slid her chair back and stood up. "Maybe I can catch some comments about my work."

"Try to catch Julie's eye," Stephie suggested. "She could acknowledge you. People like to meet the artist."

Michael watched Kathy for a moment. She was more formal than Stephie, in a black, sleeveless dress with a below the knee skirt that flipped a bit as she walked. She also wore a thick necklace that appeared to be silver and glass. The dress was not a good style for her stocky build. The neckline showed a little too much cleavage and the thin material emphasized her love handles. Her necklace was also wrong, seeming way too gaudy for the event. Michael thought Kathy looked as if she was trying too hard, but he would have enjoyed seeing Stephie in the same outfit. She could have carried it off.

* * *

Stephie hadn't planned to be alone at the table with Michael. It wasn't that she didn't like talking to him one on one. It was that she liked it more than she should. He seemed to be studying her, staring at her neck for a while then moving his gaze to her hair, then her hands, then back up to her eyes. He wasn't the first man to look at her like that, but with him her reaction was different. She had quickly and quite clearly let the other men know they were behaving inappropriately. But Michael's look seemed to warm each part of her and Stephie found herself raising her chin when he looked at her neck, shaking her head gently when he glanced at her hair, rotating her hands slowly when they were in his focus and staring straight back at him when he gazed into her eyes. It was a schoolgirl reaction, but it felt right. Of course, it would have felt better if Julie hadn't been in the same room.

"I miss talking to you," Michael said. His carefully phrased words could have meant that he missed her counseling, but Stephie knew they didn't. She understood their true meaning because of how *she* felt. When she was alone with Michael, talking and listening to any thought that came up, she felt as if she had found her way into a protected refuge where all the world's problems had ceased to matter. It was impossible for Michael not to feel at least some of what she felt so strongly.

Julie began to sing *Aura Lea*, a love song that was popular in both the north and the south. "In thy blush the rose was born, music when you spake, through thine azure eye the morn, sparkling seemed to break."

Michael reacted to the sweet music. He reached across the table for Stephie's hand, but she pulled back. The pounding in Stephie's chest told her to let Michael lay his hand on hers. She knew instinctively that his touch would ease the dizzy swaying she experienced when she was near him. But Julie's presence reminded her that this was not a protected refuge. They weren't alone. The world was a very real place with very real problems including people who could get hurt from their actions. God gives us temptation to test us and to build our strength.

"You're with Julie," Stephie said, "and she's my friend. We need to do what's right."

"I'm the one who needs to do what's right," Michael replied. "I'll tell Julie we're through. I'll tell her tomorrow."

Stephie should have spoken up. She should have told Michael that he and Julie had to be sure they couldn't make it as a couple before they stopped being one. She should have suggested another couples' counselor, one who wouldn't get caught up in his dark eyes and black wavy hair. She knew what God would want her to do, but she didn't do it. Instead, all Stephie did was look back at Michael and nod.

Nineteen

Julie's last regression revealed that someone else was involved with the murder of Emily's mother, someone Emily had never heard of as she was growing up. It was no great leap for her to think that the soul of Julie's current boyfriend might have once been Edwin's. If so, regressing Michael could be the key to breaking the circle.

Emily suggested to Glen that she approach Michael using his interest in history. She could bring up Glen's talents. She might even show him a copy of the magazine article that had first brought her to Glen. She thought she could get Michael's cooperation with less deception than she had used on Julie, because he would jump at the chance to know exactly what life was like at some point in the distant past. Glen initially had his doubts, but Emily managed to convince him. They decided to move forward with her plan.

* * *

When Sarah Knox Taylor died, Jefferson Davis, the man who would eventually become the president of the Confederacy, spent eight years of his life in mourning. Michael thought that story was sad, but beautiful. He had always longed to feel so much love for a woman he was with. He knew Julie couldn't affect him that way, but Stephie could.

Michael wanted to cause as little pain as possible when he ended his relationship with Julie, but he realized there was no easy way to do that. Every story of a break-up was always about selfishness. The tabloids were filled with gossip of celebrities and modern politicians who couldn't control their personal lives, who announced their separations at press conferences or showed up at wild parties without the ones they were supposed to love. He didn't want to be so shallow and calloused.

The best way to break-up would be to approach Julie in private, to take all the blame then stay away from her for at least two weeks. The problem with doing that was they lived together. Michael couldn't ask Julie to get out immediately because she would have nowhere to go and he couldn't be the one to leave because he owned the house. He thought about staying in a motel for a couple of weeks to give Julie some space, but he knew her temper and didn't want to leave her alone in his home. The best option he had was to move into the guestroom while Julie looked for another place.

"Last night went well," Julie told Michael the morning after singing at the restaurant. She was sipping her coffee while he made breakfast for both of them. They were still dressed in what they'd slept in. She had slipped a robe over her short sleeved, light green nightgown. He was wearing gym shorts and a tee shirt, which was his normal nighttime attire. The room smelled of frying bacon. It was part of his plan to make the house warm and comfortable before he told her she had to look for another place to stay. There was certainly irony in that decision, but Michael hoped it would improve Julie's mood.

Michael had always known that Julie had a good voice, but the quality of her show at the restaurant compared to her singing in the choir was as different as the military talents of Grant compared to those of Burnside.

"Everyone I spoke to was raving about it," Julie continued. "There could be potential with this. I don't mean a fortune, of course, but maybe enough money to quit my job."

"How many people need a nineteenth century singer?" Michael asked her. Then he regretted sounding so negative, so he added, "Of course, you were great."

"I could do classrooms or museums, maybe culture clubs. And I don't have to stick with the civil war. I can sing anything."

"I'm sure you can."

"Dressing up in period costumes would be my hook. I think it's simply a matter of getting the balance. I need to be entertaining for the kids, but educational to give the parents what they expect. If I can get that combination right it might work well."

"There's something else I need to talk to you about," Michael said.

"Can it wait a while?" Julie asked. "Maddie told me to pick up my check this morning. I've got to get dressed and get over there. Meanwhile, could you take my costume over to Stephie's? She's going to ship it back for me. That was a cute dress, wasn't it?"

"This can't wait," Michael told her. The last thing he wanted to do was to see Stephie again before he had settled his situation with Julie. He needed to resolve everything now.

"All right," Julie told him. "But I've got a very busy day lined up, so try to make it quick."

Michael was once on the other side of the fence with a thoughtless girl he had dated in his freshman year of college. She gave him the break-up talk in his dorm room while another guy she had been seeing waited for her out in the hall. The way she handled that situation had hurt his pride. Michael cringed as he thought about the previous night and how he had instinctively reached for Stephie's hand while Julie was singing. He didn't want to be the guy Julie thought about years later as an insensitive son-of-a-bitch.

"Things haven't been fun lately," Michael told her. He couldn't look in her eyes as he spoke. "We always seem to be at odds, always pulling each other down to get an advantage."

"Fun?" she asked. "Fun is one thing I thought we were good at."

This wasn't starting out the way Michael had envisioned. Although they'd been at each other's throats recently, in the past they'd had a good time. Julie wasn't the bare your soul kind of friend that comes to mind when you're in a relationship. She was the race you to the corner, play poker on Saturday night kind of friend, the person you went to when you wanted to get your mind off relationship issues, not the person you wanted to have those issues with. In a perfect world Michael would be able to lose the girlfriend, but keep the pal.

"Stephie probably wasn't the best counselor we could have found," Julie said. "We should get a professional, someone we don't already know." Her eyes were squinting and her brow furrowed, giving her an appearance of being concerned rather than angry. Michael was surprised by that response. He had expected her to be more aggressive.

"Stephie did the best she could. We were the problem." He knew what he said was true, but he also felt the need to defend Stephie. He was careful not to elaborate on her efforts. If he talked about her too much, Julie would sense his feelings. Julie could read him like a map and hurting her pride would send things out of control.

Michael hadn't expected Julie to smile and say goodbye, but he had hoped for a response that might make his task easier. If she was angry, he could be angry back. If she denied that she'd been hard to live with, he could accept all the blame and move on. But her sad, almost pleading response was very un-Julie like. Yet he knew what he had to do. He'd studied. He had read advice columns and surfed through relationship blogs. He didn't have an instinct for the right way to proceed, but he knew what experts repeatedly said was the best thing to do in this situation. He was supposed to avoid hemming and hawing. He was supposed to get everything out in the open. Honesty was the only way to act fairly. But honesty could also be mean.

"I think it's for the best if I sleep in the guest room tonight," Michael told her, forcing the words out. He thought he had said what needed to be said without hitting her too hard.

* * *

There had to be someone else. Julie knew that, because Michael was trying to tell her he wanted to break-up and she knew him well enough to be certain he wouldn't leave unless he had someone else to go to. She decided to string him along. If he had to explain himself, he might leave her with a hint or two about her competition.

"Aren't you feeling well?" she asked. During the two years they had been together the only nights they ever spent in different beds were on the days when one or the other of them was sick. Misunderstanding his intentions was an easy sell.

"I'm not sick," he told her.

Simone Gaboury was a possibility. Julie had never noticed Michael giving her a second look, but she did seem to have a crush on him. She was always stopping him in the hall to talk to him. Simone was a young French teacher from Quebec City, a small woman with a dark complexion and straight black hair that she wore with long bangs. She was pretty enough to justify Julie's jealousy. Julie had heard a rumor that Simone had some problems with an expired green card. If she turned out to be the other woman, a couple of phone calls to immigration services might be enough to get her out of the way.

"We need to be apart for a while," Michael told her. His voice trailed off as if the *for a while* part of that statement was thrown in to dampen the blow. If so, it didn't work.

"If we're going to work our way through this thing separate beds won't help," Julie said.

There was also Beth, or Beth Ella, as she liked to be known, an ex-student of Michael's who had kept in touch with him through email. Julie hated the way Beth Ella insisted that everyone refer to her with both her first and middle names almost as much as she hated the young woman's pretentious habit of writing everything in italics. Beth Ella was out of college now and working for some software company, doing something related to marketing. Julie had searched the internet and had discovered a couple of photographs on a fraternity site that Beth Ella wouldn't want her employer to see. So if she turned out to be the other woman there was a little ammunition to go after her, too.

"I think it would be best if I move to the guestroom," Michael repeated.

"You said that," Julie told him.

"I'm just making sure you understand."

"You think I'm an idiot?"

"I didn't say that."

"For God's sake, it's what we were talking about. But here's what I want *you* to understand. Moving out is giving up. I don't give up."

"You can't give up on something that's over."

"Over! Damn it! When were you planning on telling me that revelation?"

"I'm telling you now!" Michael yelled. Then he appeared to control himself and added, "It's my fault. We've been at each others' throats for a long time, but I'm not blaming you. It's me. I'm the one who's changed."

"Then change back!" Julie shouted. Michael stepped away from Julie as if he was frightened by her loud voice. She turned sharply to follow him and when she did, the belt of her robe caught on the knob of partially open drawer. She pulled her belt loose then shook and slammed the drawer shut, creating an unnerving noise. Michael seemed to react to the sound and when Julie saw his reaction she reached out and knocked a set of salt and pepper shakers and a sugar bowl to the floor. She stood next to the mess, panting fiercely, her robe askew and one of the straps of her nightgown down off her shoulder. She didn't care what she looked like and wide-eyed Michael appeared too shocked to say anything.

"I'm not going to let you give up on me," Julie said, her voice cracking like a tree about to fall, "not without a fight."

"The fight is over," Michael said in a soft but determined voice. "It's time for peace."

Julie knew the way Michael thought and was certain that with his *fight* and *peace* language he was relating their argument to Lee and Grant at Appomattox. He always did things like that and it aggravated her more than anything else he could have done.

"Forget about the guest room," she said. "I'm out of here as fast as I can pack my bags. I wouldn't spend another minute in this house if you begged me."

He glanced down at the sugar all over the floor, then looked back at Julie and nodded.

* * *

That evening Michael was alone in his living room with the TV turned on to CNN headline news. They were running a story about polar bear cubs in some European zoo, but he wasn't paying attention. He also wasn't reviewing his lesson plans for the next day's discussion on the ironclad ships of the Civil War, the *USS Monitor* and the *CSS Virginia*. His personal situation was all that filled his mind. Julie had been part of his life long enough for their separation to come with a reminiscence that had already begun to blur the pain of the relationship they had shared. But there was also a sense of hope, because Michael knew that Julie's departure was the only way he could ever expect a relationship with Stephie. He was glad he'd had the guts to take the first step.

The phone rang, startling Michael a bit and causing him to jump to his feet. He went into the kitchen where the cordless receiver was sitting in its saddle. He didn't feel like explaining himself to one of Julie's friends, so he glanced at the display before answering it. The call was from Emily Vinson, an elderly woman in his church. Julie had been spending some time with her recently, but Emily was someone to whom he wouldn't mind explaining the situation. He picked up the phone.

"Hello," he said.

"Michael?" The little quiver that is typical in the voices of elderly women was there. "I want to talk to you about life and history."

If Emily had been interrupting Michael's normal routine, he would have probably brushed her off and laughed at the concept of an old woman rambling on about past lives. But instead she caught him at a vulnerable time, at a time when he was wondering where his life would be just a short distance down the road. He wanted to do something different, something that would pull him away from thoughts of the break-up. The concept of a path toward the future that is directed by events of the past was enticing. He told her he would come to her house and talk to Glen with an open mind.

"Wear loose clothing," she told him.

Twenty

When Michael arrived at Emily's apartment he had on tennis shoes, a pair of Khaki shorts and a wine colored College of Charleston T-shirt that seemed a couple of sizes too big. He looked innocent enough to Emily. If he was the man she thought he was, the one with the soul of the man who killed her father, he certainly didn't show it.

His outfit appeared comfortable, except for the belt. She told him that it might present a problem. "It could be a distraction," she said. "If Glen starts to pull memories from a time when you didn't wear a belt like that one, there would be a conflict." Michael removed it, coiled it and set it on her coffee table.

Emily had been concerned that Michael might be too large for her couch. He was, after all, the first man they were regressing. But he lay down comfortably. He seemed a little vulnerable, spread out on the couch as if he were sleeping. The position made him appear trusting, which was too nice a characteristic for the man with Edwin's soul.

"Pick a spot and concentrate on it," Glen said as he started the routine Emily had watched so many times. "Breathe easy. Try to relax."

The plan was to guide Michael using specific details they had learned from Julie about the day Emily's mother was murdered. Edwin's soul could not have forgotten such a traumatic event. The plan seemed to be working when Glen asked him about Anne.

"Anne seemed nice enough," Michael told them, "but she had an odd little smile, a bit mischievous. I used to wave to her when I saw her, but we rarely talked."

The fact that he knew Anne indicated they were on the right track, but Emily was surprised by his last comment. Edwin was Anne's lover. Waving to her when they happened to run into each other didn't make sense. She looked at Glen who seemed equally confused. He continued to ask questions. "Anne wasn't someone you knew well?"

"We'd known each other since we were teenagers and we even kissed once, when we were young, by the ravine where Mary was found years later. Anne was more experienced than I was. I doubt she remembered it. And now the kiss seems too pleasant a reminiscence to associate with such a horrible place."

Emily couldn't understand what Michael meant by *kissed once*. The connection to the people Julie had talked about was there, but the facts weren't adding up.

He continued, "I died along with Mary at that site, but I forced myself to keep going because of Emily."

She caught her breath when he mentioned her name.

"Mary was all I wanted from life and she was gone. Perhaps Anne was involved. It makes sense, since she disappeared around the same time. None of that mattered. It couldn't bring her back. I wanted to curl up someplace and forget. I wanted to join Mary in heaven. Instead our child forced me to remain in hell and to try to function one day at a time. I don't know what I regret more, Mary's death or Emily's existence."

Emily stood up when she heard Michael say those words. She didn't speak but she felt like screaming. She had prepared herself emotionally to hear the voice of the man who had killed her mother. She wasn't ready for this, not at all. It was weird that she hadn't considered this possibility. Her father was fifty-nine when he died. There had been plenty of time for his soul to exist in purgatory or wherever it is that souls go while they wait for their chance to return.

"Nobody realizes how quickly life can change," her father continued though Michael's voice. "Everyone says they do, but it's different when it actually happens. I lived my life for Mary. Everything about that life had a magical, romantic purpose. Emily was two when that ended. I couldn't talk to her or explain what I felt. I suppose it wouldn't have mattered if she'd been twenty-two. I couldn't even explain it to myself. People say there isn't just one person for us in this life, that if circumstances lead us to someone else we can be just as happy. For me that talk is shit."

Emily had a pen and paper that she was to use to communicate silently during the session. She scribbled on the paper and thrust it toward Glen. "Stop this!" she wrote. "Send him to some other life in some other time. Please! I can't bear to hear any more!"

Glen nodded and she could tell he understood her pain. He turned back to Michael and started to speak. "Release yourself from those memories," Glen said. "We're going back further. I've been told that you love to study the history of the civil war. Let's travel back to there. Let's find out why you love that time. Let go of Harry's soul. Relax and drift."

Michael didn't come out of the trance, but he immediately stopped speaking in Harry's voice. His eyes stayed closed, but Emily could see them gently twitching, as if he was asleep and dreaming. She gave a puzzled look to Glen, but he didn't acknowledge it. He didn't seem upset, so she was confident that Michael was reacting as he should. Then Michael started to tell his story.

* * *

There was a strong smell of sweat, grass, and dirt, mixed with a slight stench of urine. There seemed to be so many men around, soldiers, all dressed in union blue, some talking, some pacing nervously, a few praying.

"Where did you move, Charles?" The question came from the man across from him. They were sitting on wooden supply boxes at a makeshift table made from a third box. The officers had folding chairs, but they had to make due. They were in front of a square, canvas tent that they shared. The tent was tall enough to stand up in, but too crowded to spend much time inside. Their bedrolls were off to the side while most of their other possessions were kept in the middle. It was identical to dozens of tents that covered what most likely had been a wheatfield a few months earlier. There were some trees 50 yards or so from the camp site, but this was an open area.

"I moved my knight," Charles said. "This one. From there."

Michael remembered growing up with his sister in their house in Albemarle, North Carolina. He remembered the lazy summer days he spent skimming stones on Badin Lake and how those times probably did more to bring him to God than the Sundays he spent in church. He remembered school. He remembered the first girl he had kissed and the first time she'd let him touch her. He remembered college and attending worship services at Faith Presbyterian. But here things got a bit murky. Faith Presbyterian was in Maine, in Penobscot County. He remembered growing up in Maine as well as North Carolina.

Michael was also Charles and Charles had been raised in a family of eight. He had six sisters and a brother, but Charles's closest friend was not of his family. It was Samuel Fickett. The two of them had been inseparable as young boys, hunting in the pine bowers and discovering ice fishing on Fields Pond. Charles had taught Samuel about music and had tried to share his love of recent composers, Mendelssohn, Chopin and Weber. Samuel returned the favor by showing Charles how to make animal traps with only rope and a sapling. He was a wizard with ropes. He always knew the perfect knot for every purpose. It was, he often said, a much more practical talent than Charles' ability to play the clarinet.

They enlisted together, Samuel arguing for adventure and Charles extolling the virtues of fighting for the right of all men to live free. But their journey had turned into a long period of waiting. The day was cloudy and cool for that time of year. Rain came often in weather such as that, but at that moment it was dry and the sun was trying to poke out from behind the clouds. They were now sitting in this Pennsylvania field that was covered with short scrub bushes and long grass. There were also white tents across the field and countless men milling about like fire ants. Samuel and Charles were fighting the boredom with a game of chess. Samuel had brought the game along. Charles was glad since he enjoyed having a bit of home with him, but he secretly believed that Samuel's love of chess came mostly from his jealousy of the joy that Charles derived from his clarinet. Samuel used chess for his own distraction.

"Are you thinking of something, Samuel?" Charles asked his friend. "It looks as if I have a chance to beat you. That doesn't happen very often."

"I'm thinking of the Rebs," Samuel told him, looking in his friend's eyes. "How there are boys down there right now waiting just as we are. They might be playing cards. They might even be playing chess."

"It doesn't do any good to think about that," Charles said, as he looked at his stocky friend. Samuel had an overgrown brown mustache and a tiny beard under his lower lip. His facial hair thinned his plump face somewhat. "They'll be coming at us eventually and thinking of them as real could make us hesitate."

"Oh, I won't hesitate. You can count on that."

Samuel moved a pawn to attack Charles's knight. He already had a bishop in striking position of one of the squares Charles would have to move to if he was to protect that piece. So Charles had no choice. He retreated, causing Samuel's moustache to rise in a smile. Samuel's ability to counter each move Charles was considering amazed Charles. They had been together too long. His friend always seemed to know what he was thinking.

"Get your guns! We're moving to Little Round Top!" The boy who was shouting could not have been more than fifteen. He was running from man to man as fast as he could move.

"Where?" Charles asked.

"To that hill over there." The boy pointed toward the south then continued running and yelling to the other soldiers.

"Looks like this game will have to wait," Samuel said. He began putting the chess pieces into the leather pouch he had tied on his belt.

"I don't think there's time to clean up," Charles told Samuel, while he reached for his gun.

"Double time! Hurry!" the boy shouted. "We've got to get there before the Rebs do!"

"These pieces have brought me luck. I'm not going into a battle without them."

Charles waited while Samuel slipped the last one into his pouch and grabbed his rifle. The two then took off together, running double time. All the men were darting about grabbing their Bibles and their guns, and pushing against each other as if no one wanted to be last. They had been waiting for this fight and now it was here. Most of them had been in earlier battles, but that didn't dim their excitement. Charles knew why.

These men wanted revenge for the beating the union had taken at Fredericksburg.

Little Round Top was more of a mound than a hill. It was covered with large rocks and small trees that might provide some protection. It had an open face to the west and northwest and also a farm path leading up to it. The Rebs would come along that path. It was their job to meet and stop them.

When Charles and Samuel reached Little Round Top, the stones and a couple of long ditches had already been taken by the first soldiers. So they jumped behind a cluster of slender Birch trees, checked their rifles, and prepared to fire from there. Charles knew their protection would have to come from the Lord, because the thin trees were poor shields.

The noise was ferocious, with guns exploding, bullets flashing by and men screaming. A foul smell rose from the huge numbers of men whose bowels could not handle their fear. And there was also the smell of blood.

Half of the men on both sides were in their shirtsleeves. And there was so much dirt everywhere that the only way to tell the Rebs from the Yanks was by which way they were running. Charles shot at the ones coming up the hill and he thought he hit one or two. He couldn't be sure because everything was happening so fast. The battle noise was so intense he felt as if it was tossing him about like a wind storm. He had stopped thinking and was reacting through adrenaline and a primitive instinct to survive.

There was someone lying about 100 feet in front of him. The man was on his belly, so Charles could not tell who had been killed. He turned to the right and then to the left, trying to account for as many of his friends as he could.

Charles saw someone else die. It was Will Nichols, a twenty-one year old who had grown up in Cold Brook about three miles east of Charles's family. One winter, when Will was a five year old boy, his mom had taken sick. Will had spent a week living with the Stevens family while his mom recovered. Ten year old Charles had felt so big and so knowledgeable as he introduced his little friend to the best sledding hills and skating ponds in the area. Now his friend was gone.

Will's death was quick and painless, but it was also gory. He stood up to fire a shot and was hit in the face. The impact spun him around while he spouted blood like an erupting volcano. Charles fell to the ground and lay there shivering, too afraid to cry or shoot.

"Get up, Charles!" The voice was Samuel's. "We fight or we die," he shouted. He was standing and firing.

Charles struggled to his knees and grabbed his gun. "Damn you all!" he shouted as he fired one shot, then another.

"I'm moving down there!" Samuel shouted. "Where Will was!" He started to go.

"No!" Charles yelled, but his plea came too late. A shot caught Samuel in the right arm and sent him falling. "Oh, God! No! Not Samuel!"

Charles ran for his friend and luck was with him. Bullets seemed to be flying everywhere, but none came his way. He reached Samuel, then dragged him to the trees, the only shelter they had.

Samuel's face was pale white, except for the spots of blood that had splattered on his cheeks. He was still and unresponsive. Charles put his head to Samuel's chest to confirm that his friend was breathing and that his heart was beating. Then he looked at the wound. There was a great deal of blood, but the bullet had gone straight through without hitting bone. He thought Samuel was suffering more from the shock of being shot than the effects of the wound, but Charles was no expert. He had to get him to the doctor's station to know for sure. First he opened his jacket, ripped off a section of his shirt, and wrapped it around Samuel's arm.

"Leave me," Samuel mumbled as he regained consciousness, but Charles ignored his command and instead started to half carry, half drag him away from the fighting. "Where are you taking me?"

"I'm going to get you help," Charles told his friend. "I'm bringing you to a doctor. You're not going to bleed to death over a bullet in your arm. You understand me? I won't let that happen."

Charles left the fighting, with Samuel draped over his shoulder. Soldiers are not supposed to leave a battle, but some bonds are stronger than others. To Charles, Samuel's life was more important than the order to fight. It was also more important than preserving the union or freeing the slaves. His first loyalty was always to his friend.

Twenty-One

Samuel said he wanted to get back to the fight, but despite his words he kept walking beside Charles. *God works in strange ways,* Charles thought. *Samuel's injury may be what keeps him alive.* They headed toward the field hospital at a slow pace.

As they walked together, Charles thought about the history they shared. He remembered how a few years earlier he and Samuel were sitting quietly in the summer sun, fishing for a huge catfish that had been seen in their favorite pond. They had listened to the water lapping against the stones on the shore. When they talked, they spoke in gentle whispers, so as not to frighten the fish. They caught it, but they threw it back, even though it would have made a good meal. Releasing the catfish meant that they could have another chance someday to sit at the pond's edge as they tried to catch it again. Of course, any chance to fish or hunt or simply walk together would never come again if Samuel bled to death on this distant battlefield.

Charles led Samuel past dozens of fresh soldiers headed in the opposite direction. Those men would have their own stories about why they were late to the fight and wouldn't be concerned about the two walking away. The explosions of the guns and the cannons still shook the land and the acrid smell of burnt gunpowder made it hard to breathe even as the distance grew.

"Take care of him please," Charles pleaded with the first doctor they met in the hospital. "He's lost a lot of blood and the wound needs dressing."

"Find a nurse. I need to help the ones who are hurt worse than him," the major replied. It was clear he was a surgeon because he was wearing a blood stained apron over his uniform. He was likely headed to the latrine area, at least that's what Charles thought. In any case he was walking away from the surgeon's table where the screams of the soldiers made it clear that amputations were taking place. Charles glanced at Samuel and was shaken by the thought that bringing his friend to the hospital might hurt him worse than the gunshot had.

"Don't let them cut me," Samuel pleaded.

"They won't. There's no need."

"Then let's keep going."

"We've got to find a nurse to bandage that arm of yours," Charles said. "While you get help I'll head back to the camp. I'll collect our stuff then meet you here. After that we'll see what happens. We have to be careful. A few of the officers have been eyeing me already. I'm not wounded and to them that means I ought to be at the front."

Charles left Samuel in a crowd of recovering soldiers. There were tents around the hospital area, but the soldiers were sitting in the open air. They were mostly amputees but some, like Samuel, had wounds that weren't severe. The nurses, who were as ragged and blood stained as the men, were looking after them. They would look after Samuel, too. As Charles walked away he prayed for his friend. Charles remembered the way Samuel had looked as a boy using that arm to skim stones or set one of his traps. The truth was he didn't know if Samuel would keep his arm. The bullet had passed through cleanly, but only a doctor could determine the chance of a serious infection and they were quick with their knives.

A few soldiers were scrambling about in the spot where Charles's brigade had camped. Presumably those boys were taking a short cut to the front line. No one was sitting still. Charles would have known something major was happening even if there had been no battle noise.

He went for his tent and found that everything was exactly where he had left it. This was the most dangerous time. He hadn't looked suspicious as he had hurried to the campsite and once he was through he could also pass for a soldier moving from one spot to another, even while carrying his gear. But packing while a battle raged would surely label Charles a deserter.

Charles hadn't left the fight to save his skin, but he'd left it to save Samuel and now that he was away from it he wasn't going back. Did that make him a coward or a loyal friend? He wasn't sure, but he knew what others would think.

He pulled the flaps down on his tent to hide his activity as best he could. He grabbed his knapsack and started shoving things in. The first item he packed was his clarinet, then his cooking gear, a few personal things, and all his clothes. He rolled his blankets as tightly as he could then tied them up on top of his back pack. He was ready to check on Samuel. After that, he wasn't sure where he would end up.

When Charles returned to the field hospital he discovered four officers milling about where he had left Samuel. They scared him. It was the wrong time to try to rejoin his friend so Charles headed away from the hospital. The further he walked the more he thought that there might never be a right time to go back.

Charles was experiencing a mixture of shame and fear, but those sentiments were overwhelmed by his confusion. He wanted to stay with Samuel, but he didn't know how to do that. Getting either killed or forced back to the front wouldn't help his friend. It was as if Charles was walking because there was nothing else he could think of doing, as if the physical act of placing one foot in front of the other somehow could keep him from dwelling on how helpless he was.

No one spoke to Charles as he marched away, moving east across Taneytown Road and Rock Creek until he reached Baltimore Pike. The soldiers he passed must have thought he was on a mission. They didn't try to stop him. The sun was setting, so a couple of miles away from the battle Charles stopped in a field, took off his backpack, and lay down.

He was far enough off the road to be fairly well hidden in the long grass. But Charles was uncomfortable. So much had gone wrong that day. When he had enlisted he'd had this romantic notion of what fighting to free the slaves meant. Some of his ideas had come from reading Frederick Douglas and Harriet Beecher Stowe, but most had come from sitting in his church and thinking. Negroes were different than he was, but Jesus spoke of love for people who are different. That's what the parable of the Good Samaritan is about. Now Charles was a deserter and, in a way, a deserter three times. He had abandoned his brigade, left his best friend to fend for himself and forsaken his principles. He wasn't worth the dirt he was lying on.

Charles pulled his backpack close to his body. He closed his eyes and thought about the clarinet in the pack and the music he had made over the years— so much beauty, so much comfort. He wished he could play, but the sound would draw people to him, people who might not look kindly on a Union soldier lying alone in a field. He thought of the melodies for *Jeanie with the Light Brown Hair*, *Amazing Grace* and *When I Survey the Wondrous Cross*. Then he thought of the *Clarinet Concerto in F minor* by Carl Maria von Weber. He had memorized all three movements. He started to hum softly and the notes soothed his heart. He stared up at the stars that had started to appear in the broad sky above him. No one had come. He was still alive. He allowed his mind to wander to better times.

Thanksgiving was Charles' favorite time of the year and twice Samuel had joined his family for the feast. Charles' mom always cooked a turkey with chestnut stuffing. She would also serve ash-pone, fried potatoes, squash, turnips and pumpkin pie. There was always plenty of apple brandy and ginger beer to wash down the food. Charles's dad would tell stories at Thanksgiving dinner, mostly tales of a time when he had no money and had to live off his wits and whatever game he could trap. Samuel was a little jealous of Charles's dad because his own was a drunk. After dinner the entire family would go outside for their annual croquet game. The first year Samuel was there he joined in, but he grew frustrated because he had never played the game before and quickly fell behind. The second year he wouldn't even try. Samuel always hated losing, no matter what the circumstances.

Charles woke when the sun rose and that is when he decided he had to go back to Samuel. It would be less risky heading toward the battle than it had been walking away, but the amount of risk was not the issue. He had to head back no matter what.

* * *

"I met an angel." Samuel said when Charles returned. "It was worth getting shot to discover her."

Samuel was the type to become bitter when circumstances ran against him, so it was shocking for Charles to find him in a good mood. He generally blamed God for whatever went wrong. Once, as a teenager, he had been angry for two months when a small cold had made him miss a town shooting competition. Charles had won third prize while Samuel, a much better marksman, had cursed fate for keeping him home.

"Is this woman a nurse?" Charles asked.

"She is. She lives about 10 miles to the east, but she came here to take care of us. She knew we needed her, so she left the security of her home to walk into a war."

Charles believed it, since they had naively done the same thing. But he kept those thoughts to himself.

Perhaps Samuel was hiding the trauma of being wounded by fixing his attention on this woman. Yet that seemed unlikely. He wasn't hurt as seriously as most of the men around him. He still had both his arms, although that could change if the wound infected. Of course, his pride had been hurt, as it had years earlier when he missed the shooting competition.

"Tell me about her," Charles said. "What does she look like?"

"She's pretty."

"Of course."

"She has light brown hair that lies on her shoulders like a soft blanket, though she generally wears it up." Samuel smiled as if he knew some wonderful secret.

"She let her hair down?" Charles asked, surprised that Samuel could have already reached a certain level of intimacy with this woman.

"It fell down as she was helping me. She just pushed it back and kept on working. She has an incredible amount of energy." Samuel lifted himself up on his left arm to look more closely at Charles. He was clearly in some pain, but his excitement seemed to be as good a pain reliever as whiskey. "The doctor wanted to take my arm, but she fought for me, convinced him to give it a chance. She keeps moving about, helping

126

everyone. The most beautiful part of this wonderful woman is her eyes. You've never seen anything as spectacular as Alexandra's blue eyes."

"I'd like to meet her."

"She had to go home. Her mother needed her for something. But she'll be back tomorrow."

It sounded to Charles as if the woman lived alone with her mother. Two women alone wasn't an unusual situation with the war going on. He wondered if there was a man in either of their lives, someone in the fight. There were plenty of locals in Gettysburg and, he supposed there were also Pennsylvania men with Grant in Vicksburg.

* * *

Emily scribbled another note and handed it to Glen. "Can we find out more about her?" it read.

Glen nodded then started speaking to Michael, steering him forward in time to the memories of the day after he was speaking with Samuel, the day Charles first met Alex.

* * *

"Are you Alexandra?" Charles asked. He looked at the young woman and he immediately saw that Samuel's description of her was accurate. There was something magical about her, a kindness that bounded out from among the horrors of the war. Charles understood why Samuel had fallen in love so quickly. He glanced down at the ground and waited for her answer.

"Call me Alex," she said, using the familiar form of her name.

"I'm looking for a friend of mine, Samuel Fickett. I believe he was under your care."

She wore a light blue dress with a diamond pattern in the material. It had long, loose sleeves and a skirt that looked as if it were designed to be worn with crinoline. But crinoline would not do for a nurse in a battle. The dress was tattered and soiled. The skirt had a rip up the front that was at least a foot long. Her chemise flashed through the torn material, as white as her smile, but it was also torn a little. Yet she stood proud in her ragged attire. She had brought water to a young boy from a Maryland regiment. The boy had been shot in the face and his eyes were bandaged. Charles wondered if he was blind. He also wondered if the boy had been a spy. Half of the Maryland troops were Rebs at heart. But even a spy didn't deserve what he had received. Alex was attempting to make the young soldier believe he was lucky to be alive. If anyone could do that, she could.

"Samuel's down the hill, beside a stream. Are you Charles?"

He nodded.

"He talked about you. You saved his life."

"I don't think his wound would have killed him, but I had to be sure."

"You were right not to leave your friend on the field," she said, speaking softly. Her voice was like music, like the notes of his clarinet, but more captivating. Her words seemed to penetrate his skin. "He lost a great deal of blood and would have lost more. You also shouldn't leave him now. He needs your friendship. I don't know where you went or why, but he was asking for you."

She had blue eyes, perceptive, penetrating blue eyes that seemed to dig so deeply into him he felt as if she were diving into his soul. There was something special about her and Charles had an intense need to find every detail of what it was. But he realized what that desire meant. Alex was Samuel's angel, the person who had given him hope and kept him from growing bitter. Anything Charles felt for this woman was a betrayal of his lifelong friend and of everything he believed in.

* * *

"I'll count to ten, Michael. You'll wake and you'll remember everything you have been through. One...Two..."

Charles was fading, but Michael didn't want him to. He wanted to stay. He wanted to gaze into Alex's eyes.

"Six...Seven..."

If he could bring her back, there would be no Samuel and no war. He and Alex would be free to live out their lives together in the twentieth century. Then he remembered Stephie and he was confused.

"Nine...Ten..."

"Oh, my God," Michael gasped as he struggled to sit up. So much had been running through his head and it had all been clear. It was as if the events he had just remembered had happened minutes before, not back in another time and another life. Alex and Samuel were as real as Glen and Emily and they were as much a part of his life as anyone alive today, even Julie and Stephie.

"Are you all right?" Glen asked.

"Your first regression is an emotional experience," Emily told him. "But after you recover you'll want to go back again and again."

She was right about the emotions Michael was feeling. He had heard of regressions and past lives, of course. But he had always thought of those things as carnival side-show acts. This had been in his own head and much too detailed to be a fake suggestion. He had been there. He'd been in another man's body, living another man's life, but the memories were every bit as real as any from last year or last week or even yesterday. This was far beyond anything Michael had studied in books. This was perfect, true history.

"I'll go back right now, if you'll let me," Michael replied.

"It's too soon," Glen said. "You need to rest."

"I can heat some soup," Emily offered. "I've got Minestrone and also some cheese and crackers. First I'll pour you a glass of wine. It'll calm you down. You're too emotional to drive home."

"The woman I met," Michael said, "the one called Alex. I've seen her before."

Emily and Glen both raised their heads at that comment. Their eyes went wide, as if they were hearing about a miracle.

"Stephie has a friend who paints murals. There's no mistake. Alex is there, in one of Kathy's works, wearing the same blue dress she wore in my head."

Twenty-Two

"I was an atheist," Kathy said, "and proud of it."

"Was?" Stephie asked. She wore a slight smirk because she was certain Kathy still considered faith to be fiction. But oddly enough Kathy nodded when Stephie questioned her. Stephie felt her grin turn quickly to an expression of confusion.

She had been updating a participation list for an annual youth group canoe trip when Kathy had shown up at her office door. Stephie closed out of Excel and invited her friend in to chat.

"I'm opening up to you," Kathy told her. "Please take me seriously."

"Of course," Stephie said, but she had intended to tease her friend. Years ago Stephie's faith had often been the butt of Kathy's ribbing. Stephie would have happily turned the tables if Kathy hadn't explicitly told her not to.

"I wanted to have this conversation with you, face to face. You're the most spiritual friend I've ever had and if anyone will understand my confusion, you will."

"I'm not following you."

"This is a spiritual crisis, even if it's backwards from the way most people would define one. And it's tearing me apart."

"Let me get this straight. You now believe in God. And that upsets you?"

Kathy had come to Greensboro and contacted Stephie after years of not seeing each other or even talking on the phone. It appeared that there was more to that reconnection than Stephie had first realized.

"For years I took pride in believing only what I could see with my own eyes," Kathy told her. "I refused to accept the religion of an ancient mid-eastern tribe just because everyone around me did. But now I'm not certain. I no longer know what I believe or who I am."

"For people who lose their faith, the experience is a deeper tragedy than an identity crisis. I don't think what you're talking about is equivalent."

"You're being dismissive, just as I worried you would be."

Kathy was right and Stephie knew she would never have spoken that way to anyone else. It was as if Kathy's presence brought back the college student Stephie had once been, with all the youthful self-importance she had shed over the years.

"Perhaps if you explain how all this started," Stephie said as she settled back to listen to her friend's story.

"Do you believe in ghosts?" Kathy asked.

Kathy's haunting had occurred in her dreams over a period of a little more than five years. The ghost was a twenty-five year old woman with light brown hair and very blue eyes who kept showing up on the porch of a farmhouse Kathy owned in the dream.

"This person tells you to believe in God?" Stephie asked.

"I won't change my beliefs because someone tells me to," Kathy replied, "not even someone in my dreams."

"That's the Kathy I remember. But if it isn't this woman then what brought you to God?"

"Depression, overwhelming depression."

"Oh, Kathy," Stephie said. "I'm so sorry to hear that."

"The dreams are horrible, but not so much for what I see in them. They are horrible because they leave me with the sensation that the world is falling apart. The woman is my daughter, I think."

"A twenty-five year old daughter?"

"I'm a different person in the dream."

"And something bad happened to this daughter?"

"All I know for sure is that when I dream I'm scared— horrified actually. I've spent most of my life thinking of religion as a crutch for people too weak to handle their problems. I can't just dismiss that feeling, even if I'm now one of the weak ones. I hate myself for needing God and the self-loathing adds to the depression."

Stephie stood up and walked around her desk so she could put her hands on Kathy's shoulder to comfort her friend. "I've counseled many people who have gone through a crisis of faith. Their feelings almost always come from events that are beyond their capacity to control. They believe God has betrayed them and they're resentful about that. What I try to get them to understand is that God can be perfect even if the world is not. I'm guessing that what you are going through is more than an identity crisis. That's why you came to me. Maybe you feel that if you had turned to God earlier, you wouldn't have experienced the same depression. I need you to understand the same thing I tell the others, that the world isn't perfect. That there's no pact that says if you pray every day your problems will disappear. God can help you through the rough times, but they will still be there. That's because free will exists. The difference between your crisis and a normal faith crisis is that the others are at risk of losing their strength while you are gaining yours."

"Is your faith always strong?"

If Kathy had asked that question before Stephie had met Michael, Stephie would have answered it with a qualified yes. She had often asked herself the question about how God could allow so much pain and suffering, but the normal answers were sufficient. Now her life had changed. There were suddenly two different sets of right and wrong. One was what came to her when she thought through her situation. The other was what came when she allowed her heart the freedom to feel. How could God allow free will while also pushing her in two directions?

Stephie opened up to Kathy as if all the years they'd been apart made no difference at all. She explained how seriously she took her responsibility as a counselor, yet how wonderful she felt when Michael was near. The conflict was unfair and, in Stephie's eyes, that made God unfair.

"Did you lie to them?" Kathy asked.

Stephie was surprised by the simplicity of Kathy's question. It was forthright and easy to answer. "No," she replied.

"Did you think of your own needs first, before you made any suggestions?"

"I didn't make any suggestions. But there were times when I would have spoken up if I hadn't been conflicted. That's the problem."

"No it's not," Kathy said. "It's hard to find someone you care about. You shouldn't second guess the situation when you do."

"You think so?"

"Of course I do. Let him know what you feel. If it's right, it will happen. If it isn't, you can move on without thinking you've let something go that was meant to be."

Stephie nodded as she listened to her friend's common sense advice. Why hadn't she thought of things in that way? It was strange how Stephie could be a good counselor for others, but not for herself.

"I do have one question," Kathy said.

"What's that?"

"How did this conversation end up being about you?"

Stephie had been dwelling on her feelings for Michael so much that when the first chance came to spill her guts she took it. It wasn't why Kathy had come to see her and she was wrong to have changed the focus, although Kathy's tone could have been less antagonistic. Stephie walked back around her desk and took her place in her office chair.

"The trouble with modern atheists is they're self-righteous," Stephie told her friend. "The people who claim the only valid arguments are intellectual are the people who believe they have all the right answers and the ones who let everyone else know it."

"You're saying I was arrogant?"

"Not with me, but possibly with yourself. Think of your new found faith as a skill that can add to the person you were before. Whenever you have a problem from now on think it through, just as you always did, but also pray on it, give it up, let a greater force speak to you about it. You'll discover there are many ways to find answers."

"Like art?" Kathy suggested.

"Yes. Exactly. Answers that can't be expressed in words."

Stephie and Kathy talked for over two hours, covering most of the things Stephie would normally talk about with young people in a communicant's class. It was interesting discussing them with an adult, especially with someone who was an old and dear friend. The ideas exchanged were intellectual and challenging and the process reminded Stephie of the talks she and Kathy had when they were in college. Those old conversations probably played a part in leading Kathy to art and Stephie to God.

When the two women separated they each made a resolution. Kathy said she would open her mind to the pull of her new found faith. Stephie agreed to speak to Michael and to tell him what she felt.

* * *

Julie spent a few days getting through her anger so she could focus on her plans for the future. She wasn't going to let a setback in her relationship with Michael destroy what she'd worked so hard to achieve. That would be giving up and Julie didn't do that, ever. She refused to accept the label of the jilted woman or of the girlfriend no man would want to keep. She needed to get Michael back to deal with that image. If they broke up after that it would be on her terms. The first step was clear. She needed to find out who was the other woman in Michael's life.

Julie began to spy on Michael. It wasn't that difficult to do. She lived with him long enough to know both the house and his habits. She knew the places in the backyard to hide and the window shades that didn't close completely. She watched him for a couple of hours each night for four nights without seeing anything unusual. Still, the sensation that he didn't know she was out there left her feeling as if she was in control.

On the fifth day Michael was working in his kitchen, opening a can of soup and microwaving a frozen dinner when Stephie arrived at the front door. Julie was surprised that the young minister was visiting him. The counseling had ended when the couple had broken up. Julie circled the house keeping an eye on what they were doing as well as she could. Michael brought Stephie into the kitchen which was convenient since that was the room where Julie had the best view. Stephie sat at the kitchen table while Michael put on a pot of coffee. Apparently she intended to stay a while.

Stephie was dressed in a light blue skirt with a brown sleeveless top. Julie thought the mismatch was an odd combination, but Stephie looked good. Her long brown hair was so striking that she would always have a hard time not looking attractive. Stephie was doing most of the talking. Julie wished she could hear what was being said.

Michael pulled a couple of mugs out of the pantry while the coffee continued to drip. Then Stephie must have said something unexpected. Michael seemed to jump a bit, as if he was surprised. He turned back to Stephie and stepped toward her. As he did that she stood up to meet him. Then he wrapped his arms around her and they kissed.

Julie's throat went dry. She could feel her heart pounding, even hear it pounding. Damn! This was her minister, her counselor, her friend. Stephie backed away from Michael and started talking again, but he grabbed her hand, pulled her toward him and kissed her again. Julie's head was swirling so violently she had to sit down on the grass. She could still see the kitchen from that position. Stephie wasn't fighting Michael. That was clear. She was leading him on.

Stephie broke from Michael then took her purse from the kitchen table and walked out of the room. He followed. Julie wondered if they might be headed upstairs to the bedroom, but the front door opened and they came out onto the steps. They stood there for a while, talking. Julie wished she was close enough to hear what they were saying, but that wasn't the case. Michael kissed her once more, this time on her cheek. Then Stephie left and, after taking time to recover from what she had seen, so did Julie.

* * *

Julie was able to live in a Quality Inn after she left Michael because he had neglected to take the mastercard. The day after she watched him kiss Stephie, she went to a Kinko's where she rented a computer to search for Neil Raiford's current address. She put that cost on Michael's card as well. The internet search for Neil's address was successful, but Julie had to add forty dollars more to the card to get extra information about him. That would have been worth it even if she had paid for it herself. She discovered that Neil had grown into the type of man she had expected he would, a registered sex offender and a petty thief. He had been in and out of jail repeatedly for as long as the public records went back. The deviant part of his background frightened her at first, but she decided it meant that Neil was weak, which implied he would be easier to manipulate. From her perspective that was a good thing. The last thing Julie did with the card was to get a five hundred dollar cash advance from an ATM. She tossed it after that because she knew the bank would contact Michael and he would cancel it. Also, she didn't want anyone tracing her through its use.

As Julie drove up route 52 toward Surry County, the picture of Stephie and Michael kept running through her head. Each time it did, the image was as clear as if she was watching it fresh and so was the horror of what she was seeing. They both had hair so dark and so similar that when they brought their heads together to kiss they seemed to merge into one person, which made her feel even worse. All the things she should have done kept filling her mind. She should have barged into the house. She should have gouged out Stephie's green eyes with her thumbs and squeezed the bitch's long neck with her bare hands until she suffocated. No one would have blamed her. The level of Stephie's betrayal was that extreme.

"I need your help," Julie told Neil when he opened the door to his rusty trailer home.

"Who the hell are you?"

"I bet you'd recognize Trent if he was at your door."

"Julie?" There was surprise in his voice. Apparently he still remembered her after all these years. That was nice to know even if it did take her brother's name to kindle his memory.

"Would you get my suitcase out of the car?" she said. "I'm going to be here a while."

Twenty-Three

When Michael arrived for his second regression, Emily answered the door, but jerked it back, nearly shutting it in his face. He wasn't alone. Stephie was standing beside him.

"She's not here to prove you're wrong, she's here to see for herself," he explained after Emily gained her composure and invited them in.

"Having a skeptic in the room isn't a good idea."

"Why would you think I'm a skeptic?" Stephie asked.

"You've been trained to think a certain way," Glen said as he stepped into the living room from his bedroom.

Stephie turned to him. "There are ministers who question tradition."

Stephie had a point. Yet Emily was uncomfortable with the idea of an audience. She looked to Glen for the next argument.

"You're the ones who are closed minded," Stephie said.

Emily knew that Stephie's nurturing side was strong. Some people in the church had become so dependant on her that she seemed to be a de facto parent. That trait could be good for Michael. It was also true that they hadn't found Emily's mother's soul and here was Stephie, a woman who was certainly a candidate. Stephie was religious and so was the mother who had been in the battle Emily had seen in her regression.

"I'll try not to jump to conclusions." Stephie told Glen. Emily was starting to change her mind about Stephie's presence.

"Michael lies on the couch and tells us what he's experiencing," Glen told Stephie. "That's all there is to it."

"I know what to expect."

Michael said he was comfortable with Stephie's presence. "I wouldn't have brought her along if I wasn't," he added.

So Stephie took a seat beside Emily as Glen began to send Michael back. Having her in the room didn't appear to interfere and Michael was soon describing his life as Charles.

* * *

"I don't know what we're doing here," Charles told Samuel. "I miss the ponds and the forests of Maine and, most of all, my home and my family."

"We're fighting for the union," Samuel said. He was sitting within spitting distance of a gently flowing creek. It would have been a peaceful scene if it wasn't for the sound of the battle, the smell of the gunfire and the cries of the wounded soldiers who were being treated in the field hospital.

"That's what they tell us. But I don't want to watch anyone else die, especially you. I'd rather die myself. I'm tired, Samuel, real tired."

"I'm the one who lost blood."

"I know that."

"I'm glad to be here. I would come back in a heartbeat."

Charles understood why his friend wanted to be in this place at this time. "I met Alex," he said.

"It's strange how someone can change a person's outlook so quickly. The plans I made were for a life spent without anyone. I thought I'd always be alone. Now everything is different."

"You were never alone," Charles said. "You always had me." He knew that Samuel was talking about feelings for a woman, but it hurt to hear their friendship discounted.

"I mean the type of relationship where you become that person, where half of her wakes up in your head every day."

"Did you hear about the fight?" Charles asked him. "I understand they held Little Round Top."

"I want you to listen to what I'm saying," Samuel said. "I've given this a lot of thought. Before I met her I had this vision of heading out west or maybe even staying in the army for years. My life didn't seem to have value. Now I want a life where I don't have to travel. I want to spend as much time as possible in one place, with Alex."

"You need your bandage changed?" Charles asked, again trying to change the subject away from the blue-eyed woman. This time Samuel gave in. He nodded and held out his arm.

* * *

"Wake up and come back to us," Glen told Michael. "Open your eyes and remember what you've experienced."

Emily was surprised by how quickly Glen had ended the session. Perhaps he was more concerned with Stephie's presence than he had let on.

"This isn't good enough," Glen said. "Stephie can't understand what we do here by listening to Michael's words. It isn't possible."

Emily had a good feeling for the way the process had been going, but she didn't say so.

"I wanted to know about the battle," Michael said. "You should have at least let me stay until they spoke about it more."

Glen shook his head and said, "People understand regressions only if they participate." He was talking to everyone in the room, but looking straight at Stephie. "Will you do it? You say you have an open mind. Will you demonstrate it?"

Emily wasn't sure what Glen was thinking, but she was impressed with the way he could be flexible as well as stubborn in pursuit of his goal. She smiled at his words.

Michael spoke. "I didn't bring her here to put her on the spot."

"We're offering her a chance to learn something," Emily told him. "It's the same chance we offered you."

"I'm not dressed right," Stephie said.

Her clothes weren't too tight although she was a little too formal in her pink blouse and white slacks. Emily thought her outfit would do. However, if she was concerned about her clothing her nervousness could interfere with the regression. "I have a sweat suit you can use," Emily suggested.

"Let's do it," Stephie said.

Emily took Stephie into her bedroom where she pulled the sweat suit out of her bureau. She handed the outfit to Stephie then gave her some privacy to change.

* * *

Stephie folded her slacks and blouse neatly and placed them, along with her pantyhose, on Emily's bed. The sweats fit Stephie perfectly despite the fact that Emily was smaller than she was. She kept her underwear on under the outfit, but she was barefoot. She hoped they wouldn't object to that. Her shoes were new and not yet comfortable. She opened the door and stepped out into the living room.

Stephie was pleased that Glen had suggested this. She understood why he thought some preachers were rigid in their beliefs, but that was not the case with her. Past lives was a concept she had always been curious about. Her interest had grown out of dreams she had experienced that contained unexplained emotions and brief glimpses of places she shouldn't have known.

"Lie down where Michael was," Emily told her.

"You're sure you're okay with this?" Michael asked.

"Glen's right. I won't find the truth any other way."

When Stephie prayed she often used a method she referred to as "perfect prayer." Instead of words she used pictures in her mind to reach out to God and to turn her problems over to him. Sometimes she visualized Christ standing in front of her, waiting for her to walk to him. At other times she visualized God as a giant hand. She would curl up in his palm and rest. As she listened to Glen's instructions she had to be careful not to slip into her prayer mode. The total relaxation was very similar, but this time she was moving in a different direction, following Glen's gentle voice back in time to a world hidden in her own head. After a few minutes passed, she arrived.

* * *

Alex was walking toward her home when the first clap of thunder sounded. Could she be mistaken? Could it be cannon fire? No. That sound was different and, thank God, the cannon fire was finally gone. But thunder meant rain. After all these boys had been through, would God send rain?

She lived on a small farm outside of Barlow, so she was headed south on Taneytown Road, passing open farmlands with a few patches of woods here and there. Before the thunder sounded, her thoughts were centered primarily on Samuel's friend Charles. She liked the man's looks with his square, strong chin and high forehead. He was a little taller than average and had thick brown hair that was disheveled when she saw him. She wondered if that was always the case. He was very masculine and looked as attractive from the back as he did from the front. She hoped she would see him again. The thunder pulled her away from her thoughts of Charles.

Alex stopped suddenly. "The creek!" she shouted out loud. She had positioned as many boys as she could by Rock Creek. Most of them couldn't move far without her help, so she had shifted them closer to the fresh water they needed. All the doctors and nurses had moved their patients and no one had thought of rain. She started to run back. She was enough of a country girl to realize that a creek can flood quickly and with enough force to do a great amount of harm.

Samuel was one of the boys by the creek. He wasn't so badly wounded that he couldn't get away, but even for him rain was not good. What if he tried to help? He was in too weak a state to resist the currents and his arm needed to stay clean and dry. She didn't want any of the wounded to get hurt more than they already were, but Samuel was the one she thought of first. She had developed quite a friendship with him during the short, hectic time she had known him. He had told her about his fondness for chess and he had promised to teach her to play. Charles was his best friend. If she allowed Samuel to get hurt, Charles would hate her forever. Alex would not allow that to happen.

She was exhausted. She hadn't slept while the fighting was going on, not for the last three days. Her sleep would have pulled her away from the soldiers she was there to help and Alex wouldn't do that. The reason she had headed home was to reassure her mother, who didn't know if she was hurt or even if she was dead. That would have to wait. She was over a mile from the place she had left the wounded. There was little chance she'd get back before the rain came, but she would do all she could. She prayed hard and moved quickly.

God presented the rainbow to Noah, along with a promise to never again destroy the world with a flood. The torrential rain and the wounded soldiers that Alex had so carefully nursed now seemed to be evidence that God had broken that promise. She started running as soon as she heard the first yell for help and she didn't stop until she was at the bank of the creek turned river. A few healthy soldiers were helping the maimed ones, but since most of the men in the area were patients, the task seemed overwhelming. She didn't see Samuel.

Alex threw off her shoes and stepped into the creek. The water was rushing by with a force that rivaled the explosions that county had seen over the past week. Was God simply reasserting his power? She stepped back and put her shoes back on.

She was not afraid, but she hadn't lost her senses either. She could see strong men who were losing the battle against the currents. If she tried to swim out to help, one of them would soon be spending his time pulling her out.

Instead Alex ran along the bank until she reached a spot where a soldier was pulling one of the wounded out of the water.

"I'll take him!" She shouted. She wrapped her arms around the half drowned man, grabbing him under his shoulders. She started to pull while the healthy soldier went back into the creek. Alex moved backwards. She slipped a half dozen times as she dragged the wounded man to dry land. Each time she fell, she landed flat on her back with the man on top of her. But she struggled up time and time again, ignoring her cuts and bruises, making certain that the wounded man had not suffered any further injuries, until the man was in a safe spot. Then she ran back to help another.

The rain was still coming down with a force that sometimes seemed as powerful as the creek. Alex's clothes were thoroughly soaked. The tear in her skirt now reached her waist, but since both her white petticoat and her blue dress were covered with brown mud, it was hard to tell which was which. As she ran, the wet material of her clothing slapped against her legs, chafing the skin on her upper thighs.

Alex reached the creek then stopped and looked around. The current was fast and the wind strong. Because of the hard rain and turbulent water, she was having difficulty finding the soldiers who were bringing the wounded to shore. She finally spotted one about ten feet upstream from where she stood. She ran to meet him.

"I have this one," she said, as she grabbed the wounded man who had been shot in the shoulder. Apparently he had been too weak to move out of harm's way despite having two healthy legs. His situation reminded her of Samuel. The soldier from whom she took the man turned and headed back into the rushing water to find another person to help.

This man was fat. Alex was weak from pulling the first one up the hill. Now she was dragging a man who was half again as heavy. The man also did not appear to be breathing. It was possible that she was struggling to save a dead man, but things were too hectic for her to know so she wasn't going to let him stay downhill. She slipped a number of times as she dragged him, but one time was particularly bad. She fell backwards with the man landing between her legs. His weight fell against her right leg forcing her calf against a large rock, causing a sharp pain and tearing her skin. Alex got up, grabbed the man once again, and worked her way to where she had left the first man. She put him down, caught her breath for a short moment, then ran down to help some more.

The third soldier she met at the bank was Charles.

"Where's Samuel?" Alex shouted. She prayed to God he wasn't dead.

"I haven't found him. I'm still looking." Charles was panting hard and having trouble speaking. He was soaking wet and out of breath, but he was performing like a hero. She took the man Charles had brought to shore and dragged him up to the area where she'd left the other two. He was an amputee. He'd lost his right leg. That made him lighter and easier to drag. It also increased the flow of her adrenaline by raising her emotions to a peak. She didn't slip while dragging him, not even once.

Alex ran back to the creek and met Charles again. This time he had a soldier who had suffered a head injury. It did not appear that the man had been hurt in battle. It looked more like a wound he'd suffered when he was battered around by the current. Alex stared at the man's cut while she dragged him. His wound needed tending, but others needed her more. She left him at the top of the hill and went back.

Alex and Charles became a team. Together they pulled seven more men out of the creek. When they were done, they paused for a moment, looked at the horrendous situation around them, and collapsed together out of sheer exhaustion.

Alex could feel Charles's arms around her. She liked how his body felt and wondered what it would be like to kiss him. And with that thought set firmly in her mind, they both fell sound asleep.

Twenty-Four

Michael felt a little awkward as he drove Stephie home. He could tell from the way she kept staring out the window that she was also slightly self-conscious. Alex's desire to kiss Charles made the few kisses Stephie and Michael had already shared seem to be karma for their souls. This was one of the strangest connections he could imagine having with a woman. It put a great deal of pressure on their relationship. Hopefully, the pressure would be a good thing.

"I've studied reincarnation," Stephie said, "But the concept of souls traveling together through time always seemed a bit too convenient, as if it had been made up by a bunch of romantics who liked stories with happy endings. Yet now I find that I knew you in this other life we shared. It scrambles some of my beliefs."

"In a nice way."

"I suppose."

"I'm glad they want us again, both of us," Michael said. His voice shook slightly although he wished it hadn't. The experience had added a dramatic sense of inevitability to his desire to spend more time with Stephie. He wasn't sure he should reveal that thought to her. It was powerful and emotional, but also a little frightening like saying *I love you* too soon in a relationship. "I've been in Charles' head and I've met Alex. So when Glen put you in that trance and I listened to you describing what you were experiencing it wasn't just words. The pictures were clear and detailed. I found I could discover almost as much about those two people through your experience as I had through my own. Does that make sense?"

"It does," Stephie said. She was smiling slightly. Michael wished he could figure out what she was thinking, but it was only as Alex that she revealed her most intimate thoughts. "I was surprised by Emily's reaction to my experience," Stephie continued. "She was grinning like a kid on Christmas morning."

"She should have been pleased. The session went well for both of us."

"There was more to it than that. I could tell."

When they arrived at Stephie's apartment Michael walked her to her door. But she didn't invite him inside and he didn't try to kiss her goodbye. They made plans for him to pick her up the next day, for their next session with Glen. He was already looking forward to it.

* * *

Emily thought they had finally found the woman they were after, the woman who had her mother's soul. It was an unreal sensation that made her dizzy, especially considering the fact that she had known Stephie for years. Thankfully, Stephie was someone Emily liked. It would be hard to suddenly be thrust into an intense personal relationship with someone she didn't care for.

"It's her, isn't it?" Emily asked.

"Here's what we know," Glen told her as he flipped through his notes. "Your mother, or more accurately her soul, had an existence during the American Civil War which ended in one of the battles, one that included fire as well as the normal horrors of war. We also know that Julie's soul was around during the nineteen-twenties as one of your neighbors and that neighbor was involved with the death of your actual mother, although she wasn't the one who killed her. That was a man named Edwin. We don't know what became of him or his soul. Also we know Julie's soul had a Civil War existence as a man who was with a pregnant woman who gave birth to her child in a barn. We're not certain that woman was the same woman who died in the Civil War battle. We don't even know if the battle came before or after the birth. We also know that Michael's soul was your father's and that soul also had a Civil War existence during which time he knew and liked a woman named Alexandra. Alexandra's soul is now in Stephie Howell, someone Michael knows and likes well enough to bring to something as intimate as a regression session. In addition to that we know that Charles, the man who had Michael's soul, had an intense friendship with a man named Samuel who was in love with Alexandra. We know Michael and Julie had a relationship that appears to have ended recently. But we don't know what happened between Charles and Samuel. We don't even know if Charles and Alexandra had a relationship beyond working together to save wounded soldiers from a flooding creek. So to answer your question, we don't know if Stephie is the woman we're looking for. But I believe she is."

* * *

On the second Saturday morning in Neil's home, Julie got up early. It hadn't taken her long to find a place in Neil's routine. That place was unpleasant, but ultimately she believed it would be useful. He was, as she suspected, a weak man. He tried to compensate for his lack of strength through acts of violence and she was the object of his aggression. But she was willing to put up with the things he did because later he would beg for her forgiveness by doing whatever she asked him to do.

Julie locked the bathroom door so she could be certain he would not barge in if he happened to wake up before she was done checking the bruises on her thighs. They didn't hurt as much as she had thought they would and as long as Neil confined his punches to parts of her body she could cover, she was content to let him act out his little fantasies. To be honest it was the kissing she disliked the most, but that was part of the routine. He would push her down, on their bed or couch or even the floor. Then he'd tear her clothes off and had even ripped a few pairs of her panties. He would punch her a few times then finally calm down. The violence was never out of anger, just a strange thing he liked to do. They'd only screwed once. He hadn't seemed interested in traditional sex, so she was able to discourage that. But after the violence came the apologies and along with the words the sloppy, stale, whiskey-breath kissing. She had to put up with that or he wouldn't listen to her the next day.

She had three medium size bruises on the inside of her right thigh and one big one on the outside of her left that was as hard as a bone and extended around to her ass. It looked a lot worse than it felt even when she sat down. She would have to be careful to keep her jeans pulled up when Neil was around. Seeing what he had done would turn him on and she would be going through it all over again. He was a strange man, but since her goal was to scare the shit out of Michael and Stephie, strange was what she was after. She zipped and buttoned her jeans then walked out of the bathroom. Hopefully, she would have some peace before Neil got up.

* * *

Glen wanted to continue with Stephie as his subject. Michael seemed to be disappointed, but Stephie agreed. Glen's reason was simple. He wanted to go back to the precise time they had left off the day before and that was easier if he had the same subject. This time she had dressed in loose clothing, a T-shirt and her white running shorts, so she didn't have to change. She had her hair pulled back in a ponytail, but Glen suggested she let it down. She was even more responsive than she had been the day before and it was only a few minutes from the start of the session until she was back at Gettysburg.

Twenty-Five

Their sleep lasted no more than five minutes. Alex woke when a heavyset, blonde soldier shook her arm. "Are there bandages, Ma'am?" he asked her. "These men are hurtin'. The water reopened their wounds."

"Oh, yes," she said, startled. She sat up, waking Charles and causing him to jump slightly. The rain had let up. It was now only a fine sprinkle. "I'm sorry. I should be helping. The bandages are kept in crates. There should be one in that cluster of trees up there." The soldier thanked her, then walked away to look for the medical supplies.

As Alex stood she let out a small cry. She was reacting to pain in the calf of her right leg. She realized that she hadn't tended the wound she'd received when she had fallen against the rocks.

"What's wrong?" Charles asked.

"I hurt my leg."

"Is it bad?"

"I'm not sure. I didn't have time to look."

"Then let me."

Charles got down on one knee in front of Alex and lifted the hem of her mud soaked skirt. She knew the cuts had to be examined, but she could have treated them herself. She was a volunteer nurse who'd been thrown into the work without any medical training but she certainly knew enough to clean up a few cuts. She probably knew more about treating injuries than Charles did. She doubted he had any experience beyond the lessons he had learned from his mother when she dealt with the normal scrapes and bruises all young boys get during their day to day adventures. Yet Alex wanted Charles to take care of her. His gentle touch on her calf sent shivers through her leg all the way up her spine, as if she had suddenly jumped into a cool lake. That intense pleasure combined with the image of Charles on one knee at her feet made her own knees wobble.

"You did a job on yourself," he said, his voice as gentle and as strong as his hands. "But most of it is just surface scratches. Sometimes they hurt worse than the deep ones. You still have a few here that are open. I'll have to clean you up and stop the bleeding."

He let her skirt fall back down over her leg then stood up and looked around. "I need to get bandages from the soldier who woke us. "I'll be right back."

She watched him walk off then looked around. She noticed that there were few nurses near by and those were a good distance away. For all intents and purposes she was the only woman in a field with what appeared to be more than a hundred soldiers. Of course most of those men were more concerned with their own problems than with a lone female who looked a mess. She was covered with mud, under her petticoat, inside her chemise and throughout her hair. Still, the emotions she had just experienced left her feeling vulnerable and she was glad when she saw Charles returning with the bandages.

"Sit down then imagine you're someplace else," Charles said. She did as she was told then he looked at her leg again. "Put yourself in your dry bedroom. Make the day a spring day. Look out your window and see the flowers coming up. Whenever something hurts it is important to remember that God is powerful and the world is good." His voice was gentle but firm, letting her know he would take care of her.

Alex felt the cloth on her calf, as he wiped the mud from her cuts with soft even strokes. Then he applied a gentle, but firm pressure to the wound. His touch seeped up her body again, causing her heart to beat hard.

"The bleeding has stopped," Charles said, as he pulled her skirt back over her ankle. He offered his hand to help her stand. She took it and got back on her feet, trying to straighten her clothes as she stood. She lifted her hand to her hair, pushing it back behind her ears.

"You look beautiful," Charles said with a soft and sincere tone to his voice.

"Are you mocking me?" she asked, but she didn't think he was. The look in his eyes told her that.

"That mud can't hide what's inside."

She hoped that was true, but the world around them seemed ugly enough to hide everything pleasant. *What an irony to meet someone like Charles in a place like this,* Alex thought. She reached for his hand then turned to look at him. "What do we do now?" she asked, her heart still pounding.

"We look for Samuel," he told her, "if you feel well enough to walk."

She nodded then they started up the hill. She kept up with his easy pace, refusing to drop his hand.

People can get lost in a battle, Alex thought, wondering how Charles would react if Samuel never showed up. "I should help the wounded," she said.

"Samuel is wounded," Charles told her. "We need to help him first."

She was certain that this was the place where she had left Samuel about two hours earlier. He probably had walked away, but he could have been carried off by the creek, God forbid. Charles suggested searching down stream from where they were, so they headed that way. They passed at least fifty half drowned, maimed soldiers, but didn't see Samuel.

"What now?" Charles was the one asking this time.

"Did Samuel have money?"

"I believe so, unless he lost it in the flood."

"Look over there." A farmer was loading one of the wounded onto a horse drawn wagon. "There are always people who look for opportunities. We have our share of them here in Gettysburg. If he had money to pay his way he might have been picked up by that fellow or one of the other local farmers. They sell rides to the trains or to the buildings that have been converted into hospitals."

"Where do the trains go?"

"Harrisburg, mostly, but some take the boys to Philadelphia. They go where they'll receive care."

"And these hospitals you spoke of?"

"The union army has taken over a church and a couple of homes that were empty. The families who lived there have fled the battle area. It's possible Samuel was taken to one of those. He might even have gone before the creek flooded, but I can't imagine Samuel going too far away without letting me know. We've become good friends. And remember, Charles, I saw him about twenty minutes before the rain started."

"We need to find him. That's all there is to it."

Charles took Alex's hand once again and started leading her toward town. She followed quietly.

* * *

The first hospital they stopped at was the converted church. Alex's thought as she entered the building was that if Christ ever designed a place of worship it would be simple and holy, like this one. It was a small, rectangular building, with plain white, lap siding outside and two large brown doors, one in front and one on the left side. The windows were also plain, decorated only with black shutters. It seemed fitting that this structure should become a hospital, because hospitals and churches were the institutions everyone was now depending on to heal the wounds from the war.

Her family had moved to their farm when she was twelve and since that year she had made more trips to Gettysburg than she could count, but she had never been inside this building. Perhaps that was because it was a German Calvinist church. Her mom had been raised Presbyterian, but her father and she had always been Episcopalian.

Inside the building, the pews, the flooring, and the posts and beams that held up the roof were all dark brown. The church walls were white, the same shade inside as they were outside. The pulpit was brown and rose up two steps higher than floor level. There was a simple brown altar table behind the pulpit, on which there stood a wooden cross, also brown. Behind the table, was a magnificent stained glass window, with greens, blues, reds, yellows, and every shade in between. Under normal conditions this window and the church vestments had to be the only colors the congregation would see. *How fitting,* Alex thought.

The window was a picture of Christ, standing on a hillside surrounded by spring flowers and green trees with mountains and a clear sky in the background. The background reminded Alex of the scene Charles had told her to visualize while he tended her wound. Jesus had his left hand raised in a gesture of blessing and his right hand outstretched as if he were beckoning to everyone he could see, especially the wounded soldiers beneath him.

The pews had been twisted around so they were positioned face to face to provide a number of long beds. They were occupied by at least thirty patients, most of them with serious wounds.

Alex whispered to Charles as they stood in the door. "I've always thought that I would like to die in a church, but this changes my mind. I'd rather be alone. I'd rather be someplace where I could have dignity."

"Maybe some of these soldiers won't die. Maybe they've traded a little of their dignity for a few more years in this world."

"Maybe," Alex agreed, but the hesitancy in her voice revealed her doubt. As a military nurse she knew how many of the soldiers died after they came to places like the one they were looking at.

Alex and Charles walked into the hospital together, but as he moved around the wounded she stepped up to the cross and the stained glass window. She dropped to her knees and prayed for the wounded. She prayed for Samuel, specifically. And she prayed for Charles. She asked God to help him understand that it was not his fault that Samuel was hurt. That he had done everything anyone could have done. She finished the prayer by saying, "I pray this in the name of Your blessed son, Jesus Christ. Amen."

Alex stepped back from the altar and joined Charles as he was walking between the pews. "He isn't here." Charles told her.

"I could tell from the look on your face."

"You said there were other hospitals in town."

"I can't go on like this," Alex said. "I'm tired and I'm filthy. I have cousins who live in town. If we go there we can clean up, get some fresh clothes and maybe some rest, too. After that we can look for Samuel with renewed strength. I'm sorry, Charles, but I can't do any more."

Charles paused as if he were weighing his options then he nodded. Alex could tell he was torn between her needs and his need to find his friend. She was surprised but pleased that he chose to follow her.

Twenty-Six

The town house that Alex's cousins lived in was on the north side of town, a forty-five minute walk from the makeshift hospital. Along the way Alex and Charles told each other about their likes and their dislikes and about the people they loved: their parents, Charles' sisters and his brother, and, of course, Samuel. Alex loved hearing the stories Charles told, but she also found she could open up about her own life in a way she was not able to do with other men she had met. She told him how before the war she hated blood. The sight of it had once made her so queasy she had been unable to move.

"You hide it well."

"It's awful to say, but I guess I'm used to it now. And when I work quickly I don't have time to dwell on my fears."

"Certain fears are necessary," Charles told her. "You need to listen to those. But other fears have to be confronted. The trouble is knowing which is which."

"This is a fear I needed to face. That's why I chose to work as a nurse."

"That's not what I heard. I heard that you did it for the soldiers. The men you helped believe that God sent you."

Alex smiled. Charles knew how to say the words that made her heart swirl. The sun's position indicated it was late afternoon when they reached the house. Alex was very hungry and imagined that Charles was also, but he didn't mention that to her. He acted as if the conversation with her was all his body needed to keep going.

They walked up the steps to the front door and knocked. No one answered.

"I thought this might be the case. Aunt Jenny and Uncle Louis must have taken the cousins and moved out during the battle. But I know where a key is hidden. They won't mind if we use their house and borrow some clothes." Alex led Charles back down the walkway.

She found what she was looking for tucked behind a shutter, although she had to climb through a patch of ivy and stand on her toes to reach it. Their key was still kept in the spot they had shown her a couple of years earlier, when she had spent a week visiting.

The living room was elegant with gray striped wallpaper, hardwood floors, and a large, dark gold throw rug that had a floral pattern woven into it.

"I'm scared to step in," Charles said. "I'm drenched and I'll spoil anything I touch."

"You're not half as bad as I am," Alex answered. "You're just wet. I'm filthy. But if we take off our shoes and avoid stepping on the rug, we won't do too much damage. We need to head to the kitchen. I'm certain we'll find something there to eat and we can also start a fire in the stove to heat some water for our baths. I intend to take one and you're also welcome to. I'll look better when I'm not in this state."

"No one could look better," he said, touching her shoulder as she helped him take off his boots. She felt so naïve, like a child, as her heart started pounding again. She hoped Charles wouldn't notice.

There were carrots, turnips, onions, cucumbers, and potatoes, all stored in the pantry. There were also biscuits that were a little hard but free of mold and a slab of pork that could be sliced up for bacon.

"I'm sure there's more food in the cellar," Alex said, "also tea and coffee. I suggest we each eat a biscuit or two to stave off our hunger. Then we can get cleaned up and get some rest. In the morning I'll make you a meal, but I'm much too tired to even think of cooking."

Charles agreed, but he also ate a couple of carrots. They finished their improvised supper and started a fire in the stove. Then they filled up a couple of the largest pots they could find and placed them on top to heat.

Alex led Charles to the master bedroom, still carefully avoiding the rug. They found the bedroom to be as interesting as the living room was elegant. It was filled with furniture that had a rough look about it. Alex told Charles that her Uncle Louis had made most of the pieces himself. Those included the bed frame, a rocking chair, a small table, a love seat, and two chests of drawers.

"They bought that mirror." Alex pointed to a full length looking-glass in a brown wooden frame and stand. It could be positioned anywhere in the room and adjusted to stay put at any angle. "He built the other items to match. I think it gives the place a wonderful look. Do you agree?"

"I do," Charles told her then he looked at a glass case containing a dozen dolls. Each one of the dolls had an intricate, ceramic head on top of a stuffed, cloth body. They were all female and all dressed up, with bonnets, full skirts, shawls, and aprons. They were beautiful, but Charles spoke of the case they were displayed in. "And did he build that, too?" he asked.

"No, but Aunt Jenny made every one of those dolls. Except for the heads. She bought the heads."

"Talented family," Charles said.

"My parents aren't too bad, either," she replied smirking slightly. "You must meet them someday."

"I'd like that."

"Then you will. My father's working the railroad in Harrisburg. It's necessary work to keep the army supplied, but we miss him, my mother and I. She's home alone. You can see her whenever you wish."

"That would be a good thing to do— after we find Samuel."

For a moment Alex had forgotten their friend. "Yes," she said. "Samuel must come before my mother, but first comes my bath. Help me find the tub."

Charles opened a set of double doors and found what they were looking for stored in the closet. It was a fat, oval metal tub attached to a base for an overall look similar to a squat hour glass. Alex and Charles each grabbed a side and carried the tub out to the middle of the room. The base was about nine inches high and spread out far enough to keep it from tipping over when someone was climbing in. One side of the tub was built a foot higher than the rest, to provide a backrest. The other edges were all gently curved, so the bather could sit in the tub, lean against the backrest and dangle his or her legs over the side. It was designed for comfort.

Inside the tub Charles discovered something he hadn't expected. It was a copy of Charles Darwin's book, "On the Origin of Species."

"What's this?" Charles asked, picking up the book and thumbing through a few pages.

"I suppose it belongs to my Uncle Louis. He's an insatiable reader. He also prides himself in being a progressive thinker, although I believe he follows the current trends too much."

"Then you don't accept Darwin's ideas?" Charles asked Alex.

"I haven't read enough about them to make up my mind."

"He says we're all descended from apes."

"That much I know, but I don't understand what led him to believe such a thing."

"He visited some islands in the Pacific where he found species of animals that weren't anywhere else in the world. He said the animals that survive are the ones best suited for a particular environment. His point is that the smarter apes survived and became us. It's an interesting idea, but only a theory. I'm sure you've heard how upset some people are over his theories. They want him silenced."

Alex circled around the bathtub and placed her hand on the backrest. "I wonder," she said, looking pensive, "if what he says is true, then how will our environment change us? Will we be different for having lived through a war?"

"Darwin seems to be saying that might makes right, which is certainly true in wartime. If the rebels win this one, the union soldiers will be remembered with a much different perspective than if we win.

I'm sure that whatever way this thing ends you and I will have to deal with the results for the rest of our lives."

"We better check on the water," Alex said, changing the subject as she walked away. Charles followed.

The water was at a rolling boil. They carried the two kettles to the tub, dumped them in then returned to the kitchen for two more kettles of cold water to mix with the hot. Alex found a cake of soap in the pantry and was all set for her bath.

Charles left Alex alone, but just as she was about to undress, she glanced in the large mirror. He had left the door ajar and was standing outside the room, watching her reflection. *That little scoundrel,* she thought. *He's spying on me.*

Alex's first reaction was to go to the door to close it. Charles had no right to try such a trick and she should scold him for it, but then she had a second thought that grew inside her like a fire. Her glance at the mirror had been brief. She was certain he hadn't noticed. She could let his little trick succeed without him thinking any less of her. She felt a flush come to her cheeks as she mulled over this crazy idea. This wasn't something that a woman raised the way she had been raised should do. Yet life could end tomorrow. The war had proven that and had left everyone with a sense that anything goes. Still, that was more of an excuse than a reason.

She didn't need to look in the mirror to know what was happening. Charles could not take his eyes off her and that realization made her feel wonderful. She bent over and splashed some bath water onto her face, to clean off some of the mud that was covering her. Then she stood up and opened the first button on her blue muslin dress. I have nothing to lose, she thought, swallowing hard and staring away from the mirror. He doesn't know how much I want to do this.

She opened the second button. Her exhaustion mixed with the emotional thrill she was experiencing and made her sway slightly. She could feel Charles staring. She opened the third button, the fourth, fifth....

* * *

"...Six. Seven. Eight. Nine. Ten. Come on back, Stephie," Glen said, speaking softly. "You've been under for a good length of time. It's time to talk about what you've been through."

Twenty-Seven

Stephie's perception of life, a set of beliefs that had taken most of her thirty-two years to develop, had been abruptly redefined by the experience of her regression. Yet her faith wasn't shaken. If anything, this clear proof in the existence of the human soul had strengthened her belief in God and had validated her decision to live a life in pursuit of spiritual goals.

She shook off the groggy, post-hypnotic sensation as she shifted her legs down from the couch and twisted her way into a sitting position. Then she caught Michael's eye. As soon as that happened she was hit with a wave of embarrassment that overwhelmed all her other thoughts. She was one with Alex, so revealing the attraction Alex had experienced for Charles exposed her own feelings for Charles' counterpart, Michael. And that wasn't something she was comfortable doing, not yet.

"How are you feeling?" Michael asked. There was a peculiar, forced quality to his voice that exposed his own emotions and made it clear to Stephie how he understood the connection they had with Alex and Charles as well as she did. She was certain she was reading him right.

"I'm alright, a little shaky perhaps, but fine otherwise."

Michael would assume Stephie felt the same attraction as Alex had and he would be right. She didn't mind him knowing that she liked him and, Lord knows, she hoped he liked her. It was just that she would prefer they had a deeper emotional connection before Michael understood how he made her hormones pump.

"You need to rest for a while," Glen told her. "We can take a break, perhaps have some coffee."

"I have peanut butter cookies if you'd like something sweet," Emily added.

"Coffee sounds nice. I could use the caffeine."

"Perhaps you two could switch places for the next session," Emily suggested. "Michael could give us Charles' perspective."

Stephie nodded and Michael smiled. It seemed to Stephie that he liked the idea.

"Is that possible?" Emily asked Glen. "Can you send Michael back to the time where Stephie left off?"

"I think so. We were all listening to her describe what was happening, so his focus should be right. Are you willing to try?" he asked Michael.

"I'd love to take a turn."

The regression had been an amazing experience for Stephie, but it would be nice to hear Michael reveal some of what was going on in Charles' head.

* * *

Emily had ice cream in addition to the cookies— butter pecan with chocolate sprinkles. It was like a little party with an innocent atmosphere that relaxed everyone. Soon they were all chatting as if this day was like any other day. But it wasn't and Glen knew that better than anyone in the room. He had identified the souls of a family in these people, a family that had existed many times throughout history. And here they were sitting around this simple kitchen table as they had so many times before, in distant years. What he had achieved was the greatest success of his career, but it would be meaningless if he couldn't break their tragic cycle.

Michael set his coffee down and talked about the feelings he had after his first regression. "When I was in high school and even middle school I was bored with the names and dates we covered in history classes, but fascinated by the stories of individuals living in the periods we studied. It was the realization that all the people who had lived before us were individuals with loves and hang-ups of their own that drew me to history for a career. Suddenly I can go into the head of someone from more than a hundred years ago, from a time I've spent years studying, and I want more of that experience. I want as much as I can get."

As Michael spoke, Glen wondered if his usefulness might have waned. Michael's soul was in Emily's father, Harry, whose only relationship to his wife's murderers was the motivation brought on by Anne's jealousy. Glen didn't know enough about Alexandra's death to understand Charles' role, but he had a feeling it would be similar to Harry's. So did it make sense to switch the regression from Stephie to Michael? Wouldn't Charles' point of view provide less information than Alexandra's? Glen wondered if he might have given in too soon to Emily's suggestion for Michael to take a turn on the couch. Yet it was true that Stephie was new to the process and pushing her too hard, too quickly could cause harm.

"For me the motivation is religious curiosity," Stephie responded to Michael. "That's also why I became a minister."

"You fooled me there," Michael told her. "You are so good at solving people's problems. It's a natural assumption to think you became a minister so you could spend your life helping others."

Glen dwelled on Michael's words for a moment. He could see altruism as another tie between Stephie and Alexandra given the reason Alexandra had become a nurse. Yet the connection didn't appear to follow through with Mary Vinson. She was a mother and mothers all help their children, but was that enough for the tie to be something other than a simple coincidence? Glen couldn't answer that. He wondered if Emily could. She only knew her mother through the regressions. She had no idea how the woman spent her time when they were apart. Glen also wondered if Mary Vinson shared Stephie and Alex's religious nature. That was another question he couldn't answer.

Glen knew that Mary, Alex and Stephie were three separate women, physically. But Stephie was the connection he had with the other two and, for that reason, when he thought of them he pictured Stephie. He knew, for example, that Alex had light brown hair, but in his mind he couldn't stop seeing her hair as black. This had happened to him with previous regressions, but this time it bothered him more because Stephie was exceptionally beautiful. Picturing Alex pulling soldiers from a flooding creek was less realistic when her image had long, soft hair and a Barbie doll figure. He wondered if Stephie's beauty had ever hurt her ability to be a successful minister. Those green eyes of hers would make most any woman she knew envious. He imagined her looks might keep some people from choosing her as a counselor or others from concentrating on her sermons. Ministers are supposed to teach about God. They're not supposed to look like goddesses.

"Everyone I've observed Glen regressing has had a different explanation for why they were interested in the process," Emily said. "I'm not sure I understand why they need any explanation. Regression is a beautiful experience that is spiritual and fulfilling. I don't have an excuse. I simply love the opportunity to know more about who I was and who I am."

Although Emily avoided explaining her true interest in regressions to Stephie and Michael, Glen already knew her real motivation. He was glad she was politically astute enough to keep the story of the circle to herself. Scaring Stephie and Michael would be counter productive. *Perhaps*, he thought, *the time to regress Emily again has arrived*. It wasn't a decision Glen could make quickly. He knew how much strain the process could cause, especially to a woman of Emily's age. But he also knew that being too careful could cause harm. He looked across the table at Stephie and Michael and thought of the part of the circle that meant they would have a child together. Then he shifted his focus to Emily.

Glen's feelings toward Emily had grown over the course of their friendship, convincing him that he also had a repeating role with her spiritual family and specifically with her. It was an odd sensation. She was forty-five years older than he was and that age difference made her older than his mother would have been if she was still alive. In fact, Emily was old enough to be his grandmother but the age mismatch didn't stop the connection he felt. Glen understood that after life comes more life and this perspective enabled him to envision relationships that most people would not even consider.

"Well," Michael said addressing Glen as he rose from the kitchen table and took his coffee mug to the sink. "I'm ready when you are."

Twenty-Eight

The bathwater was brown from the mud that had once covered Alex, but to Charles it felt as clean as the water at home in Fields Pond and a great deal warmer. He leaned back in the tub and closed his eyes, thinking how sweet she had looked when she had lain in the same water. Alex had gone upstairs to her cousin's room and had left him instructions to sleep in her Uncle Louis and Aunt Jenny's bed. She had also left him a pair of her Uncle's drawers and a long cotton shirt to sleep in.

When Charles was done he toweled dry and put on the shirt, but he skipped the drawers. He looked at the bed she expected him to use. It was comfortable and he was exhausted, but the image of Alex was running through his mind. He longed to be near her, to touch her. He left the master bedroom and walked to the front of the house where the stairs were. The wood in the steps creaked a bit as he crept up, and so did the floorboards in the hall once he reached the top. It was possible that Alex knew he was coming. There were three doors off the upstairs hall, but only one was ajar. Charles reached for it and slowly opened it, avoiding most of the squeal of old hinges that he had expected. She was there, in a double bed against the far side of the room, lying on her side, facing the wall, covered by a mostly pink patchwork quilt. He could see her clearly because she had left a candle burning. He wondered why she would have done that if she had not been expecting him.

He blew out the candle then gently lifted the bed covers and crawled in beside her. Her nightgown had pulled up and he could feel the skin of her legs against his own. Although he realized she was exhausted, he believed she was pretending to be asleep so she wouldn't have to ask him to go. Slowly he moved his arm around her and buried his face in her brown, wet hair. He lay there, in that position, feeling as if he could hold her and protect her forever. When he was certain she was asleep he allowed his own body to rest.

Alex was still asleep when the morning light came through the window and woke Charles. He slowly pulled his arm from her waist where it had remained all night long. He felt stiff and tingly as the blood started to return, but the thrill of touching her for such a long time was well worth the slight discomfort. He carefully avoided rousing her as he swung his legs over the side of the bed and sat up. Then he stood and went downstairs to look for more clothing. He thought he might surprise her by cooking the breakfast, but he remembered how she had been looking forward to making a meal for him. He left that task for her as he went back to Uncle Louis' room to find a pair of pants.

Charles had a fire going in the stove when Alex came into the kitchen. Her hair was dry and brushed, so she had been upstairs for a while making herself presentable. She was wearing a light blue robe with white lace trim over her pink nightgown. Apparently her relatives had a great deal of clothing for her to choose from. Charles wondered how rich they were. Yet having money before the war didn't assure a comfortable life afterwards. Charles had found a pair of light brown trousers and was wearing those in addition to the white, pull-over shirt Alex had given him to sleep in.

"Did you rest well? Charles asked, after they said their good mornings. He asked the question as a bit of a tease. He knew she was too much of a lady to discuss their sleeping arrangements in the light of day and he liked the little game they were playing.

"I was asleep as soon as my head was on the pillow and I didn't wake up until just a short time ago. I don't think anything could have woken me, short of another battle."

Charles noticed that Alex's light brown hair had a slight hint of red in it. He hadn't noticed that subtle color previously, even before it was filled with mud. It was as if spending time with her and getting to know her better helped him to look at her closer. He felt as if he needed to study each little part of her so he could file the images in his head and retrieve them whenever he needed a boost from a beautiful thought.

"I see you have the stove stoked," she told him. "I'll make us something to eat. After breakfast we need to decide where we should go next."

"You said there were other hospitals set up in town. We should look for Samuel there."

"Yes. But most of the wounded have been taken out of town and I'm not prepared to follow you to Philadelphia or Harrisburg. I need to get back to my mother. She's alone. I have to be sure she's all right and I have to let her know how I am. She has enough to worry about with my father being away."

"Samuel will be there, Alex," Charles said, his voice cracking slightly. He refused to say out loud what they were both thinking. Thousands had been killed in the battle. There was no way to know who those people were, no list of names or places the young men had come from. People can get lost in the time of confusion that follows a battle and Samuel could be one of those. He also could have been injured in the aftermath of the rain or hurt in some isolated fight with rebel soldiers who were still hiding out there.

* * *

They did not find Samuel in the first hospital they searched that day, but they found something that made Alex cry. She had weathered the entire battle without a sign of a tear, so Charles knew how upset she was. What they discovered in the hospital was the dead body of Ginny Wade, a young woman about Alex's age who had been shot by a stray, sniper's bullet. The bullet had passed through a wooden door and into Ginny's back. Alex told Charles that she had not known Ginny well, but that she had met both her and her sister, Georgia, a few times. Gettysburg was not a big town. Most everyone knew everyone else. The two sisters had been the subject of conversation recently because last week Georgia had given birth to a son. It had been a moment of beauty amid the horrors of war. Everyone had been glad that Ginny was there to take care of her sister while her husband was off fighting for their country. "Now look at what has happened," Alex said more to herself than to Charles as she stared at Ginny's lifeless body.

Charles wondered what it was about this woman that seemed to shake Alex more than all the other horrors she'd witnessed. He imagined that gender and familiarity both played a part in the reason. It certainly seemed easier for Alex to identify with a woman who was killed while working in her own home than with any of the soldiers, including Samuel.

"It's all right," Charles said in his gentlest voice. "Don't let it break you."

Alex smiled back, but seemed to shutter inside. "Shall we go to the next hospital? she asked. "I'm ready if you are."

* * *

The second and last hospital Charles and Alex searched that day was in a square, two story brick building. The wounded had been distributed throughout the building with the worst cases kept on the first floor. They saw death and blood and pain. But they did not see Samuel. It was time for Charles to make his choice. They stood together in front of the house as she turned to him and waited for his response.

"Samuel is family to me," he told her with a steady rhythm to his voice that indicated he knew exactly what he had to say. "I spent my entire life with him. When he was shot I felt as if I were the one who had been hit. Now, I want to find him and do everything I can to help him. But suddenly there's something I need even more." Charles reached over and grabbed Alex's hand, pulling it back toward his chest. "I want you, Alex. It will weigh on me forever if I don't find him. I know that. But when I try to tell myself that I shouldn't stay with you it's like telling water to run uphill."

Alex reached out and gently touched his mouth. "It won't be long," she said, her voice almost as soft as a whisper. "I just need to let my mother know things are fine with me and that I love her."

* * *

Alex and Charles stopped back at her cousin's house before starting the hike to her family's farm. She said she wanted to leave a note to her aunt and uncle, explaining that they had spent the night and thanking them for the food and clothing she and Charles had taken. Charles was happy to follow her there. His time was her time now.

Alex found ink and stationary among her uncle's papers. She filled the pen and leaned over the desk to start her note. Charles stood behind her, looking over her shoulder as she wrote. "My dearest Aunt Jenny and Uncle Louis, I have stayed one night in your home and have also granted lodging to a soldier who is in search of a friend. His friend was wounded and separated from him during the storm that followed the battle. I wish to...."

Charles couldn't help but think about the night they had spent together in the small room upstairs. She had felt so soft and had smelled like a fresh spring rain. He needed to touch her again, to feel her body next to his as he had the night before. Charles slipped his arms around Alex's waist and when he did she stopped writing. "Don't stop your note," he told her. "I just have to hold you."

"I like it when you do." Alex set the pen in the ink and turned around in his arms. "I liked it last night, too."

She had acknowledged the night they had spent together and her voice made Charles' head swirl. Her words were gentle music echoing through his soul, acknowledging her feelings for him. "You are the most wonderful person I have ever known," he said. Ordinary words couldn't come close to expressing his feelings, but his heart was racing so hard he didn't know what else to say.

Her face was close enough to his to feel her breath on his skin. That sensual feeling caused him to lose his own breath for a moment, but at the same time Charles felt an overwhelming need to move even closer. He leaned toward her as she reached up toward him. Their lips touched softly at first then harder as he pushed toward her again. She was soft and smooth but tasting her put fire in him. He reached his hands to the back of her head and filled his fingers with a blanket of her hair, still kissing her hard.

"Don't speak," she said after pulling away from him. "Follow me." She took Charles' hand and led him back to the master bedroom. When they reached the bed she lay down and pulled him on top of her. Charles had trouble with the buttons in the back of Alex's dress so she had to help. Her chemise had to be pulled over her head and there was a knot in the tie string of her drawers that was absolutely maddening. But they kept working at each other's clothing between the kisses and caresses until they were naked.

When Charles had fantasized about this moment it wasn't so clumsy but none of that mattered as long as Alex wanted to be with him the way he wanted to be with her. It wasn't the way she looked or the feel of her body against his that had him shaking in ways he had never experienced. It was more than that. It was her soul wrapping around his as if she were a sanctuary from a world that was too cruel and too violent. He kissed her neck then worked his mouth down to her breasts.

Alex was tight, yet in an instant she was open as her virginity gave way. She let out a little cry that scared Charles when that happened, but at the same time she tightened her hold around his waist as if she were trying to crawl into his chest. Even if Charles had wanted to stop, he couldn't have. He was too caught up in her power. He moved with a steady, smooth rhythm until his body couldn't hold back. Then he lay on her, exhausted, taking in the feel of her delicate body breathing under his weight as if she were his own pounding heart.

Twenty-Nine

Stephie knew of other couples who believed they had been together in past lives, but her relationship with Michael was different from theirs. The regressions had given them evidence far more powerful than intuition. She was Alex and he was Charles and they had made love at Gettysburg. Knowing that made Stephie scared of what Michael could be thinking and even more of what her own thoughts should be.

"We need to talk to Kathy," Michael said as they rode home in his Grand Prix. Stephie was glad he wasn't bringing up their nineteenth century affair. The subject had to be as awkward for him as it was for her.

"Why?" she asked.

"Alex is in one of her murals."

"You think Kathy was part of our past life?"

"I saw her painting before I saw the Alex in my memories, but I'm certain she was the woman in it. If it was anyone else I might have been mistaken, but I was drawn to her portrait and now Alex is in my head like a melody I've played a thousand times. How could Kathy have painted her if she didn't know her?"

Michael's comment about Stephie's past life version left her with mixed feelings. She felt both proud and resentful, like a middle aged woman hearing from her husband that twenty years ago she was the most beautiful woman he had ever known. Stephie wanted the image that was stuck in his mind to be her own black hair and green eyes, not Alex's light brown hair and blue eyes.

"Kathy said she had a twenty-five year old daughter in a recurring dream," Stephie told him. "Do you think she could have been Alex's mother? That would explain the strangeness of our relationship back in college. She also said that many of her paintings came from that dream." What Stephie didn't say was that Alex's presence in Kathy's art was not nearly as strange as the concept that she and Michael were meant to be together in countless lifetimes. Stephie had never doubted the existence of another soul that was the perfect match for her own, but this was not the way she had expected to find that soul. She knew she was attracted to Michael and when she held him she felt as if he fit her body like a perfect pair of jeans. But they hadn't had time to discover each other or to work through day to day problems. Instead, they had just been placed in each other's arms and told that they belonged there. There was beauty to that, but an awkward beauty.

Now Michael was expressing an interest in Kathy and how she related to their past lives. Perhaps Kathy would give them another way to get to know each other better.

"Should we go talk to her?" Michael asked.

Stephie glanced at the clock on the car dashboard. It was getting close to six. "She might be eating," Stephie answered.

"Give her a call. If she's free we'll buy her a dinner, unless you have somewhere else you need to be."

"I don't" Stephie pulled her cell phone out of her purse and tapped in her friend's number while Michael continued to drive. Kathy was happy to hear from her and thought dinner would be fun.

* * *

Kathy was wearing a white T-shirt with blue lettering that read "Art is life and life is art." She liked the shirt because it kept her focused on what she considered important, but the words read too much like a commercial for her to wear it in public, so it had become one of her lounge around in shirts along with her souvenir shirt from *Wicked* and two *I love New York* shirts she had received as gifts from her mother. She took off the Tee and her gray sweatpants and changed into a pair of black jeans and a red blouse that gave the impression of being dressy without actually being dressy. Stephie had said dinner, but not where. This outfit was a choice she often made when she wasn't sure where she was going.

Michael seemed nice, but there was something ominous that surrounded Stephie and him. Kathy had always been a skeptic concerning subjects that had to do with the less than tangible aspects of her life, so evaluating Stephie's relationship based on her intuition was not something that made her comfortable. But she was concerned about her friend. She wanted Stephie to end up with a man who cared about her and was strong enough to protect her. She thought Michael met those criteria, yet she wasn't certain.

They took her to an Italian restaurant that was a step or two above a pizzeria. It had a dining room with yellow, stucco walls that were decorated with photos of Italian scenes. The menu was a mixture of pizza and pasta, but Kathy was pleased to have a wide range of meatless choices. She decided that Stephie had probably suggested the place since her friend knew she was a vegetarian. "There is someone from my church who can help explain your dreams," Stephie said as she and Kathy sipped on glasses of Merlot and Michael drank a beer.

"A psychologist?"

"Not exactly, but she's knowledgeable."

"She works with a hypnotist," Michael said. "He's the one who will impress you."

"Did he help *you* with a problem?" Kathy asked.

"He helped me understand things about myself that I had never imagined could be true."

Kathy's dreams were personal. Under normal circumstances she wouldn't consider discussing them with someone with whom she didn't share a long history. But the subject provided an opportunity to talk to Michael and she intended to find out more about him. She wanted to be sure Michael was someone who could make Stephie happy. Stephie's happiness had always been more important to her than her own.

"I considered trying a hypnotist a while back, but I wasn't sure how to avoid the frauds. You can vouch for him, I assume."

Michael nodded.

"If the dreams were normal I wouldn't be so upset. It's just that they seem more real than the rest of my life and the memories of them don't fade the way most dreams do. Does that make sense?"

"If anyone could tell you what makes sense, Glen could."

"What do you think, Stephie?"

"There's nothing to worry about. It was an incredible experience for me and we'll be there to make sure you're treated right."

Stephie's promise to be there was a powerful argument for Kathy. The years during which they had lost contact had felt empty much of the time. Kathy's career had taken off. She had attended countless parties with more friends than she had ever imagined she would have, but there was always something missing. Twice she had thought she was in love and one of those men, Philip, had moved in with her for a while, but both those relationships had grown flat— the routines had seemed empty and the conversations stale. It had never been that way with Stephie. She might have talked about something as mundane as a math quiz, but Kathy had always hung on her words.

"The dreams have to come from somewhere," Kathy said. "If I just had a hint of where that somewhere might be... If I could understand why they keep coming, I wouldn't care if they continued. In fact, I think I might miss them if they did stop. Has this friend of yours ever worked a similar case?"

"He touches memories you don't even know you have," Stephie told her. "Dreams do the same thing, don't they?"

The waitress came out with everyone's meals, including the baked ziti Kathy had ordered. They each had refills on their drinks and after Kathy finished half of her second glass of wine she agreed to have Michael set up a session for her.

* * *

"Dreams can come from countless sources," Glen told Kathy when Stephie and Michael brought her to Emily's apartment. It was Thursday, the day following Michael's previous session. Glen and Emily had both been eager to see Kathy as soon as they had heard she was willing to come, so they didn't let much time pass. "I can help you with one of the sources," he said, "past lives. If something traumatic happened when your soul was in another incarnation, impressions of that event can carry through to where you are today. They can influence how you think and what you do. And they can certainly show up in your dreams."

The experience that had brought Kathy to see Glen was not an unknown past life from some time back before she was born. It was the time she had shared with Stephie. Despite Kathy's career success and perhaps to some degree because of it, she still longed for the simpler times of one on one conversations about feelings and ambitions and the confusion of being young. In their sophomore year Kathy and Stephie had been lab partners for an astronomy class. One night they had met the class at two in the morning to use the university telescope for a perfect view of Saturn and three of its moons. On the way back to their dorm they stopped by a pond on campus. They sat in the grass, tossed pebbles in the water and stared at the stars until the sun came up. They didn't talk much that night and that was part of what made the experience so beautiful. Stephie was the only person Kathy had ever known who always understood when it was best to talk and when it was best to remain silent.

"You said I needed to keep an open mind, but this is unexpected," Kathy said.

"It will be a wonderful experience," Stephie told her friend. "I learned a great deal when it was my turn."

"And you think I'll learn something, too?"

"Yes."

Kathy knew that Stephie thought of her as a skeptic in all things spiritual, but this was different. She had always been drawn to concepts that were unusual. "I never could resist a chance to try something new," Kathy said hoping her words surprised Stephie a little.

Kathy was wearing a red, floral skirt with a black knit top. The outfit was loose enough, but it was modern and Glen thought it could affect the success of her regression. Emily suggested she keep the top on, but change the skirt to one of the pairs of sweatpants they kept for such an occasion. Kathy agreed and was soon ready to be sent back into her most distant memories.

Kathy was uncomfortable lying on the couch in front of so many observers, but she was determined to go through with the process. She wanted to experience this for herself because she was concerned that Stephie might be caught up in something that wasn't what it appeared to be. Stephie had always been gullible and, for that reason, vulnerable. But she'd also always been independent and resentful of Kathy's attempts to protect her. So Kathy had to be careful. This was the issue that had kept them apart for years. It would break her heart if she finally brought Stephie back into her life only to chase her friend away again.

Glen was speaking in his slow, gentle voice, directing Kathy to stare at a spot in the ceiling and telling her to let all her thoughts drift off into space. She breathed deeply and followed his words. It took her very little time to relax into the easy, swaying mood of the regression and to travel back in time.

Thirty

Margaret was in her garden when she noticed Alex walking up the dirt road that ran in front of their house. She had been thinking of her daughter, but that wasn't a coincidence. Alexandra was always on her mind, especially when Margaret was working on mindless projects such as weeding. She worried about her husband, Andrew, as well, but even when he was in her thoughts Alex was also swirling around there with him. Alex was her only child. She had conceived her and carried her and birthed her. She had fed her and disciplined her and loved her. When Alex went into the battle to serve as a nurse, Margaret experienced a level of pride and fear that she couldn't have felt for any other person.

Her daughter and the man she was with were quite a distance off, but Alex was easy for her mother to recognize. It had to do with a confidence evident in her stride. Margaret put down her hoe, lifted her long skirt slightly and hustled out to greet her daughter and her companion. When she reached them, Alex broke away for a quick hug, but after that she went quickly back to the man's side.

Margaret could tell from the way Alex touched the hand of the man she was standing beside, that there was a bond between them. She was perceptive enough to recognize that, but she couldn't tell how intense their feelings were. She also didn't know why the man was there. He wasn't like the other one. He wasn't wounded. Did that mean he was a deserter or was there some other reason? If he was a deserter she admired him for that choice. She wasn't like Andrew who went running off to work the railroads in Harrisburg because he had a sense of obligation to the union. In her heart she thought that young men standing in a field and shooting at each other was about as foolish an act as any of God's creatures could commit. Women wouldn't do that. If women ran the country there wouldn't be slavery and there wouldn't be war.

As Alex was introducing Charles, Margaret couldn't help but stare at their intertwined fingers. She watched him grow uncomfortable. He tried to release her daughter's hand, but Alex wouldn't allow it. Alex was acting stubborn, as usual. Her stubbornness was how she had always approached life. It was both her finest quality and her biggest flaw. She would always pick a solution to a problem quickly and keep on hammering away at that approach until it worked. She often succeeded in situations where others would have failed because she wouldn't give up. Yet she also often worked twice as hard as she had to because she wouldn't admit that her approach wasn't the best one.

"You have a guest," Margaret told her daughter. She spoke softly. "He arrived yesterday, to ask for your hand in marriage and to explain how he intended to provide for you. He's a soldier who has been shot in his arm. We talked all morning, but when I offered to change the dressing on his wound he wanted none of that. He said he would wait for you."

"Oh, my Lord!" Charles yelled. He pulled his hand away from Alex. "Samuel is here!"

"Yes. That's his name," Margaret continued. She turned back to Alex. "He told me that you and he were in love. I believed him, because I could read the love in his face. But now I don't understand what's happening."

"He's our friend," Charles told her. "Of course we love him. We both love him."

"He spoke of a special attraction to you, Alex, and of how you had taken care of him after he was shot. He said you love him in the way he loves you."

"Mother. That's not true." Her eyes grew wide as she shook her head and took a half step toward Margaret. It was clear she was frustrated and unsure how to respond. Meanwhile Charles still seemed focused on the fact that Samuel was alive and well. He kept looking at the door to the house.

"Whatever you two decide to do, please be careful. Samuel appears fragile to say the least."

Her concern for Samuel's well-being was sincere, but not her greatest fear. If Alex had somehow become part of a lover's triangle she wasn't in a safe place. Margaret had an idea as to what had happened, because she knew her daughter. Alex most likely threw herself into the goal of caring for Samuel with such abandon that he mistook her dedication for love. She had been that way as a little girl, especially around the farm animals, always caring for the weak and sick ones more than the others. That aspect of Alex's personality was the reason that Margaret had accepted Samuel's story. But her daughter had apparently made a different choice. Margaret turned and went back toward the house. Charles started to follow.

"Charles," Alex said, stopping him as she spoke. "We can't appear to be together when Samuel is here. At least not at first."

"I understand. I know how Samuel would suffer if he saw you with another man and I couldn't stand to see him in that kind of pain."

It isn't going to be easy, Margaret thought as she entered her home. She had noticed the way they looked at each other right away. Those feelings would be difficult to hide.

* * *

Charles was ecstatic as he greeted Samuel, but his wounded friend responded in a matter of fact manner. Charles told Samuel that he had thought his friend could be dead or off in a distant hospital where an overworked doctor might be amputating his arm. He hadn't expected him to be sitting in Alex's home, in as good health as he had been since the time when he was shot. That was all well and good, but Margaret knew that Samuel had been waiting in the house to see Alex, without any doubt that she would arrive. He probably hadn't thought about Charles much at all. At least that's how Margaret saw the situation and she was good at figuring these things out.

"How did you get here?" Charles asked his friend.

"I asked for the Stevens' farm then I walked. Alex had already pointed me in the right direction by where she looked whenever she spoke of her mother." He turned toward Alex and added, "I can tell what you're thinking more than you realize."

Samuel's comment worried Margaret, but she was careful not to show it in her expression. She looked at her daughter and saw that Alex was concerned and not hiding it well.

"We searched for you," Alex said. "We looked up and down the creek. We went to the hospitals in town. We never imagined you would be here."

"Where else would I go?" Samuel replied. "You know how I feel about you." He reached for Alex's hand and when he touched it he held on. She didn't pull away, but she appeared to be grasping his in a limp manner as if she was prepared to release it whenever he was ready. Margaret turned her gaze toward Charles. He was watching them nervously. She hoped he wouldn't let go of his emotions. "I came here to ask your mother if I could have your hand in marriage." As he spoke, Samuel smiled at Alex.

"That's what she said. You asked her, but you didn't ask me."

"I knew what you would say. I can feel what you feel."

Charles took a small step backwards. Margaret could tell that he was trying to handle the way his life seemed to be unraveling. She didn't think he would start a fight, especially with Samuel being injured. Their friendship was also clear in his expression.

"I don't want to marry," Alex said. Margaret could see her daughter shaking slightly as she spoke. She could remember a time when Alex's voice had never quivered, not even slightly. She was always confident as a child, so sure that the right choices would lead to the right results. Perhaps the war had shaken that optimism, but it was more likely that this situation was simply too complicated for her to envision a good outcome. "I've been through too much," Alex continued. "The war has made everything so hard and depressing. I can't make any decisions while it's still raging. Please try to understand."

She would want to marry if it were Charles making the offer, Margaret thought. She could see that written all over her daughter's face.

"I have you both here," Samuel said as he released Alex's hand. "There is nothing more I want than the companionship of the woman I love and of my best friend. I can wait for marriage forever as long as I have those things." This time the quiver was in Samuel's voice, which worried Margaret even more.

"Everyone must be hungry," Margaret said. "Alex, I'll start a meal while you look after Samuel's wound. Charles, you can help me."

* * *

Margaret showed Charles where the few chickens were that she had managed to keep out of the hands of wandering soldiers. He went out to slaughter one while she peeled potatoes and carrots. The day was cool with scattered clouds. It was very similar to the days that had led up to the battle, days that were perfect for Yanks and Rebs to march toward the place where they would kill each other. She hadn't known where the soldiers were until the fighting began and Alex took off to help the wounded, but during the days preceding Margaret had felt that something powerful and devastating was about to happen. She had that same feeling now.

Samuel was getting around quite well, so the fever that could come with a wound such as his hadn't happened to him. Margaret was glad about that. He had allowed Alex to change his bandages and she hadn't said anything to Margaret to indicate there were complications. Although he kept his right arm down by his side, Samuel didn't show any indication of pain when he used his left hand to hold a cup, shake Charles' hand or hug Alex. Margaret hoped Samuel missed Charles' pained expression when the hug occurred, but she didn't think that could be possible.

Charles started the conversation after everyone was at the table and the blessing had been said. "I was talking to Alex on the walk over here, telling her about that catfish we caught. You remember that one, don't you, Samuel?"

Samuel struggled a little as he tried to spoon boiled potatoes onto his dish with one hand. Charles made a gesture that indicated he would help his friend, but Samuel turned away. Alex made a similar gesture and Samuel accepted her help. Margaret noticed that Samuel breathed in deeply as Alex leaned toward him. He sat up a bit and his eyes fogged as if he were trying to remember her scent. She remembered Andrew doing something like that years ago, then talking about how sweet she smelled. That was after they were married. Margaret wished her daughter would be a little more careful or perhaps less naïve.

"I remember you were there with me," Samuel told Charles. "But I don't see how you had much to do with that fish."

"I showed you the spot."

"You want white meat or dark?" Alex asked.

"White," he said then turned to Charles. "I allow you were there that day, but that's about it. I knew that pond for years before. I was the one who led us there and I was the one who pulled that fish in."

"You said you'd never been there and I helped you take that fish off the hook. It was big and it was jumping about like it was possessed. I had a heck of a time grabbing it. Remember how funny that was?"

"I remember how you ripped it off the hook and tossed it in the pond. You were jealous, Charles, because I caught the biggest fish in the county. That would have been two dinners for me and my mom. We needed the food and you tossed it."

"I have some coffee," Margaret told them. "I almost gave it up to company E when they passed, but I kept it to celebrate the day that Alex returned. I know that sounds selfish, but I thought how I'd given up my husband and my daughter. At least I could keep a few coffee grinds." She smiled hoping they would see her gesture as sweet or perhaps a little humorous. They didn't pay any attention to her.

"We said we'd go back and catch it again," Charles said. "I wanted to spend another day fishing with you and I thought you wanted the same."

"You wanted to catch it because I had caught it. You were always that way, always wanting what was mine, even though you had so much more."

* * *

Kathy was twitching and twisting about on the couch as if she were feverish. Her motions caused Stephie to worry. "Bring her back," she told Glen. "Look at her. It's too much."

He must have agreed, because as soon as Stephie spoke he said, "I'm going to count. When you hear me reach ten, you will wake up. You'll remember everything you experienced."

Thirty-One

Kathy sat on the couch for close to a minute before she spoke. She was trying to get her feelings straight. "Hypnotists put thoughts in people's heads for a living," she said at last. She saw the session she had just been through as an inherently unequal power relationship. She didn't approve of Glen determining what memories would be in her head while she lay on the couch as if she had been drugged. And now, in the aftermath, she felt as if she had just woken up in bed with a man she didn't like very much. "How do I know the difference between what you pull out of my mind and what you put there?" she asked Glen.

"You dreamed of Alex before we brought you here," Stephie said. "Doesn't that prove this is real?"

"I'm not sure."

"We were listening to everything he said to you. Glen guided you to the time we needed to know about then we all listened to your story. It was a very elaborate and detailed story."

"Details can be real even when the total picture isn't. I've painted countless scenes that way, by grabbing bits and pieces from everywhere and putting them together the way I want them."

"I can't do that," Glen told her. "I'd be a hell of a hypnotist if I could."

"Maybe you are."

* * *

Stephie tried not to talk as Michael drove Kathy home. Once again her friend was putting down things she believed in; acting as if hope and faith were sins as serious as ignorance and indifference. Kathy made her feel as if she were an eight year old. "I should have known you would react like this," Stephie said half under her breath. "You pretend you're playing the part of a skeptic, but this is just your way of putting down what others believe in."

"I'm looking out for you, that's all. You don't know Glen from Adam. And how about Emily? My guess is you don't know much about her either."

"She's been in the church for longer than I have."

"So?" That was typical, too. Every time Stephie made a point Kathy would just shrug her shoulders and make it sound as if her opinion was too stupid to even consider. She wouldn't let her get away with that attitude this time.

"I've sat with her in Bible studies and I've worked with her on mission projects. She's a good person. I know her well enough to know that."

"And gullible?"

"You're determined to put this down no matter how much the evidence points to the opposite conclusion."

"Evidence?"

"Yes, evidence. We went back into our heads and we all saw the same things. If it wasn't based on truth, Michael or you would have said something about Alex that didn't jive with the way I knew her and I would have had to sit up and ask why. But that didn't happen. Everything was the same from the way it felt to walk along a dirt road in July to the feelings we had for each other."

"Feelings?"

"You were my mom in that life. That is a powerful relationship and it explains why I keep on loving you even when you are the worst pain in the neck I can imagine. We are a family, a spiritual family which is even stronger than blood."

The argument was not done when they arrived at the motel where Kathy had been staying. But Kathy got out of the car and Stephie was left feeling unsettled. Michael said they could continue to explore the past even without Kathy, but his words didn't stop Stephie from feeling abandoned.

* * *

When they reached Stephie's apartment, Michael asked if he could come in. They hadn't talked much after Kathy left and there was a great deal he wanted to say. Michael was determined to move Stephie past the negative feelings so they could consider what they should do next. Stephie got out of his car and stepped toward her home. She tilted her head to indicate that he should follow.

"I know it's real because I feel it's real," Michael said as Stephie started a pot of coffee. He was sitting at her kitchen table, watching her as she pulled the filters out of a cabinet and measured the coffee spoon by spoon. He thought about how it had felt to make love to Alex and he couldn't help but wonder how similar Stephie would be. Her hair, her skin, her stature, all that was different, but the experience had been so much more than physical and her spirit, the part of her that would last throughout time— that was the same.

"Feelings are not enough," Stephie told him.

Michael wanted to shout back that feelings were more than enough. When they had first met he was drawn to her in a way he had never experienced. There had to be a reason for that, a history. Feelings were not just enough, they were everything. But all he said was, "They're a start and a good one at that."

The coffee had started to drip and its deep aroma filled the kitchen. Stephie reached up to get a box of cookies from the cabinet above her refrigerator. When she did that, her pink blouse pulled up slightly revealing the smooth light skin of her back. *Feelings*, Michael thought.

"How can we convince Kathy that there is more to this than she is admitting?" Stephie asked.

"We need something concrete to tell her, something that confirms a part of our current lives Glen couldn't know."

Stephie put two brown, ceramic mugs on the table and when the pot of coffee was done brewing she walked around to Michael's side to fill his cup first. He had noticed her light perfume when they were in his car, but now she was close and her scent was so sweet that he took in a deep breath as a reflex. Her hand seemed to shake a little as she poured the coffee and that made him wonder if she was as nervous as he was. He wanted her to feel what he was feeling. Michael reached for a couple of packets of Sweet and Low.

"To me it is more important that *you* accept the reality of what we've been through," Michael told her.

"Me? I'm not so stuck on church dogma that I can't accept evidence that's as strong as what we experienced."

"I'm not talking about the impact on your religious beliefs, Stephie. We've been shown a bond, a link between us that's more powerful even than death. I can feel the power of that connection and within that feeling is where the truth exists. Alex lived more than a hundred years ago, but I can tell she still lives in you and I can feel for you what I felt for her. When you say you accept the reality of our history, that is what you're acknowledging and you are saying that Charles lives in me."

Michael understood that their relationship had started long ago, probably many lifetimes before Charles and Alexandra. He was counting on Stephie knowing it, too.

"I know who you are and I feel what Alex felt," she told him in a soft, shaky voice. She was swirling her coffee and looking down at the cup as she spoke.

Michael wanted to make love with Stephie as Charles and Alex had in their past life, but the situation was complicated. For one thing she was a minister. Although she was a beautiful, young minister who had just indirectly professed her love for him, there were still expectations that wouldn't be there if she had any other occupation. And there was also the whole *soul mates throughout eternity thing* that he might have trouble living up to. Michael didn't get up or even reach out for Stephie's hand. But he did do one important thing. He told her he loved her.

She smiled and said, "Me, too."

* * *

As soon as Michael, Stephie and Kathy had left her apartment, Emily had turned to Glen. "Doubt like hers is contagious," she said.

"It's not as bad as you make it sound. I don't believe we'll lose Michael or Stephie. Kathy would have helped, but without her we still have a good chance of stopping Julie before she can hurt Stephie. That's what will break the circle."

Their road had a detour, but at this point Emily wasn't sure how far out of the way it would take them. "So what's next?" she asked, setting her resolve to keep moving forward.

"We need to go back to find out what happened that night after Margaret's dinner. Who do you think we should regress next, Michael or Stephie?"

"Stephie is the most susceptible to Kathy's opinions," Emily told him, answering quickly. "We need to keep her involved."

"Then that's what we'll do. I'll call them both tonight."

Thirty-Two

Michael picked Stephie up the following day for her next regression. The time they had agreed to was 9:00 in the morning instead of after school, as the previous sessions had been. Michael had to call in sick and that concerned Stephie. Her own schedule was flexible. As long as she worked her way through the lists of events she had to organize, made the phone calls she had to make and dealt with the isolated extra problems that always came up, it wouldn't matter if she worked normal hours or late hours. But this was the first time Michael had skipped out on a class. And as if that wasn't bad enough, the woman he had to leave the message with was the temp they had hired to replace Julie. He said it made him feel awful when he had to talk to her.

Emily offered them coffee and pancakes as soon as they arrived, but they had both eaten breakfast and didn't want to waste any time. Within ten minutes of their arrival, Stephie was on the couch and back in the nineteenth century.

* * *

Alex was restless. She was lying in the bed she had slept in since her mother had moved her out of her bassinet twenty-some years earlier, but the feelings that were keeping her awake belonged to the grown woman she had become. She hadn't been able to spend time alone with Charles since they had found Samuel in the house and the few times she was able to talk to the man she had fallen in love with, she had been forced to keep the conversation formal and impersonal. Now she was aching for him. She wanted to feel his arms around her and enjoy the touch of his skin against her own. Even more than that, she needed to hear him tell her how deeply he cared for her in his own simple words.

Alex sat up on the side of her bed. It was a warm night, so there were no covers to push off. She stood and gathered her thoughts. It was dark and late. Her mother and Samuel were both in their rooms. If she was quiet she could slip down the hall to Charles' room.

She was wearing her summer gown due to the July heat. It had flutter sleeves and a v-neck, but despite those feminine touches the cotton material kept it modest. She went straight for the door instead of reaching for her robe. The iron hinges on her door squeaked slightly when she pulled it open as she had expected they would. She opened it slowly with her right hand, steadying it with her left in a manner that managed to keep the sound to a minimum. There were boards in the hall floor that made sounds when they were stepped on, but Alex knew her home well enough to know how to avoid those. She crept past the door to the room where Samuel was staying and made it to Charles' room. The hinges on his door were quiet, so she was able to push the door open without any revealing sounds. Some starlight came in through the open window and revealed that Charles was on the bed with no covers, sleeping on his side, dressed only in a pair of white cotton drawers with long legs. Alex closed the door behind her then quietly went to him and touched his shoulder.

Charles woke from the soft stroke of her hand and turned to look up at her. He smiled, took her hand in his and pulled her down beside him. He kissed her and lifted her gown so he could touch her body. Her first inclination was to reach out to touch him, but she held back. Instead she took a few deep breaths and lay very still, relaxing as much as she could, letting him make all the advances. Her body shook as she fought the desire to wrap herself around him, but her resistance was worth it. As he slowly caressed and kissed her body she could feel the power of his need for her and when he wriggled out of his drawers and moved on top of her she felt as if she had given over to him everything that was her. In the process she had become one with the most wonderful man God could create and in that moment she knew heaven.

After they made love, Alex lay curled up next to Charles with her arm over his side, enjoying the feel of his breathing until she could tell from the even rhythm that he was asleep. Then, as gently and carefully as she could she moved off the bed and, after finding her gown and pulling it back on, she left his room.

The darkness of the hall enveloped her like a protective blanket. She felt alive and warm and full of a sense of peace she hadn't known since the war had begun. In a time of brothers fighting brothers and maimed young boys facing hopeless lives, she had found a small, beautiful niche filled with peace and love and a sense of optimism about the future. There could be nothing in the world that came close to the wonder of love.

She took a few steps then stopped when she heard a tiny sound from the direction of Samuel's room. It might have been her imagination or perhaps he had turned in his sleep, but the noise brought her down a notch or two from the reverie she had been experiencing. She took in a breath and started again toward her room walking as softly as she could, heel to toe. Her eyes had adjusted to the small amount of light and now she could see something unusual, Samuel's door was cracked open slightly. She thought it had been closed when she passed by earlier, but she wasn't sure. So much had happened that night. Maybe she had that one small detail wrong. She took another step forward, again heel to toe.

That's when the door swung open and Alex found herself just inches in front of Samuel's face. It was hard to see his expression in the dark, but she knew he was there to confront her. She glanced at her mother's room and prayed that he wouldn't make any noise. If her mother discovered that Alex was walking the hall at that time of night she would know that Charles had been her destination. If that happened Alex would never be able to face her again.

Samuel reached out and grabbed Alex by her left arm. He held her with a tight grasp that pinched. She flinched but she did not cry out. It was his right hand that he was holding her with and that was his wounded arm. He had much more strength in it and much more mobility than she had thought possible. She also knew that using that arm would be causing him a great deal of pain. The fact that he was ignoring the pain showed her how upset he was.

Samuel gestured with his head to indicate the stairs and pushed her in that direction. She went where he wanted her to go as quietly as she could, still praying her mother wouldn't hear them. They passed the closed door to Charles' room and she glanced over at it, hoping against hope that he would come out to see what his friend was doing to her and then stop him, quietly. But Charles didn't come out and Samuel pushed her again. His fingers on her arm felt like a sacrilege because such a short time earlier she had felt the joy of Charles' hands touching her skin.

They moved down the stairs and out the front door. She was a little scared now, but she still didn't think he would hurt her. He was Charles' friend and she had helped him when he needed care. All of that had to account for something. They were under the stars now, so there was enough light to see. Perhaps he had pushed her out here so he could see her expression when he confronted her about Charles. Samuel must have seen her leaving his friend's room and guessed what was going on. She turned her head to look at him and stopped short at the sight of his left hand. He was holding a Bowie knife with a blade that had to be close to ten inches long. He had it pointed at her back.

Samuel pushed her to one of the rockers her mother kept on the porch. There was a dress on the chair and Alex noticed right away that it was hers. He must have taken it out of her room and brought it outside. That meant he had planned this. Perhaps Samuel saw her when she went into Charles' room and took her clothes out of her room while she was with Charles.

"Get dressed," Samuel commanded, squeezing her arm hard before letting go.

Alex took the dress, a gold colored working dress with a red flower print, and she pulled it on over her head. She wasn't used to wearing her nightgowns as her underclothes, but she knew that many women did.

"The shoes, too," He told her. He had brought out her black working shoes along with a pair of wool knit socks. Alex finished tying her belt in back of her dress then she sat in the rocker to put on the socks and shoes. It took her a while to lace up the shoes and Samuel appeared to grow impatient as time progressed. Alex began to worry more as he became agitated. The knife had changed the way she thought about him. She was afraid that if she didn't do everything exactly the way he instructed her, he might hurt her.

Samuel had left something else on the porch. He pushed it toward her with his foot and said, "Pick it up." That is when Alex's concern changed into true fear. It was a bag that had been in her room, a carpetbag that was stuffed with something, probably more of her clothing. He planned to take her somewhere and to keep her there for a long time.

Alex jumped back. Her body shook and she started to scream, but before she could make a sound Samuel had his knife to her throat. "Pick it up and walk," he said. She could tell from the angry spit in his voice and the brutal strength of his grip on her arm that he meant more than that. He was demanding that she move quickly and without even the slightest sound. She did as she was told. He forced her down the five steps of the porch and pushed her away from the house, out toward the road. Alex had no choice but to comply.

* * *

"Are you okay?" Emily asked her. Stephie wasn't sure she was. She didn't answer. She just sat up on the couch and tried to control her breathing.

Michael came to her and dropped to one knee. He took her hand and held it on her lap. Even if he wasn't there when she needed him in her past life, he was here now and that felt wonderful.

"I have a lot of explaining to do," Glen said, "and it's time I did it."

Thirty-Three

The one aspect of living with Neil that Julie actually enjoyed was access to his gun collection. He had two handguns, a black one and a silver one with a black grip. He had told her some specifics about them, but she hadn't paid attention other than to note that the black one was a Glock and the silver one was a Kahr. She was more interested in his rifles. He owned two Remingtons, a Kimber, two Winchesters and a Browning. Julie was drawn to the Browning, although it was the simplest and probably the least expensive. She liked it because it was a .22 that was very similar to the one she had used when she was learning to shoot. She discovered that she hadn't lost a bit of her talent despite years of not touching a gun.

The woods behind Neil's trailer were perfect for shooting. The area had very little scrub growth and lots of tall, long-needled pine trees with high branches. It was easy to find a place where Julie could tape a target to a tree then step back a good distance and still have a clear shot. Holding the rifle again was like returning to her childhood and for some reason the good memories had persevered while the bad ones had faded. She thought about the times she spent walking in wooded areas and wading in creeks. And she also reminisced about the first rabbits and squirrels she shot as a young girl. She considered picking off one or two for practice, but decided she wouldn't want the carcasses to rot out there and it was too much trouble to bury them. Growing old brought a sense of practicality that ruined a lot of the fun.

Julie was practicing with the Browning when the thought came to her that she might use guns to scare Michael and Stephie. There would be too much chance for trouble if she did anything as reckless as shooting at them. Yet there were other ways to get to them. They knew of her love of guns. If they started getting catalogs and literature from random gun shows, they would know she was the one who had filled out the forms. They would wonder why and they would also wonder how foolish she could be. She might also use Neil to put a little fear into them somehow. He could be scary when he chose to be.

Julie squeezed the trigger of the Browning and was certain the bullet ended up in the black area of the target. That was good, either a bulls eye or about as close as anyone can get without hitting the center. She wondered if Stephie had ever picked up a gun. Probably not. She was too much of a girly girl.

* * *

It wasn't hard for Stephie to accept that she had lived a past life. She had always had a desire to believe in reincarnation even when she was around the teachers in seminary who had tried to steer her in a different direction. It was more of a stretch to accept the concept that Michael had shared her past lives and that they'd had a relationship in each of those occurrences. After that revelation the idea that Kathy had been her mother in one of her past lives was startling to say the least. But if those things weren't weird enough, these new concepts definitely were. Stephie was now being told that Emily, a woman in her eighties that she had known for years, might be the child of her last incarnation. And Glen was also saying that if she was the woman they were looking for, she had been murdered in every one of her past lives, at a young age. That meant she would also be murdered in this one. Yet, when Glen told her all this it was as if a professor had been talking to her about some distant tragedy like the destruction of Pompeii. She was so overwhelmed with the implications that she didn't react emotionally until she was back at her apartment, alone with Michael. Then she started to cry and her voice cracked with emotion as she confessed that she had begun to hope that Kathy's skepticism would turn out to be justified.

Michael hugged her. "We don't get to choose what's real and what isn't, but you are not going through this alone. I was Charles and you were Alex. I'm as certain of that as I am of anything in my life. And if that's true, then the rest is, too. Glen also said that we have an advantage this time because we know what to expect. That means we can protect you and we will. I swear that on my love for you."

Michael's promise to protect Stephie eased her fear. Even if they couldn't change what was to be, Michael's love made life wonderful. She remembered the anonymous quote she had used in a few of her sermons. *Life is not measured by the number of breaths we take, but by the moments that take our breath away.* Stephie turned her head slightly to bring her lips to his and he kissed her. His promise was one of those moments.

* * *

"I need to contribute to the process," Emily told Glen over their supper the night of Stephie's last regression. It was just fast food. She hadn't had time to cook, so he had run out and picked up a couple of chicken wraps. That was a nice change. She didn't mind cooking, but they both hated to clean up. "We've probably got the right people now, but we aren't certain. I can help with that. Regress me. I was there."

"You were a baby," he said, seeming to shrug off her offer. That didn't seem fair to Emily.

"I had eyes and ears. I can tell you what was happening around me."

"Stephie had to stay on the couch for five to ten minutes before she could stand or even talk about what she'd been through. And she's in her thirties. The stress could hurt you."

She appreciated his concern, but the result was unfair. It was ageism and that is as repugnant as any other form of bigotry. She wanted to tell Glen that, but she had to be political. Besides, she was afraid he would get angry or, worse yet, start to sulk.

"Of course it will be stressful," Emily said, keeping the argument impersonal. "I know that. But what's important is not what happens to this old body of mine. It's what happens the next time around and the time after that. You taught me that. You know it better than I do."

"Kathy doesn't believe in what we're doing and she'll be trying to influence the others. Somebody has to keep Michael and Stephie on the right track and you've proven yourself exceptional at convincing people. If something happened to you I don't know how I'd function."

"Something *has* to happen to me. We don't ever talk about it, but we both know it's true. There are, after all, rules to this circularity you always speak of and one of the main ones is that souls can't be in two bodies at the same time. Stephie's going to have a child and I expect that will happen soon, since her biological clock is ticking. That's part of the circle; the child is born and the mother is killed. You, Stephie and Michael are going to change the last part of that. I'll be there, too, but I'll be a helpless infant."

Glen looked away from her and out the kitchen window. His eyes were tearing up and she could tell he was trying to control his emotion. That was sweet, but unproductive. "I'm an unusual person," she went on. "Most people who live a long life don't suffer through such a lonely one. Yet right now I can only think of one good, close friend I've ever had. That's you. I'd like the next time to be different and I'm counting on you to do whatever you can to see that it happens. As for me, there must be a reason I've been around this long. Regress me. I can help."

Glen nodded slowly. His neck was tight and he seemed unable to speak. Emily was surprised by how much she had touched him. She wasn't afraid to die. She'd had more years than most people could hope for and she was supported by what Glen had taught her— that life went on. But his sadness was contagious. When she understood how much he would miss her, she found that she would also miss him in ways she hadn't considered. She wondered if he might be a part of her spiritual family and, if so, what her relationship with him might be in a life when their ages were closer.

"Come on," he said, "before I change my mind." Neither one of them had finished their sandwiches, but Glen got up from the table and walked toward the living room. Emily followed. When she got to the couch it took some doing to lie down. Part of that was the problem she always faced because her body was stiff and weak, but part of it was because she was shaking a little from emotion. "Relax," Glen said. "You know the routine. Pick a spot on the ceiling and focus. You'll be back there soon, back to the long walk in the woods."

* * *

When Emily's eyes opened she was lying on her mother's bare stomach in what appeared to be a barn stall. Her mother was trying to clean the blood off of her tiny body using a cloth that seemed to be a shawl, although Emily wasn't sure of that. What she was certain of was her own helplessness. Her body was weak, but free of pain, except for the pain of hunger. Her mother sat up and lifted Emily to her breast so her baby could fill her belly. Emily remembered the experience of feeding in this manner from the other regression, but this was different. For one thing there was the smell of manure and straw around them. She couldn't hear any animals in the barn, but she could tell they had been there recently. The other, more important reason that this regression was different was that this mother was tired and Emily could sense that she was also consumed with fear. Feeding from her body was not comforting in the way it should have been. The baby stopped suckling and began to cry.

"Please be decent and allow me to be with my daughter alone, for just a short time," her mother called out. "We're too weak to run away."

"You have the night to rest," a man's voice replied from outside the barn stall. "But if the troops leave in the morning, we need to follow."

Emily was experiencing everything the baby was going through, but there was still room for her own thoughts. At that moment those thoughts were focused on Julie's description of waiting outside a barn stall for a woman to give birth. She was confident that this was that same event, but she wasn't positive. She also believed that the man was Samuel and the woman was Alex. Yet she couldn't tell by what she could see through the infant's eyes. The woman was dripping with sweat and her bloody clothes were half off. But even if she had been cleaned up and dressed neatly, Emily could not have known if this woman was the same person based solely on the descriptions of Stephie and Michael. She hoped she could make that connection somehow. That would be major and would prove to Glen how valuable she could be.

Her mother started to sing very softly, "What a fellowship, what a joy divine, leaning on the everlasting arms." The song was for comfort and Emily understood that, but it was also a gift to her and she was flush with emotion over the love behind her mother's sweet voice. "What a blessedness, what a peace is mine, leaning on the everlasting arms." Then Emily remembered more of what Julie had described. This was the hymn that was sung by the woman in the barn of her regression. That was the proof Emily needed. This was the scene Julie had witnessed from a different perspective, the viewpoint of the man.

"I have water in my canteen," the man outside the stall told the mother. "You can use it to clean yourself up."

"Keep your water, Samuel, just give us time alone."

Samuel. She called the man *Samuel.*

Thirty-Four

Glen was generally reserved and professional to a fault, but not this day. His almost giddy behavior surprised Emily. She assumed he was so thrilled with the proof that Julie was Samuel that he couldn't contain himself. Julie had run off and no one had any idea where she had gone, but despite that setback they were better off knowing who they were after. It might still be like looking for a needle in a haystack, but at least they knew which needle they were after.

"I was worried," Glen told Emily. "I thought the regression would be too much for you. I had this picture in my head of you never waking up." He smiled broadly and grabbed her shoulders. "You can imagine how thrilled I was when you opened your eyes and spoke to me."

Emily stepped back. She had known he was worried about her. That was why he had kept her off the couch for so long. But she hadn't expected a reaction like the one she was watching. He was acting like a child.

"Get control of yourself," she scolded. "You worried for nothing."

"We have a connection, you and I. This time around I'm your teacher, but next time who knows? I could be your child or you could be mine. Or maybe we'll be closer in age. We could be partners in some elaborate project that makes this one seem small. I don't know, but I do know I am part of your spiritual family. So this task of ours is important to me and I don't want to do it alone."

"We've been over this before. You *have* to do it alone. No other possibility exists. Promise me you will see this through when I'm not here."

"I promise, of course. I understand reality, but that doesn't mean I can't celebrate the time you remain with us. Right?"

Emily took a deep breath and looked at the pale loose skin on her hands. All this talk of connections bothered her. Their goal was much too important for her to allow her life to be a distraction. It had been long, perhaps too long. The time had come for her to leave the responsibility to Glen as well as to Michael and Stephie. She had done everything she could do. If they did the same, the next time would be better.

* * *

"I was going to call you," Stephie told Emily.

Emily had come into Stephie's office two minutes earlier. This was the first time they had spoken in more than two weeks.

"And I was going to ask you why you hadn't," Emily replied. She was dressed as if it were a Sunday, in a floral print dress that had bright pink and blue daisies against a black background. Stephie had on jeans and a casual top with pink and white horizontal stripes. She had thought today would be a paperwork day. If she had known Emily would pick this day to visit, she might have worn something a little more formal.

"Michael and I haven't lost faith in what you've shown us. We just needed time to think."

"So you took it."

"Yesterday something weird happened. A brochure came in the mail for a gun show at the coliseum. I wouldn't have thought twice about it except Michael received the same notice. The cards were mailed to us, not to resident or any other label that might indicate they were part of a bulk mailing and on the same day Michael received a catalog for gun accessories. It was a fairly bulky catalog, the kind people generally have to pay for. It was frightening, considering what you and Glen told us."

Emily was on the striped couch, across the room from Stephie. She was leaning back in a relaxed manner that seemed odd given the way she was dressed and what they were talking about. Stephie was studying her somewhat suspiciously because there seemed to be two options concerning the new influx of junk mail. The most obvious was that sending the brochures and catalog was a scheme of Julie's. But the other possibility was that someone else had wanted them to think the mail was Julie's scheme. If the second reason was true then Emily and Glen were the most likely culprits. Stephie was fairly good at reading people and Emily didn't look guilty, just tired, very tired.

"Are you all right?" Stephie asked.

"Very much so. I'll explain later, but first tell me more about the mailings. Do you suspect Julie?" Her words were slightly slurred.

"I don't doubt the regressions," Stephie said, changing the subject. "My senses are too full from those journeys. I can smell the gun powder and the rain. I can feel the strain of dragging full grown men to safety. And the touch of my hands on so many soldiers' wounds is such an emotional experience that I will probably feel it on the tips of my fingers for the rest of my life. Kathy is wrong. Glen couldn't have put those sensations into my head, not all of them, not even some of them. But how can I accept you as my child? No matter how many times I tell myself to believe what you say, my common sense tells me that a woman your age can't be the child of a woman my age. God doesn't play those tricks. I try to figure out what it is I'm supposed to think and everything comes up blank."

"You haven't experienced Alex in a time after her child was born," Emily says. "I've been there and that's why I know what I know. The love between a mother and a daughter is almost like loving yourself, but more powerful. I'm more aware of that because I've spent so many years alone."

"Are you sure you're all right?" Stephie asked. Emily's words were once again running together. It became more evident when she strung more than two sentences together.

"There are things I want to tell you about me, things that will make it easier for you when I come around again."

"Come around?"

"Exactly. I like routine. I suppose all children do, but I never grew out of it. Even when I was a teenager I didn't want change, except for wanting my father to pull out of his depression. But that wasn't change as much as it was healing. What I am saying is I was never a rebel, like so many young people are. Also, pay attention to who I am as I grow up. Nothing hurts worse than being treated as the person you want me to be instead of the person I am. It was my father who did that, not you. But still…"

"Have you been drinking?"

"No. All I've done is act on what's real. Knowing that should strengthen your beliefs. That's why I waited until I was here, to show you the strength of my beliefs. But it's not why I came. I came because I want you to know me better before I die. That's the only reason."

"What do you mean you've acted on what's real? What have you done?"

"I took Darvon."

"No!" Stephie yelled at Emily. She jumped as if an electric shock had just shot up her back then she reached for the phone and dialed 911. When the operator answered Stephie spoke quickly and in clear concise language. "We have a woman here who has taken pills. We need an ambulance." The dispatcher confirmed the church's address and said he would send one out immediately. He told Stephie he would stay on the phone, but she needed to keep Emily awake by getting her up and walking.

"I have a prescription for my arthritis," Emily said. "I took them all at once."

"Give me your hand," Stephie said after she stepped around her desk to the couch where Emily was sitting. "We're going to move around a bit. People will be here soon to help you."

Stephie grabbed Emily and pulled her into a standing position. She was much lighter than Stephie had expected. She was also wobbly, so they stood there as Emily got her balance.

"At first I thought it was Julie," Emily said, her words slurring much more now. "She seemed wrong and to be honest I was disappointed. But you know what? You are perfect. That's right. Perfect. You are caring and thoughtful. And you look like a model, with that long black hair of yours. It shines, you know, like you just washed it, only always. And you are just the right weight and just the right height. You and Michael look like a Hollywood couple. That's right. You two could be on one of those red carpets, Michael in a tux and you in a long black gown, strapless, of course, with diamonds embroidered into the fabric."

"Take a step, Emily. You need to keep walking. We're going to move out of the office and walk toward the choir room." The door was open so Stephie didn't have to let go of Emily's arm to get out of the office. That was good since Stephie wasn't convinced the woman could stand on her own.

"Look at you now, so caring and so efficient, always doing the right thing. I want you to know something, Stephie. Kids say what they feel, but only about selfish things. And babies, they can't say anything. So I'm telling you now that I love you. Remember that when you get frustrated over the things children do. You will be a perfect mom and I will know it in my heart. That's a promise."

The hall floor was vinyl over concrete. It could get a bit slippery. But Emily had worn black moccasin style shoes with what appeared to be rubber soles. The shoes seemed to give her some stability. They reached the choir room door and turned around to walk past Stephie's office again.

"Did you really think that doing this would convince me circularity is real?" Stephie said to Emily. She was trying not to sound as if she was scolding, but she was and she knew her emotions were affecting the tone of her voice. "You say life is precious. That's why you want to protect me. But then you try to cut your life short. If you really believed in Glen's teachings you wouldn't try to force your soul out of the body you have. Instead you would have confidence that the natural order of things would take over and your soul will be free when I am ready to have a child."

"You're growing older every day," Emily told her.

"I'm not *that* old."

"Well I am, so cutting off some time from the dull life I've led is well worth it if by doing that I can help the next time work out better."

"If you're gone who will protect me?"

"I never said it would be me who saves your life. This walk has been good. I've had a chance to say what I needed to say. But it's not going to keep me alive so I need you to promise me something."

"What?"

"That you'll make a child with Michael."

The request made Stephie so dizzy that she stopped walking. For a moment it seemed as if Emily was holding her up instead of the other way around. But Stephie recovered quickly and started pacing again. What had surprised her about Emily's request was not that it was unexpected. Maybe the path Glen had spoken of was pulling her or maybe it had to do with the experiences she and Michael had shared through Charles and Alex, but Emily's wish was Stephie's as well.

"Do it as soon as I'm gone. I don't want to wait forever to come back."

* * *

Stephie called Glen after the ambulance took Emily away. She didn't get through to him, but she left a message on Emily's machine telling him what had happened and which hospital they had taken her to. She also called Michael. She couldn't talk to him because he was in a class and she didn't want to wait for him to be paged so she also left a message for him. Stephie asked Michael to join her as soon as he could.

A grey haired doctor in a white lab coat came out to speak with Stephie soon after she let the nurse in the emergency room know she was there. "We're keeping her overnight," he told her. "We made sure the pills didn't kill her, but the stress was a lot for a woman of her age. Are you family?"

"No. I'm her minister." Stephie didn't want to elaborate about her role in the church, so she left it at that.

"I didn't realize. Did you tell the nurse? They should have sent you back right away."

"I didn't mention it," Stephie said. "Emily's circumstances are very different than a normal suicide." It wasn't much of an explanation, but it would have to do.

"They always are," the doctor told her. "It will take some time for the staff to transfer her to a room. You can go back if you wish to speak to her. I hope you'll consider it. Ministers can be as important in saving lives as doctors are, especially with the elderly."

"No. I'll wait here." Stephie had been through a pressure situation and had reacted efficiently. Her actions had saved Emily's life. But she wasn't sure Emily would see that as a good thing, so she wanted to wait a little while before she spoke to her again. Stephie was also confused and needed to talk to Michael. If the things Emily had said to her were just the ramblings of someone on too many pain pills, they would be easy to slough off. But they were personal concepts that Stephie had been trying to make some sense out of before Emily's frightening visit.

Michael ran into the waiting room just as the doctor turned to leave. "How is she?" he asked. He was winded. Stephie could tell he'd run in from his car. She wondered if he cared more for Emily the friend or Emily the soul who would someday be their daughter.

"They pumped her stomach," Stephie told him. "She's alive, but they're keeping her overnight."

"Oh, God," he cried out then he hugged Stephie.

Stephie held him for a short time then pulled back to speak. "She tried to take her own life," Stephie said.

"Why?" Michael's voice shook with emotion.

"She wanted to free her soul." Stephie touched his arm and looked in his eyes. "There's something else as well, Michael. Emily made a last wish when she was convinced she was going to die. It's something we need to talk about."

"I'm glad you two are here." Glen had come running in when they weren't looking. He interrupted their conversation. Stephie heard a quiver in his voice and saw that his eyes were puffy. "I thought Emily understood what I'd been telling her," he said. "Circularity is about fate. You don't have to push fate." When he said the last sentence he spoke each word separately, clearly and with emphasis.

"Sit down," Stephie told him. "They're moving her to a room, so for now we have to wait. There will be plenty of time to talk about this later."

* * *

There was no longer a need for Stephie to deal with a crisis. There were nurses and doctors to care for Emily. Stephie let her guard down a bit as soon as she stepped into the hospital room and saw how frail and tired Emily looked. She felt her throat tighten and her eyes grow damp. She reminded herself that she was a minister and that it was her duty to remain strong and clear headed, but her heart told her otherwise.

"It's wonderful to see you alive," Stephie said choking back her tears. "There were times when I didn't think this moment would occur. But it has and I thank God." Michael put his arm around her. She was glad he did. She needed his support.

Emily turned to her without raising her head. "I will be your child," she told Stephie. "You will love me unconditionally as mothers always do. Please believe that the way I do." Her voice was soft and weak.

"You don't act as if you believe it," Glen said. "We're in a circle of fate, a tragic one that we are going to do our best to break. The last thing we need to do is force the events. Michael and Stephie are going to have a child and your soul will be free before that happens. It isn't something to look forward to. It is just the way things are. I'm trying to deal with it the best I can. We all are."

Stephie felt Michael's arm become tense as Glen spoke of their child. Her emotions were going crazy over that, too. Everything was so mixed-up with their relationship. Maybe they would fall in love. Maybe they already had. Maybe they would marry someday. Maybe they would have the child Glen spoke of. But knowing the future made everything awkward and strangely unclear. She couldn't be sure if knowing where they were going might not be what brought them to where they were. Emily had made that clear as she tried to demonstrate her faith.

"I'm tired," Emily said. "I need to get some rest."

"Tell me you understand what I'm saying," Glen told her.

"I do," Emily replied.

"Then close your eyes and relax."

"Yes," Stephie said, smiling slightly. "No need to walk you in circles anymore."

Thirty-Five

"How old would Trent be now?"

That was the question Neil used to broach the subject of Julie's brother. It seemed carefully planned; at least, that's what Julie thought. She wondered if Trent had ever told Neil that she had seen them together— probably not. Trent was a boy back then, a ten year old boy, and Neil had been old enough to understand what he was doing. He never would have allowed Julie back into his life if he had even the remotest inclination of what she knew.

"It might be fun to talk to him again," Neil said.

What a stupid man Neil was. Trent had aged, but he wanted to see him anyway. He was allowing his actions to be controlled by thoughts of the smooth skinned child Julie's brother had once been. She hadn't seen Trent in years, but she pictured him as overweight and balding as their father had been.

"I could call him and ask him to meet us somewhere." She couldn't invite him to the dump they were living in, so meeting someplace else was the only choice they had. Neil would know that, but neither of them would put it into words.

"That would be good," Neil said. "How's he doing?"

"It's been a while since we talked."

Neil did not respond to what she said. Instead he seemed to concentrate harder on his current project. He had brought home a couple of window screens he'd found at the county dumpsters and was using material from them to patch a torn spot on the screen in the bathroom window. He cursed as the thin wire pricked his fingers a few times, but he kept working. Julie doubted his effort would solve the fly problem. There were other ways the bugs were getting in.

"My mom will have Trent's number," she said. "I'll call her from the Exxon tomorrow. We'll see what happens."

"I guess we will."

Julie's call to her mother was brief, as she had expected it would be. Her mom claimed she couldn't talk because she was busy cleaning the downstairs bathroom. That seemed a fairly lame excuse given that Julie hadn't spoken to her for a couple of months. What made her feel worse was the way her mom recited Trent's number without having to look it up.

"Hello." That was the first word Julie had heard her brother speak in years. It brought a rush of family events back to her from times spent in front of the television to holiday dinners, which were the only memories she had of all four of them sitting down together. Some of those remembrances were good, but mostly she recalled only one constant— a life without respect from either Trent or her parents. He had told her parents something about that incident in the woods and she had not been given the chance to defend herself. That was clear. They didn't know that she was just in the wrong place at the wrong time. Neil was the guilty one and that was the best thing about bringing him back into her family. Maybe they would remember the truth if they had to look in his bloodshot eyes.

"It's me, Trent, your sister," Julie said.

There was a pause before he replied. "It's been what? Five years?" He was always a master of understatement.

"Phones work both ways, you know. At least they did before my situation changed. The man I'm staying with now doesn't have one." She called Neil *the man*.

"Your situation changed?"

"Yes. I left the teacher." Trent would assume she wasn't the one who walked out, but at least she could put up a front.

"There's a surprise. How long did this one last? Three years?" So he had kept up with her personal situation.

"Not quite. But if you're after a surprise my new guy will do it for you." Surprise wasn't the right word, but it sounded better than sick or degraded. She was certain Trent would get those feelings back.

"I'll bet," he said.

"He wants to see you. That's why I'm calling." As soon as the words came out of her mouth, Julie realized she had said too much.

"Why would he want to see me?" Trent didn't miss much.

"He just does."

"I wouldn't have thought you would even mention having a brother. What is it you've been telling him, Julie?"

"I thought we might meet you for dinner someplace. You could bring your wife and kids. I'm reaching out to you here." She didn't want to see his family, but if that was what it took to get him out, she would make the offer. She might have overreached. He was getting suspicious.

"Who is this guy?" Trent asked.

"That's the surprise."

"Tell me who he is."

"Come to dinner with us. You'll find out."

"There's no way I'm going to meet him if you don't tell me who he is."

Julie knew her brother well enough to realize he meant what he said. She considered lying for a moment. But if she did, she would no longer be able to feign ignorance of how much this situation would hurt him.

"It's Neil," she said, "our old neighbor. I thought you might want to see him again to set some things straight."

There was a long pause then he told her, "You and he can rot in hell. You've both earned it." And he hung up the phone. Julie smiled as she left the Exxon station and headed back to Neil's trailer.

*　*　*

Michael asked Stephie out on a date. He did this while they were standing in the parking lot of the hospital after they had left Emily's room. So much was happening to them and all of it seemed to be happening too quickly. She told him this and he agreed. They needed to slow things down and to take time to get to know each other. Michael made the suggestion, but Stephie jumped on it as if it were her own. Now all he needed was the perfect first date idea.

They had been to an art show together, but that didn't count because it was Kathy's and in an unopened restaurant. They had also been to a war together, but that had been in their heads while they had each, separately, reclined on the couch in the security of Emily's living room. Where do you go from there?

If Michael was picking a place to go with a woman he had just met, he would choose a concert or a play. The idea would be to have something to focus on in the event that the conversation waned. But he never had problems talking to Stephie; in fact, the easy way they talked to each other was one of the prizes of their relationship. Dinner was an option and he thought about a place he had heard about in downtown Greensboro that had rooftop dining and a wide menu of desserts, but he wanted something special and just taking Stephie to dinner didn't demonstrate much thought.

He was in his kitchen and the mailer for the gun show at the coliseum was lying on his counter. For one, bizarre minute, he considered that as an option. He had gone with Julie to a flea market and to the annual Christmas craft show a few times. There was something pleasing about moving up and down the aisles and listening to the people in the booths trying to hawk their wares. If the show had only been boats or RVs instead of guns. Michael didn't mind guns. He had even been to a rifle range a few times and that was fun for the novelty of the experience. But he knew they made Stephie uncomfortable and she had a good point about Julie's connection with them, especially given the predictions Glen was making.

The idea of a boat show at the coliseum got Michael thinking about outdoor play and that thought led to the idea of a late afternoon canoe ride. It would be peaceful and romantic. He would pack a cooler with sandwiches, chips and sodas, so when they got off the lake they could find a picnic table and watch the other boaters. He was quite proud of that idea. It would impress Stephie exactly the way he wanted to impress her.

"I was a little concerned about being on the water with you," Stephie said when the day came and they were sitting in the canoe, paddling toward one of the bridges that spanned the lake. "I have memories of the time when you were Charles and we were pulling half drowned men out of a rushing creek. I thought it would be hard to get past that, but this is beautiful."

Stephie was dressed in white shorts, the long kind that reached her knees and a brown tank top that made her look so good Michael considered it a sin when she put on the required life preserver. Her hair was pulled back and she wore sunglasses and sandals. It was spring, but warm enough to be summer, and she was dressed to suit the temperature. In Michael's opinion the lake was nice, but Stephie was what made the afternoon beautiful.

"You mentioned a request Emily made of you when she thought she was dying," Michael said. "What was it?"

"Of us, not me," Stephie told him. "You probably have it figured out by now."

"I have a general idea." Michael was in the back of the canoe, so he was controlling the direction they were paddling. There was a breeze that would blow the boat off course if he stopped, but it wasn't so strong that he had to work hard to keep them going straight.

"She wanted to die," Stephie said, "to free her soul. Then she wanted us to have a child, so she could return as our baby. That's it. As strange as it sounds, it makes sense in the context of what we've been through recently."

"So you're saying you want to have our child?" Michael paddled a little deeper on the last stroke. His right hand touched the surface of the water and he noticed that it was surprisingly warm.

"No, I was saying that it makes sense for Emily to want us to have a child. Beyond that everything gets complicated."

"In what way?" Michael switched his paddle to the left side. Stephie was keeping hers on the left, but sometimes he pushed a little too hard and had to help her get things headed right again. It had something to do with leverage from the back of the boat.

"For one thing, I want to know Michael better than I know Charles." She had made love to Charles when she was Alex so that was quite a statement.

"That's why we're here," he told her. Generally the process of making a child either involves too much passion or practically none at all. Since they were planning their family already, Michael thought their efforts would end up leaning more toward the latter. He hoped not.

"I always thought there would come a day when I would sit down with a man and talk about the family we wanted to raise. I never imagined that it could happen on our first date." They reached the bridge they had been paddling toward and floated between two of the large columns that held it up. There was a water line on the cement surface of the columns that was about six inches higher than the lake's surface. It was from the splash of the waves and indicated that a motor boat must have been through there fairly recently.

"As Glen said, whatever happens has to take time, so don't be too stressed out."

"That's not what Emily told me. She said my biological clock is ticking."

"I hate that saying."

"That doesn't make it wrong."

"Look over there," Michael said as their canoe came out from under the bridge. "That's a blue heron. They love to stand in shallow water where they can just lean over to eat. Imagine a life like that: flying, swimming and eating. How peaceful."

"Peaceful and beautiful, but also lonely. I like my life, at least the way it's headed now."

"And we'll do everything we can to keep it headed in the right direction. That's a promise from the man steering the boat."

Thirty-Six

Kathy agreed to meet Glen for coffee. She consented partially because she felt guilty about the way she had reacted when he had regressed her and partially because she knew Stephie was still working with him. She still wanted to be certain that Emily and he weren't taking advantage of her friend.

"You and I are wild cards in this situation," Glen told her over two cinnamon lattes. "Emily is the child, Stephie the mother and Michael the father while Julie is always involved in the death. But although you and I travel with them, we have different roles with each go round. I'm in the outer circle, but that isn't true with you. You were Alex's mother and now you are Stephie's friend. You were and are central to what happens. That's why I need you."

"I don't believe in regression."

"We don't need your belief, but we do need your help to keep Stephie alive." The tone of his voice was not bitter or sarcastic, just hopeful. If this was some elaborate scam, Glen was doing an excellent job of presenting it. But that's how good scammers act.

"What do you want me to do?" she asked.

"Julie's in hiding. We've got time to find her, but we don't know where to look. I want to send you back to multiple lifetimes. The idea would be to see if patterns from the past can help us in the present."

Kathy had pulled the lid off her latte, so when she sipped on it the froth left a residue on her upper lip. She reached for a napkin and wiped it off as she thought about Glen's suggestion. Emily's attempted suicide hadn't improved her confidence in Glen's mysticism. But she wanted to do what was best for Stephie. If there was anything to Glen's belief in reincarnation then she would do what she could to alter her friend's fate. If there wasn't, she needed to be part of the process anyway, to prove Glen was a con man.

"Where do you plan to send me?" Kathy asked.

"We won't know until you get there," Glen answered with a smile.

* * *

Kathy knew to wear loose clothing to the regression, so she had on a long skirt and a green pull-over top. When Glen met her at the front door, he nodded his approval and told her that her outfit could fit in many time periods and in many places throughout the world. It would limit the regressions as little as possible. She thought that his compliment was one of the oddest she had every received and she smiled at that thought. He led her to the living room then left her with Emily while he went to the kitchen to get them both something to drink.

Kathy was taken aback by how frail Emily seemed. It was as if her near death experience had added ten years to her age. Her hair had been grey and her pale skin interlaced with wrinkles. Now her hair seemed whiter. There was a yellow tint to her skin and her wrinkles appeared deeper. Kathy had tried to convince Stephie that Emily's actions were clear evidence of the harm that could be caused by crazy beliefs. But, as in so many of their discussions about Christianity, Kathy had trouble understanding Stephie's opinions. Stephie called them faith, but to Kathy her concepts seemed like lunacy.

Emily was wearing a light blue housedress with a pattern of purple and dark blue stripes. The dress buttoned up the front as if it were an oversized shirt. If it wasn't for the buttons it would have looked like a nightgown, which gave her an impression of having just stepped out of bed. Emily remained sitting and Kathy noticed that her legs seemed insubstantial. There was a cane in a corner of the room, but it wasn't near Emily. Apparently, she used the furniture to maintain her balance while walking inside.

"Thank you for agreeing to do this," Emily said. Her voice was more confident than Kathy expected. "This session is going to be a little different. At least that's the way I understand what Glen has in mind. He said he plans to turn you loose rather than trying to steer you to one time or another. If fate is good, you come back with information we can use. If it isn't, we try again."

To Kathy this scene seemed like a bad date story. Things hadn't worked out well the first time, yet the guy was begging for a second chance. If she could have placed the blame entirely on Glen, she would have known how to react. But she couldn't do that. She had been predisposed to a bad experience and that's what she had received. She had promised herself that this time would be different, that she would at least try to open her mind.

Glen rejoined Kathy and Emily in the living room and brought them each a glass of water. Emily sipped on hers, but Kathy downed hers quickly so they could move forward with the first regression. She lay on the couch and the journey started.

The first place Kathy returned to was a rural area of Spain in the eighteenth century. She kept house for her husband, worked their garden and raised the ten children who had managed to live past their first years. She had lost two who had not. Her husband was a sailor who was only home long enough to keep her pregnant. But he was a good man and managed to bring home enough money for his ever expanding family to survive. There was a possibility that the souls of Stephie, Michael and perhaps Julie were all present somehow in the woman's home as some of her many children, but Kathy couldn't be certain of that. After a little more than an hour Glen pulled her back from that regression and sent her on another.

The next regression led her to China during the Han dynasty. Once again she was a peasant with very little money and lots of children, so her life in the Orient was not so different from her life in Spain. After that she experienced an existence in ancient Egypt and one in a tribe in an Amazon rainforest, which could have taken place during any time period from twenty thousand years ago to the twenty-first century. Glen told her that Stephie, Michael and Julie had to be present in all of those regressions, but Kathy wasn't so sure and there was no clear evidence one way or the other.

Kathy seemed tired after the voyage to the Amazon, so Glen suggested that they put off sending her anywhere else. But Kathy insisted that she felt fine and he gave in. It was good he did, since the next regression finally produced signs of the tragedy they were looking for. Kathy went back to a place in an area of sub-Saharan Africa during the hunter-gatherer period.

* * *

On the morning of the day Onye died Ekah had reminded her friend that they were supposed to gather figs. They had walked to the same trees the day before, but Ekah had not picked as many as her family needed. So, although they gathered every day, going back to that place was something they did for Ekah's sake. That's why they were in the forest when Onye fell into the boar trap. It wasn't an unusual request for Ekah to make and the two young women always went out together when they picked wild fruits or vegetables, but it made Onye's death harder for Ekah to deal with. She also felt guilty for ignoring the smell of fire. It should have been a clue. Fire is used to drive animals.

"I like that place," Onye had said. "Sometimes I go there late in the day when I want to pray. It's quiet."

It wasn't quiet on the day she died. The branches broke with a sound as loud as a buffalo stampede and Onye screamed. But the heartbreak of hearing her voice was gone quickly. It sounded as if her mouth had been covered. That wasn't the case. Ekah ran to the edge of the pit and looked down. There was her friend, her body torn open leaving no air to push through her throat.

There were many dangers in the life Ekah knew. This wasn't the first time she had experienced the death of someone she cared about, but this disaster affected her more than the others. There were sharpened stakes on the floor of the pit. They were there to kill the boar, but they killed Onye instead. One came up through her lower back, near the antelope skin she wore around her waist. The wood pierced her entire body and came out of her chest slightly, just a thumb's length. There was blood over all the pit, as there was when a boar was trapped. Another stake pierced Onye's thigh and one stuck in her shoulder, but it was the one in the center of her body that had killed her. Perhaps that was good. Onye would not have wanted to live a life crippled from injuries.

Ekah looked at her friend's dark eyes. They were open and seemed larger than they had been when Onye was alive. Ekah wanted those eyes to move, but they just stared blankly, not at her, but at the white clouds that floated peacefully over the forest. Ekah started to cry uncontrollably and did so until her own eyes were drained. Then she turned away from her friend and went back to her camp.

* * *

"She was as close to you in that life as Stephie is in this one?" Glen asked Kathy after he brought her back. Kathy was still on the couch, but she was sitting up and had been out of the hypnotic state long enough to get a sense of the world around her. Glen had instructed her to remember everything she could about her life as Ekah and the people she shared that life with.

Kathy was too shaken up to reply quickly. They had spent a great deal of time discussing Stephie's impending catastrophe. But their talk was clinical, like a weatherman tracking a hurricane. And that made the disaster seem unreal. This was different. She had loved Onye in that life. She had experienced what it would feel like to see such a close friend die.

"There were differences in that life. Ekah and Onye were never apart, while Stephie and I were separated for years." Kathy was trying to be honest and thorough. She explained that although she and Stephie had gone their own ways for a long time, they were always emotionally connected. "Relationships between women can be intimate. That isn't something Stephie and I have a monopoly on."

"No, but it is what we were looking for. Who dug the trap?"

"There were between seventy and eighty people in the nation. I can't be certain."

"But you have an idea?" Glen was asking all the right questions. It was as if he could hear the confusion in her responses.

"Yes," she admitted. "There was a woman who was jealous of Onye because of the man she was with. One of the trappers was a brother of that woman. He could have been the one. It was dug in a place where Onye and Ekah often gathered fruit and it was dug at night. Whoever did that should have warned them, but didn't. Perhaps it was intentional. I just can't be sure." This happened tens of thousands of years ago, but Kathy still didn't want to accuse anyone falsely.

"A brother?"

"We were a close knit group of people. Many of us were related and I have no evidence, just intuition."

"I'd like to send you to that lifetime again. You must have talked to the woman who was jealous of Onye. I'd like to hear what she had to say." So would I, Kathy admitted to herself as she lay back down on the couch.

He sent her to a day when Ekah discovered the woman practicing with her brother's battle axe. Ekah hid behind a tree and watched for a while. She never revealed herself, because a woman practicing with a battle axe was not an acceptable thing to do. If the woman knew Ekah had witnessed what she was up to, she would have been very upset and might have attacked her. That was especially frightening because she handled the weapon better than most men.

"You didn't give us specifics," Glen told Kathy when he brought her back again. "But practicing with that axe indicated a willingness to break rules and a tendency toward violence. If she was the one and she involved her brother, then there was a family connection. That isn't in every regression, but if it is often enough it might help. I'd like to send you back to the lives we discovered in Spain, China and the Amazon forest, so we can look for family connections there as well."

By this time all doubt had left Kathy's thoughts. There were too many lives involved and the image of Onye's death was as clear and as real as if it had happened yesterday instead of in another world and time. It took them another couple of hours, but Kathy and Glen discovered women in both the Spanish and Chinese lives who had died and left behind daughters. In both of those cases the murdered women had been involved in love triangles and the principal suspect in the killing of the Spanish woman was a cousin of someone who hated her husband. They didn't finish the regressions until late at night, but it had been a productive day. Glen and Kathy were exhausted, but Emily had slept through most of it.

Kathy was about to walk out the door when she thought about Emily. "Do you need a hand with her?" she asked Glen. She wasn't sure how much Emily could do for herself. She seemed so weak.

"No," he said, shrugging off her offer. "I'm used to what she needs." That was an amazing statement especially considering how short the time had been. There was something about what Glen said that impressed Kathy more than his regressions and even more than his tireless efforts to change Stephie's fate. It takes a special person to be a willing and self-sacrificing caregiver and Kathy hadn't pegged Glen as the type. She could trust him with Stephie's life. She was sure of that now.

Thirty-Seven

Stephie did not believe that Kathy's approval was necessary before she could continue working with Glen and Emily, but she felt more comfortable when it came. Exploring past lives was a radical idea for a Presbyterian minister. And although she took pride in her open approach to all things spiritual, she was sticking her neck out somewhat. There were people in her congregation who would consider it offensive, even blasphemous, for their preacher to experiment with something so foreign to their traditions. Having the support of her friend helped her move forward.

Stephie called Glen to schedule another session after she learned that Kathy had changed her opinion of the process. And after she spoke to Glen she talked to Michael. He was in his last couple of weeks of school and couldn't take a personal day. She told him she would reschedule so he could be there, but he said it was too important to wait. He would catch up with what happened later.

Stephie arrived at Emily's apartment the next morning for the regression. Emily said "hello" and smiled, but Glen had to help her to her seat in the living room. Stephie noted that it was taking a while for Emily to regain her strength. She supposed that was normal for a woman in her eighties, but it worried her. Stephie followed them then went straight to the couch where she closed her eyes, listened to Glen's soft, steady voice and went swirling back into the nineteenth century.

* * *

Alex's life with Samuel had settled into a strange routine. They survived by stealing and avoided being caught by never staying in one place more than one day. When Samuel needed to leave her to break into a barn or someone's kitchen, he would find an out of the way wooded area, then gag Alex and tie her to a tree. Over time he became very quick with the rope he carried, especially after his arm healed. Alex maintained a hope that someone would discover her while he was away, but that never happened. She often heard people walking on the roads near her, but she could never get their attention. She would rustle about and make as much noise as possible, but no one investigated the sounds. They probably thought she was a deer or a squirrel. Her greatest fear was that someone would shoot Samuel while he was stealing their food and she would be left to starve. She had become so dependant upon her captor that she was happy when he returned.

In the evenings they slept side by side. He tied their ankles together with enough slack that he could turn over without disturbing her, but with enough knots in the rope to be certain she couldn't free herself without waking him. Most nights they simply slept on the ground, but if rain seemed imminent he would pitch the army tent he had stolen. He tried to speak with her as if they were loving companions and he never got mad when she refused to talk back. He also allowed her some privacy when she changed her clothes or relieved herself in the woods. He would stay where he could be certain she wouldn't run off, but he would turn his back so she could maintain a little dignity. Most of the time Samuel acted like a gentleman, but a gentleman kidnapper is still evil and Alex hated him for what he had done to her life.

Alex was pregnant, but she had kept her condition hidden. She feared what Samuel's reaction would be when the day came that he discovered her secret and that time was arriving quickly. She had begun to show. She was surprised he hadn't picked up on the signs yet. He had shown concern when she had trouble keeping food down, but had never associated her problem with a baby. The time to reveal her state finally arrived when they faced a challenge that was dangerous.

"We've got to cross it," Samuel told her. They had caught up with the Army of the Potomac and had begun to follow. He found that he could steal from the soldiers and the other camp followers and, if he was very careful, still keep Alex hidden. "This is as good a spot as any," he told her. What Samuel wanted to cross was a river. He had chosen a place that wasn't ideal, because he couldn't risk exposure. The water at their crossing was fast and there were few stones to step on.

"I can't risk falling," Alex said.

"We don't have a choice," Samuel told her. "I don't want you to hurt yourself, but that's the way the army is going so it's the way we will go as well."

Alex looked at the river again. It didn't appear to be more than waist deep, so even if she had to walk on the bottom she could get through it. But if the current caught her she would be in trouble. Some of her fear came from the memories of pulling soldiers out of the creek at Gettysburg. She knew how powerful water could be.

"I could die if I fall wrong."

"You're not going to fall."

"You intend to tie my hands, don't you?"

"Yes."

"How will I protect myself?"

"I'll have the end of the rope and I'll keep pulling you forward. You won't slip."

"There's more to this than you realize."

"We need the soldiers. That's all I have to realize."

"I've listened to everything you've said as you've led us into every backwoods town in Maryland and Virginia, but there has to be a point where I say no. I can't cross this river, not in my condition!"

"Your condition?"

"There's a wall of stone on the other side. Look at it. It's bordered by thick brush. Even if I made it across, how would I get up?

"You hang on to the rope and I pull."

"I can't."

"You will."

"I'm pregnant."

Alex's confession stopped Samuel as if she'd hit him with a pile of stones. She wished she had. He paced in front of her, turning to speak but unable to get the words out as if the wind had been knocked out of him. He grabbed the coil of rope then he lunged for her. Alex hadn't been expecting that and didn't try to protect herself. He grabbed her around the waist and started pulling her toward the river. This was the opposite of what she and Charles had done at Gettysburg. She kicked and tried to pull away, but he was so much stronger than she was. During the first week of her captivity she had tried to escape three times and had learned how futile her attempts were. Samuel had absolutely nothing to lose and that ruined state had left him with the focus and the power of insanity. He was even more dangerous now that his arm had healed.

Samuel jumped in the river and pulled her after him. They both slipped and sat on the bottom, soaking all their clothes. Alex jumped up to try to get back to the shore, but Samuel grabbed her around the waist again. She had swallowed a mouthful of water and was choking, but that didn't slow him down. He held her with his left arm then moved across the river by half walking and half paddling with his right arm. He slipped a few times, dunking them both, but never losing hold of Alex. She stopped struggling and let him carry her. When he reached the opposite side of the river, he went straight on to land through one of the thick bushes, pulling her after him, tearing her clothes and scratching her from head to toe. They finally reached a place where Alex could sit on the ground and breathe, but her arms, legs and face looked as if she'd been attacked by a pack of dogs. Samuel took the coil of rope off his shoulder, tied her to a tree and went back across the river to get the rest of their belongings.

Alex leaned against the tree and watched Samuel making his way back across the river. She was crying now and unable to wipe the tears from her cheeks because her hands were tied. She wanted Charles to find her and save her. God forgive her soul, but she wanted him to show up with his rifle in his hand. She wanted him to kill Samuel so the man would never bother her again. But when she had time to think, as she did at this moment, she wondered how much of her situation was her own fault. She had nursed Samuel when he was wounded and that was what she was supposed to do. But had she done more than that? Had she flirted with him? Had she given him reason to believe that she had more to offer than any other nurse? And had it been wrong to go to Charles that night at her mother's home? Was it wrong to give in to her desire? Was God punishing her for weakness and lust? And was God punishing her baby as well?

* * *

When Glen brought Stephie back, she sat up quickly, but stayed on the couch for a moment thinking about what she had learned from Alex's life. She had picked up a perspective on her current life by learning of decisions she had made in a past life, decisions that had worked out terribly wrong. Her past life history was probably the reason she was indecisive at times. But for each issue on which she had gained an understanding, there were multiple new questions that arose. Had she become a minister because Alex felt she had somehow betrayed God? Was it possible that every element of her life from her career to her feelings for Michael were just leftover emotions from other lives? And if so, would that make everything about her somehow inferior or just different? It was hard to take all of this in. Physically she wasn't the same as Alex, so there had to be other differences. How much of her current life, of the Stephie Howell that existed today, was unique? Was her soul like a drop of water in the rain/evaporation cycle that goes on and on? Or was it different somehow, like the drops that become snowflakes and crystallize to unique shapes?

"Are you all right?" Glen asked.

"Yes. I'm sorry. I'll get up."

"Stay there as long as you need to. That wasn't why I was asking."

"I'm a little dizzy from everything. That's understandable, isn't it?"

"Of course it is. It is just that you were describing how you felt when you were Alex and some of those feelings seemed troublesome to me."

"In what way?"

"Try to separate yourself from Alex. Think of her as someone who has come to you for counseling. What happened to her could have happened last year or even last month instead of in the nineteenth century. The war might have provided Samuel with more opportunities, but it was his nature, not the circumstances, that bears the blame for what happened. What would you tell a rape victim who came to you for help? Would you criticize what she wore or where she was when she was attacked?"

"Alex wasn't raped. At least she wasn't at the point in time I was remembering."

"Rape is about violence and power. Those things can happen without sex and the response of the victim is often the same."

Glen's words could have been Stephie's. When it came to counseling she was like the cobbler's son who goes barefoot. She wished the person giving her the advice was a woman instead of Glen. There was something awkward about receiving advice from a man concerning men's misuse of power in their relationships with women.

"Guilt is a powerful emotion," Glen told her. "It can carry from life to life as much as love, anger or hate."

Stephie looked over at Emily to see how she was reacting to Glen's words. She seemed to be staring, not at Stephie or Glen but off into space as if it were she who had been hypnotized. Stephie squinted a bit and leaned forward to see if she could tell why Emily was acting so strange.

"Emily?" Stephie asked, as she got up from the couch and crossed the room. There was no expression at all on the woman's face. She wasn't staring as Stephie had thought. Her eyes were glazed over. She wasn't looking at anything.

"Oh, God," Glen called out when he saw what had drawn Stephie's attention. He ran and dropped to a knee in front of her. "She's breathing," he said, his ear to her chest. "Call 911."

Thirty-Eight

Stephie and Glen followed the ambulance to the emergency room, but this time Stephie told the triage nurse that she was Emily's minister. They still had to wait about ten minutes before they were allowed to go to where Emily was being treated.

The doctor was a big boned woman of about forty with a round face and shoulder length brown hair. The room had four beds in it. Emily was lying in one. The other three were empty, but nurses and attendants were walking through. She had a small amount of privacy provided by a partially closed curtain on a ceiling track. Emily was attached to an IV pole on one side and what appeared to be a heart monitor on the other. She was dressed in a white hospital gown with a pattern of blue flowers on it. Apparently, the nurses had changed her clothes when they had brought her in even though she hadn't been assigned a regular room. They must have determined she was going to be there a while.

The scene caused Stephie to think of the nineteenth century makeshift hospitals she saw when she was Alex. They were primitive and filled with an overwhelming amount of wounded young men, but there were similarities. There was still the patient and the doctor, the former lying as still as possible while the latter attempted to work efficiently. In Emily's case the doctor's work was over. "She's dying," she whispered to them. "She's still breathing, but only very weakly and her organs are beginning to shut down. We've done all we can do. I'll leave you with her, so you can say your goodbyes."

Stephie reached for Emily's hand and began to pray, "God, your will is always perfect, even when it is hard for us to understand what is happening or why. We ask that you be with this woman as she passes from this life and guide her as she moves forward." Stephie opened her eyes and looked at Glen. He licked a finger and held it in front of Emily's mouth so he could tell if she was still breathing. He nodded to Stephie indicating that their friend was still alive. Stephie looked around for the doctor, but the woman had left the room. She leaned over and glanced under the curtain to be sure no one was close enough to hear the rest of her prayer. "We thank you for the promise of the resurrection and pray that if it is your will we will someday have the gift of Emily back in our lives. Help us nurture her when she returns so she can be happier and stronger and can live a life blessed with love from the first day to the last. We ask this in the name of Jesus Christ, your son. Amen." It was a strange feeling to be concerned that others might hear her prayer, but the words were from her heart. She was certain God would understand.

Emily's hand was cold and limp. She was lying on her side and if her chest moved as she took in each breath, it was imperceptible. Finally, she made a last little sigh and she was gone. It had taken her much longer than Stephie had thought it would, but Emily had killed herself with the overdose. "It isn't suicide when it's done for a love of life," Stephie whispered. She wasn't sure if those words were part of her prayer or just reassurance for her own sake.

* * *

There are few things in life that are as difficult as speaking at the memorial service for your child. Talking at her daughter's memorial service is what Stephie believed she was about to do, but the life of her child was in the years to come not in the years that had passed. Emily was gone. Yet the part of Emily that was her spirit, the part that had determined her strength and guided her decisions, would return and would deal with a new set of circumstances. Hopefully Stephie, with the constant help of Michael, would make those circumstances much less difficult than what Emily had faced during her eighty-three years in this lifetime.

The service was sparsely attended. Glen was there, of course, and so was Michael. The regulars from the church were there to help with the food and to offer their support. There were also two others whom Stephie didn't recognize. Glen told her they were people Emily had met during the time when she was searching for her mother's soul. It was a strange feeling looking at those women. There was something about them that had drawn Emily, something Stephie shared with them. She wondered what it could be.

One of the women was sitting about halfway back on the side of the sanctuary to Stephie's right. She had light brown hair that was poker straight and about shoulder length. She was dressed in a dark brown jumper with a yellow top underneath. The outfit had a country feel to it, which seemed appropriate since Glen told Stephie that the woman was a gardener. The second one was a postal employee who was sitting on the same side as the gardener, but all the way in the back. She was a muscular looking woman in her late forties with long blonde hair and a dress that was black. Due to its lace sleeves and mid-thigh skirt the dress was inappropriate for the service. Still it was nice the woman came. It was nice they both came.

After a pause Stephie's words began to flow. "I've known Emily for most of the four years I've been with our church," she said. "But I only grew close to her recently. Before that we would say our hellos on

Sunday mornings and every once in a while we would chat about the meaning of a biblical passage or a concept of church philosophy. I gave her what she asked for, but not much beyond that and, what's worse, I rarely asked for anything in return. It's only recently that I discovered how much she had to offer. Sadly, I don't believe I was alone in looking past Emily Vinson.

"God's will is in Paul's letter to the Philippians chapter two verses three and four, *Don't do anything from selfish ambition or from a cheap desire to boast, but be humble toward one another, always considering others better than yourselves. And look out for one another's interests, not just for your own.*

"Our world has many quiet people in it who have a lot to give and are rarely granted the opportunity. We need to touch them, yet if we approach them as projects rather than as friends, we're cheating ourselves. It isn't enough just to shake their hands and ask how they're doing. We need to listen and we need to hear what they have to say.

"The most personal and loving contact I ever had with Emily occurred on a day when she was telling me how to raise my child." Stephie paused for a moment. "The few gasps I just heard tell me I need to clarify that statement. I don't have a child. Emily was giving me advice for the future when I may be a mother. I guess you could call it hypothetical advice, but it was worth listening to. What was most impressive about the things she was saying was how her words were personal and straight from her heart. Her mother died when she was two. Growing up without a mother is difficult, of course, especially for a young girl. Emily lost love, wisdom and a role model. She told me how she felt about that, how if affected every relationship she had over the course of her life, how it made her angry, how it made her sad, but mostly how it made her lonely. Emily was a woman who didn't deserve to be lonely. She wasn't the first and she won't be the last, but she was one I grew to know and care about in the last year of her life.

"If there is a message from God in the loss of Emily Vinson, it is how important it is to care for our children and our friends, to teach them, to learn from them and to love them with the entirety of our souls. That's what life is about."

Stephie sat down as the choir started to sing "For All the Saints." Only then did she begin to cry.

* * *

Glen sat with Michael in the center section of the sanctuary. He was thinking of how much he would miss Emily, how even though he had known this day was coming he still felt shocked when it arrived. He had known Emily just a few months, but he had grown accustomed to life with her. It was special having someone who shared his goals and helped him work toward them. It wasn't the first time he'd experienced that feeling, but this time had been more intense than all the others. He had become a caregiver for her during the last couple of weeks and that intimate relationship had made them even closer. Now all he could hope for was that they might share an existence again someday— possibly when their ages would not be so far apart.

Glen was concerned with how little time there was left. Emily's soul was free. Stephie and Michael were now a couple. Those two facts meant the pregnancy that would drive fate was at least theoretically possible. In fact, she could be pregnant already. He couldn't be certain of the timing for a soul to enter an unborn child. It was hard to believe that a fertilized egg had one and just as hard to believe that a fully developed baby did not. Somewhere between those two events there was a broad expanse of possibilities.

But there was also the relationship between Stephie and Michael. He had reasons to believe it wasn't sexual yet. She had reacted with nervous embarrassment to the regressions that had revealed the affair between Charles and Alex. That could have been due to his and Emily's presence, but it had surprised him at the time. And then there was the fact that she was a minister. Their relationship might still be physical, but there was no doubt that her profession complicated things. Her congregation wouldn't be pleased if her pregnancy wasn't preceded with a marriage. They had made that sentiment clear just minutes earlier, when she was speaking.

Glen leaned toward Michael and whispered, "Stephie's words were lovely. I could tell she was speaking from her heart."

"Yes," Michael whispered back. "She loved Emily."

"She'll have a chance to love her again," Glen told him. "You both will."

Thirty-Nine

"I'd like you to stay with me," Stephie said after Michael brought her home from the memorial service. Her voice was soft with a little waver in it. He'd heard the same quality in some of her most emotional prayers from the pulpit. She looked down as she spoke rather than straight in his eyes as she normally did.

"Are you certain?" Michael asked. He surprised himself with the question. He and Stephie had shared more in the short time since Julie had left than most couples share in a lifetime and each moment they had experienced together caused him to desire her more. But he needed to be sure of how she felt.

"I don't want to be alone tonight."

"Remember what Alex felt for Charles?" Michael asked. "How she was impulsive and passionate. I miss Emily, too, but grief isn't the right reason, not for our first time together. Hopefully, there will come a day when you feel the same intense infatuation for me that Alex felt for Charles. I can wait."

"But I can't," she told him. She took his hand and pulled him toward her. "You and I will bring Emily back. That's what we've learned. We need to do that as soon as we can."

It was the answer Michael had dreaded. "When I make love to you I don't want it to be about a love for someone else, not even for our child. Is that too selfish?"

"I love you, Michael, and our love will grow. But that's no reason to make Emily wait."

Michael shook his head and stepped away from her. They were standing in her living room. He crossed to an armchair that was next to a floor lamp and sat in it. It was a perfect place for reading. She probably spent hours there relaxing with a novel or studying her Bible. He wondered if she ever just sat there, thinking about him the way he thought about her. "For all the times I've imagined making love to you," he said. "I never thought it would be like this."

"Neither did I," she replied. She went to him and held out her hand. He took it. She pulled him up then led him out of the living room and down the hall to her bedroom.

"Wait here," she said. He sat on the edge of the bed while she turned off the ceiling lamp and stepped into the bathroom. There was still light in the room, but it was a dim light from a nightlight in an outlet near the door. She seemed to be taking a long time. He glanced at a statue of St. Francis that was on her bureau and wondered why a Presbyterian minister would have a statue of a saint. He thought that if there was such a thing as a normal minister, Stephie was not it. That's when the bathroom door opened and she came out, looking far lovelier than she had been in even his most vivid fantasy.

Her thick hair was loose and long enough to touch her shoulders. It had a wave in it from being pulled back and pinned up. She had taken off the short-sleeved black dress she had worn to the memorial service and whatever she'd been wearing underneath. All she had on now was a pink bath towel that she had wrapped around her body. Covering her body made her seem a little shy and that increased Michael's desire for her. She sat beside him, leaned over and kissed him. He was overwhelmed with pleasure, as if this moment was all that mattered in this life or any life he had ever experienced. He lifted his arm around her and pulled her towel loose. It fell to her waist. He shifted his hand to one of her breasts as they continued to kiss. It was firm with skin so soft and smooth he could feel it through his soul. He felt that holding her was new and exciting; yet at the same time it was as if they'd always been together and he knew then that this was an experience powerful enough to pass through all his future existences. He knew that without any proof except the way he felt.

Stephie pulled her mouth away from Michael's and leaned back, but he wasn't ready so he leaned toward her in an attempt to keep kissing. She held a hand up in front of his face. "Take off your clothes," she told him. The tone of her voice didn't imply a command or a plea, just a simple request that would make the moment better. He had left his suit jacket on her couch in her living room, but he still was dressed in everything else he'd worn to the memorial service, even his shoes and tie. He was such a fool. He should have undressed while she was in the bathroom, instead of sitting on her bed looking around the room like a school kid. Still, he didn't want to stop kissing her, even to take off his clothes. He pushed her arm to the side and started to kiss her breasts. She smelled sweet and fresh as clear spring water. She had no perfume on, just a faint odor of bath soap. She put her fingers in his hair and gently pulled him away from her chest. "Take off your clothes," she repeated, looking in his eyes.

Michael twisted away from Stephie then stood up. He undid his tie, pulled it off and dropped it on the floor. He started to unbutton his shirt, cuffs first then the ones down the front. He had a white T-shirt underneath. He felt so overdressed. He looked at Stephie as he slipped out of his shirt. Her breasts were larger than he had thought they would be, perhaps because she generally dressed conservatively. He couldn't think of any top she had ever worn that was low cut or tight. Stephie pulled the towel back up to cover her chest and Michael realized he had been staring. He was still acting like a kid.

"I'm sorry," he told her.

"Don't be," she said. "I like looking at you, too." Michael wasn't sure if Stephie said that because she meant it or just to make him feel less awkward. But after she spoke he pulled off his T-shirt and tossed it with a little flair, as if he was placing an exclamation point on her sentence. Michael wasn't a body builder, but he jogged and kept in fairly good shape. He thought he looked good for a thirty-four year old man in a culture filled with fast food restaurants and microwave popcorn.

His shoes were next. He thought about sitting beside her on the bed to remove them, but decided it would be quicker to pull them off while standing. He tried and they were too tight so he bent over, untied them then pulled them off. There was a gap in the conversation and Michael felt as if he needed to fill it. He said, "Tomorrow's the next regression, right?" Stephie had wanted to wait until after Emily's memorial service and Glen had agreed, but only if they could proceed immediately afterwards. Michael knew that and Stephie realized he did. That meant she also knew his words were pure small talk.

"Yes," she answered. "He wants to regress *me* again, but I'd like you to be there." Michael hadn't realized he wouldn't get the next turn, but the decision made sense. Alex was the one on the run with Samuel. They needed to get into her head, not his. Michael pulled off his socks, one at a time, while standing. He stood up after he had tossed them onto the pile of his clothes and he looked at Stephie looking at back at him. She had her hands in front of her, holding the towel. Her head was tilted slightly and her lips opened a bit. She was looking at his body, not his eyes. It did seem as if she was studying him in the dim light as closely as he had looked at her. He smiled, slipped out of his pants and boxers in one motion then went to her. She handed him her towel, which he tossed without thinking. He sat beside her, wrapped his arms around her body and pulled her back on the bed in one motion.

* * *

"Will you marry me?" Michael asked as he lay beside her. The covers were thrown off the bed and they were naked. She was on her back and he was running his fingers along her body, tenderly exploring each tiny curve and crevice. Every so often she shivered from his touch. Sex had been like coming home to a place that was at the same time both familiar and brand new. It was about love in a way that he had never experienced with another woman and that was what had made it more glorious than he had imagined it could be. He finally understood Stephie's need to bring Emily back and sharing that need with her had wrapped their experience with another layer of love. He wanted to keep Stephie with him forever.

"For all the times I've imagined you proposing to me," Stephie said. "I never thought it would be like this." Michael smiled at the way she used his words. He leaned over and kissed her again. "Marriage isn't a constant in our other lives," Stephie continued. "Emily told me her mother was married to her father, but Alex was not married to Charles."

"So?" Michael asked.

"So fate isn't directing us on this one. We're free to choose our own path."

"We're always free. That's what Glen says. We're going to change the outcome of the circle. We're going to save your life and I'm going to spend the rest of my days with you, Emily and another one or two children that never made it into our other lives. Circularity is an aberration the three of us will fix.

"And marriage?" she asked.

"It's just a piece of paper, I suppose, and I won't love you any less without it. Still, it's a magical piece of paper that will make our lives easier and it's what I want. Will you marry me?" he asked again.

"Yes," she said. "I will."

Forty

Michael slept at Stephie's apartment on the night of Emily's memorial service. He left very early the following day so he would have time to swing by his home to shower and change before another day of teaching. That afternoon he picked Stephie up, took her to dinner at a seafood restaurant then brought her to Glen's for the next regression. Glen preferred starting earlier in the day to have time to explore anything interesting they might discover. He had suggested they could proceed without Michael as they had the last time, but Stephie was determined to have him by her side, especially since this would be the first time that Emily wouldn't be with her. Glen gave in without an argument.

"Would you do me a favor?" Stephie asked Michael as she sat on the couch where the sessions took place.

"I'll do whatever I can." He took her hand as he spoke.

"Would you sit in Emily's chair? I'd feel more comfortable if you were there."

Stephie glanced at Glen while she talked to Michael. She had been concerned that he would see her request as an attempt to push Emily's memory away rather than an effort to honor her. But Glen didn't appear to be paying much attention to what she asked for. Instead he was smiling and looking at her hand in Michael's.

"Lie down now," Glen said. "We'll get started."

* * *

Alex heard voices and the sound of footsteps in the woods. At first she thought Samuel was returning, but he wouldn't be talking to himself. There were no more flames in the fire, just a layer of red coals. It was getting cold despite the fact that Samuel had given her the heavy coat he had stolen. He had also wrapped her in a wool blanket. The sun was down but she could still see well because the full moon was bright on that cloudless night. She thought it was December, but she wasn't sure exactly how long they'd been traveling. She had been tied to this tree for more than an hour. He'd tied her in a sitting position, so her legs were rested, but her back and her seat were sore. She had swelled from the pregnancy to the point where Samuel had to change how he tied her. Now the rope was higher, just under her breasts. Staying in one position was more difficult and he told her he wished he didn't have to hurt her. But if he didn't tie her, she'd run away. That's what he said. Truth was she thought she would die if she was on her own in the middle of nowhere. She didn't care for herself, but she had the baby to think of. She told him that. He still tied her up.

"My hands are slipping. I need to set it down, just for a minute." The voice sounded like a boy's voice. He had to be fairly young to stay out of the war, unless he was a soldier. They were following the Army of the Potomac, but he could be a confederate. She wondered if she should try to yell. Samuel had stopped gagging her over a month ago, claiming he was showing how much he trusted her. But what if he was trying to trick her somehow? Yet that didn't seem like him. He had hurt her many times, but only by pushing her too hard or tying her ropes too tight. He'd never intentionally injured her. That would just slow her down.

"Can you hold it a bit longer? Over there would be good." The second voice was a woman's. That was good. If a man found her tied up like this he might rape her. A woman though— she might trust a woman.

"Over here," Alex shouted. "I need your help."

She heard someone walk in her direction then saw the person poke her head out from behind a half fallen tree. It was a woman. She was dressed like a man, but it was clearly a woman.

"I've been kidnapped," she shouted. The woman stepped out where she could be seen.

"Where is he?"

"Untie me. I need to get away."

"Where is he?"

"In a farm we passed. He's stealing things he needs."

"That's my home."

"I'm sorry, but I need to escape before he gets back. Please untie me."

Alex could see the boy behind the woman. He was half hidden behind a small fir tree, but she could tell he was eleven or twelve. That was about the youngest age for soldiers on either side. If he waited much longer someone would grab him and put a gun in his hands. He was standing beside a barrel. Apparently, that's why they were in the woods, to hide whatever that barrel contained.

"This man, is he a soldier?"

"He was."

"A deserter?"

"Yes."

"My husband's in the war, if he's still alive. He would never run off like yours. But I wish he would. I do."

"He's not my husband. He just took me."

"He's a Yankee, right?"

"Yes."

"Stay back, William," she said to the young boy. "I may be crazy but I'm going to help this lady." She approached Alex, but stopped a couple of yards from her. "Lord," the woman said. "Are you with child?"

"Yes." Alex had thought the blanket and the coat would prevent the woman from noticing, but the rope must have pulled the material tight enough for the woman to detect her condition.

"And he keeps you like this? What kind of a monster is this man?"

"Please untie me. He'll be back, soon."

She moved around Alex quickly then dropped to her knees to work on the knots. "What's your name?" Alex asked.

"You don't need to know that."

"I guess not."

"When I get these ropes off I need you to help me bury something."

"He'll be back soon."

"It won't take long. I dug the ditch already. We just need to throw it in and put leaves on top. If we don't hide it, the soldiers will take everything we have."

"Yes. Of course."

There hadn't been another chance like this since the day Alex last saw Charles. Her heart was racing, but it wasn't going to be easy. When Samuel untied the ropes he never took as long as this woman was taking. Every second that went by increased the risk of Samuel catching them.

"Don't squirm so much," the woman said. "You're pulling it tighter."

"Light a stick in the coals. If the knot's too hard then burn the rope loose."

"No need. The knot's loose. It won't be long."

"It can't be long."

"There you go," she said.

The rope fell off Alex and she rolled to her knees to get up. For the last month or so that had become the easiest way to stand. "God bless you," she said.

"Now you help us. If your man gets back before we hide that barrel, it will be hard for me and my boy."

"He's not my man."

The woman led Alex toward the boy and what they were trying to hide. It was a big load for either of them, especially for such a small boy. She could see how it had been a struggle.

"Where to?" Alex asked as she stepped up beside the barrel. She pulled on the top leaning it into her belly. She hoped this wouldn't be too much for the baby. She carried some of the things Samuel had stolen, but he generally took the largest load. She wasn't used to lifting much weight. "Can we roll it?" she asked.

"It would leave a path. We're just going beyond that rock." She indicated a direction by nodding her head then bent over. "That's my marker." Alex felt the weight shift as the woman picked up the other half of the load. It was very heavy. It was probably filled with salted meat. That made the most sense. Lately food was worth more than gold.

They had taken just a few steps when the woman dropped her half of the load. It fell back on Alex's right leg, but glanced lightly off her thigh and didn't hurt her badly. The woman was running now and when Alex turned she saw that Samuel was coming full speed in their direction with his Bowie knife in his hand. Alex looked for a weapon, a branch or anything she could use, but before she could move Samuel grabbed the woman by her hair, pulled her to the ground and stuck his knife in her chest. She was dead and Alex hadn't done a thing to help. Maybe she was too scared to move. It had all happened so quickly she didn't even know what she was thinking. She looked for the boy, but he was nowhere to be seen.

"My God, Samuel!" Alex shouted at him. "She was an innocent woman. You killed an innocent woman."

"I'd say you killed her," Samuel answered as he cleaned off his knife. "I shouldn't have left you without a gag. Let's see what's in that barrel."

"You are going to rot in hell for sure."

"I'm already in hell, Alex and you are right beside me."

* * *

Stephie was thankful she had insisted that Michael be with her, since this was the worst regression she'd been through. She was shaking so much she had to stay on the couch for nearly an hour while Michael held her hands, massaged her neck and told her how he would always be with her. He knew what to expect so he wouldn't be asleep as Charles had been or busy in another room as Emily's father had been. But Stephie knew Michael couldn't watch her every minute of every day. They would deal with this together, or course, but her strength was more important than his because she was the one Julie would be coming for with all the satanic power of Samuel's soul. Stephie would be the one who had to protect herself.

They held each other that night as they lay in bed and Michael drifted off to sleep. But Stephie couldn't ease her mind enough to rest. The picture of Samuel thrusting his knife into the chest of the woman kept racing through her head, over and over. In her head she could also see the boy watching his mother die. He was cowering behind the fallen tree. Then, when the act of violence was over, he crawled away, shaking like an injured animal. Stephie wasn't sure if Alex had seen the image that was rushing through her mind or if it was just a reaction to the fear and wretched pity she had experienced, but she was certain of one thing. That boy did not deserve such pain and must have been forever changed from such an experience, just as Emily was changed from the death of her mother.

Forty-One

Over the next month Stephie and Michael went through five more regressions. Four of them were Stephie's. Those didn't teach Glen much, except how horrible it was for Alex to be tied up like an animal. Michael's one regression also didn't teach Glen anything that would help him understand Julie, but it was interesting. Glen sent him back to the morning after Samuel took Alex.

* * *

Charles's life finally had hope, hope that it would turn out the way it was supposed to, full of warmth and satisfaction. General Meade had won the battle and was now in pursuit of Lee. Charles felt pride in that even though he had walked away from the fight. Samuel was the reason he had deserted and it turned out that his friend was alive and on the mend. That was reason enough to celebrate but what gave him the most joy he had ever known was Alex's midnight visit. She was in love with him. Alex was the most remarkable woman he had ever known and for some crazy reason she wanted to be with him.

Charles slipped his shirt on, pulled his trousers over his drawers and headed downstairs to where Alex's mother would be preparing breakfast. He was hungry, but he would try to eat as little as possible. Food was hard to come by in these times and although he appreciated the way Margaret was willing to share what she had, he didn't want to take more than he should.

He was about to leave the bedroom when he heard someone shouting. He could tell it was Margaret, although he couldn't understand what she was saying. He stepped out into the hall.

"She's gone," Margaret yelled. Her voice was coming from Alex's bedroom. Charles ran down the hall to see what was going on. He found Margaret looking through Alex's closet and bureau. "Her clothes are missing and they're both gone. She's run off with Samuel." Margaret turned to Charles and in a voice that mixed fear and anger, she screamed. "He forced her. She wouldn't go like this if he hadn't. I know my daughter and I swear by God that the man you call your friend has taken her."

"If Samuel has hurt her I will shoot him myself," Charles said. He couldn't tell her about the night visit and how he knew that Alex would not want to run off with Samuel, but he could agree with Margaret's words. "I promise you that here and now."

"Would he hurt her? You know him. Would he do that?"

"The Samuel I grew up with wouldn't do this to a defenseless woman. I can only hope that part of him hasn't changed completely."

"Samuel never talked about himself." Margaret had been crying, but was able to speak rationally. "He talked about Alex without taking time to breathe. He spoke freely of love, saying she was his angel, his reason to live. That's why I warned you both when you came up the road holding hands. I am certain Samuel knew how Alex felt about you and it was anger over that situation that drove him to do what he did. I saw how my daughter looked at you. She would never leave you unless something horrible occurred."

"They're on foot," Charles told her. "We might catch them if we can get a horse."

"I've sold most of them," Margaret said, "but I might be able to get one back." She was breathing heavily. Charles wanted to calm her down so they could figure out what to do, but he was just as nervous as she was. "Hazel is a five year old mare that I couldn't bear to sell, so I paid a friend to hide her from the soldiers."

"How soon can we get her?"

"He's got her tucked back in the woods, where the soldiers will never look. He has about five acres of fenced in land and ten horses he's hiding. He told me I would have to wait until the end of the war to get her back, but if he hears Alex is in trouble he'll make an exception. He's known her since she was a child."

"While we're talking they're getting further away. How soon can we get her?" Charles could tell how upset Margaret was. She was starting to lose focus and they couldn't afford that.

"His home is about a forty minute walk from here," Margaret said. She had started to pace. Charles was standing still but watching her circle. "If he's there when I get there and he agrees to bring her to me it will take a few hours to do that. If everything goes right I can have Hazel back here in four to five hours."

"They could be halfway to wherever by then."

"To wherever?"

"I don't know where," Charles said. "Samuel might be headed south. The war has left that area in chaos, so he might be able to hide if he goes that way. But he knows the far north. He might be headed back to Maine where he's as familiar with the forests as the deer are. And there's always the west. He would have an easier time keeping a kidnapped woman west of the Mississippi because there's more open space and less law."

Charles felt tremendous guilt over the situation. It wasn't his idea for Alex to sneak to his bed. She had surprised him, but even so he should have been the sensible one. He should have turned her away. He was weak because she was beautiful. The real problem was that he had no idea what Samuel was capable of doing. They had known each other since they were children. Charles should have understood the situation better and reacted with extreme caution.

"Go get that horse," Charles told her. "Meanwhile I'll start circling the area on foot. I'll make wider and wider circles around your home, but I'll be sure to return when you expect to get back. Hopefully, I will have found something that will tell us what direction I should ride in once I have a horse."

Margaret had on a casual frock that would be perfect for a walk, but not for the ride back. She said she had to switch to her split skirt and put on some shoes before she could leave. Charles wasn't about to wait. He told her to get over there as quickly as possible. Meanwhile, he would start the search.

Charles went out the front door of the farm house and down the steps. He went to Margaret's garden first. It was possible Samuel had picked some squash or beans or even dug some potatoes prior to confronting Alex. They couldn't carry too much with them, but even a little food would change their pattern of escape. Charles didn't see any unusual signs, so he walked around by the side of the house. There was a row of scruffy bushes and small trees surrounding most of the building. Apparently, the shrubs were there for looks, which was unusual for a farmhouse. They hadn't been cared for recently, probably since the day when Alex's dad went off to Harrisburg. There was nothing unusual on this side, either.

Charles moved to the back of the house. From there he had a clearer view of the fenced in fields where Alex's family had kept their cattle and horses during better times. He could also see a thick wooded area where Samuel could have taken Alex if he wanted immediate cover. Charles didn't think they had gone that way, but to be sure he looked for signs of two people walking away from the house. The ground was moist, but there had been no rain. He looked for shoe prints where there was a break in the grass and for broken grass where there wasn't. He found no indications that anyone had walked out that way recently. Charles was convinced that his first thought was right. They had walked straight out to the road and stayed on it, so they could cover as much distance as possible before he and Margaret started to look for them. Charles walked around to the other side of the house and had similar luck there. He didn't find any signs that Samuel and Alex had headed out that way.

When Charles made it back to the front of the farmhouse he widened the circle. This time he went out to the road. He looked for Margaret, but couldn't see her. That was a good sign. He was hoping she was too far along to see. He found some shoeprints out there that could have belonged to Alex and Samuel. They were fairly fresh, were clearly made by two people and one of the sets were smaller, indicating a woman or a young boy. Both sets were made by men's ankle boots, but Alex had a pair of those that she had been wearing in the field hospital. That wasn't uncommon since women's slippers were impractical for extended physical activity. The people who made the footprints were headed back toward the battlefield. The fight was over and the armies had left, but it was a good possibility that Samuel might try to follow the union.

Charles decided to go back to the house to look through Alex's clothing. If her walking shoes were there he would start circling the house again. If they weren't he would head down the road a bit to see if he could find any more signs. This could be the progress he had hoped for. It would be wonderful if he knew where to ride to once he had the horse.

Once back inside the house he went straight to Alex's bedroom and started rummaging through a trunk where she kept her shoes. He didn't find the ankle boots he was looking for, so that indicated to him that those footprints were most likely Alex and Samuel's.

At the bottom of the trunk Charles found something unexpected. It was a well used clarinet reed he had purchased a few years ago. It was chipped and worn which is why he had tried to toss it out. It seemed that Alex had recovered it and saved it, probably to remind her of him. He picked it up and held it for a moment. The dual emotions of longing for Alex and fear for her safety swelled up inside of him as he touched this small indication of how she had felt about him. He set it back in the trunk and headed out again to the road. She was everything of value in his life. He had to find her.

Charles walked back toward the town of Gettysburg, moving slowly so he could study the road surface and the land on either side. The closer he got to town, the greater the risk. He was a deserter and he was headed to the place where there were people who knew what he was. But the walk turned out to be uneventful. He turned around at the appropriate time to be back at Alex's home when Margaret returned. He hadn't found any additional signs of Samuel and Alex.

"Thank God you are back," Charles said when he saw Margaret. He had been watching the road from the porch of her house. "I hope you had no trouble."

"Nothing unexpected," Margaret said as she swung her leg over the horse and dismounted. "What now?"

"I know which way they headed, but that's all I know. Thanks to you, I can travel faster than they can. We'll need God's blessing, but we have a chance of finding them. All you can do now is pray." Charles placed his foot in the stirrup and swung his body onto Hazel, then he rode back to the road and off in the direction he had just been walking.

Forty-Two

"I've got some specifics on Julie's brother, Trent," Kathy said. She had called Glen to tell him what she had discovered. It hadn't been hard. All it had taken was access to the internet and Julie's social security number, which Michael knew. "He has a wife and two daughters, ages five and seven. The family lives about ten minutes from Julie and Trent's parents, who still live in the home in West Virginia where Julie was raised. Apparently the Bullard family doesn't fit the stereotype. The daughter left town while the son stayed behind."

"Do you think she's been in touch with him?" Glen asked her.

"I was thinking more of a family connection to the violence, like what we discovered in my regressions. We need to watch her brother."

"Her father or her mother could also be the connection."

"Then what do we do?"

"We go up there and check on them, as you suggested."

"Both of us?"

"I could watch the parents while you keep an eye on the brother. We could switch off after a while, to be less obvious. If the family is the key we're looking for, then this is the right thing to do and if Julie shows up unexpectedly, that would be even better. I'm not sure it's much of a plan, but we don't have anything else."

Kathy hung up the phone, but stood by it for a moment as she thought about the conversation she'd just had. It seemed to her that Glen was easy to talk to and she was pleased that he was helping Stephie. He was a good man. She wished she had never doubted him.

* * *

The trauma of Trent's childhood had remained with him in emotional waves of anger, disgust and helplessness. But over the years the waves had become further apart until the sense that his life had less value than other lives had disappeared like a ripple in a lake's surface. Then Julie called and the memories flooded back into his being. He couldn't sleep, work or relax with his family.

When Trent was a child, Neil's deviance was a force he wasn't able to fight. Neil was physically stronger and old enough to be an authority figure to a young boy. But Trent was an adult now and that meant things were different. The resurgence of the memories came with hatred and a desire for revenge. There were risks, of course, but they might be worth taking.

Trent had been watching television with his wife and daughters when he noticed that no one in the room was paying attention to what was on the set. Dora and the girls had fallen asleep while his thoughts were wandering to subjects he didn't want to share with any of them, even Dora.

Trent had chosen his daughters' names: Christina and Faith. Dora preferred names without religious significance such as Marissa or Natalie, but she understood that Trent's faith had been the power that had allowed him to overcome his history so he could lead a normal life. She told him that was why she had given in on such an important issue. Now, after years of watching them grow, the names of his daughters reminded him of nothing other than the girls themselves and he was certain that was true for Dora as well.

"It's too early," Christina said in a groggy voice. He picked up Faith, but since he could only carry one of the two, his eldest daughter had to get to bed on her own. Part of this ritual was that Dora slept through all of it.

"It's ten o'clock. I let you sleep on the couch much longer than I should have," he whispered. The dark haired girls were in their pajamas with their teeth brushed, so he could take them directly to the room they shared. Faith's hair seemed pure black, while her older sister's was dark brown. They both had dark skin and brown eyes. Trent would tuck them into their beds then go back to his wife.

After the girls were in their rooms Trent returned to the den couch where the Saturday night ritual normally continued with him giving his wife a foot massage. She would pretend to sleep through it, but he would know she was awake. After a few minutes of rubbing her feet, Trent would switch to her shoulders and then other parts of her body until he was eventually giving his wife a total body massage. As he touched her skin, he would pull off her clothing and he would kiss each place that had been hidden from his view. Then she would kiss him back and undress him as well. Their sex never deviated from the pattern they had established. There wasn't anything new or unexpected. But Trent loved the way his body shook with joy and how his worries and insecurities disappeared as long as he held Dora. Their sex was like a drug without any side effects. It was the most beautiful thing in his life.

It hadn't always been like this. Trent met Dora in high school, in his English Literature class. She asked him for help with an assignment to write a short story. He wasn't a very good student, so he was surprised but complimented by her request. The study dates became other dates and eventually they found they were in a relationship. That's when things became complicated because what Neil had done to Trent had made intimacy more difficult for him than it was for most young men.

One time, on a rainy school night, Trent and Dora were in the parking lot behind Grizzly Mountain Texaco. They were in the back seat of his Mitsubishi Mirage which was hidden by the wrecks that were being kept for parts. They had been kissing for at least a half hour. He was certain she was growing bored while waiting for his body to respond, so to keep her from pushing the issue he slipped his hand under her T-shirt. He felt awkward and quickly pulled back.

"I'd just as soon talk," Dora told him, "if that's what you'd like to do. I want to get to know you better."

"Whatever," he replied, trying to sound indifferent.

For more than a year after that night Dora spent time with Trent, listened to his problems and gradually won his heart. There were times when Trent felt as if he were a project for Dora and that caused him to react with some anger. But she always managed to sooth his temper and gradually sex began to work for them as well.

"You're someone who needs to be in love," Dora told him. "We share that trait."

Dora told him something else that he had no reason to doubt. She had experimented a little before they were together and had decided that she didn't like sex all that much. But once things started clicking for the two of them, it just kept getting better. He believed her because he felt the same way.

Dora and Trent were married a year after high school, in a service at the church they had attended together since their junior year. He did two years of college at night, but then Christina was born. Two years later Faith gave him another reason to stay home. He told Dora he wanted to enjoy his girls while they were young, but he also thought it was unfair for Dora to do all the work of raising them.

After Christina and Faith were tucked in their beds, Trent returned to the den and sat in the armchair he usually occupied when they were watching TV. Dora opened her eyes slightly and stared at him. "Are you all right?" she asked. Clearly she was surprised that he wasn't massaging her feet. There hadn't been a break in their weekly routine since four months earlier when Dora had been suffering with a nagging cold.

"I don't feel right," Trent told her. What he said was true, but he was implying a physical ailment. That implication was a lie and he would have felt awful about telling it if his anger hadn't been blocking all other feelings.

"That's a shame," Dora said. "Is it your stomach?"

"Something like that," he said.

His wife was the perfect woman for him and his daughters were two of God's most beautiful creations. Trent didn't want to lose any of them, but at the same time their beauty reminded him of the ugliness Neil had brought into his life. That was especially true of his daughter Christina, who was just a little younger than he had been when Neil had raped him.

Trent's anger swelled, attacking his body like a disease. Neil was a cancer, a malignancy that had to be dealt with to save the world. He had no right to do what he had done. He was possessed by Satan.

I have an obligation to see that he doesn't hurt anyone else, Trent told himself. But all he said to his wife was, "I'm tired now. I'm heading to bed." He wouldn't tell her any more than that.

Forty-Three

Stephie wanted to be beautiful on the day she was wed. It was part of the dream, that brides are always beautiful. She thought she would look silly in a gown with less than half a dozen people at the wedding, but she was still determined to wear something special. So she bought a sky blue, knee length dress with a ribbon tie around the waist and spaghetti straps. It had a little lace on both the bodice and the skirt that made it seem more than semi-formal without appearing overdone. What was important was that it fit well and the color suited her. She wouldn't be the princess that every woman should be on her wedding day, but she would look good for Michael.

The wedding was to be an afternoon ceremony in a small outdoor chapel on a hill behind Stephie's church. The rain plan was to move the service inside, but the day turned out to be a warm, sunny June day. Michael, along with Stephie's mom and dad, were getting ready when Stephie stepped out of her home to drive to the church. She planned to go two hours early. She wanted to fix her hair, change into her wedding dress and prepare herself spiritually for the life commitment she was about to make. But when she closed the front door of the house and turned to walk down the few steps of the small porch, she noticed a yellow and red box sitting on the wooden stoop. She looked at it closely. It was ammunition, fifty cartridges ready to use in a .22 rifle.

The gun catalogs hadn't stopped coming, although Stephie and Michael were so used to seeing them that they simply were tossed whenever they appeared. But this was new and it was a clear threat.

Stephie dropped her dress. It had taken her more than a week to pick it out and she was thrilled with the choice, but all of that was gone from her mind. The hanger slipped from her hand and she left the outfit in a blue satin clump on the dusty wooden floor. Bullets were on her porch. She was not a gun person, but she knew that bullets kill people. She ran inside.

"Michael!" she shouted. Stephie was shaking in her jeans.

"What?" he asked. He met her in the foyer after running down the hall from their bedroom without his shirt. She greeted him by throwing her arms around his neck and hanging on like a frightened child. "Tell me," he demanded.

"On the porch," she said. "Look on the porch."

Stephie followed Michael out there. He bent over as if he were about to pick up the box, but she stopped him. "It's a threat," she said. "I don't care what the police would have said about the catalogs. This is a threat and people can't do that."

"We'll file a complaint," Michael told her.

"There could be fingerprints on that box," she said. "Don't touch it. Even if Julie thinks we've committed the worst betrayal since Judas, she can't threaten us."

"I'll make the call," Michael said. He stepped back into the house and turned toward the kitchen.

Stephie picked up her dress after Michael left. The skirt was stained in front from landing in purple bird droppings. Apparently, the birds had been eating berries. It was disgusting and it meant that Julie's act had succeeded in ways she couldn't have imagined.

Stephie followed Michael into the house as her dad came out of the bedroom where he and her mom had been getting dressed for the ceremony. "What's going on?" he asked. His question was more of a demand than an inquiry. Stephie told him it was a long story, but explained the basics. Her mom was standing by his side when she got to the part about being the couples' counselor for Julie and Michael. Maybe it was her imagination, but they both seemed to cringe over that.

"We can't let Julie intimidate us," Stephie said when Michael returned. "When this day is over, I want you to be my husband."

"We have to be careful," he told her. "History isn't on our side."

"History?" her mom asked, but Stephie wasn't about to explain the regressions.

"There's got to be a way we can be brave without being stupid," she said, ignoring her mother's question.

"Julie is pushy and self-centered, but not crazy," Michael told her. "If we concentrate on preventing her from doing something that accidentally hurts you, we're going to be all right. I can't see her trying to hurt you on purpose."

"I don't understand what's going on?" her mother asked again.

"There isn't time," Stephie said. "I'll tell you later." Her mother seemed irritated that her daughter was putting her off, but Stephie's father took her hand as if to calm her down.

"We've got to let Glen know," Michael told her. "He was planning to pick up Kathy."

"Call him and get them to come by here," Stephie said. "We also need to move the ceremony inside regardless of the weather and lock the doors of the church while it's in progress."

"You want to go forward with the ceremony?" Michael asked. He seemed surprised. Stephie hadn't thought there was any other choice.

"This was our wedding day when we woke up. I want it to be our wedding day when we go to sleep. Are the police on their way?"

"Yes."

"And after they do whatever they have to do?" Stephie asked him.

"We drive to the church together," Michael said.

"How does she know about the wedding?" Stephie's father asked. "You didn't put an announcement in the paper, did you?"

Her dad had a good point. Perhaps Julie had been driving by the house and had noticed his minivan. Even so, it would be a leap to determine it was their wedding day. She might have a friend in either the church or the school office who could be feeding her gossip, but that was unlikely since Julie was as much of a loner as Emily had ever been. For now, though, it was more important for Stephie to deal with what Julie knew rather than getting bogged down with how she knew it.

* * *

The police, who arrived around the same time as Glen and Kathy, weren't much help. Stephie filled out a couple of forms they handed her and explained their story from the time when she used to sing in the choir with Julie to that morning when she dropped the dress she had planned to be married in. They had stepped around the box on their way in, so she took them back to the porch to show them what was there.

There were two officers, a young, petite blonde woman and an overweight dark haired man who was at least fifteen years older. The woman reacted to Stephie's confession that she had been Julie's counselor with more visible surprise than her parents had shown. Then she told Stephie, "Bullets aren't illegal. I don't think we could charge your friend with anything more than littering and we would probably have trouble making that stick." Stephie's feeling was that the woman's attitude about the way Michael and she found each other was influencing her opinion about the seriousness of Julie's threat. She wanted to explain to the officer and to her parents that what Michael and she felt for each other wasn't just a simple attraction, it was something that had been building in all the lives they had shared over countless centuries. Yet it would take her weeks or even months to try to explain that concept to her mom and dad. As for the officer, explaining her past lives to her would make Stephie seem like a candidate for an asylum.

Meanwhile, the other officer managed to pick up the box of bullets with his ungloved hands. Glen didn't say much during the process, but every time Stephie glanced in his direction she could see he was shaking his head. He had always told them they were on their own and calling these cops just seemed to prove his point.

"What do we do now?" her dad asked after the police left. It was interesting that the question came from him. Stephie wondered if Michael was figuring out the answer without voicing the question. Both the men in her life seemed to be concerned for her safety. That knowledge made her feel good, but not secure. She knew how little they could do if Julie decided she was going to attempt some real harm.

"I can't wear this," Stephie said, holding up the soiled dress.

"Do you still want to?" Michael asked.

"I don't care if we're dressed in bathing suits," she told him as she headed down the hall to their bedroom, "but we're going to the church and getting married today."

She found a black, sleeveless dress with a v-neck top and a pleated skirt. It was simple yet pretty. Although it's bad luck for a bride to wear black, it would have to do.

They drove to the church in her dad's van because it was the only vehicle they had that would hold all of them. Stephie sat in the middle while the rest of her family served as body shields. She didn't like that, but they all insisted. When they arrived, Michael went out alone to be sure the door to the church was open. When he found it unlocked, he came back for everyone. They ran in single file, hunched over, like war refugees on the evening news. They locked the door behind them.

Tom, the church's senior minister, greeted them in the church foyer. "I've presided over many weddings, but I don't believe I've ever seen an entrance quite like that."

In other circumstances his words might have been funny, but no one was in the mood to laugh. "We're here and we're ready," Michael said. "Marry us as quickly as you can."

* * *

Stephie worked in the church and prayed in the sanctuary almost every day, but when she stepped into that dark room on her wedding day, that room lit only by the glow of the stained glass windows, she felt the deeper peace that she desperately needed. Most brides plan their weddings with careful attention to every aspect. They hope for perfection and are upset if even one small detail doesn't work out. Stephie didn't believe those brides could understand the intensity of what she had experienced. She rejoiced in being alive, gave thanks to God and celebrated the joy of being one with Michael.

Tom took over the ceremony with the gentle authority he was used to showing. As part of the ceremony he tried to define marriage. He spoke of working through the hard times in order to appreciate what was good. Stephie looked at Michael as Tom said those words and she thought of how true they were, not only for that day but for all their lives together.

They would get through the bad and would go on to love each other forever and ever, long past till death do us part.

"I do," Stephie said, when it was her turn to do so. Two simple words with only three letters, shorter even than "Jesus wept," the shortest verse in the Bible. Yet the sentence was one of the most powerful phrases she would ever say.

"You may now kiss the bride," Tom told Michael. As they sealed their love by wrapping their arms around each other and gently touching their lips, Stephie prayed that they would live through whatever came next.

Forty-Four

Stephie and Michael had reservations at the Grove Park Inn in Asheville, but staying there seemed like a bad idea. Michael stated the obvious, "There's a chance Julie knows our plans."

Stephie started to speak, but she was too angry and frustrated to find the words. Even if there was no violence, she didn't want to spend her honeymoon constantly looking over her shoulder.

"We need to go somewhere other than where she expects us to be," Michael said.

"Let's just drive," Stephie suggested. "We can stop when we find a place that looks interesting." She thought she would be happy no matter where they went, as long as they were together and alone.

They waited until two-thirty the following morning before sneaking out of the house. Her parents had requested that they wake them before they leave, so that's what they did. Her mom and dad said goodbye and wished the new couple the best of luck, but they didn't turn on any lights while they spoke because they didn't want to reveal activity in the house. The story of Stephie and Michael's marriage continued to read more like an espionage thriller than a romance.

A little more than a half hour after they left the house, Stephie sat in the passenger seat of Michael's Grand Prix watching the dark scenery slip by. They were headed north on US-220 toward Virginia. At that late hour it seemed that there were more trucks on the road than cars, but they were making good time, no matter where they were going.

The first motel they tried had no night service, so they went on to a Best Value Inn near Lexington, Virginia. They booked a room for three nights and settled in as quickly as they could. Michael brushed his teeth then stripped to his boxers and collapsed on one of the two double beds. Stephie was too hyper to feel tired. Instead of lying next to Michael, she sat in one of the chairs and stared at him. There were lots of things that had gone wrong. Not making love to her husband on their wedding night was one more item to add to that list. Yet she was happy. She loved Michael and knew they belonged with each other. No matter how little time they had, their days together would be beautiful.

Something crossed Stephie's mind as she watched Michael sleeping. In this life she and Michael were running from Julie, while in her life as Alex she and Samuel had run from Charles. She wanted to escape, but Alex wanted to be caught. It seemed to Stephie that the differences were proof that events could change from one lifetime to another. The thought gave her hope.

Stephie got out of her chair, used the bathroom, then washed up and brushed her teeth. She changed into a yellow cotton night gown she had packed. She had bought something special for her wedding night, a pink satin chemise with a contrasting trim. She hadn't been able to wear the dress she wanted to wear for the ceremony and now the timing was wrong for her sleepwear as well. But it was the person that mattered, not the outfits and Michael was the perfect man. She took one last glance at her husband before she shut off the light and curled up beside him.

* * *

Michael found a family restaurant in the morning where they had pancakes and coffee. They weren't surrounded by opulence as Stephie had expected, but she was happy to be staring in Michael's eyes as they talked about the way they felt about each other. Then the subject changed.

"This place is absolutely perfect," Stephie said.

"No it's not," he replied. He was scratching his head a little too hard, digging at his skin and staring down at the table. She could tell he had something to say and he wasn't sure she would want to hear it. He didn't contradict her very often. All of this had to be related: the bullets on the porch, the abbreviated ceremony, the hotel where they were staying and the honeymoon night without touching each other.

"Why?" she asked. She knew the answer, but she wanted to open the door for him to express it. She kept her question as simple as possible to avoid putting her own words into his head.

"We're running and we're being manipulated," he told her. He looked at her eyes as he spoke. She could see his confidence slowly coming back. "Yet no matter how much we sneak around to avoid the confrontation, it will come. And if we're feeling too comfortable when it does, we lose. That's what happened to Charles and Alex." He paused and looked down at his coffee. "So what if we take a different angle. What if we give Julie the opportunity she's looking for? If we're prepared properly we could break the circle and be free of all this."

It was the same advice she had given many couples during counseling sessions. Avoiding confrontation causes problems to fester until the problems are so massive that nothing can be done to change the situation. This was not a counseling session and the problem with Julie had already grown to threats of violence. But none of that changed the basic truth. The longer they waited the more dangerous the situation would become.

"How do we do it?"

"Our history is pushing us in a direction we haven't chosen, but Julie is a part of that history and she is being pushed every bit as hard as we are. If Glen helps us learn where that direction leads we can be prepared. That's our one advantage"

After breakfast they went back to their room so Stephie could change her shoes. She wanted to switch from her flats to her ankle boots, because they planned to hike some of the local trails. Her jeans were fine, but she changed from her T-shirt to a long sleeve Tee that would protect her arms from low hanging branches. Michael was comfortable with the sneakers and jeans he was wearing, so they were ready to go.

The idea of walking through a wooded area was a strange one considering what they had been through as Charles and Alexandra. It wasn't either Michael's or Stephie's idea. Instead it was something they had come up with together. It had to do with where they were, but it also had to do with something deeper. It was as if sharing this experience might exorcise some demons. Stephie wasn't scared of Julie, because she was confident Michael's ex didn't know where they were. But she was scared of the feelings that might be stirred up as they experienced sensations that were similar to what had happened more than a hundred years earlier.

They talked to the woman at the front desk and found the name of a park with some decent walking trails. It took them about fifteen minutes to find the place, but once they did they parked the car and started hiking right away. The trail was well used, so there was no chance they would lose it and get lost. Most of the leaves had been pushed off into the woods by runners or bikers, but there were still a few scattered on the path. The trail wasn't flat, so Stephie could feel her calves tightening as she went up and down the little ravines. That was good. She liked the exercise.

A girl with a round face, long legs and a thick, dark ponytail jogged passed them and smiled. She looked about high school age and Stephie wondered if she might be on a track team. The girl was wearing a loose T-shirt that flipped up as she ran each step, revealing a tight, well conditioned belly. Stephie's own stomach was almost as flat as the young jogger's, but it wouldn't be that way for long. Her period was about a week late. She didn't know for sure because she hadn't bought a test kit yet, but she believed she was pregnant. Stephie glanced over at Michael to see if the young girl had caught his eye. She hadn't.

Everything about the walk felt good to Stephie and that surprised her at first. But the sensation made sense when she analyzed it. The déjà vu she had expected was of a time when she was being forced to run from the right man. Now she was *with* the right man. It was as if their souls had traveled through time to find each other. Michael was right about doing whatever they could to break the circle.

The trail wound back into the woods and for a time followed along a creek. The path was narrow there, so they had to walk in single file. Michael still held onto her hand. He was in front with his hand behind, so her fingers were interlaced with his and touching the lower part of his back. It was a natural way to touch him, but also very intimate. The sound of the water flowing passed rocks and fallen tree trunks was soothing and the creek smelled sweet, like honeysuckle. Yet when she looked around at the wild plants she could not find any that were fragrant. Perhaps the smell wasn't real. Perhaps it was a memory from her other life.

* * *

After the walk they returned to the motel to wash up. The entire path had been shaded, but it was a warm and muggy day so they had worked up a bit of a sweat. They had hiked for more than two hours.

Stephie fell into a chair as soon as they entered the room. "Do you want the shower first?" she asked.

"We could share." She was glad he said that. His voice was slightly softer than usual with a hint of insecurity, but the man who always wanted to hold her had returned.

"Run a tub instead," she replied, smiling as she spoke.

Michael got into the bath first. Stephie followed, positioning herself between his legs so she could lean back on his chest. He rubbed some soap on her back, her shoulders and her chest. His hands felt smooth and slick, but also strong. His touch was sensual and made all the thoughts of Julie fade away. Then he put his arms around her and settled his hands on her lower belly.

"Someone might be in there," Stephie said, placing her own hands over his and pushing down lightly, "someone who is growing and waiting for the right time to come to us."

"I know — and I dream of that day. But more than that, I swear to you that when it is here we will be ready. Our family will be safe."

"I know we will." Stephie understood that this was a promise from the core of their hearts to the child that would someday be theirs. They would do everything to keep that promise.

Forty-Five

Michael and Stephie made love after their bath, then lay on the bed for a few moments. His hand was in hers, resting on her stomach. Neither of them spoke, while Stephie gently played with his fingers then pushed his hand down her body until it was over her womb. He understood what she was telling him, about the possibility of a baby and what that would mean to the life they shared. He whispered, "I love you," then pulled Stephie on top and kissed her again.

"I don't want to lose the feeling that we're in our own world," Stephie said when they were done kissing. "Let's just eat in the room then spend the rest of the afternoon by the pool." Michael pulled his clothes on and headed out to buy a couple of sub sandwiches. It wasn't until he was in the car that he decided to make a stop at a drug store to pick up a pregnancy test.

When Michael returned he found Stephie in her swimsuit. It was a dark brown one-piece with straight straps and an embroidered pattern of beads at the center of the bust. It wasn't tight and it was cut in a conservative style, a minister's swimsuit, if there is such a thing. Yet she looked fantastic.

"You are like a Hollywood starlet in that suit," he told her as he ran his eyes up and down her body.

She smiled, but didn't say anything.

"I'll set up our table for lunch while you take care of this," he said. He smiled as he handed her the testing kit.

"Oh, Michael, you're kidding. I'll have to take this suit off completely to pee on this thing."

Michael laughed a little as he thought about how some of the older women in the church would react if they heard Stephie talking about *peeing*. Then he thought of how a pregnancy at this time would mean that when the baby was born those same women would be counting the months from the wedding and shaking their heads. They needed to learn that the world had changed, even for ministers. Still, Stephie and he probably wouldn't make too big a deal about the wedding date.

"Taking your suit off doesn't sound too difficult," he told her, "considering all the trouble I went through to get you in this condition."

Stephie rolled her eyes and said, "Right."

"Seriously, the idea of having a child with you is more exciting than anything I can imagine. I can't wait any longer."

"You are sweet, Michael. Have I ever told you that?"

"Not often enough."

"Wait here. I'll do it."

"As if I'm going anywhere…"

Stephie stepped into the bathroom while Michael unwrapped the sandwiches and set them on the table along with the sodas and chips. She came out quicker than he had expected.

"Well?" he asked.

"It takes five minutes. I haven't looked yet."

"I'm sure they mean up to five. If it's positive, it could be showing now."

"I don't want to jinx it."

Michael was in no mood to wait, but Stephie had done the test as he'd asked her to. It seemed fitting that he humor her request.

Michael had asked for mayonnaise and mustard as well as oil and vinegar, so his sandwich was a little soggy. He tried to eat it as neatly as he could, but he wasn't doing a very good job of that. Onions, olives, tomatoes and green peppers were all slipping out from the edges of the bread. Since he didn't have a fork he was picking the toppings up with his fingers and stuffing them back in the sandwich. Meanwhile Stephie was taking delicate bites of her sub and not having any trouble. Hers was turkey breast while his was ham and cheese, but that shouldn't have affected their neatness. Michael thought it was just another indication that she was as perfect as any person could be.

"I guess it's time to look," Stephie said after she glanced at the clock radio. She slid her chair back and walked toward the bathroom. He sat and waited, nervously. It seemed to take her a long time, although it couldn't have been more than a half a minute. She stepped back where she could be seen and said, "Congratulations, daddy, the pink band is as clear as the smile on your face."

Michael jumped up and wrapped his arms around her. He said, "I swear I will protect you both and love you forever." Then he kissed her.

* * *

On the day after the wedding Kathy and Glen drove in the same general direction as Stephie and Michael only they went a little further to the west, to West Virginia where they could spend some time observing the activities of Julie's parents and her brother. They took adjacent rooms in a Days Inn and decided to attempt their first stakeout after dark that evening. They waited for a couple of hours after dinner before Kathy went to spy on the parents and Glen went to Julie's brother's home.

The two houses were in different settings and required very different reconnaissance styles. Julie's parents were still in the home where Julie had grown up and it was still surrounded by woods. Glen left Kathy at the front of the long driveway and watched her walk up it. She was dressed in dark clothes and carried binoculars. Her goal was to find a place where she could be well hidden while she spied through whatever open windows she could find. Glen would pick her up at the foot of the driveway three hours from the time he dropped her off.

While Kathy was trying to learn something about Julie through the activities of her parents, Glen would sit in his car on the street outside Julie's brother's home. He also had binoculars and fully expected that he might have to circle the house on foot, in order to see any activity. The homes of the neighbors were close, so spying on this home would be more dangerous than what he had asked Kathy to do. But the potential to learn something that could lead them to Julie was there, so Glen felt he had to do it. They planned to repeat the same process the following night. Three nights was the limit Glen had set, since each day they stayed increased their chances of being caught. .

He waited in his car until a little after ten. A few people walked by where he was parked without noticing him, but eventually his luck ran out. A heavyset woman who was about forty years old was walking a Shih Tzu with a red ribbon tied at the top of his head. The woman, who was dressed in jeans and a plaid blouse stopped to allow her dog to relieve himself on a small tree. While she was waiting for the Shih Tzu to finish his business she glanced into Glen's car and saw him slouching down in the driver's seat. The woman hustled her pet away as fast as the little dog's legs could move.

Waiting in his car after he had been discovered was foolish, but Glen didn't want to give up on his task. He drove a couple of blocks down the street, turned a corner and parked there. Then he walked back, keeping an eye open for the dog walker or anyone she might have sent out to check on him. He couldn't stay on the street without arousing more suspicion. Instead he circled to the back of the house, hoping he would not be seen by the neighbors. He discovered that he had stumbled into a golden opportunity to learn something about Julie's brother. Trent and his wife were in the middle of an argument. The blinds were drawn so Glen could not see the couple, but he could hear them. He sat down on the ground under the window, leaned against the brick foundation of the house and listened.

"I can't tell you," Trent said.

"That's where the problem is," Dora replied. "We've lost something. There was a time when you could have told me anything. And you did."

"It's something I have to work out on my own."

"Tell me this. Are you having an affair?"

Glen decided that Dora and Trent were alone in the room, given the personal nature of the conversation. He listened for Trent's answer.

"Of course not."

"You can be honest with me. I would much rather you tell me there is someone else in your life than to have you tell me nothing. I can contend with anything other than being closed out."

"There will never be anyone other than you, Christina and Faith. This is something personal. It's something I have to do."

"Oh, God, it doesn't have anything to do with what happened when you were a child, does it?"

"Lots of things happened when I was child."

"You know what I mean, Trent. You're not involved in anything wrong, are you? People who have had that happen to them sometimes fall into similar behavior. You told me so yourself. You didn't do anything wrong, did you?"

"Never, Dora! Never!"

The back door flew open and Trent stepped out. He didn't move off the small back porch. Glen tried to squeeze up next to the house as closely as he could, but there was nowhere for him to go. He was lucky, though. The night was dark and Glen didn't look in his direction.

"Come back and talk to me," Dora told her husband. She wasn't where Glen could see her, but he had a clear view of Trent, a burly man in a green shirt and khaki cargo shorts. Trent had thick, curly hair and an unusual goatee that had two long extensions pointing from his chin to his ears. That part of his beard looked a little like racing stripes. Glen looked away because he was worried Trent would sense him staring. Trent took a couple of deep breaths then went back inside. He left the door open.

Glen rolled to his hands and knees and started to crawl. He made his way around to the side of the house then stood up and walked at an even pace. When he got to the street he started to breathe a little easier. He headed back toward where he had parked. It was time to pick up Kathy. When he reached the car, he dusted the dirt off his pants and got in.

Kathy was standing by the end of the driveway. He glanced at the time on the car radio. He was early by more than fifteen minutes and hadn't expected her to be waiting. He stopped the car and she got in quickly.

"What happened?" he asked.

"It was a total fiasco."

"Someone saw you?"

"I snuck up the driveway and found a spot at the edge of the woods where I could hide fairly well. Julie's parents were in the den and there were no shades on the windows. I could see them perfectly. I thought everything was going well and it was, for a while. But they were watching TV and they didn't move from their spots. It was about as informative as watching grass grow. Then this cat discovered me."

"A cat?"

"That's right, a big tabby that was wandering around their backyard. It didn't have a collar so it might have been a stray. But when it found me it started to meow. It came over to rub against my leg. I pushed it away with my foot, but it kept coming back. And it was making loud noises, not just a purr. If Julie's parents hadn't been so involved in the shows they were watching I'm certain they would have heard it. I was annoyed and scared someone would see me, so I decided to leave. I wasn't getting anything out of watching them sit on the couch anyway. That cat followed me halfway down the driveway. I had to yell at it and even toss a few stones in its direction to get it to stop. It finally turned around and I went out to the street alone. After that I just waited for you to come."

"You did the right thing to get out of there," Glen told her.

"I wonder if there's something about me the cat is attracted to. Maybe the motel soap I used smells like something a cat would eat. You haven't noticed anything, have you?"

"You're asking me if you smell bad?" Glen felt a little awkward with the question, but not as badly as he would have if she did stink. He glanced at her and she nodded. "You're fine. It must have just been a watch cat."

"There's no such thing as a watch cat," she said, laughing. He turned a corner to head back toward the motel, glanced at her again and started laughing with her.

"I don't think we should risk another night like this." he told her, turning serious again.

"What if Julie shows?" she asked.

"The chances of that happening before one of us gets caught are slim at best. We need to rethink our plan."

"We have a plan?"

"Ouch." Glen knew Kathy was kidding, but he also knew there was some truth in her words.

"We learned something through all this," Kathy told him. "We're not detectives, but you have an amazing talent that can teach us more than we could get if we spent a lifetime in the backyards of Julie's relatives. You can tell us what happened before and what's likely to happen again. That's where we need to focus."

Glen knew she was right. But the time wasn't wasted. He had learned that Trent had some issues. That might be useful in the future.

"All right," he said. "We'll head home tomorrow."

Forty-Six

The question that had been bothering Trent since the conversation with his sister was, "Why was Julie with Neil?" His name brought back a flood of horrible memories and the worst was the picture of Julie walking away. She was twelve at that time, still a child. Yet her age seems more of an excuse than a reason. She was Trent's older sister. He depended on her, and all she had to do was scream.

Trent couldn't talk to his wife about the need to have his question answered. Dora believed, rightly, that anything concerning his sister would bring them pain. He knew she would try to prevent him from contacting Julie. He knew her attempts to protect him would lead to arguments that would be much more serious than the ones they had been having lately.

Finding Julie wasn't hard. Neil Raiford was listed in the sex offenders' registry for North Carolina, the second state Trent tried, right after West Virginia. The address of his trailer was listed alongside his crimes, including one conviction for collecting child pornography and one for indecent liberties with a minor. It didn't say if the minor was a boy or a girl.

Trent kept an eye on Neil's home until he saw Julie come out and get into her car. He followed her until she stopped at an Exxon. He pulled his car up to the pump next to hers and said, "We need to talk. Park your car over there." He indicated a place at the side of the convenience store then he pulled into one of the spots there. She hadn't started pumping her gas, so she drove over to the spot next to where he was parked. Julie got out of her car and into his.

"This is a surprise," Julie said. Her voice sounded even and controlled, without a hint of sarcasm.

"Things didn't work out with you and the teacher, right?" Trent didn't give her a chance to respond. "And if things aren't right in your life you want to bring me down. That's what you always do." Trent was trying not to shake but his emotions got the best of his body and he trembled as if he was afflicted with palsy. Meanwhile Julie seemed at ease, sitting beside him as relaxed as she might be in a park on a Sunday afternoon.

"I called because Neil wanted to talk to you, just as I said." Trent heard Julie's words, but he knew she was lying. When Julie was in pain she did everything in her power to push that pain onto others. It was a coping measure and he was her most common victim. She had been doing it for as long as he could remember.

The memory of a young Julie, so many years ago, abandoning him to Neil flashed in his head again. The image made Trent shake and he yelled. "Oh, God, Julie, why him?"

"Not so loud," Julie said, smiling in a way that infuriated him. She was looking at a couple of high school girls who were standing at the gas pumps, staring. But Trent knew she didn't care about making a scene. That wasn't her style. "Neil is someone I can manipulate. That's what I need right now. It isn't always about you."

"You made it about me when you called. This has to do with the teacher, doesn't it?"

"The woman he's with, she was counseling us. Can you believe that? He left me to fuck the counselor."

Trent could hear a level of emotion in Julie's voice that was unusual and unexpected. She had always suppressed her emotions, at least outwardly. This time, her anger was so intense that she was allowing her pain to show. That most likely meant there was truth in what she was saying. The phone call was about him, but her choice to move in with Neil seemed more complicated. "You're planning something?" he asked.

"She was also our minister. She still is his, I suppose. She's his wife now, too. I live with him for years. We go through a little problem, just small stuff. So we set up a counseling session and he ends up marrying the counselor! Don't tell me about problems that happened to you years ago. You have Dora. You have your girls. I'm the one whose life is falling apart." Julie opened the car door and started to step out. "I've got things to do, so I'm going to get my gas then get out of here. You can follow me if you want. I don't care."

Trent sat in his car until his sister left the station. He had contacted her to try to understand why she was hurting him and to plead with her to stop. That would never work, but there might be an opportunity to do something to stop the sense of powerlessness he had lived with for as long as he could remember. He knew Julie. He knew her anger was focused. If what she needed from Neil was an act of violence, as Trent suspected it was, there might be a chance to turn it in a direction Julie didn't want it to go. He intended to keep an eye on them both. Something would come of this mess, something that would finally put an end to it all.

* * *

"We don't want to keep hiding," Stephie said when they were back with Glen and Kathy in the apartment that was once Emily's home. "Michael and I talked it over. We think we can take away Julie's advantage if we learn the time and place of her attack. Hopefully more regressions will show us the way."

Glen agreed. "We can start right now if you're willing."

Michael nodded as Stephie said, "The sooner the better."

They moved to the living room. Stephie took her spot on the couch while Michael and Kathy watched. Kathy took the place where Emily used to sit.

"I'm going to send you back to the life of Charles and Alex," Glen told Stephie. That was exactly what she wanted him to do. "I'll steer you to the time right after Samuel kidnapped Alexandra. Charles was looking for you, but Samuel had a fairly significant head start. All right?"

"Yes." Stephie took a deep breath, lay back and concentrated on the spot in the ceiling that she used for her point of focus. It didn't take long before Alex's memories came flooding back.

* * *

Alex kept turning her head to look back even after her home was gone from her view. She was hoping and praying that she might see Charles on his way to save her, but she didn't. She had been walking for hours and Samuel was still forcing her to keep going. She felt like the little girl in the book she had read many times as a child: *The Red Shoes*. In that story a vain, self centered girl was forced to dance continuously. She understood why that little girl was punished and she wondered if God might be punishing her in the same manner. Her fate seemed to be retribution for the sin she had committed with Charles.

"Step off the road," Samuel ordered. His voice was not bitter or angry. Instead it was flat, almost devoid of emotion.

"Why?"

He pushed Alex toward the woods and threatened her again with his knife. He wasn't going to tell her why, but she learned soon enough. They were hidden behind a tree when a man on horseback went riding by. He was wearing a Union uniform, but she couldn't determine his rank.

Alex had not heard the hoofbeats until minutes after Samuel had. Perhaps he was attuned to the sound, but even if that was so he must have better hearing than she. That was odd considering the fact that he had just been in a battle. Many men hurt their hearing from the noise of a battle. She knew that from her work as a nurse.

Samuel started to push her out of the woods, but he changed his actions quickly and pulled her back. There was another horseman. When he came close enough she recognized Charles on her mother's horse.

Samuel's knife was at Alex's throat before she had a chance to make any noise at all. She wanted to yell. She wanted to go running toward the man she loved, but all she could do was stay in Samuel's grip and hope Charles would discover her.

Charles stopped Hazel and looked toward the woods. But Alex could tell that he was only staring in their general direction as he searched the woods with his eyes. He looked desperate and sad, like a lost boy searching for the path home. She felt her stomach grow tight and her entire body shiver as she watched his head turning slowly. She wanted Charles to see her and come to her, but she was scared of what Samuel might do if she made the slightest sound. There was no choice but to remain quiet. Charles turned his horse in a slow, small circle then headed on in the same direction he had been traveling before he stopped.

Alex had led the life of a righteous young girl for most of her life. She had attended church regularly, including funerals and weddings. She had prayed daily, always being careful to thank God more often than she asked for His help. When the war started she became a nurse because she believed that helping others was what God was calling her to do. Then along came Charles and she was drawn to him from the first time she saw him. He was her gift, a part of her life that was, at the same time, both generous and selfish. She thanked God for Charles in the same way that she had always thanked God each time she was blessed.

The sin of lust was real. She understood that. But Jesus was generous with the woman by the well. Why wasn't God generous with her?

Samuel forced her back to the road and they started to walk again.

* * *

"Why did you pull me back?" Stephie asked when Glen woke her. She sat up on the couch.

"What you were going through was stressful. I was concerned."

"I'm sure Stephie appreciates the concern," Michael told him, "but the stressful situations have all the lessons we need to learn. Alex didn't cry out because Samuel had a knife at her throat. Was that a bad choice? Apparently so, given the way things turned out."

"Send me back," Stephie said.

Michael stood up and touched Stephie's shoulder. He looked at Glen. "Think of the stress Stephie will be under if Julie shows up before we're prepared."

Glen looked over at Kathy who didn't say anything, but nodded to him.

"All right," Glen said, then turning to Stephie he added. "I'll move you forward in time."

* * *

Samuel and Alex were following the Army of the Potomac. They weren't the only ones. In fact there was a large group of camp followers. Alex longed for human companionship other than Samuel, but he kept her some distance from the others. There were primarily two types of women among the followers: laundresses and whores. The women who did the soldiers' laundry appeared as tough as the prostitutes, so Alex wasn't sure she could trust any of them. Samuel had hurt her with rope burns and with the way he often pushed and held her forcefully. He had never carried through on his threats with his knife, but the way he controlled her indicated that he might. She lived her life a day at a time and did not call out to any of the people that were close enough to hear.

There was another reason for Alex's caution concerning Samuel. She wanted to bring her baby into the world so that she, Charles and the child might live a normal life after this mess was over. She was showing, just a moderate bump but enough that people would have noticed if she wasn't wearing a wool coat, one that Samuel had stolen for her. It was a man's coat, but it was warm. That was important since it was now the beginning of November. The leaves had turned bright colors, mostly reds and yellows, but the majority had not fallen yet. This day was bright with just a few clouds and a brisk temperature that felt good on Alex's cheeks and her nose. If she had been with Charles instead of where she was, the day would have been perfect.

"I have to find dinner," Samuel told Alex. They were sitting on a couple of stones near an abandoned farm the followers had taken over. The army had camped in a farm community that had enough open fields to offer plenty of space to pitch tents. The followers were a good distance behind the soldiers, perhaps as much as a mile.

"Nothing there, right?" Alex asked, nodding at the abandoned farmhouse and barn.

"Can't be, not with this many people milling around."

"That's what I thought."

"We're going to have to move further into the woods this time, just to be certain."

Alex had thought that was coming. Compared to where they had been for most of their walk, this was a crowded area. He wouldn't want anyone finding her where he left her. It seemed ironic to Alex that she understood Samuel in ways she might never know Charles.

"We found a moose calf once when we were kids, Charles and I. It was nursing off the body of its dead mama, so it wasn't going to live long. We wanted to bottle feed it to keep it alive. Charles' family had a cow that was giving milk, but his mother said we couldn't share. She said her family needed everything they had. We had to leave the calf where it was even though we knew it would die."

"What's that supposed to mean? I already know what will happen if you don't make it back."

"That isn't what I meant. I'm just saying that I'm not always the person you have to hate. Sometimes things beyond my control define my actions, things like Charles' mother refusing to share with a moose calf or you acting like a dog in heat even after I opened my heart to you. If you want to hate someone, remember that and hate yourself."

Alex got up and started walking toward the woods. There was nothing she could say to that.

Forty-Seven

Three months had passed since Stephie and Michael were wed and Glen performed a regression almost every day of that time. By far the majority of those had been of Stephie, although he sent Kathy back to her life as Margaret a couple of times and Michael back into his memories of Charles three times. The regressions of Kathy and Michael brought a clearer understanding of the frustrations Margaret and Charles felt, but they didn't offer any information that could keep Stephie safe. All four of the friends agreed to concentrate on Alexandra as Samuel continued to hold her by force.

Glen performed the regressions in chronological order, but he skipped periods of time if he thought the opportunity to learn wasn't likely to be there. Stephie could feel everything Alex had felt when she was under Glen's hypnotic state, so she had experienced both pregnancies simultaneously. That was interesting and something no other woman could have ever experienced. But it also doubled all the discomfort and awkwardness of a pregnancy. And it depressed her, because she knew the fate of Alex's child. Yet the experience had a silver lining. It kept her focused on the need to protect her own baby.

"My morning sickness is lasting too long this time," Stephie once complained to her obstetrician, who reacted with some confusion.

"This time?" Dr. Newsome asked.

"I can't remember anyone ever telling me they had experienced it this long." Stephie replied. She hated being deceptive, especially with her doctor, but it was necessary. Dr. Newsome would never, in a thousand years, think of a past life pregnancy, but she might wonder if Stephie had been through a teenage pregnancy. Stephie didn't want her thinking that since it wasn't true.

"It's not at all unusual for nausea to last into the second trimester," Dr. Newsome told her. "Every woman is different."

Stephie noticed other differences. The most prominent of those was the difference in their health. Alex was gaunt and weak. Stephie took vitamins and carefully watched all elements of her diet while Alex ate only food scraps and on most days she did not get enough of those. Alex was also under constant stress. The conditions she lived through were so bad that it was surprising she didn't lose the baby.

The day came when Glen decided to send Stephie back to the birth of Alex's child. He told her that it would be interesting to him because he had already experienced the birth from the perspective of Samuel. Interest was a part of what Stephie was feeling, but only a small part. Mostly she felt scared. She knew Alex's baby would live through the birth, but she had no idea how difficult the delivery would be. Alex was in the most frightening, primitive conditions. Now, more than any other time since she had been abducted, she missed her mother. Stephie could feel the fear that went hand in hand with Alex's loneliness as if it were her own.

* * *

The straw on the barn floor smelled of mildew. It hadn't been tended recently, but it was soft and warm. It was a cool April day and Alex needed the warmth of a bed of straw thick enough to bury her legs in. She and Samuel had walked through the entire winter. She was tired and the cold had been inside her body for so long she often worried it would freeze her baby. That hadn't happen and the child was ready to come out. Her training as a nurse hadn't covered birthing babies, only the specifics of treating wounded soldiers. But her mother had told her about the process. Her mother's efforts prepared her somewhat, but Alex was afraid. She would have been a fool if she hadn't been.

"Can I do anything to help?" Samuel asked. He sounded sincere, but he had treated her like an animal for so long she could only feel hatred toward him.

"You can leave me," she said. "That's what I need."

"Nothing else?"

"Something to tie the chord with, then leave me alone, please. I can't run off. You can see that."

He took one of his laces from his boot and handed it to her then he stepped out of the stall and closed the gate. She knew he was still guarding her from outside the gate, but another contraction came on her. The pain was so intense it was all she could think of.

The barn was made from split logs and seemed to be a good sturdy shelter. It was a clear day, so Alex could not tell if the tin roof leaked. Still, she was more comfortable than she had been in months. She had no underwear on under the mud stained blue dress that Samuel had stolen from some place she couldn't even remember. Since they started to follow the army, they often stopped in places long enough to do a laundry. But the creeks were gathering places and Samuel kept her away from those. Rain was about the only way her clothing was cleaned at all. Her dress was wet this day, but not from rain. Her water had broken about an hour earlier.

It was a surprise that Samuel had allowed her to come to this barn for the birth instead of forcing her to have her child behind some fallen log in the woods. *Thank God for that*, Alex thought. These days it was hard to find anything to thank God for, but her child would be something. She was certain of that.

The stall was larger than ten foot square, perhaps as much as twelve foot. There was no window to the outside. One of the other stalls had a window, but Samuel had chosen this one. She was in no condition to have climbed through it, but that had to be his reason. Along one of the walls there was a wooden hay rack positioned fairly low. Before the war the farmer had most likely kept smaller animals, goats or sheep perhaps. The straw was a sign that there had been animals in the barn. There were also some clusters of pellet droppings.

Alex lay in the straw as a contraction came on her again. It was a strange feeling, as if her body had a mind of its own. They were coming at even intervals now, but still a good length of time apart. Alex knew what to expect. They would come on her more frequently until, as the birth time approached, they would bring on an overwhelming desire to push. She had no hot water or rags. She had nothing but her own body and the straw she lay on. That would have to be enough.

* * *

Stephie was suddenly pulled out of Alex's memories by Glen's urgent voice, finding herself back on the couch. "Come to us, Stephie," Glen was repeating. She opened her eyes to see Michael and Kathy standing beside Glen. The return was abrupt this time and left her feeling as if she were stepping off a carnival ride.

"What happened?" she asked, pushing away the sensation that she was more Alex than herself. She straightened her sweat suit. Apparently, she had been pulling on her loose pants as if they were Alex's skirt.

"You were writhing about," Michael told her. "We were worried about your health. The memories of Alex's contractions could have started your own birth process."

"It's too early for that," she said, sitting up on the couch. She was still groggy, but not so much that she didn't remember four months was too early to give birth.

"We weren't certain, but we were concerned," Glen said. "So we stopped you. I know it must have been difficult. But we had to look out for your baby's health, no matter how jarring it felt to pull you back."

"Thank you for that," Stephie said. The pain had been intense and she had left Alex's memories a good length of time before the actual birth. She was glad the pain would be over until it was her own contractions she was suffering through. There was nothing to learn from experiencing two births, nothing that had anything to do with Julie.

* * *

That evening Stephie lay on her side in bed with Michael's chest pressed softly against her back. She felt his arm reaching over her as he slipped his hand under her cotton gown, reached up and gently rubbed her small baby bump. He squeezed her a little as if to say, "I'm here and I love you." She was happy to be having Michael's baby. He was the perfect man for her: gentle, thoughtful and strong. It made sense that Julie was angry enough over losing him to do most anything.

"I was the one who told Glen to bring you back early," Michael whispered. "He was getting so caught up in the process that he was losing sight of the goal." He paused for a moment. "To protect you," he added.

"You were scared for me?"

"Yes."

He kissed her on the side of her neck. Her head started to swirl a bit. She caught her breath then twisted around so he could reach her lips. He reached up to her breasts and caressed them. She was sore up there, but she could feel how much Michael needed to touch her. The sensation of this wonderful man wanting her was so great she could hardly feel the pain. He pulled her up into a sitting position and lifted her gown over her head. She raised her arms to help, then lay back down on the bed.

He took off the boxers and T-shirt he was wearing before he started to kiss her again. Stephie loved the way Michael's skin felt against hers. She wrapped her arms and her legs around his body and tried to pull his soul into her own. It felt as if she was succeeding.

* * *

When they were done making love Michael rolled off her. They had kicked the blankets off the bed. But even though they remained on their backs lying naked on the single sheet, she wasn't cold. The physical exertion of love-making had left her with a warmth throughout her body. The only way they were touching was by holding hands with their fingers interlaced, but the sensation of being one with Michael remained in Stephie's heart and she knew from past experience that it would stay there in a way that would sustain her through whatever she had to face.

"Tomorrow I want to jump forward to the battle," Stephie told Michael.

"Where Alex dies?"

"Yes."

"You know what Glen says about that. He wants to keep the experience chronological, so we can understand it the way Alex understood it."

"I'm tired of waiting. I don't feel any more prepared for Julie than we were three months ago."

Michael released her hand, sat up on the side of the bed and reached for his boxers. "You're right," he said, as he stood up and started to dress. "We'll talk to him tomorrow."

Forty-Eight

The next day's regression started at a different point than Stephie had expected. Glen agreed to skip to the battle scene as she and Michael requested, but, when the regression started, Stephie found herself tied to a tree, waiting for Samuel to come back with stolen food and clothing. She could hear the fighting off in the distance, but it wasn't where she was. That meant she wasn't where she expected to be. This memory was also different from what she had expected because of the appearance of a woman.

* * *

"What's this?" the woman asked, stepping into view from behind a large boulder. Alex had seen her before. She was a middle aged camp follower, someone who made her living washing the soldiers' clothes in the creeks. After Samuel killed the woman with the barrel, Alex lost hope of being discovered. Ever since that confrontation he took her deeper into the woods, to tie her far from the traveled paths. But this day was different than the others. There was the sound of gunfire, just as there had been at Gettysburg. And there was also the smell of smoke. A battle was going on and Alex was certain that the woman was looking for a place to hide.

"Help us please," Alex said, but she was gagged so her words were inaudible. "Help us," she repeated.

"Sakes alive, young lady, what are you doing like this? And with a child by your side?" The woman tried to untie the gag, but the knot was too tight. "Hold on there. I can get this off you." She pulled a knife out of her skirt pocket and cut the material Samuel had tied across Alex's mouth.

"You found us. Thank you so much."

"I wasn't looking for you."

"Nobody was. That's why I'd given up hope. But here you are. Untie my hands before he comes back. I'm worried about my daughter. She could be cold on the ground like that."

"Before who comes back?"

"Samuel, the man who kidnapped me and tied me here."

"What if the child needed you? You couldn't help her with your hands tied."

"He knows that."

"There had to be a reason he would do this to you, especially with the baby." There was some confusion in the woman's voice. Alex could tell she was wary about helping the wrong person. There was a war going on.

"He had his reasons, but they weren't my fault. You're doing a good thing. I'm not a criminal or a spy. You have my word."

"A spy's word doesn't mean much."

"If I were a confederate I wouldn't be tied up here, I'd be turned in to the army." Alex knew the camp followers stayed alive by backing the union. "Samuel claims he loves me and this is how he shows it. Please help us. If you wait too long he'll be back."

"Oh, yes. I've seen that kind of love. Let me work on those ropes."

For a short time Alex had some hope, but the timing wasn't good. Samuel was already back. He jumped out from behind the same boulder that had hidden the woman. His Bowie knife was drawn. The woman was on her knees, so it was easy for him to pull her by her hair and slice her neck. She was dead before she could have known what was happening. Alex screamed and the baby started to cry.

"Quiet! Both of you!" Samuel flashed the bloody knife in Alex's direction. She caught her breath and stopped yelling, but she couldn't control the baby. Samuel' eyes were wide and he was panting as if he had just run ten miles. He was looking down at the child.

"Leave her!" Alex yelled. "Untie me. I'll keep her quiet."

"We've got to get out of here now!"

It took Samuel very little time to get the rope off Alex and to coil it so he would have it when he needed it again. As soon as she was untied, Alex comforted her daughter who stopped crying in her mother's arms. Alex had chosen the name Charlotte, in honor of Charles. But she didn't say it out loud, because she feared the name would make Samuel violent. Instead she used terms such as "her" and "she" and "my daughter." Those words felt good when she said them, but sometimes she whispered Charlotte's real name. Her little girl was all Alex had of Charles and could be all she would ever have. It felt good to say her name out loud.

Samuel wiped his knife with a handful of dead leaves then put it back in its sheath. He grabbed Alex by her arm and forced her to move. She didn't try to resist. "This way," he told her. They started walking in the direction of the gunfire. They left behind the crumpled body of the woman who had tried to help her.

They moved closer to the road, but stayed in the woods. They couldn't walk the road because there were too many union soldiers, all moving at a fast pace and all headed for the sound of the battle. Samuel kept following and didn't even stop when the woods turned into an open farm field. Some of the soldiers looked in their direction. A woman moving toward the fight with a child in her arms was a strange sight. Yet although many men looked in her direction, none stopped to ask if she understood the danger. Perhaps it was because Samuel was keeping her some distance from the soldiers. Perhaps it was because the men were all thinking of the fight they were approaching. Or perhaps it was because Samuel was with her and moving forward with determination. This was true until they reached a ford in the river.

The troops were consolidating at a narrow crossing in what seemed to be a fairly powerful river. Shore to shore was no more than thirty to forty feet. Alex remembered the last time Samuel had forced her to cross a river. That was when she had told him she was pregnant and he had responded with anger, forcing her into the water. At that time she would never have believed her situation could be worse.

"Don't go over there, ma'am," a soldier called to her. He was standing on the other side of Samuel.

"She'll do what I say," Samuel said to the man. "You fight the war. We're both on the same side."

Alex wasn't sure why Samuel added the last part. He must have been trying to imply that they had some purpose related to the war effort. Who would believe that, with a baby in her arms? She should have spoken up, but she had been scared into total submission for so long there seemed to be no other choice.

The soldier turned and took a step toward her, but one of the others turned him back and pushed him toward the river. "Think of the child," he yelled as he stepped into the river.

The growth had been thick on both sides of the river, but the soldiers had trampled on most of the brush. There were a couple of places where the shore protruded out into the water. Alex and Samuel followed some men over one of those and stepped into the flowing water. It wasn't deep. Alex could see from those around her that at the deepest part it only came up to their mid thighs. For the first few steps she held her skirt up a little with her left hand while she held Charlotte with her right. The current wasn't fast, but it was strong enough to make her uneasy. She let her skirt drop into the water so she could hold her baby with both hands. She made it across without falling, although she was soaked by the time she was on the shore. Unfortunately, Samuel also made it across.

The soldiers were running now, so they did the same. The gunfire was louder than anything Alex had heard at Gettysburg. She had been in the field hospital during that battle, now she was in the middle of the fighting. The heat and smoke from the fires were intense and Charlotte was crying loudly. Alex held her baby against her wet dress in hopes of cooling her somewhat, but the effort was in vain. They were walking toward the fire while it was burning toward them.

"I'm not going on!" Alex shouted. "I'd sooner risk your knife than what's ahead of us."

"Then here is where we'll stay."

"Why?" Alex had long since given up asking Samuel that question, but it came out this time because what he was forcing her to do was lunacy. They had to shout at each other just to be heard.

"After all these months you still don't understand?"

Alex shook her head to let him know that *understand* was a word she had given up a long time ago.

"When we first started out I didn't know where we were going. I kept moving because it was the only way I could think of keeping you with me. Then our path crossed the path of the soldiers and I knew they would lead us to our destiny. We're close enough to the fight now. The battle will reach us here and it will test us. If you die, I will go with you. I'm ready for that, if it is God's will. But I lived through one battle and we may live through this one. I hope so. If it happens we'll be purified in a way you can't understand yet, not until you've lived it. Life will be precious. We'll go forward without any thought of our past. I've been there. I know how it works. We will start over— you, me and Charles' bastard. We'll raise her as our own. This battle is God's blessing. It will tie you to me in a way my rope never could."

The sound of the fighting and the heat of the fire told Alex that it was no time to tell Samuel how insane he was. She turned away. She couldn't stand to look at him.

Alex saw three or four confederates passing by. They fired in her direction. But if they were aiming at her, they were poor shots. She saw a union soldier raising his rifle to shoot, probably at the Rebs who had just passed. She thought it was the man who had briefly tried to help her at the river, but that could have been her imagination.

Charlotte was crying, so Alex sat on the ground and held her to her breast. She started to sing to her daughter. "In Scarlett town where I was born there was a fair maid dwellin'." It was *Barbara Allen*, a folk song that Alex knew well enough to sing most of the words. Through the few short months Charlotte had been alive, Alex had sung it to her repeatedly. Now it was the only balm Alex had to ease her daughter's fear, and she would use it.

The confederates came back. Alex saw them and thought they were the same young men who had passed by a few minutes earlier. They were all still alive and she was glad of that. One of the soldiers raised his rifle and pointed it at her. Alex twisted her body to protect Charlotte. There was a loud crack then everything went black.

* * *

"Come back!" Glen shouted. "Come back now!"

Stephie opened her eyes slowly, her head swirling. Michael went to her and stroked her hair.

Glen spoke again. "I let you go on too long. I shouldn't have done that. Alex's death was too powerful a memory for you to experience. I made the same mistake with Emily once."

Stephie had a lump in her stomach, one so tight it felt like a knot in the rope Samuel used to tie Alex. And her stomach was the only part of her body she could feel. Her arms and legs were weak, and her head was swirling like water in rapids. She heard Glen's words, but she knew he was wrong. He was right to let her go on that long. "I was never so scared in my life," she told him, as she moved her feet to the floor and slowly sat up on the couch. Michael helped her then took the seat beside her. "But we had to go there," she continued. "It was the point where the circle comes together. Still, I never want to feel anything like that again."

"Never again," Michael told her as he put his arm around her. His touch made her feel more secure.

"Can I get you anything?" Kathy asked. "Coffee perhaps?"

Glen turned to Kathy. "Good idea. Why don't you put on a pot? There are danishes above the refrigerator." She stepped out of the living room into the kitchen and he turned back to Stephie and Michael. "Let's run through what we know. Think about every regression we've done, what's the same and what's different."

Michael answered first. "One thing that's different is that Julie is a woman and Samuel was a man. That has to affect their decisions."

"I'm not sure it does," Stephie said. "Women can be just as aggressive, especially women like Julie. But there's another, related difference that I think is crucial. Samuel was in love with Alex, while Julie was in love with Michael. How do we know I am the one she'll come after?"

"We don't," Glen told her, "but we know you're the one she'll hurt." His words made Stephie cringe. He kept on talking. "Remember this isn't about just you two. It's the mother and daughter bond that's at the center of the circle. It's about Charlotte's relationship with Alex, Emily's relationship with Mary and your relationship with the child you're carrying. That's where gender is important. Michael can be there for you, but he can't be you."

"But Emily didn't die," Stephie said.

"Part of her did," Kathy said as she stepped back into the living room. The coffee had started to brew, filling the apartment with a pleasant aroma.

Stephie knew her friend was right. Emily was alone throughout most of her long life. There might have been multiple reasons for that, but growing up without her mother was one of them.

"Alex was kidnapped and held for months before she died," Michael said. "That didn't happen to Mary and hasn't happened to Stephie. Could that be a difference in the thought patterns of men and women?"

"You're harping on one thing," Kathy told him.

"That's a good thing," Glen said. "We have to harp on every detail we can think of. What else was different?"

"Mary and Anne weren't in a war zone," Michael told him, "unless you consider bootlegging to be a private war."

"Also Julie likes guns and Samuel used a knife," Stephie added.

"A weapon's a weapon," Kathy said.

"Tell that to the people of Hiroshima," Michael said sarcastically.

Stephie could tell he was irritated over Kathy's remark about harping. "Take it easy," she scolded them both. "We have to work together on this."

"What about similarities?" Glen asked. "We know both Alex and Mary were killed and we know that the killers were not Samuel and Anne. I think that's important. Someone's going to be with Julie and *that's* the person we need to watch."

"The bonfire!" Michael said. His head went up with a start as he spoke. Stephie could tell that he had an idea he thought was important.

"What are you talking about?" Kathy asked.

"The forest was burning around Alex when she died and Mary was killed near the campfire Anne and Edwin had started. There's got to be a connection."

"Oh, my God," Kathy said. "You're right. There was fire in another regression, too, the one where Glen sent me to Africa. Stephie's soul was in a woman named Onye, who died when fire was being used to drive animals into traps."

"You're talking about the pep rally, aren't you?" Stephie asked Michael. His idea had become clear to her and it made sense.

"Yes," Michael told everyone. "It's to be held at the high school in about two and a half weeks. They do it every year, to raise support for the first home football game. There will be a giant bonfire. The place will be filled with high school kids who won't be paying attention to anything other than having fun."

"And Julie knows about it?" Glen asked.

"Of course she does," Michael answered. "She helped organize the last two. She was the one who suggested the fireworks last year."

"Fireworks?!" Glen and Kathy exclaimed at the same time.

A shiver ran up Stephie's spine. She glanced down at her belly, wondering if her baby was far enough along to have felt her fear. She hoped not.

Forty-Nine

Trent tore open the plastic bag to pour the garbage into the motel bathtub. The contents smelled, as they had each of the other nights, mostly of stale beer. Along with a half dozen empty Miller cans there were two catfish skeletons and paper, lots of paper. Much of the discarded paper was crumpled napkins or towels smeared with catsup or syrup, but there were also receipts and bills. Those were among the items that held promise. There were gas and grocery receipts from the Exxon station and Food Lion that gave a few hints about how Neil and Julie were living. This day he wasn't as lucky as he had been a few days earlier when he had found a receipt for ammo from a firearm store on the opposite side of the interstate. Apparently one of the two had a 45 millimeter handgun. He could get one of those without any trouble at all.

They didn't have garbage pickup. Instead, Julie made two runs each week to the roadside dumpsters. She was a creature of routine which made it easier for Trent to be there when she arrived. He would watch from the woods then, when his sister had left, he would walk out, take the bag and head back to where he had left his car. It was simple to pick the one she had dropped off. It was always the white bag on the top of the pile, the one with the cans in it.

The next things Trent found were the two torn halves of a grease-soiled letter. The letter was on high school stationary. *Dear Julie,* it read. *It was good to hear from you yesterday. I checked on this year's bonfire. It's scheduled for Friday night, October eighth, like I thought. They're supposed to light it at nine o'clock. I hope you can make it. It will be good to see you again and catch up. Michael Stuart has been involved in the planning of the pep rally, just as you thought, so he'll definitely be there that night. See you then. Sincerely, Kim.*

Julie had kept in touch with someone she used to work with. She wasn't the type to hang onto old friends, so Trent knew she had a purpose and keeping up with her old boyfriend had to be it. She was most likely going to the bonfire to harass the guy. If so, she would bring Neil along, who would be good at harassing. Trent was pleased that he had figured out their plans, but the bad memories that came with any thought of Neil also brought a chill that stopped Trent's smile.

* * *

The thought of putting Stephie at risk made Michael feel as if he were cutting into his own heart, but he knew her life would be in more danger if they did nothing. The new school year had started so Michael and

Stephie had to arrange their meetings with Glen and Kathy around Michael's teaching schedule as well as Stephie's work at the church. The four friends spent as many evenings as possible in Glen's living room, running through every scenario they could think of. Michael also spent extra time at his school because he had volunteered to help organize the planning for this year's bonfire. He did that to be sure they would know what to expect that night.

"Should we buy a bullet proof vest?" Kathy asked during one of their planning sessions. Michael appreciated the suggestion, but Glen shook his head.

"She would look odd if she covered it with a coat, since she will be standing by a bonfire. For this to work, we can't do anything even remotely suspicious. If Julie sees something that tips her off, the circle won't come together. That doesn't mean it won't ever. It just puts the event off until a day when we aren't prepared and that wouldn't be good for us."

The details made Michael shake. The more he heard, the more it seemed that all they would be doing would be hoping for the best, while Stephie was out there risking her life. Once again their souls had found each other, just as they had in countless other lives, and once again their happiness would be cut short. What good was it to know, if there was nothing that could be done? "How do we protect her?" he asked.

"I'm certain Julie will show," Glen said. "We have to be prepared to act if anything starts. That's what it comes down to."

"And although we'll be looking for Julie," Kathy said, "the person we have to stop will be someone else, someone with her. Samuel didn't kill Alex, one of the confederate soldiers did. And Anne didn't kill Mary, Edwin did."

Glen added, "There's consistency, which is good. It's our edge."

It was clear that Stephie was scared. She had been quiet most of the evening. Michael took her hand and squeezed it to let her know he would do anything he could to protect her. She held on tightly. Michael knew that Stephie's faith enabled her to get through situations that would break other people.

Michael hadn't told anyone this, but he would have a handgun by the evening of the bonfire. He had already bought it and was waiting the required thirty days before he could pick it up. He didn't know how to use it, but he planned to take a class at a gun range to learn the basics. That would force him to make up a story so Stephie wouldn't suspect. He hated lying to her, but not nearly as much as he hated being unprepared to protect her. Fate had put her in a horrible circumstance. Michael would do whatever he had to do to get her through it unharmed.

"It won't look suspicious for us to stay by Stephie's side," Michael said. "You're her friends and I'm her husband. It would look strange if we did anything else. So I say we arrive together, stay in a group and keep our eyes open."

Michael thought of the Secret Service and wanted to say he would take a bullet for Stephie, but that sounded too macho. Besides, he knew any one of them would, if the situation reached that point. Kathy loved her almost as much as he did. And Glen knew that Stephie was the key to breaking the circle. Her life would affect what happened to all of them in the next life and all the lives that followed.

* * *

Stephie lay in bed that night with Michael by her side. His lower leg was touching her calf in a familiar, gentle manner that was intimate, yet apparently unintentional. His steady breathing indicated he was asleep. Sometimes she would try to stay awake, so she could enjoy this quiet time with the love of her life resting beside her. Even if things didn't work out and her life was cut off too soon, she was still lucky to have had Michael in it, as well as the other friends that stood by her.

Her thoughts drifted to Kathy and to a February night back in college when the two young women stayed in the library until they were chased out at midnight. They talked as they walked back to their dorm, carrying their books. It was a cold night. The campus was quiet, but Stephie could see some activity in the lighted rooms they were passing. She remembered the long, warm jacket she wore that night. Wearing that coat on a cold night made her feel as if she were in her own world. Kathy was also wearing a heavy coat and might have felt the same way. Stephie thought at the time it was the mellow sense of being alone and apart from the rest of the world that led to their conversation. Now she knew better.

Kathy spoke quietly as they walked, "Sometimes I feel as if all that truly matters in this life is you and me, as if we are the same flesh and blood. I feel a connection with you I don't feel with anyone else, even when we're just sitting in the library with our noses buried in our books."

"I was working on my report for Western Civilization, so I was more connected to William the Conqueror than you." Stephie said with a giggle in her voice. "But I do know what you mean. We're best friends forever, you and I. That will never change."

Stephie had used humor to shrug off Kathy's attempt to say something important. Now, looking back on that night, she felt as if she had betrayed her friend. That intimacy, that important relationship their souls held with each other, was back and Kathy was once again the one reaching out, this time potentially with her life.

Stephie rolled onto her side to try to get some sleep. But when she did, she felt how her womb had begun to grow and thought of Emily. Was she back, inside Stephie's body? If so, Stephie was certain that what they were about to go through was critical to the soul that would someday be her daughter. Before she allowed herself to drift off to sleep, she prayed, as she always did. Her prayers were for herself, for Kathy, Michael and Glen, and for the child growing inside of her. She prayed for survival, but more than that, she prayed for an eternity that could hold a promise of peace and joy for all of her spiritual family.

Fifty

Fear began to take over Stephie's every thought. She was ineffectual at work and Tom, the church's senior minister, had to speak to her about it. He asked if she was all right. "I am," she lied. She could tell from his expression that he wasn't fooled. She was supposed to preach on the Sunday of the week before the bonfire, but he didn't bring it up and she pretended she had forgotten. Stephie could not sleep at all on the night before the bonfire. So on top of everything else, when that evening arrived she was exhausted.

Stephie's pregnancy was just under five months along. In her case that was far enough to show. Although she wasn't wearing maternity clothes, the choices she could make from her wardrobe had been limited by her increasing size. She had two pairs of jeans she could get away with if she left them unsnapped and if she wore long tops to cover them. The evening of the bonfire she had on one of those long tops, a large T-shirt from the church's last fall festival. She wore sweat pants with it. She wanted to have on loose clothing in case she was forced to run or jump from trouble.

Michael could not take off from school on the day of the bonfire, because he had volunteered to work on the preparations. "I'm going to know that area better than I know our own house," he told Stephie. "I'll check out how high the wood for the fire is piled and walk around the entire field looking for any spots where Julie might hide. We're going to come out of this all right. I promise."

"Thanks," she said in a voice that was meeker than she had intended. *Thanks* wasn't what she wanted to say, not at all. She wanted to hang on to Michael and keep him in her arms until the nightmare was over. But she knew he was doing what he had to do. Instead of screaming out a protest, she told him goodbye as if it were any other day. She went to the kitchen to fix a cup of coffee. When she stepped into the room she found she couldn't bear to go through the routine of making a pot. She sat at the kitchen table, put her head down and prayed.

* * *

Michael's classes blended together that day like mud. He was working on a lesson on the Soviet Union and twice had to be corrected for confusing Kruschev with Brezhnev. *What difference does it make?* he thought. All he had on his mind was the night they were about to go through. Among the four friends he was the one who knew Julie best. He would be the one with the most responsibility. If he failed to react then Stephie would die.

The field where the bonfire was to occur was on the north side of the school, next to the football field. There would be lots of places to hide: a tall row of Leyland Cypresses, cars that would be in the parking lot, stadium stands and a wooden fence around the school dumpsters. Michael walked along the chain link fence that separated the stands from where he was, checking it for places someone could crawl through if they wanted to badly enough. He found two. The first one had been repaired, but it looked as if a sharp pull would break the repairs. Two people could get through the other break if one held the fence back while the other crawled.

Michael went back to his car to get some tools and heavy wire he had brought along for this purpose. He would keep them from using those places, but there were kids in the school who could break through if they wanted to. And as soon as they did, the entire area under the stadium seats would be open to Julie. He would have to keep an eye on it along with the other places.

There was no way Michael could predict what kind of cars would be in the lot that night, so there wasn't much he could do to prepare for that. He was most frightened by vans and SUVs. He would have to keep an eye open for them, too. Maybe Glen or Kathy could do that. He walked around the Leyland Cypresses and the dumpsters. There were some scary aspects to both those areas. A few of the Leyland Cypresses were close enough to the school to provide a place where someone could hide without being seen and the dumpsters were covered by a wooden, slat fence that someone could hide behind while looking at people through the cracks.

"Mr. Stuart," a girl's voice called to him from across the yard. It was Kate Bennett, a sophomore who was on the bonfire committee. "Do you want to inspect the wood?" One of his roles was to make certain they didn't have any precarious logs that might roll toward students after the fire was lit. He begrudgedly left the dumpsters and walked toward the students.

* * *

"This is crazy," Neil told Julie as he turned the car down Roosevelt Street toward the high school. "I've got a record. They'll throw away the key if someone catches us."

"You're scared?" She knew he'd never admit to fear.

"No way. It's just that everything is wrong with this. I'm not supposed to be anywhere near a school. Being there is enough to get me locked up. Bringing a gun is asking for real trouble."

Julie had expected this discussion. Neil would agree to most anything from a distance, but when he started getting close he had to be convinced.

"You said you'd do whatever I asked. You want me to lift my shirt and show you the bruises. You broke skin, you know."

"I said I was sorry." She had him when he told her that.

"Words are cheap," Julie said. They were both silent as Neil drove the car into the school lot and took a spot beside a Mustang. "Remember the plan. I'll point out Michael and Stephie then all you have to do is scare the shit out of them. You're not to hurt anyone. Show them the gun somehow. Make them think you're going to shoot. That's all I ask. If you fire it without getting caught or accidentally hitting anyone, that would be good. But I don't expect you to do that."

Two boys pulled a Honda Civic into the spot on the other side of their car. One of them glanced at Neil as they got out.

"He saw me," Neil said. Julie had to reassure him again.

"People are going to see us. That's more my worry than yours, since I know most of them. But it doesn't matter. If we follow the plan we'll be alright. Just follow the plan."

They walked into the crowd. Julie noticed there were a few cops watching over the students, but there was no metal detector. That would have been a game changer.

* * *

There had been times in Trent's life when the anger had subsided a little. Dora brought him those periods of peace and after Christina and Faith had come along, they helped as well. But despite the blanket of calm that covered his fury, he always knew it was there. When Julie brought Neil back into his life, she pulled that blanket off and exposed his naked rage. He knew the time had come to do something. This evening, he would have a chance to put an end to the monster who had forced him to live his life with a constant sense of shame. If things went right, the police might think Neil killed himself or maybe that Julie did it. If they figured out the truth, he would have to pay the price. But anything would be better than allowing Neil to go on living.

* * *

Kathy drove to the bonfire with Glen, Michael and Stephie, so she would be by Stephie's side the entire evening. She would put the safety of her friend over her own. She made that promise to herself enough times that it had become a mantra. Protect Stephie. Protect Stephie. Protect Stephie.

Margaret had not been able to do anything after Samuel took Alex away. When Kathy came out of the regressions she had brought that sense of impotence back with her, like a mother sending a child off to war. This time things would be different.

Michael parked the Grand Prix and they all got out. Students were swarming all over the field. There were students in cheerleader outfits intermingled with the others. There had to be football players in the crowd as well. They weren't wearing jerseys but Kathy had a good idea who they were based on their size. She wished she could recruit a few of them to protect Stephie.

It was about eight-thirty. The fire was set to be lit around nine. The sun had set about an hour and a half earlier, so all twilight was gone. But the lights around the school field were on. They could see well enough. They joined the crowd of people heading up to where the fire would be lit.

* * *

Here we go, Glen thought as he watched Michael light the fire. The flames took off quickly because the wood had been soaked with kerosene. Glen turned toward Stephie and studied her for a moment. She seemed to be concentrating. Her eyebrows were down, her brow slightly furrowed and she was holding her head low, so her long, black hair blocked part of her face. He hoped she wasn't planning too much. She needed to react rather than plan. That was critical. Hopefully, the extra weight she was carrying wouldn't slow her responses. He knew she'd been exercising, trying to keep in good shape. That would help.

Glen looked down at Stephie's swollen belly. The baby wasn't born yet. That was a substantial difference between this go round and both Alex's and Mary's. He wasn't sure if that would change the situation too much. Emily had lived decades after her mother was killed, but with the quality of her life destroyed. Charlotte had lived only a few minutes longer than Alex. Those were very different situations, so it probably wasn't a critical aspect of the circle. This time, if Stephie was killed the fetus would go with her and that meant Emily would miss out on her next life entirely. Glen would do everything he could to keep that from happening.

286

The fire was burning strong now and the smell of smoke was everywhere. Glen was still looking at Stephie. He could see the flames in her dark eyes. He wondered how much of Stephie's natural beauty the next Emily would inherit— if she was born. The band started to play the school pep song while the cheerleaders and some of the students sang. The tune was "On Wisconsin" with the high school name substituted in place of Wisconsin. That wasn't very original.

Michael came back to the group after fulfilling his obligation to supervise the lighting of the fire. "What next?" he asked Glen.

"We wait and we watch."

* * *

They were standing in the crowd of students, about three rows back. There were lines of traffic cones and a group of teachers keeping the students away from the flames, but Stephie could feel the heat. It was intense on her front while her back remained cool, as if she were being grilled. The sensations took her back to what she felt as Alex no matter how hard she tried to resist the fear. It seemed as if images of Charlotte were floating among the flames, crying out for her mother to save her. Stephie turned her face away from the flames and reached down to touch her belly. Her T-shirt was damp. She was sweating more than she had realized and more than anyone else since she was pregnant. Stephie felt a flutter as her baby seemed to move a bit. It was foolish to believe that the baby was reacting to the heat because she was kept at a constant temperature inside Stephie's body. Still, Stephie couldn't help but think that her child was trying to communicate the only way she could.

"I need to move back from the fire," Stephie told Michael. "It's too much for me."

"You're safe in this crowd."

"Exactly why we need to move," Glen said. "We're not here to avoid the attack. We're here to meet it and win."

Stephie understood Glen's need to treat things clinically, but this was her life they were talking about. She wished he would show a little more compassion. Michael took her hand and started to walk out of the crowd. He was different. He always showed compassion. It was also good that Michael was leading because the students knew him and quickly moved out of his way.

* * *

"Who is that?" Kathy asked. Most of the teachers were alone, but this was an adult couple. They looked as if they were in their early thirties. Kathy was the only one of the foursome who had never met Julie. She had seen photos, of course, but that was different from meeting someone in person.

"Where?" Glen asked, but the couple disappeared behind the pep band before Kathy could point them out.

"I lost them. They moved to the other side of the fire. I think they were looking at us."

"Michael's a teacher," Stephie said. "Lots of people are looking at him."

"I know," Kathy told her. "But this couple was too old to be students. Does it make sense that Julie would be here with someone else?"

"Someone's got to pull the trigger," Glen said as he started to walk in the direction Kathy had indicated.

Kathy looked over at Stephie after Glen spoke and noticed that her friend seemed to catch her breath. But Michael and Stephie followed Glen, so Kathy did the same.

* * *

Trent saw Neil and Julie and knew his theory about their plans was correct. He recognized the intensity that took over his sister's body whenever she was competing. There had to be a good reason for Julie to be wandering around the schoolyard with a pervert by her side. She had to be seeking revenge.

He touched the gun on his hip. He was wearing a loose pair of jeans with an elastic waistband and no belt. He could pull his .45 without too much trouble, but that would take some time. He would need to have it drawn when the opportunity came for a clear shot at Neil.

He noticed a group of four adults who seemed to be following Neil and Julie. Two of them had to be the teacher and his wife. Trent had no idea who the other two were.

* * *

The band was playing "We Will Rock You" while the cheerleaders led the singing. Everyone seemed to know the words. That didn't surprise Stephie, since all they sang was the chorus, which was just one sentence. Stephie felt a desire to sing, but not something hard and furious like that song. She wanted to clear her head of anything like that type of music and fill it with "Barb'ry Allen," as Alex had. She tried to hum the old folk song, but it was hard to do with students around her shouting out the other tune. Yet she persisted. From her baby's inside perspective, anything she was humming would drown out the angry music.

Three of the cheerleaders were holding a fourth above their heads, supporting her by one of her legs. The girl they had up in the air had her free leg bent and her arms spread in a wide V. She stayed up there until the "Rock You" song was done then she yelled, "Go Rebels" and jumped down.

Glen turned abruptly toward Michael and asked, "The team name is Rebels?"

"That's right. I hadn't thought about it before. Does it mean anything?"

"Another sign, I suppose."

Stephie believed in signs and prayed they would get one soon that told them this night would not be a replay of what had happened so many times before.

* * *

As the group of four followed the woman they thought could be Julie and the man she was with, Glen noticed something that was more important than a sign. There was a husky man with a distinctive beard who seemed to be walking in the same direction they were headed. The beard was a goatee with side extensions that could best be described as racing stripes. Even from a distance that man's identity was clear.

"There's someone else here," Glen said to Kathy who was walking next to him. The other two were a couple of steps in front.

"Who?"

"Julie's brother. I can't point him out because he can see us, but I saw him up close when we were in West Virginia and there is no question that he's the man I see now."

Kathy reached out to put her hand on Stephie's shoulder. When Stephie and Michael stopped walking, Glen explained the situation. "I'm going to keep an eye on him," Glen told them. "He could be important."

"As important as Julie?" Michael asked.

"I believe so."

Glen stayed back as the others resumed searching for Julie. He noticed that Trent had kept walking while they were talking. He seemed to be following someone. *Like a Rebel tracking a Yankee,* Glen thought.

* * *

Michael led Stephie and Kathy around the row of Leyland Cypresses and straight into the presence of Julie. The man she had been walking with was standing beside her with a large pistol drawn. It was pointed in their direction. He held it by his hip, apparently to keep it from being seen by anyone who might peek around the trees. There had to be over two hundred people in the field, but on this side of those tall hedges it was just them— face to face with Julie and the man with the gun. Michael stepped in front of Stephie then he looked to both sides for help. That was useless. The first of the fireworks went off at that time and Michael knew the sound would cover gunshots. The situation couldn't get worse.

Julie smiled. "There's something you need to know, Michael. I'm different than I used to be, a little crazier I suppose. But that's my advantage. Welcome to your new reality. It's very simple, really. This is Neil. He's my friend. He and I are going to be watching you, always. And one of these days you and your little preacher are going to be sorry for what you did."

Julie stepped away from Neil and slipped between the first two Leyland Cypresses. Neil cocked his head slightly, but kept smiling and staring. Then, after he had given Julie a little time to get away, he turned and walked quickly in the direction she had gone.

"Are you all right?" Michael asked. "Both of you?"

"A little shaken, that's all," Stephie told him. Kathy nodded in agreement.

Facing a man with a gun was something Michael had done before, at Gettysburg. The memories from that regression were whirling through his mind. He was Charles back then and Julie had been with him, as Samuel. In that war they were on the same side. He had even risked his own life to save Samuel's. So much had happened since then, in all their lifetimes. Michael hugged Stephie then reached in his pants for his pocket holster and took out the small pistol he had there.

Stephie gasped. "No, Michael. When he sees that he'll kill you." She reached for his gun, but he pulled it back.

"I'm going to protect you."

"They said they'll be watching," Kathy told him. "What do you suppose they'll do when they see you have a gun?"

"I won't let Julie scare us."

"You say so," Kathy said, "but she's been watching you both for months and she's been pretty good at scaring you so far."

"Maybe it's over," Stephie said. "Maybe the circle broke when Neil didn't pull the trigger."

"I don't think so," Michael told her. "Glen said to expect a close call and that was just another threat. We've got to find them again."

"You need us to go with you?" Kathy asked, her voice ringing.

"The way this thing works Stephie has to be there, but you have a choice. I'm hoping you'll make the right one. We can use your eyes."

"Don't," Stephie said to her friend. "Get away from this place. We'll be all right."

"I'm coming with you," Kathy told them both.

Charles knew how to handle a gun, Michael thought as he led the two women back toward the crowd of students. *That knowledge will come back to me, because I need it. I'm going to protect Stephie and get those sons-of-bitches without waiting until the next time the damn circle comes round.*

*　　*　　*

Stephie saw the scared looks on the faces of the students they passed. Michael had his gun hidden under his shirt, so that wasn't what was causing them to react. It had to be the intensity of his expression and his body language. They didn't run; they just stared at him with their jaws dropped. The fireworks were in full force now. Sometimes they were green, sometimes red or blue. They changed the color of everything under them.

Stephie had a bad feeling about how this scene was playing out. And where was Glen? They'd lost him. She craned her neck and tried to look over the heads of the crowd of students.

"Julie's on the other side of the fire," she told Michael.

"I've got an idea where they're headed," he said. He grabbed her hand and pulled her toward the fire. The flames scared her. She turned to be sure Kathy was still following. She didn't want to put her friend in danger, but she felt good having her beside them. *It's the mother-daughter thing,* she thought, shaking her head. They were cutting close to the bonfire. The smoke and heat mixed with her fear to leave her feeling as if they were in hell.

* * *

Julie was so pumped with adrenaline she was shaking like a kid on a carnival ride. She had told Michael exactly what she'd been planning to say for months. All he could do was stare at her and listen. "Welcome to your new reality," she had said, while Neil pointed his Glock at their heads. That was so perfect!

She was tucked in the space between the dumpsters and the fence that hid the garbage. Neil would join her any minute then they would sneak away from the schoolyard. So far everything had gone exactly as she had hoped. The place was faultless: students everywhere, fireworks going off and everyone staring at the bonfire.

Neil darted in beside her. "The teacher is headed this way," he said. "He looks as if he's ready for a fight."

That wasn't like Michael. He was always nonviolent and self-righteous about it. "Are you certain?" she asked.

"He was pushing through the crowd as if they weren't even there. The kids were parting in front of him like squirrels running from a dog."

"We got to get out of here now!" she said.

"If the teacher wants a fight, he's got one." Neil drew his gun again and checked it. What was happening wasn't what Julie wanted. She poked her head out behind the dumpster and saw Michael and Stephie heading in her direction as if Michael knew exactly where they were. Everything she had planned was falling apart. She ducked back in and stood behind Neil.

* * *

Stephie hung onto Michael's shirt to be sure she didn't separate from him. She also reached back and grabbed a handful of Kathy's T-shirt.

"Get some help," she told Kathy. They were headed for a couple of dumpsters that would provide a perfect place to hide. She had a bad feeling about this. Those two could be setting a trap. Kathy nodded then took off.

When they reached the dumpsters Michael pulled out his gun and started around the first one, lunging forward without any sign of caution. Stephie released her grip on his shirt and took a step back. She was frightened even if he wasn't. An instant later a powerful arm was around her neck and she was being pulled backwards toward the far side of the other dumpster.

"I got your wife, teacher-man," a voice yelled from inches behind her head. Stephie could feel his hot breath on her neck and the barrel of his gun in her hair.

Michael came back around the dumpster and stood there, his eyes wide. Stephie could see the anger all over his face, but he didn't seem capable of speaking. He looked around, but once again there was nobody near them. She was scared he'd do something foolish, more scared for him than she was for herself.

"Throw the gun down," Neil demanded. "I'll kill her. I swear I will."

"This wasn't the plan," Julie shouted from behind Neil. "I didn't want it to go this way."

Michael tossed his gun, but as he did a shot rang out. "No!" he yelled. He lunged for Neil. He pushed Stephie to the ground and started to wrestle Neil's weapon away from him. But Neil's gun wasn't the one that had gone off. Stephie knew it because the sound wasn't deafening and, what's more, she was alive.

Stephie looked around to find two other men fighting. It was Glen and a bearded, burly guy that had to be Julie's brother. She knew immediately that this was the one. He had been the confederate soldier who had ended Alex's life. He had been Edwin, the man who had killed Emily's mother. And now he had fired his gun. But the bullet had hit the fence not her. His shot was supposed to bring her death, but this time Glen had stopped it. There was a second shot and Stephie saw that the two men stopped fighting. She saw Glen stand up slowly. He was alive.

Michael held Neil to the ground as Kathy returned with two police officers. One of them went to Glen while the other arrested Neil. Julie tried to step away while the police were distracted, but Stephie blocked her path. There was no longer any reason to be afraid. The circle had been broken.

Fifty-One

Michael received Stephie's call while he was working at the gallery. He immediately contacted Kathy. She had her cell phone with her as she had said she would.

"Put the sign up and lock the door," she told him. "I'll be there in fifteen minutes. If a customer complains I'll say my goddaughter needs her daddy."

The gallery was Kathy's. The response to her work in the restaurant had been encouraging enough to convince her to open it. Her inventory included a dozen or so of her own pieces, but most of the work was done by artists she had met over her years of painting. Her business was successful enough to provide a small, but steady income.

Michael was her first and only employee. She couldn't pay him as much as he had earned as a teacher, but it was sufficient when combined with Stephie's salary. The opportunity was mutually beneficial, since Kathy needed the help and Michael needed a job. The school system had asked him to resign after he pleaded guilty to bringing a loaded firearm onto the school premises. The principal said he respected Michael's need to protect his wife, but he wasn't able to make any exceptions.

Michael paid a two thousand dollar fine, which was nothing compared with the twenty year sentence Neil received. Neil was convicted of assault, along with the same gun crime to which Michael had pled guilty. Neil also agreed to testify against Julie, who was prosecuted for issuing a threat of violence. She pled guilty, paid a fine, and agreed to never contact Michael or Stephie again. There had been a possibility of a jail sentence for Julie, but she had managed to avoid it by convincing the judge that she was not aware of her brother's presence at the bonfire. Trent was the only one who had actually fired his gun, so determining that he had been acting alone was important to Julie's defense.

"Gladly," was what Julie said when she agreed to stay far away from Michael and Stephie.

"Do you think the restraining order is enough?" Michael asked Glen after Julie's sentencing.

"I think it's irrelevant. Two souls were necessary to complete the circle of fate, Trent's as well as Julie's. That doesn't mean all problems are gone. Things can happen that are independent of anything that happened before. But the tragedy that occurred in life after life has been altered. Stephie and you are no longer predestined for disaster."

Glen had not been convicted of a crime, although he was the only one who had killed anyone. Trent had been shot while Glen had been wrestling the gun away from him. There was no reason for the police to suspect anything in what had happened other than an act of heroism.

"I worry about Trent's family," Kathy said.

"Worrying is all right, but don't try to help them," Glen told her. "The police would see that as a suspicious. Guilt is an easier emotion to understand than sympathy."

"Suspicious? They know I didn't have anything to do with Trent's death."

"But they also know we're all friends. And if you *are* feeling guilty remember that Trent was part of the circle that has finally been broken. In his future lives he won't have to go through circumstances that lead him to kill someone. That's a blessing."

"True."

Michael was not concerned about the way the police would react if Kathy tried to help Trent's family. But the fact that those girls were Julie's nieces worried him. The circle was broken by Trent's death. And the restraining order meant that if Julie ever threatened them again, they could have her locked up. Yet it still didn't make sense to aggravate her by contacting her family.

"I understand," Kathy said after Michael explained his concerns. "I won't do anything risky."

Glen returned to Charlottesville for a few weeks then traveled up to Vermont to work with a woman who claimed she had once been Annie Chapman, an English prostitute murdered by Jack the Ripper. Glen would be the first person called after Emily was born. That was a promise Michael made when Glen left.

Michael put up the sign as Kathy had instructed. Then he pulled his coat on, locked the door and walked so quickly to his Grand Prix he was almost jogging. His car was in the place he always parked, across the lot by the street. Michael made it a practice to leave the spots directly in front of the gallery for the customers. If he had known today was the day when Stephie's water would break, he would have made an exception. But he couldn't complain. They had been able to see the future when it really counted and, thanks to that, Stephie was alive.

* * *

Stephie had pre-registered at the hospital, so it took her very little time to have a room assigned. She sat in a wheelchair while Michael pushed her to the maternity ward. She had been in the birthing room about a month earlier when a tour of the hospital facilities had been arranged for all the students in their Lamaze class. The dominant piece of furniture was the maternity bed. It could crank up like any adjustable bed, but it also had a section that slid down and out of the way, so that Dr. Newsome would have plenty of space to do what she needed to do. There was also a couch in the room which was a place for Michael to sit and even lie down if the labor took a long time. Stephie hoped that wouldn't be the case. The rest was very much like any other hospital room, with a sink near the bed and, behind the sink, a small, private room with a commode. There was also a rolling tray for meals and buckets of ice chips and, beside the bed, a monitor to keep tabs on the health of both Stephie and her child.

Michael closed the door and helped Stephie up from her chair. He picked up a hospital gown that had been left on the rolling tray and handed it to her. It was the type that tied in the back and had mid length sleeves. The material was light blue cotton with a pattern of dark blue diamonds. Stephie changed into the gown then Michael helped her into the bed and they began the process of waiting.

Dr. Newsome arrived after Stephie had been in the hospital for close to a half hour. The doctor knew to come because Stephie had called her from home. She also knew not to rush because she had been through the process enough times to understand how long labor could be. She checked Stephie's dilation and found she was a little over five centimeters.

"You're in active labor," Dr. Newsome told Stephie, "but it will still take some time. The nurses will keep track of your progress and they will call me when your baby's ready to come. I don't plan to leave the hospital today, so I can get here when you need me."

After Dr. Newsome left the room Michael said, "I can't tell you how much I've looked forward to this day."

"I just want it over," Stephie replied. She tried to keep any sarcasm out of her tone, but her words appeared to affect Michael. He didn't come up with any other optimistic statements and he turned his attention to Stephie's needs. He brought her ice chips if she pointed at her mouth. He offered her a sip of water if she looked at the cup. And he gave her a back rub when she stretched in a way that indicated she was sore. He did what she wanted him to do before she could ask. She found that her need for Michael to help her bear the pain along with her anticipation of the miracle happening within her body created one of the most intimate moments of her life— intimate but almost unbearably painful.

She felt another contraction starting. There was a slight sensation, like a rope lying on her body. Then that rope began to tighten, as if her body was trying to strangle itself. The pain peaked and then flowed over her like an ocean wave and then it was done and she was fine again. She used her Lamaze techniques to withstand the pain, breathing deeply and focusing on a spot during the contraction in a manner that wasn't very different from what Glen had asked her to do each time he had regressed her. But this time she didn't go back into another life. This time the other life was coming out on its own.

"Call somebody! Now!" Stephie shouted at Michael after the last, intense contraction. He ran out into the hall and came back with a nurse who checked on Stephie's progress and confirmed that she was fully dilated. She left the room to page Dr. Newsome.

"Our baby's almost here," Michael told Stephie as he wiped her brow with a tissue. "Be strong." That was the last thing Stephie wanted to hear from him, but then he said, "I love you." Those magic words gave her the strength she needed.

"Me, too," she replied. She thought her body might have tingled a bit when she said that, but it was impossible to tell because another contraction was starting.

"Don't push yet," the nurse said as she stepped back in the room. "The doctor will be here in a few minutes. You're doing just fine." The nurse's name began with an *R*, but Stephie couldn't remember if it was Randy or Rena or something else that sounded similar. She had been in and out of their room repeatedly for most of the morning and was a sweet young woman who was very helpful, but her name just hadn't sunk in. That was odd for Stephie. She was generally good with names. Of course, she had been distracted all morning. "Everything is proceeding well," the nurse continued. "It won't be long now.

The nurse removed Stephie's blanket then positioned leg extenders in the back of the bed and helped Stephie get her legs up in them. Her gown was pushed above her waist and a small blanket placed across her abdomen. Stephie looked over at Michael to see what he was doing. He was getting the camera ready. She had asked him to take pictures, but now she wasn't sure she wanted them. The concept of giving birth had seemed so beautiful. Now she felt grotesque. Another contraction started.

"Don't push," the nurse told her then she turned to Michael and told him to make her blow in his face. "She can't push and blow at the same time. Dr. Newsome will be here soon. Keep at it until she gets here."

Stephie had learned about the blowing thing in the Lamaze class. Michael had learned what to do at the same time. He leaned over her and yelled, "Blow!" She did what he told her to do, right in his face. But she didn't want to. She wanted to push that baby out of her body.

Alex didn't have either a doctor on the way or a husband waiting with her for the doctor's arrival. All she had was a kidnapper. The experience was as clear in Stephie's mind as it had been on the day of the regression. She could smell the straw and feel the way it poked and pricked at Alex's naked legs. She could also smell the remnants of manure from the animals that had been there before the war changed everything. Glen had stopped the regression before the birth happened, but Stephie knew it was successful. Alex had brought Charlotte into the world without any help. She had no water to clean her baby and she had most likely used her teeth to cut the cord. It was as primitive as a birth could be, but they had both survived— that day at least.

Dr. Newsome arrived and Stephie was free to push. It was her moment now and this time would be better than Alex's had been. Michael was beside her, his hand touching her shoulder with a firm indication of how much he loved her. The room was clean. She was on a bed with cotton sheets, not a bed of soiled straw. There was a nurse and a doctor in the room with her. And what was more important than anything else was that the world was free from the fate her child's soul had endured so many times before. Life for her daughter would have the potential for joy and fulfillment that all God's people deserve.

"I see the crown," Dr. Newsome said. "She's positioned right. Push now. Push hard."

Stephie leaned forward and tightened every muscle in her body. She could feel the mass of the child inside her, slipping slowly forward. Michael had his hand in hers and she squeezed it as hard as she could. Her thighs tightened. Her buttocks tightened. Even the muscles in her feet tightened and her toes curled. The baby came out just a little further, just fractions of an inch. Then everything gave way and she felt her daughter slide into Dr. Newsome's hands and into a world that was new and fresh.

"Look at her," the doctor told Stephie as she held the baby up. "She's beautiful."

"Oh, yes. God bless her. She *really* is beautiful." Stephie struggled to say the words. She was weak and out of breath from the tremendous effort of giving birth. But she was also filled with more joy than she had ever known.

The nurse took the newborn, held her for a moment as Dr. Newsome clamped and cut the umbilical cord then moved her to a small table where she cleaned her and wrapped her in a blanket. As soon as she was finished the nurse handed the child back to Stephie. Stephie looked up at Michael who reached down and gently touched his daughter for the first time.

* * *

Emily Charlotte Stuart arrived on the twenty-third of February at 3:57 in the afternoon. She was named after two of her previous selves, which was probably the first time in history that had happened. But Michael and Stephie intended to call her by her nickname, Emma, to give her an identity of her own. Stephie knew that Emma would be unique and special. Yet she also knew that deep down, in the core of her soul, Emma was the child she had loved and would always love through eternity

Kathy arrived at the hospital after Emma had been around for a couple of hours. "I finally feel like a grandma," she joked as she held the baby. Stephie smiled, but she understood the reference to Margaret, who never saw her own grandchild.

Emma had a scruff of dark hair and blue eyes. Stephie hoped her baby would keep the eye color, but she knew that eyes often darken as babies grow. *It will be fun to find out*, she thought, as she took her daughter back from Kathy. She leaned forward to kiss the top of Emma's head. Stephie loved the baby smell of new hair and skin mixed with a little talc. She had smelled a lot of newborns when visiting church members who had just given birth, but it seemed to her that Emma's smell was unique and more enticing than that of any other child. The aroma seemed to fill Stephie's body like freshly baked cookies. It made her spirit soar.

"God bless you, Emma," Stephie said. Then she bent forward and kissed her daughter. She kissed both of her eyes, then her cheek, three long, deliberate kisses. In most ways the kisses were no different than the ones they'd shared in their past lives. They were messages of dedication and love. But this time there was something unique, something extra in the warmth of soft skin touching her lips.

Stephie breathed deeply, lifted her eyes to God, and allowed the difference to fill her heart.